Robert G. Barrett was raised in Bondi where he has worked mainly as a butcher. After thirty years he moved to Terrigal on the Central Coast of New South Wales. Robert has appeared in a number of films and TV commercials but prefers to concentrate on a career as a writer.

ROBERT G. BARRETT

The Godson

PAN
Pan Macmillan Australia

The author is again donating a percentage of his royalties to Greenpeace, an
organisation he deeply respects.

This is a work of fiction and all characters in this book are a creation
of the author's imagination.

First published 1986 by Pan Books (Australia) Pty Limited
This edition published by Pan Macmillan Australia Pty Ltd
1 Market Street, Sydney

Reprinted 1988, 1989 (twice), 1991, 1992 (twice), 1993, 1994, 1995, 1996 (twice),
1998, 1999, 2000, 2001, 2002, 2003, 2004, 2006, 2007, 2009

National Library of Australia
cataloguing-in-publication data:

Barrett, Robert G.

The godson.

ISBN 978 0 330 27162 2

I. Title

A823.3

Typeset by Post Pre-press Group
Printed in Australia by McPherson's Printing Group

Papers used by Pan Macmillan Australia Pty Ltd are natural, recyclable
products made from wood grown in sustainable forests. The manufacturing processes
conform to the environmental regulations of the country of origin.

This book is dedicated to John Sinclair for saving Fraser Island and to Dr Bob Brown for saving the Franklin River.

ACKNOWLEDGEMENTS

The author would like to thank the following people for their help in the writing of this book:

Anthony and William, two brothers who wish to remain anonymous, who have been friends of the author for over twenty years. Thanks to them for their hospitality and for sharing the freedom of their magnificent Tweed Valley property.

Ms Virginia Greig, headmistress of Spencer State School.

The management and staff of the Pelican International Resort, Coffs Harbour.

The management and staff of the Sebel Town House, Sydney.

Mr Barry Pearce, curator of The Art Gallery of New South Wales.

'HEY, Price. Wake up, mate. We're almost there.' Eddie Salita was smiling softly as he reached across the front seat of the Rolls Royce and tapped his boss gently on the shoulder.

'Huhh?' Price blinked his eyes open just as a large blue sign saying Australian Capital Territory whizzed past the window of the car. 'Shit!' he blinked again. 'I must have dozed off.'

'Yeah,' chuckled Eddie. 'You started to nod off the other side of Goulburn.'

'Did I?' Price yawned and stretched. 'What time is it?'

'Just on five. It's almost dark too.' Eddie nodded to the radio playing softly in the dashboard. 'I've been listening to one of the local radio stations — 2CA or something. They said it's two degrees with southwesterly winds and they're expecting light rain, possibly snow.'

Price peered out of the window as another sign set in stone blocks saying Canberra flashed past in the bleak twilight. 'Bloody Canberra,' he mused, rubbing his hands briskly together. 'I could think of a lot better places to be in August.'

'Yeah,' nodded Eddie. 'So could I.'

The previous day Price had got a phone call at home from an old friend, Laurence O'Malley. 'Laurie' and Price went back over thirty years to when they were young louts doing their best, running around Glebe and Balmain. Price got into a bit of minor crime and gambling, and ended up owning an illegal casino. Laurie got into law and politics, and ended up Attorney General of Australia. As a politician, O'Malley was one of the more popular figures in Australia: friendly, warm and a bit of a reformist with a lot of good ideas. He wasn't particularly corrupt, but if he could he didn't mind doing a favour or two for his old mates, and he'd done Price quite a few over the years. Now the Attorney General needed one himself. He didn't elaborate over the phone and he couldn't get to Sydney as the budget session was in progress. It was a little urgent, so could Price very discreetly come down to Canberra? Price being the sort of man he was, the bags were packed and in the boot of the Rolls and he and his number one hit man were on their way to Canberra not long after getting the phone call.

Eddie put his foot down gently on the accelerator to pass an old panel van, then eased up a little further on in the light traffic as The Federal Highway curved slightly to turn into a long, wide, tree-lined boulevard flanked by motels and government office blocks.

'You know where this joint we're staying at is?' asked Price. 'The Country Club Motel?'

'Yeah,' nodded Eddie. 'It's on this Northbourne Avenue. I don't think it's much further.' A couple of Motels went past — The Rex, Park Royal — when Eddie spotted what he was looking for. A large white neon sign in front of a dark blue, vine-covered building. 'Here it is. Country Club Motel.'

He hit the blinker and turned left into a pebbled driveway facing a very opulent-looking establishment. The spacious white driveway, gables and long columns out the front almost gave it the appearance of an old Southern mansion in Georgia. Eddie cut the engine and they both sat there staring at each other for a few moments. Each knew what the other was thinking. Climbing out of the air-conditioned warmth of the Rolls Royce into two degrees of sleet with a sou'westerly behind it was going to be a bit of a shock to the system to say the least.

'Well,' Eddie finally said. 'We gonna make a move or what?'

'Yeah,' Price nodded grimly. 'Let's go.'

They pulled their tweed caps down tighter, zipped up their sheepskin jackets and burst out into the frigid Canberra evening.

'Christ almighty!' roared Price, almost disappearing in the clouds of steam coming from his breath. 'It's colder than a well-digger's arse.'

Eddie didn't reply. He grabbed the two bags from the boot as quickly as he could, slammed down the lid and they both sprinted for the motel foyer.

'And how are you, Mr Kelly?' smiled the blonde girl behind the desk after Price had introduced himself. 'Did you have a pleasant trip down?'

'Yeah. It was all right, thanks,' replied Price, still shivering slightly in the warmth of the foyer.

'Two nights, Mr Kelly. Is that right?' she said, checking the reservation. 'Tonight and Friday night?' Price smiled and nodded. 'Would you just sign here please.' As Price signed the book the girl moved a hand towards a bell on the desk. Eddie reached across and gently pushed her hand away.

'That's all right,' he said, picking up the key. 'We'll be okay.'

Eddie couldn't have been more gentle or polite but there was something in the way he touched her and the dark stillness of his eyes that slightly unnerved the blonde receptionist.

'Oh . . . all right then. Well, if you should want . . .'

Eddie gave her a brief smile. He picked up the two bags and her voice trailed off as he and Price stepped briskly across to the lift.

'Not a bad digs,' said Eddie, after throwing their bags on the double bed in each room.

'Yeah,' agreed Price. 'Don't look too bad at all.'

The motel room was quite spacious and beautifully appointed. Two separate bedrooms faced a lounge room and a curtained verandah giving extensive views over the east side of the city towards Black Mountain Reserve. There was a bathroom and spa and a small kitchen with a well-stocked bar running off it.

'Christ! There's plenty of piss here if we want it,' said Eddie, opening and closing the fridge. He moved into the kitchen. 'Fancy a cup of coffee, Price?'

'Yeah. But not that instant shit. Ring room service and get some percolated stuff sent up. And book a table in the dining room. I'm gonna get cleaned up then make a few phone calls.'

'What time do you want to eat, Mr Kelly?' smiled Eddie, picking up the phone.

'Ohh, around seven'll do,' replied Price. He unzipped his jacket and went into his room.

PRICE AND EDDIE had finished their meal by about nine, and were seated in the motel dining room sipping a bottle of wine. The dining room was comfortable and uncrowded, tastefully furnished in blue and white with a bowl of blue gardenias on each table. The service, like the food, was excellent. Eddie and Price didn't go for anything exotic from the menu, each preferring, because of the cold, a nice New Zealand mussel bouillabaisse and a New York cut with pepper sauce and vegetables. Price ordered a bottle of '76 Penfolds St. Henri claret which went down exceptionally well. In fact it went down that well he ordered another one after the meal. They were now both halfway through that bottle, feeling an inner glow of warmth and contentment as they contemplated their first night in Canberra and the circumstances that had brought them there.

'So,' said Eddie, keeping his voice down a little. 'You still

11

don't know for sure what it is O'Malley wants you to do?'

Price reflected into his glass of wine and shook his head slightly. 'No. Not really. He couldn't say much over the phone. But from what I can gather he just wants me to look after some young pommy bloke coming out for a couple of weeks. That's all.'

Eddie took a slow sip of wine. 'Seems funny though, him bringing you all the way down here just to ask you to do that.'

'There could be a bit more to it. But it wouldn't matter if Laurie wanted me to drive to Gobe Island for him. I'd do it. I owe him. And he's been a good mate for over thirty years.'

'Yeah. He's a top bloke all right,' agreed Eddie. 'Nothing wrong with him.'

'One of the best, Ed.'

They paused as the waiter appeared and topped up their glasses.

'Anyway,' continued Price, once the waiter had left. 'I said I'd be out at his place at Red Hill at ten tomorrow. I'll probably be there most of the day, so you can drop me off and pick me up at five.' Eddie nodded. 'That gives you seven hours to yourself in beautiful downtown Canberra. What do you reckon you'll do?'

'Probably drive round and round in circles like everyone else does here,' shrugged Eddie with a laugh. 'No. I'll spend a bit of time in the War Memorial. Then go down the National Gallery — I promised Lindy I'd get her a decent print she could frame. I'll get something for the kids too.'

Price smiled. 'I tipped you'd go to the War Memorial.'

'May as well while I'm down here,' shrugged Eddie.

'Won't bring back any bad memories?'

'I never had any bad memories of Vietnam, Price. It was grouse. I'd go back tomorrow. I don't mind killing people at all,' he added with a sinister smile.

'I know,' said Price, flashing a smile as sinister as Eddie's. 'Why do you think I've got you working for me?'

They raised their glasses just as the bill arrived. Price signed for it and slipped the waiter a twenty.

'Well, Eddie,' he said. 'What say we finish this then I'll give you a few games of German Whist and we'll hit the sack. You can wake me up at eight thirty. Okay?'

'Yeah. That sounds like a good idea.'

They lingered over the second bottle of St. Henri then went

to their room. After several games of cards, a bottle or two of beer and a bit of TV they were in bed by eleven. Feeling warm and comfortable and knowing it was like the Siberian Steppes outside, both men slept like the dead.

EDDIE WOKE UP around six feeling pretty fresh. After he'd finished in the bathroom he made a cup of coffee which he took out on to the verandah — for about five seconds. That was all the time Eddie needed to know that although it wasn't raining or snowing, it was bleak, miserable and absolutely icy out in the open. He finished his coffee in the warmth. Miserable and cold it might have been outside, but it was also good for something else — a run. He got changed into a tracksuit and his Tiger Trainers and put a beanie and a pair of gloves in the front pocket. Using the bar as a bench he swung his legs up and did a few stretches while he studied a map of Canberra. Ten minutes later Eddie was out the front of The Country Club Motel, heading towards Braddon and Limestone Avenue. He didn't bother to take a gun with him, but force of habit made him slip a switchblade knife down the inside of his left glove.

Anybody watching Eddie run would have probably thought he was the fittest bloke on God's earth as he sprinted along, crossing streets in three steps and leaving clouds of steam from his breath in his wake. Wiry and light-framed, Eddie was a fast runner at any time but all he was trying to do now was warm up. He was going for twenty minutes at a cracking pace before even his blood seemed to start circulating let alone him getting a sweat up. It was a pleasant run, though. Wide, flat streets lined with hundreds of trees which accounted for what seemed like an endless carpet of brown leaves at every turn. Hedges in front of the houses and old fashioned street lamps gave it an almost old English, countryside look. After a while a copper-domed building, looming up on a tree-studded hill to his left told him he'd found the War Memorial. He sprinted across Limestone Avenue, up the driveway and into a park before coming back to stop at a display of tanks, artillery and a piece of old Bailey bridge to the left. With its two machine guns on top, a chipped armoured personnel carrier which had been blown up by a mine in Vietnam brought a smile to his face as he checked it out. But it was too cold to be standing around for long so he took off again.

He went straight down a long, landscaped boulevard which

headed towards Lake Burley Griffin and Parliament House with the sou'wester whipping along behind him. So much for the scenery, he thought, glancing at his watch. Arms pumping, he headed back to the motel.

Eddie had only meant to go jogging for thirty minutes but it was after eight when he got back to The Country Club. He got showered and woke Price right on 8.30.

'You been for a run, mate?' said Price, noticing Eddie's tracksuit and joggers in the lounge.

'A run? It's more like trying to survive out there. Christ, it's cold. How'd you sleep?'

'I didn't move.' Price yawned and stretched. 'I'm gonna have a shower. You ordered breakfast?'

'No, not yet. What do you fancy?'

'Ohh, bacon and eggs, coffee — the usual. And get some porridge and prunes.'

'Coming up,' said Eddie, picking up the phone. 'Or as the yanks say — you got it.'

'Whatever. But tell 'em to hurry. I'm starving.' Price disappeared into the bathroom.

An hour or so later they were standing outside the motel next to the Rolls. Of all things to happen, the sun suddenly came out and for a few brief moments several skinny shafts of blue seemed to appear behind Black Mountain.

'Hello, look at that,' said Eddie, tilting his face towards the sky. 'I knew I should have brought my cossies.'

No sooner had he spoken than the sun disappeared again and a cold blast of wind whipped around their necks, almost snapping their ears off.

'Eddie! Open the bloody car door, for Christ's sake,' said Price through gritted teeth.

Eddie turned the heater on full while he warmed up the motor. Across his lap was a street map of Canberra.

'You know where this place is?' asked Price.

'Yep.' Eddie pointed to the map. 'See. La Perouse Street, Red Hill. I go through the city, past Parliament House, round that golf course and O'Malley's place is right there. On the corner of La Perouse and Harvey Street.'

'Right. Well let's get going.'

Eddie found driving in Canberra easy. There wasn't much traffic and the streets were so wide and well-planned that even the worst driver in the world would be flat out to have an accident. The only annoying thing was that every street or road seemed to curve or finish in a circle, ending in roundabouts as big as football fields. Finally he found La Perouse Street, a quiet, curving road full of poplar trees turned brown and dotted with Olde English-style street lamps set on wide, green median strips. The area gave the distinct impression of wealth, style and cultivated elegance.

'Jesus Christ!' muttered Eddie, as once again the street he was on began to arc into a circle. 'Am I ever sick of going around in circles. I'll end up getting car sick. And all these bloody trees. It's like you're forever driving around and around Centennial Park.'

'Yeah,' agreed Price. 'That architect Burley Griffin must have finished up with chlorophyll poisoning and curvature of the spine after he designed the joint.'

Finally Eddie found the street and house he was looking for, a white two-storey residence fronted by a small, neat stone wall. A tall Canadian pine pushed up from the front yard and a bushy tree full of red berries stood to the right of it. Glass bricks set on either side of the wood-panelled front door reminded him of some of the houses you'd see in parts of Dover Heights in Sydney. There was a double garage to the left. Eddie crunched the Rolls Royce up onto the gravel driveway and cut the engine.

'You needn't bother coming inside, Eddie,' said Price.

'Yeah, righto.' Eddie got out of the car and opened the door for his boss. 'I'll see you at five then, Price.'

'Okay, Ed. Good on you, mate.'

From the back of the Rolls, Eddie watched as Price went to the front door. It opened before he had a chance to knock and Eddie noticed a tall, willowy blonde in a tweed suit and glasses smile and beckon Price inside. He turned and nodded to Eddie; Eddie nodded back as Price stepped inside and the door closed. Satisfied that everything was in order, Eddie got back in the Rolls and started the motor. Now, he thought, checking his watch, what to do till five o'clock? He smiled to himself as he backed down the driveway. I think I might make the War Memorial starting favourite.

He pulled up near the western entrance and went straight inside. He had changed his mind about looking at the tanks and the artillery out the front, and as for the old armoured personnel carrier, you've seen one APC, you've seen the lot. A blast of hot air from the heater above the entrance nearly blew his cap off. He unzipped his jacket, picked up a visitors' guide and joined the other people heading towards the Gallipoli exhibit.

Eddie had never visited the Memorial before. His only other time in Canberra had been a quick trip in and out in a Caribou to deliver 200 stolen AK-47s to a major in the Australian engineers when Eddie went back to Vietnam working more or less as a mercenary with the US Army and the CIA. He found the War Memorial absolutely fascinating and, for someone as tough and deadly as him, even moving. The painstaking attention given to detail was nothing short of amazing. Whole battle campaigns were mapped out. There were old letters, diaries with bullet holes in them, officers' uniforms shredded from shrapnel. Old tins of biscuits and chocolates with Queen Victoria on the front. Guns, bayonets, Turkish uniforms. Dummies in full, original battle dress. He meandered on to the Sinai and Palestine Exhibits, then through the aeroplane hall containing huge, complete planes: Halifax bombers, Spitfires, old RAAF Boomerangs. A tape recording was playing over and over — the voices of an actual flight crew on a bombing raid over Dresden.

He wandered on through the other visitors taking photos and groups of kids taking notes, into the Middle East section, the South West Pacific, and New Guinea; wherever Australian fighting men and women had laid down their lives for their country. But all the time Eddie was drifting inexorably towards what he was ultimately looking for. He found himself in a small theatrette watching newsreels about the Korean war. He left that, strolled through the Korean section and he was there. Vietnam.

The first thing that caught his eye was an old black and white Admiral television set sitting in a mock-up of a 1960s style lounge room. On the table alongside were old magazines, Beatles albums and other items from that era of flower power. There was a small record player; the 45 on the turntable was The Seekers' — 'I'll Never Find Another You'. He glanced at some school children taking notes on the brown vinyl lounge, when the TV started. It was 'Four Corners' on the ABC, a journalist was reporting live from the battlefield. The kids on the lounge took notes; Eddie blinked in wonder at the film. Those soldiers on the screen, were they familiar faces? Jesus Christ! They were. The newsreel stopped and from behind a helicopter suspended from the ceiling two speakers started up with the swoosh-swoosh-swoosh of helicopters taking off and landing. It was all too real. Eddie closed his eyes and for a moment he was back there. Bin Bah. Xuoc Thoy. Nui Dat. The bodies. The heat. The dust and flies. The smell.

16

Mines, booby traps, tension. Bodies spinning like tops as the bullets hit them. Patrols. Brutality. Turning WIAs into KIAs. Brave men. Cowards. But where a lot of Vietnam veterans might have been unnerved, Eddie was rapt. Eddie Salita was a killer long before the army sent him to Vietnam.

Like a kid in a toy shop he strolled along the exhibits taking in the sights. Dummies in tiger stripes, complete with face camouflage, M16s and body armour. American uniforms. Viet Cong in their black pyjamas and Ho Chi Minh sandals standing next to pushbikes and carrying AK-47s. An old concrete road sign caught his attention: Saigon 104 kms. Yeah, chuckled Eddie. Been there, done that. Jesus, how good's this?

After an hour or so he found himself in front of a glass case with an exhibit of Montagnard clothing. There was even one of their deadly little cross-bows. This made Eddie's grin even bigger. He'd been good friends with the 'Monts'. He was taking in the details of the red and black tunic when a shapely backside belonging to a tall, auburnish blonde looking at some paintings on the far wall caught his eye. She turned slightly side-on and Eddie had to blink and shake his head. He shook his head again, but there was no mistaking that angular, haughty face, hazel eyes and tidy nose sitting above a pair of lovely soft lips. It was her, all right. Denise Richtenburgh. 'Dutchy'.

Dutchy had been the back-up singer in a group entertaining the troops the second time Eddie was in Vietnam. She was engaged to some musician back in Sydney, but Eddie had taken her out a few times in Saigon and had made three enormous attempts to get into her long, sexy pants. Once in a jeep, once in hospital and the third time he had her back in an American Colonel's bivouac, well topped-up with Jack Daniel's and ready to go. He was just about to do some furious inserting when the stinking, rotten Vietcong started mortaring the base. This was one of the turning points that transformed Eddie into such a killer because as soon as he got his fatigues back on, he grabbed a grenade launcher and took out the four mortar positions by himself. But when he got back, the colonel's tent was gone and so was Dutchy. She was all right, but the Vietcong had certainly stuffed up what should have been a good night's tooling for Eddie. The VC paid for it, though. Eddie never took another prisoner after that. They both remained good friends, but with the war as it was, Dutchy went one way and Eddie went another. But what was the long, sexy thing doing in Canberra? There was only one way to find out.

Almost like he was back in the jungle, Eddie moved from behind the glass case, snuck up on the unsuspecting Dutchy and grabbed her by the elbow.

'Righto, gotcha,' he said sharply into her ear. 'And don't try to get away.'

If Eddie was trying to surprise Dutchy, his approach certainly had the right effect. She nearly went through the roof. Her eyes widened like saucers, her jaw dropped and a look of horror drained the colour from her face. Under his firm, but gentle grip, Eddie could feel her entire body stiffen like a post.

She blinked at him for a moment as if she was trying to focus and get her breath back at the same time. 'Eddie,' she finally spluttered. 'What the fuckin' hell are you doing here?'

Eddie shrugged, slightly mystified. 'Checking out the War Memorial. What else?'

Dutchy fell back against the wall, almost dislodging a painting. She put a hand to her face and glanced furtively around the room. 'Who are you with?'

Eddie shrugged again. 'No one.'

'Meet me out the front.' She snatched her arm away and moved quickly, if a little unsteadily towards the exit.

'What . . .'

'Meet me out the front.' She tossed the last words over her shoulder and left Eddie standing there.

Eddie watched her shapely backside in the designer jeans disappear into the Korean section. Well bloody well work that out, he mused. An old mate. I have a bit of a joke with her and she just about shits her pants. Once again he shook his head. Buggered if I know. Oh well, she said to meet her out the front. May as well, I s'pose. After stopping at the Memorial shop to buy two souvenir sweat-shirts for his sons, he went down the front to wait for Dutchy.

Eddie was leaning against the statue of Simpson and his donkey when Dutchy came down the steps of the War Memorial. The colour had returned to her face but the smile appeared a little forced.

'Eddie Salita,' she said, when she got close. 'You stupid prick, you scared the shit out of me. I had to go to the loo.'

Eddie looked at her questioningly for a moment or two. The years had been good to Dutchy. There was hardly a line on her face and when she came down those steps not a part of her moved that shouldn't have. 'Your bloody nerves are going, Dutchy.'

She smiled at him and shook her head. 'You got a car?'

Eddie nodded to where he'd parked the Rolls. 'Come on, I need a bloody drink.'

They walked to the car park and got inside Price's Rolls Royce. Eddie didn't start the car straight away but sat there looking at her for a few seconds. By now Dutchy's sexy hazel eyes had started to crease into a smile, though it seemed a smile of relief more than anything else.

'So what are you doing in Canberra, Eddie?'

'I drove my boss down on business. This is his car. What about yourself?'

She looked at Eddie evenly for a moment. 'I just sold a bloke five thousand Buddha sticks outside the kiosk less than twenty minutes ago. I went into the Ladies to check the money and on the way out I thought I'd have a quick look at the Vietnam exhibit — seeing as I did my bit for my country over there,' she added with a smile. 'Anyway, I'm standing there minding my own bloody business and you come up and grab me by the arm. I thought it was the Federal Police. I bloody near died.'

'Jesus, Dutch. Sorry mate — I didn't know.'

'Ohh, that's all right, I suppose,' she sighed. 'But boy, did I shit! And you have got a way of sneaking up on people, Eddie.'

'Yeah, I know.'

She puffed her cheeks in another sigh of relief and flopped back against the head-rest. 'Anyway, what about a drink?'

Eddie started the car. 'Righto. Where's the nearest bar?'

'My place. I'm staying at the Alislie. It's just across the road on Limestone.'

'Okay.'

THE TALL WOMAN in the tweed suit and glasses was all smiles when she opened the door for Price. 'Mr Galese,' she beamed. 'Do come in. The Attorney General has told me so much about you.'

'Yeah, I'll bet he has,' replied Price.

'I'm Yvonne.' They exchanged a brief, but firm handshake. She turned to close the door and her long blonde hair swirled across her shoulders. 'This way, please.'

Price followed Yvonne through a small hallway hung with expensive oil paintings and beaten bronze plaques into a large, bright lounge room facing the back garden. There were more oil paintings, antiques and miniatures; several lamps dotted the thick cream carpet that washed against the brown and maroon velvet furniture, giving the room an almost Edwardian effect. The crackle of an open fireplace against one wall spread comfortable warmth throughout the room, and leaning against a mantelpiece above the fireplace was Laurence O'Malley. In his grey corduroy trousers, white V-neck pullover and cravat he practically blended in with a number of marble statuettes placed evenly along the mantelpiece.

There was no mistaking O'Malley; the silver hair, the large thick nose, slightly veiny from one or two Scotches too many, the drooping eyes which seemed to have a permanent twinkle in them and the slightly crooked mouth all added up to make him a political cartoonist's delight. With his head character-istically tilted to one side when he spoke and his paunch and rolling gait, he ambled across the room to Price.

'Price, you old bastard,' he grinned. 'How are you, mate?'

'Not too bad, you thieving old shit,' replied Price, returning the grin. 'How's yourself?'

'Fantastic.'

They shook hands then hugged each other in a warm embrace.

Yvonne gave a discreet cough. 'I'll be in the study if you want me, sir.' O'Malley nodded; she gave Price a brief smile then left them alone.

'By God it's good to see you, Price.'

'Yeah. You too, Loz. Bad luck we can't get together more often.'

'Yes,' sighed the Attorney General. 'But I don't think the public would like it very much.'

'No. But I'm sure those grubs on the newspapers would.' Price removed his jacket, cap and gloves and placed them on the back of one of the lounges. 'So what's doing, Loz, old pal? What's the strength of dragging me away from my nice, warm, illegal casino down to this cold, rotten prick of a joint? Do you need some of my money to help balance your shitty budget?'

'No, nothing like that,' laughed O'Malley. 'But Christ almighty, Price. Let's have a drink first. Then we can discuss what I told you over the phone.'

Price rubbed his hands together and stood in front of the fire. 'I certainly won't say no to that, old son.'

The Attorney General produced a bottle of Bowmore and a soda syphon from a bar in a corner of the room. He tinkled some ice into two crystal tumblers, gave them each a good hit of Scotch and a splash of soda water and handed one to Price.

'Here's to Balmain,' he grinned.

Price clinked his glass against O'Malley's. 'Yeah. Good old Tiger Town.'

They sat on opposite lounges and got stuck into the beautiful Scotch while they talked about their larrikin past like old mates who have made good in the world are apt to do. An hour and a half flew by — most of the Bowmore was gone, and if the Attorney General of Australia and one of the leading members of the Sydney underworld weren't half-pissed, they were making an excellent imitation of it.

'Anyway,' said Price, taking an unsteady turn at topping up their glasses. 'So much for crab-pots in Birchgrove and hanging around the Kodocks Club. What's the story with this pommy kid?'

O'Malley eased back against the lounge and closed his eyes for a moment. 'Righto,' he said. 'This pommy kid happens to be my godson.' Price raised his eyebrows slightly. 'I got to be very close friends with his father when I was doing my law degree at Cambridge. His name is Peregrine Normanhurst the Third. He's a baronet and in line to the throne, sort of. His father is Lord Armitage Normanhurst. An ex-admiral of the fleet and the third Duke of Orange. They're an old naval family.'

Price nodded dryly. 'Sounds like this kid comes from a long line of naval oranges.'

'Price . . . please.' The Attorney General held up one hand. 'Anyway, Peregrine's a nice enough kid, from what I can remember. But evidently he's now turned into a shocking Hooray Henry. He's filthy rich and he hangs around with all these other rich kids in Sloane Square in London. Sloane Rangers, they call them. The so-called upper class. All they do is spend money and make complete arseholes of themselves, and their parents always bail them out.'

Price nodded. 'I know a few like them in Double Bay. Nothing a good kick fair in the arse wouldn't fix up.'

'I agree. Anyway for a dare, silly bloody Peregrine has jumped in his Aston Martin with one of his girlfriends, Lady Shitbags or whoever, and zoomed up to Northern Ireland to see his cousin Lewis who's a captain in the British Army stationed in Belfast. You see he and his cousin are almost identical — twins, so to speak. This is all supposed to a bit of a whizzo bash and all that. You know, have a jolly good time, take some jolly good photos.'

'I can just imagine.'

'So, silly bloody Peregrine and this sheila are driving through Belfast, drinking champagne, and of all things to happen, he spots his cousin out of uniform, outside some pub talking to three blokes. He pulls up, jumps out of the car and makes a big deal of finding his cousin. But what the dill doesn't know is that his cousin's working undercover and the three blokes are heavies in the IRA: two Frayne brothers and a fellow called McGine.'

'The plot thickens,' said Price.

'Does it what. Lewis pulls out a .45 and shoots the three IRA members before they get a chance to shoot him, then he legs it rather than have his smother blown. He throws the empty gun down next to the bodies and tells the Hooray Henry to get, but Peregrine, who's half full of French shampoo, picks it up. These other Irish burst out of the pub and are about to tear Peregrine and his brush to pieces when a British Army patrol arrives and saves the idiot.' O'Malley stared at Price for a moment. 'Can you follow me so far? I've got Armitage's letter here if you want to see it. He wrote before he rang me.'

'No, that's all right.' Price gave his drink a bit of a swirl. 'I've got the picture.'

'Okay. Now there's a third Frayne brother in the hotel. He comes out and sees Peregrine with the still hot-smoking gun, so to speak. He puts two and two together, and being Irish, it comes out five, so he thinks Peregrine has shot his brothers. So now he and his little cell of killers are determined to neck Peregrine. Revenge. And you can't really blame them I don't suppose.'

'How old's this Peregrine wombat?'

'Twenty-two. But he looks eighteen and acts about twelve.'

'Fair enough,' nodded Price.

The Attorney General poured them both another drink. 'So what it all boils down to, Price, is this. Peregrine's old man wants to get his kid out of the country for a couple of weeks till Lewis can go back in and assassinate this third Frayne brother and his cell, then get something in the local paper and on TV about mistaken identity and that should clear poor silly Peregrine. The IRA have got more important things on their plate than some wooden-headed Hooray Henry. And with a bit of luck, young Peregrine should live happily ever after.'

'Happily, but not too intelligently.'

'Yeah, right.' O'Malley nodded and gave a tired smile. 'You see, Price, Peregrine's an only child and he's the one who's going to inherit his father's estate and all that. He's also my godson — which is why I'm involved.' O'Malley's sad, droopy eyes seemed to suddenly get sadder and droopier as he pleaded up at his friend. 'All I want you to do, Price, if you can, is hide this wombat godson of mine in Australia for a couple of weeks till all this Elliot blows over in England. Can you do that for me? You're the only man I can ask. And trust.'

Price gave a bit of a chuckle and shook his head. 'Of course I can, Loz. I'll just keep him at my place till he goes back.'

The Attorney General shook his head adamantly. 'No, that's no good. You'll have to get him right out of Sydney. He'd only be here five minutes and he'd be out on the town. And being an English Baronet, the papers would be on to him straight away. There's plenty of Irish in Australia, Price. I should know. O'Malley's not Jewish. And if word somehow has filtered through, some Mick out here would be a moral to take a pot at him. It's still all a bit of a lark to poor silly Peregrine. The stupid prick honestly doesn't know how much strife he's in.'

'So what do you want me to do, Loz?'

'Take him out in the bush somewhere, say up the North Coast where it's warm and isolated. You must know someone who can look after this Beecham's pill for a couple of weeks?'

'Yeah, I can fix it up. No trouble at all.'

O'Malley couldn't help but clap his hands together with relief. 'Good man. Well, I'll let you know when he's arriving and what he looks like and all that.'

'Okey-doke. Consider it done.'

'Good on you, Price.'

The silvery-haired casino owner held up his empty glass. 'So how about a drink?'

Happy and relieved at knowing that everything was now in Price's capable hands, O'Malley cheerfully topped up their glasses and once again the conversation went back to old times. Another hour or so went by — the rest of the Bowmore was gone, and Price and O'Malley were starting to roar.

'Okay, Price,' said O'Malley getting to his feet. 'Now that we've got that other business out of the way, how about I shout you to a nice lunch? You hungry?'

'Yeah. All this piss and cold weather. I'm starving,' replied Price.

'Good. Well, I'm going to shout you to the best fish meal in Canberra.'

'At a restaurant?' Price looked at O'Malley quizzingly. 'That's a bit dicey isn't it? You being seen out in public with me?'

'Hah!' The Attorney General held up a commanding finger. 'Don't think I haven't thought of that.'

O'Malley went to a cabinet at the other side of the room leaving Price staring at the fire. He rummaged around in a drawer for a few moments then walked back over and stood in front of Price.

'Well, what do you reckon?'

When Price looked up, the Attorney General was wearing a loose fitting black wig, horn-rim glasses and a false moustache. He stared at him expressionless for a moment and shook his head.

'Is that a wig, or did your cat die? You look like Lamont Cranston's father-in-law.'

'Yes. But I don't look like me — do I, Price?'

'What about the nose, Loz?'

'I've booked it a separate table.'

'And does it pay for its own food?'

'Certainly.'

'Then let's go.' Price stood up and put on his jacket. 'And where are you taking me? They got a No Names in Canberra, have they?'

The Attorney General slipped an arm around his old friend's shoulders. 'Price,' he said. 'I am going to take you where they've got the fattest, juiciest Clyde River oysters you've ever tasted. And they do a Braidwood Rainbow trout in lemon butter that'll give you a horn a foot long.'

'Fair dinkum. Where is it?'

'It's a bit of a sneak go. The Alislie Hotel. Over near the War Memorial? Yvonne,' he called out towards the study.

BARELY TWO MINUTES drive from the War Memorial, Eddie pulled the Rolls up in a small car park at the front of the Alislie Hotel, a single-storey building, spread out over almost the entire block. With its red, pink and white decor, rambling vines and well-manicured gardens, it looked like one of those gracious old hotels you would find in England or on parts of the continent. There was a covered driveway where a set of steps ran up to a polished double-oak door, but there were no parking spaces.

'Go round the back,' said Dutchy. 'There's plenty round there.'

Eddie found himself in a large parking area at the rear of the hotel. He locked the car and followed her through the back entrance and along a maze of corridors that ran past a large garden with a fountain bubbling away in the middle which the hotel appeared to be built around.

'What made you pick this joint?' asked Eddie.

'It's quiet. It's very nice. It's low key, without being sleazy and there's a lot of people always coming and going.'

'Just the sort of place you'd stay if you were in Canberra getting rid of five thousand "Stevie Nicks".'

'Right on, Eddie baby,' agreed Dutchy, as they arrived at her room. She fumbled in her bag for the key and pushed the door open.

Dutchy's room wasn't exactly huge, but it was comfortable and warm. A double bed faced a TV, a small fridge and a well-stocked mini-bar. There was a separate shower and bathroom; through the curtains behind the bed, Eddie could see the fountain bubbling away in the courtyard.

'Not too bad, Dutch,' nodded Eddie.

'Yeah,' she replied, a little indifferently, throwing her bag and rabbit skin jacket on the bed. Without any further ado, Dutchy went to the bar, grabbed a mini-bottle of Jim Beam, Green Label and poured the lot into a glass. She got some ice from the fridge, gave it the merest whisper of ginger-ale and downed the lot in two swallows. 'Ohh boy,' she said, with an appreciative toss of her head. 'Did I need that.' Eddie stood there with a slight smile on his face, and watched her repeat the performance; this time taking only one good swallow. 'Ohh yes. That's better.' She sat back on the bed and motioned towards the bar with her drink. 'Help yourself, Ed. You don't need me.'

'Yeah, okay.' Eddie checked out the bar, looked in the fridge and settled for a bottle of Reschs Premium Lager. He took the top off and raised the bottle to Dutchy. 'Well. Good to see you again, Dutch.'

'Yeah, you too Ed.'

They each took a swallow and Eddie grinned as he saw the tension leaving his old flame. 'So, Dutch,' he said. 'You're in town doing a little dope scam, eh?'

'Yeah.' She opened her bag and pulled out a large envelope full of fifty and hundred dollar bills. 'A nice, lazy fifty grand,' she winked. 'Not bad for a couple of days work.'

'Very nice,' agreed Eddie. 'And what's your wedge?'

'My wedge?' Dutchy grinned and tossed the money casually on to a table next to the bed. 'The lot.'

'The lot?' Eddie looked surprised.

'Yeah, I nicked them. These dealers have rented the unit next to mine. I've never spoken to them, but it sticks out like dogs' knackers what they're up to. I just happen to have a key to their flat and one day, when I knew they weren't home, I went in, and hello — there's a tea-chest half-full of "Stevies" and all these green plastic, garbage bags with numbers written on them. I grabbed one with five thousand on it. Made a phone call, and here I am in Canberra minding my own bloody business I might add, and then you turn up.'

'Yeah,' grinned Eddie.

'But you needn't worry, Eddie. Even though you now know all my business, I won't ask you yours.' Eddie kept grinning, but didn't say anything. Dutchy looked at him for a moment then put her drink down and got up from the bed. 'Ohh, bugger this,' she said and threw her arms around him. 'Jesus, it's good to see you again, Salita — you little shit.'

'You too, Dutch.'

At five feet ten and wearing high heels, Dutchy was a good three inches taller than Eddie. She looked down into his eyes as he returned her embrace then kissed him full on the mouth, moving her lips slowly from side to side and taking her own sweet time about it.

'Eddie, there's a bottle of champagne in the fridge and you and I are going to drink it.'

Eddie scarcely had time to nod before Dutchy had a bottle of Taittinger out of the fridge, and had popped the cork and poured them both a glass. They drank that and then another, laughing while they reminisced about old times. Dutchy turned on the radio and music drifted through the room. The first song finished and cross-faded straight into another. It was an old Tamla-Motown hit, The Foundations singing 'Now That I've Found You'.

'Oh, Eddie,' Dutchy squealed, putting down their drinks. 'I remember this from Vietnam. We used to do it in the show. Come on, let's have a dance.'

With Dutchy crooning throatily and Eddie doing his best they sang and danced their way around the motel room. The song ended, leaving them standing there looking into each other's eyes. Finally Dutchy spoke.

'I heard you were married, Eddie,' she said.

'Yeah. Got a great missus and two terrific kids,' nodded Eddie. 'And incidentally, Lindy would cut my nuts out if she knew I was in here with you. And so would my bloody boss,' he added, 'if he ever found out.'

'My marriage lasted four years. But I finished up well in front, and there's no hard feelings.'

'That's good.'

They held on to each other, smiling, looking into each other's eyes. Neither tried to break away.

'How long before you have to leave?' asked Dutchy.

'About half-past four. I've got to pick Price up at five.'

'My plane goes at 6.30. That gives us about four hours.'

'Four hours,' smiled Eddie. 'To do what? I am married you know.'

'Fair enough,' agreed Dutchy. 'But say something happened here this afternoon; you wouldn't really be playing up behind your wife's back.'

'No?'

'No. You'd just be collecting on an old debt. And I do owe you one you know.'

They kissed again. This time Dutchy slipped her tongue into Eddie's mouth, to be immediately met by Eddie's. He ran his hands up under her pullover, undid her bra and cupped his hands around her breasts, gently massaging her nipples with his fingers.

'Oh, Eddie,' she sighed and ran her tongue in his ear. She pulled Eddie in to her then sighed again. 'Oh, Eddie. Are you carrying a gun, or are you just glad to see me?' She put her hands in the small of Eddie's back and pulled him in harder against her pelvis. 'Ooh, Eddie,' she giggled. 'You *are* glad to see me.'

Eddie unzipped the front of her designer jeans. The zipper burst open and his hand quickly moved down. Beneath his touch he could feel the bristle of her ted, warm and moist through her knickers.

'And just what have we got here, Miss Richtenburgh?' he asked, giving it a gentle stroke as he kissed her breasts.

'That,' heaved Dutchy. 'That's classified. It's my army intelligence map of Tasmania.'

'Yeah?' Eddie moved his tongue down her stomach and over her navel towards her crutch. 'In that case,' he said, easing her jeans down over her backside at the same time. 'I'd better eat it. The enemy could overrun us again.' Before he started, he looked up at her and winked. 'This first one might be a bit quick, Dutchy. But like you said, we've got four hours.'

* * *

YVONNE SWUNG THE Attorney General's Fairlane smoothly up the driveway in front of the Alislie hotel, stopping without turning off the motor.

'You needn't bother opening the door for us,' said O'Malley, wriggling out of his seat belt. 'No need to make a big show of us arriving.'

'Good idea, sir,' she replied, smiling a little as she watched Price and the Attorney General climb unsteadily out of the car.

O'Malley glanced at his watch. 'Pick us up back here at, say, three o'clock.'

'As you wish, sir. See you then. Enjoy your lunch. You too, Mr Galese.' Price gave her a wink and the Fairlane moved off, then he and O'Malley walked up the front steps, weaving a little as they entered the warmth of the hotel foyer.

With its lush red carpet and polished oak panelling, the Alislie dining room had a noticeable feeling of natural warmth. The gold wallpaper, red and white decor and the vase of fresh flowers on each table gave the room a distinct air of elegance and old-world savoir faire. Within seconds of their arriving a politely efficient, but unobtrusive, head waiter appeared.

'Mr . . .?' he smiled.

'Menzies,' replied the Attorney General.

The head waiter smiled in acknowledgment. 'Of course, sir. This way please.'

He ushered them to a table next to a small, enclosed patio overlooking the courtyard and fountain, directly opposite room 306 where Dutchy and Eddie were sipping champagne, less than fifteen metres away.

'Very nice,' said Price, looking around. 'I'm impressed, Loz.'

'Yes. It's a pity it's so bloody cold. We could have sat out on the patio. It's beautiful out there.'

'Any cocktails before eating, sir?' asked the head waiter, placing a wine list on the table.

'Yes, two margaritas,' said O'Malley.

'Certainly, sir.'

'I like it here, Price,' said the Attorney General, when the head waiter was out of earshot. 'It's classy without being pretentious. You haven't got hoardes of wallies gawking at you. And,' he added enthusiastically, 'the food has got to be the best in Canberra — and no one's twigged to it yet.'

A tuxedoed waiter arrived with the drinks. O'Malley ordered a bottle of Roxburgh Chardonnay, plus a dozen oysters Rockefeller each and the Braidwood trout with vegetables in season for both of them. They finished their margaritas and the wine arrived; which they ripped into with great gusto. It wasn't long before the oysters were at their table.

'By Jesus, Loz. These are a good oyster,' said Price.

'Told you, didn't I?'

Price polished off his oysters in less than ten minutes and was starting to look at the shells. 'In fact, these oysters are that good, Loz . . . seeing as you're paying — I'm going to have another dozen.'

'Order a dozen for me, too.'

Price had just put his hand up to catch the waiter's attention, when his eyebrows knitted and he cocked his head towards a partially open window not far from their table. 'Did you hear that, Loz?'

The Attorney General cocked an ear towards the window. 'Sounded like a woman screaming.'

'There it goes again,' said Price.

'Do you think there could be a murder going on?'

Price listened intently for a moment then chuckled. 'No,' he said. 'I've heard that sound before. They're probably a couple of honeymooners.'

The waiter arrived, Price ordered and they continued with the chardonnay while they waited for their oysters.

'Maybe we should get a couple of dozen sent round to that bloke's room,' laughed Price, as another scream filtered across the courtyard and through the window. 'And a gallon of stout.'

'Whoever that bloke is,' said the Attorney General, putting down his glass to attack the second lot of oysters, 'he doesn't need any bloody oysters. In fact, I'm going to close the window — I'm starting to get a fat.'

They finished the first bottle of Roxburgh Chardonnay just as the fish arrived, so O'Malley ordered another. The trout in lemon butter sauce with chopped fish herbs straight from the garden was one of the best fish meals Price had ever had. And he told O'Malley too. Even the accompanying vegetables, which were steamed to perfection, seemed to have a flavour all of their own. They took their time with the meal, savouring every morsel while they finished the wine, and then ordered Drambuies and coffee. By three o'clock the head of state and the distinguished racehorse owner from Sydney were howling like wolves. O'Malley settled the bill and the head waiter led them to the front steps which they went down like a mob of sailors coming back from shore leave. Yvonne had the car out the front and when she saw the state they were in she decided it might be best if she did open the door for them this time.

'Home, James,' hiccupped O'Malley, as he and Price sprawled onto the back seat.

'Home it is, sir.'

As Yvonne got back behind the wheel of the car, Price caught a glimpse of her face in the rear vision mirror watching O'Malley wobbling around in the back seat. Even in the state he was in, Price could tell by the smile on her face and the warm look emanating from her eyes that this wasn't just a job to her. She had a genuine affection for the likeable, if quite drunken, Attorney General of Australia.

SOME TIME AFTER four, Eddie Salita, his hair matted, and his face streaked with sweat, was sitting on the edge of the bed in room 306 doing up his shirt. Dutchy was laying back under the bedcovers watching him through half-closed eyes. She had a look of dreamy contentment on her face; she also looked like she'd just been ten rounds with Sonny Liston. Eddie stood up to tuck his shirt in and smiled down at her.

'So, how are you feeling, Dutch?' he said.

'How am I feeling? Fucked is how I'm feeling, Eddie. And I mean that quite literally.'

Eddie chuckled. 'Well. I thought that was the idea of the afternoon.'

'Well it was. And when you said the first one would be a bit quick I thought, fair enough. And I was keen for the second. But the third and fourth. Christ! You stopped twice in four hours — and that was just to drink two bottles of beer.' Dutchy wriggled her bum slightly beneath the sheets. 'Jesus! How am I going to walk to the plane? I'm that bow-legged, you can hang me over the front door for good luck.'

'Sorry, Dutch, but I just can't help it, mate. Poking a pussy in my face is like giving Popeye spinach.'

'Tell me about it,' groaned Dutchy.

Eddie put his cap and jacket on and stood looking at his old flame for a moment. He smiled, sat next to her on the bed, put his arm around her, and kissed her.

'Dutch,' he said softly. 'I don't quite know how to say this. But I have to go. And I don't know if I'll ever be able to see you again, love.'

'That's okay, Ed. I understand. I got a bloke who runs a

shoe company in Sydney who wants to marry me anyway. I think after this I might take him up on the offer.'

Eddie kissed her again. 'I gotta get going, Dutch. And you've got a plane to catch.'

She twined her arms around his neck and kissed him for the last time. 'See you, Ed.'

'See you, Dutch.' The door closed and he was gone.

Eddie was smiling to himself as he sat in the Rolls waiting for the motor to warm up a little, then a thought hit him. Christ! I'm supposed to have been in that Art Gallery this afternoon. And that bloody print I promised Lindy. Shit! Where is the joint? He snatched the NRMA road map of Canberra from on top of the dash and quickly scanned the streets. There it is. King Edward Terrace, just on the other side of Lake Burley Griffin. And it's on the way to Red Hill. Grouse. He glanced at the clock as he tossed the map back on the dash. I've got just under half an hour.

Eddie found the National Gallery easily enough, but for the life of him he couldn't find a parking spot. He left the car as close as possible to the building and sprinted up a set of steps and along an elevated pathway to the entrance. Inside the revolving doors the ceiling was so high and echoey it was like being lost inside some gigantic cathedral. Eddie's eyes darted everywhere in the indirect lighting trying to find the gift shop. He spotted it not far from the entrance and, ignoring the stares of several uniformed attendants, almost ran across to it.

There were rows and rows of cards and posters, and stacks of books and magazines. No, that's not what I want, Eddie muttered to himself. His eyes flicked around the gift shop. Ah, there's what I'm looking for. He went to a row of art-prints on a rack built out from the wall and started flipping through them. Shit! What am I going to get her? I wouldn't know one bloody artist from another. Wait on, this one looks familiar. Eddie's mind was jogged back to a chocolate commercial he'd seen on TV. Two characters in an old painting in an art gallery come to life and eat a bar of chocolate when the caretaker walks away. The caretaker returns and they get back in the painting leaving the wrapping on the art gallery floor. That'll do, thought Eddie. He pulled it out and took it to the girl at the gift shop counter.

'Aah, yes,' said the studious looking young lady behind the counter. *On The Wallaby Trail.* An excellent choice. You're an aficionado of Frederick McCubbin are you?'

'Who?'

'Frederick McCubbin,' repeated the girl. 'The Australian artist who painted this.'

'Never heard of him,' shrugged Eddie. 'But I like Kit-Kats.'

The girl heaved a sigh of exasperation. Bloody Philistine, she muttered to herself. Typical. She wrapped Eddie's print in a cardboard tube. He paid her and sped to the car. He was at O'Malleys house in Red Hill at two minutes to five.

When Eddie swung the Rolls Royce up into the driveway, Price Galese, the urbane casino proprietor was propped in the doorway, blind as a bat. Yvonne had him by one arm; O'Malley was passed out on the lounge inside.

'Ohh, Eddie,' he groaned, when he saw him walking towards him. 'Help me to the car, will you, mate.'

Yvonne looked at Eddie and smiled. 'They've had a big day.'

'It looks it,' replied Eddie, taking his boss by the arm.

'Will you be all right now?' Eddie nodded and returned her smile. 'Well goodbye then, Mr Galese. It's been a pleasure to have met you.'

Price mumbled something and gave Yvonne a limp wave. Eddie gave her a last wink as the door closed, then placed his boss gently on the front seat of the car and did his seat-belt up.

'Ohh, Eddie. I'm so bloody drunk,' said Price, as they cruised back down La Perouse Street.

'Yeah? I'd never have guessed,' grinned Eddie.

'That bloody O'Malley. Christ! He drinks like a bloody fish,' said Price with a hiccup.

'Where have you been?'

'We kicked off drinking whiskey at his place. Then he took me out for lunch.'

'Yeah? Any good?'

'Yeah. It was beautiful. Some old pub out near the War Memorial.'

'The War Memorial?' Eddie looked at Price a little suspiciously. 'You went to some pub out near the War Memorial. What was it called?'

'The Alislie, or something,' mumbled Price.

'The Alislie.' Eddie nearly ran up the arse of a Holden station wagon as they approached Lake Burley Griffin. 'You had lunch at the Alislie?'

'Yeah,' hiccupped Price. 'T'riffic food.' He gave a drunken laugh. 'It was funny, though. We're eating away and some

32

bloke was screwing this sheila in a room just across from us. You could hear it all over the joint. Sounded like he was cutting her throat.'

Eddie swallowed hard as he remembered Dutchy going off in bed like a box of sweaty dynamite. He made a mental sign of the cross and decided to change the subject. But Price changed it for him.

'What'd you do yourself?'

'Huh? Oh, I ah . . . went to the War Memorial. Then had a look at the Art Gallery — got the kids a present, and a nice print for Lindy. It's on the back seat.'

'Good on you, Ed. You remembered your family.'

'Yeah!' Eddie gave a sigh of relief. 'Well, I suppose you won't be wanting any tea tonight then?'

Price shook his head. 'Just a cup of coffee and put me to bed.'

'Righto. What time do you want to get going in the morning?'

''Bout nine, eh?'

'Okay.'

Price rolled his head towards Eddie, having trouble keeping his eyes open. 'Oh, Eddie,' he moaned. 'I'm so pissed.'

Eddie looked at his boss, smiled and kept driving. Despite the warmth inside the car, Eddie could distinctly feel a few drops of cold sweat forming around his neck.

AT 8.30 THE following morning, Price and Eddie were standing outside The Country Club Motel. It was bitterly cold and misty. The roads were damp from some light rain and great clouds of steam hung in the still morning air as they spoke. Price's face was a little pale, but overall he hadn't brushed up too bad. He was just awfully seedy.

'So, how are you feeling after a feed?' said Eddie, slamming down the boot after placing their bags inside. 'At least you had a good night's sleep.'

'Not too bad considering. Those four Panadol did the trick.' Price shook his head. 'That bloody O'Malley.'

Eddie smiled and opened the door for him. 'It takes two to tango, you know.'

The big motor purred into life and Eddie glanced at his watch. 'We should be home not long after lunch.'

'Good,' intoned Price. 'Two days in Camelot's more than enough for me.'

'Yep,' agreed Eddie, his eyes on the outside mirror as he

33

swung the Rolls around. 'It's Centennial Park without the kiosks, as far as I'm concerned.'

It wasn't long before the blue sign they'd seen coming in flashed past; only this time it was on the opposite side of the road telling them they were now leaving the Australian Capital Territory. Eddie wasn't thinking about much, just smiling to himself about how lucky he was Price hadn't parked at the rear of the Alislie and spotted his car. Price was staring ahead in silence, obviously preoccupied.

'So,' said Eddie, turning the car radio down a little. 'How did it all work out with O'Malley? Everything sweet? Anything you want to tell me about?'

Price seemed to come to life a little. 'Yeah,' he nodded enthusiastically, 'it all worked out well. It's no real big deal. In fact I'll give you the guts while we're going along.'

By the time they'd passed Lake George and Thornford, Price had given Eddie the complete story; including the fact that Peregrine was the Attorney General's godson and it was the IRA who were after him. The only thing he didn't do was show Eddie the photo of Peregrine that O'Malley had given him, as he had put it somewhere in his overnight bag when he was drunk. Despite the seriousness of Peregrine's situation in England, Eddie couldn't help but be a little amused.

'It's a bit of a funny one, Price,' he said.

'Yeah,' nodded his boss. 'It is a bit, isn't it?'

'This Peregrine sounds like a bit of a Beechams.'

'Yeah,' nodded Price again. 'It sure looks that way. But, he's O'Malley's godson and I said I'd look after him. So . . .'

'Fair enough.' Another kilometre or so sped by. 'So what do you intend to do with him?'

'Get him out of Sydney. Send him right up the North Coast somewhere for a couple of weeks. Till all this rattle blows over in Ireland. Or England. Or wherever it bloody is.'

'Up the North Coast?' Eddie's eyes lit up as if an idea had just hit him. 'How far up the North Coast?'

'Right up. The further the bloody better.'

'Jesus! I might be able to do something there. I got some old mates from Vietnam living in the Tweed Valley. I was only on the phone to them last week. There's a big property up there used to belong to this colonel in the US Marines. There's no one living there and they were thinking of buying it. But they haven't got the money. You could rent it easy enough and snooker him up there.'

'Jesus, that's a good idea,' said Price.

Eddie put his foot down and easily overtook a line of three cars. 'You got anyone in mind to take this bloke up the North Coast and look after him?'

A hint of a smile creased the corners of Price Galese's dark brown eyes. 'Yeah,' he nodded slowly. 'I think I know just the bloke.'

SITTING IN THE lounge room of his Bondi semi, watching the Saturday afternoon football live on the ABC, Les Norton could hardly have been in a better mood. It had been a pretty good day all round. He'd got out of bed at about ten thirty and had an enjoyable breakfast with Warren. Warren then left Les to go off to the Paddington stalls for a few drinks and have a look at the elfs and goblins and other endangered species that are apt to congregate in large numbers along that part of Oxford Street on Saturday. It was a cold but clear day with a light nor'wester blowing so Les opted to ring Billy Dunne for a run on Bondi Beach and a bit of bag work at North Bondi Surf Club, which, in the crisp winter weather, was more than enjoyable too. After this they had a T-bone and salad at the Bondi Icebergs plus a few beers. In between shouts he and Billy managed to pull three jackpots on the pokies. Then on the way home Les called in to the TAB and had $200 on one of Price's horses, My Deal, which, by changing channels to 'The Wide World Of Sport', Norton was ecstatic to see it get up in the last few strides and win by half a length at 7/2. Quite a tasty result. But best of all, Easts had just knocked off Balmain with a dead set, flukeish try in the last two minutes when the Easts hooker went over from a Balmain knock-on. The Roosters missed the conversion but still managed to win by one point. Not a very convincing result and not that Norton was any sort of fanatical Easts supporter, apart from having a bit of a soft spot from his playing days with them. But when it came to football, a certain George Brennan, manager of the Kelly Club was: and his team was Balmain. He and Les had bet $100 on the game plus a carton of beer. Now Norton was even more in front. But no amount of liquor or money would be as good as seeing the look on George's face when Les walked into the club that night or the ammunition he'd have to fire at him with absolutely none coming back.

Aah yes, thought Norton, easing back happily into the lounge. How do the words go to that Louis Armstrong song? 'And I say to myself, what a wonderful world.' He raised his Kahlualaced cup of coffee to the TV screen and the players who were now leaving the field.

'You're not wrong, Satchmo old mate,' he said out loud.

Norton finished his coffee, pottered around the house for a while, then had his usual hour's nap before he got ready for work. Warren still wasn't home when he got up. The pixies have probably taken him away, Les mused. So he ironed his shirt, had a couple of toasted ham sandwiches and was at the Kelly Club around eight-thirty. Billy was standing out the front when he got there.

'My Deal,' grinned Les, as soon as he saw Billy. 'Did you get on?'

Billy nodded and returned Norton's grin. 'Reckon.'

'It paid $7.70 on the TAB.' Billy nodded again. 'Between that and our little flutter at the pokies we haven't had a bad day.' Billy winked.

'But, mate,' enthused Norton, giving his workmate a light punch on the arm, 'did you see who won the football?'

'Yes,' replied Billy. 'And I know someone else who did too.'

Norton laughed and rubbed his hands together. 'How's his face? Like a tin of condemned bully beef?'

'Worse.'

'Good. I'll go up and let the fat cunt know I'm here.'

Whistling cheerfully, Norton disappeared up the stairs two at a time. He was back about five minutes later, still whistling and with two steaming mugs of coffee.

'Did you see him?' asked Billy Dunne.

'Sort of,' replied Les. 'He saw me. Mumbled G'day or something. Then went and hid in the shithouse.'

'Did you follow him in?'

'No,' chuckled Norton. 'I left him in there where he belongs. But I'll stick it up him after work. Don't worry about that.'

The boys sipped their coffee while they nodded to and joked with some of the punters who were starting to arrive. No one stayed out the front long enough to engage them in any great lengths of conversation as the bitter sou'wester whipping up Kelly Street soon put a stop to that. Even the mugs and the drunks didn't want to hang around and argue in the cold for long. These were the sort of nights Les and Billy appreciated more than ever the scarves and gloves that Price had shouted each to wear with their tuxedos.

'Price is back,' said Billy.

'Yeah,' nodded Les. 'I saw him on TV this arvo in the winners' circle when My Deal won.'

'Wonder what he was doing in Canberra?'

'Wouldn't have a clue. George didn't know either. He might tell us after work tonight.'

'Yeah,' nodded Billy. 'He might.'

Another hour or so passed by and apart from the wind stinging their eyes and making their noses run, the boys were doing it cosy. In fact they wouldn't have minded a bit of a heated argument or even a minor altercation just to liven things up and get their blood pumping. They had just finished another mug of coffee when a beige Rolls Royce turned graciously into Kelly Street, with Eddie at the wheel and a smiling Price at the window.

'Hello,' said Billy. 'Here they are now.'

The Rolls came gently to a stop not far from the club and Eddie and Price got out. There were greetings and smiles all round when they saw Les and Billy. Eddie was wearing corduroy jeans and a windcheater, Price had on a light grey suit and blue tie; neither had their jackets done up and although the wind was going through the boys on the door like a knife, Price and Eddie seemed completely oblivious to it.

'So how was Canberra?' asked Billy.

'In a word, Billy,' replied Price, 'fuckin' cold.'

'Colder than this?' asked Les.

'You're kidding, Les,' said Eddie. 'Canberra makes this look like Surfers Paradise.'

'Jesus, that's where I wouldn't mind being right now,' said Norton, clapping his hands together.

Price and Eddie exchanged surreptitious smiles. 'You never know, Les,' said Price. 'I might just have a little something for you after work tonight.'

'How do you mean?'

Price gave Les a light punch on the shoulder. 'I'll tell you about it when we knock off. Anyway, I've got to get upstairs and make sure George hasn't robbed me.'

'I wonder what that was all about?' said Norton, as he watched Eddie and Price disappear up the stairs.

Billy shrugged his shoulders. 'Dunno,' he said. He made a gesture with his hands. 'But I imagine we'll find out after work tonight.'

Try as they might, Les and Billy couldn't find anything funny about standing around the front of the club that night and at one am Les made sure their next cups of coffee were well-laced with Jim Beam Black Label. But the cold kept the mugs away and there wasn't so much as a cross word let alone any fisticuffs all night. So apart from the weather, and with a few bourbon coffees under their belts, Saturday evening went smoother than a Mormon's haircut. However, Les and Billy were still more than pleased when at three-thirty they had the place locked, bolted and barred and were sitting in the warmth of Price's office having an after-work and end-of-week drink.

There was the usual idle chit-chat as the first two rounds of drinks went down. Price and Eddie didn't seem to be saying a great deal. Les and Billy commented on the weather and the money they'd won on the pokies and Price's horse. The big surprise of the night was George Brennan. Having lost the bet to Les and knowing he was in for a ferocious bagging, Les had expected him to have a 25 carat case of the shits. On the contrary, he was all smiles. Les hit him with a couple of barbed sling-offs early in the piece but the fat casino manager wouldn't come in at all — he simply shrugged his shoulders and copped it sweet. This took the wind right out of Norton's sails. So he quietly collected his $100 and his case of beer and even conceded that the Easts try was a fluke and Balmain should have won. Billy Dunne couldn't believe his ears. Eventually though, the small talk about football, racehorses and the weather drifted off and all eyes turned to Price and Eddie. George was the first to swing the subject around to what was on everyone's mind.

'So,' he said casually. 'How was the trip to Canberra, Price? Everything go all right?'

'The trip to Canberra? It was good. Cold. But yes, everything did go all right,' replied Price. He stared at the deafening silence coming from his three trusted employees and exchanged a half smile with Eddie. 'I suppose you're all wondering what we were up to down there. And why we left in such a hurry?'

'Well . . .' George gave a noncommittal shrug of his shoulder while Les and Billy tried to look indifferent. But it was patently obvious they were all swarming like bees.

'Okay.' Price eased back in his padded leather chair. 'I'll tell you what's going on.' He fixed his gaze on Norton. 'I would have had to anyway.'

While Eddie got them all another drink, Price told them the reason he and Eddie went to Canberra. He simplified it as much as possible. But he did mention the lunch with O'Malley, the fact that Peregrine was a baronet and the Attorney General's godson. How it was the IRA that were after him and how they were going to hide him on the farm Eddie knew

38

about in the Tweed Valley for two weeks. Eddie didn't mention what he had done while he was down there.

There was a puzzled, if not slightly amused silence for a moment as what Price had just told them sunk in. Then Billy spoke.

'Shit!' he said. 'You had lunch with the Attorney General of Australia?'

'Yes,' nodded Price. 'The Right Honourable Laurence O'Malley QC. Hard to imagine a bloke I used to SP with in pubs would finish up Attorney General of Australia, isn't it?' Billy shook his head in amazement.

'And you're going to hide this Peregrine bloke up the North Coast somewhere for two weeks,' said Les.

'That's right,' said Price, then he and Eddie exchanged smiles. 'And that's where you come in, Les me old son.'

'I come in?'

'Yeah. Who do you think's going to take Peregrine up to the Tweed Valley and put him under his wing for a fortnight?' Norton blinked as Price motioned his Scotch and soda towards him. 'You are.'

'I am?'

'That's right, Les, you big bouncing bundle of fun. You are.'

Norton stared at Price for a moment. 'Hey, hang on a sec,' he said guardedly.

Price gazed around the room at the bemused looks the others were now giving Les. 'Will you listen to this prick? He was whingeing about the cold out the front earlier. I offer him a trip up the North Coast to sit on his arse for two weeks in the sun and do nothing, and he's blowing up. Can you believe it?'

Norton made a defensive gesture with his hands. 'Wait on, Price. I didn't mean it like that. You just caught me off guard, that's all.' He shrugged and took a sip of Fourex. 'Sounds like a piece of piss, to tell you the truth. What do you want me to do?'

'Right.' Eddie placed a folded sheet of paper on Price's desk. 'That's where you're going. That's the address of the farm and how you get there.'

Norton reached across for the map just as Price dropped a large envelope on the desk. 'There's a photo of Peregrine. And five thousand in cash which should be more than enough for a two-week holiday. But,' he added, 'anything he wants, you get him. There's also the address of a car dealer I know out at Tempe. Go out there Monday and pick out any car you want for the trip. It's all sweet.'

Norton dropped the map and picked up the photo of Peregrine Normanhurst. It was a little out of focus and taken from across the street: three casually dressed young men sitting on the bonnet of a Daimler drinking a bottle of champagne. 'Which is him?' he asked.

'The one on the right,' replied Price.

Norton stared at the photo. All he could make out was that the person in question was of medium build and had fair hair. 'It's not much of a photo,' he complained.

'You'll see him on Sunday.' said Price. 'You won't be able to miss him. He arrives on British Airways flight 389 at 3.30 in the afternoon. Pick him up and keep him at your place till Tuesday. Then you can both piss off.'

While Price and the others watched him with slight amusement, Norton studied the photo of Peregrine and the other items on Price's desk. 'I don't believe this,' he said, shaking his head. 'It's like that bloody show on TV, "Mission Impossible". This is your assignment, Mr Phelps. Should you choose to accept it. This photo will self destruct in five seconds. If you are caught the agency will deny any knowledge of your existence.' He shook his head again.

'If I was you, you big red-headed goose,' said George, 'I'd cop it sweet. Two weeks in the sun. You've killed them.'

'Reckon,' added Billy. 'I wish it was me that was going.'

'Yeah, I suppose you're right,' smiled Les. 'A couple of weeks out of the cold in the peace and quiet. And all I got to do is put up with this Sloane Ranger. There's no way those Irish are going to follow him all the way out to Australia. They'd never find him anyway.'

'Hey,' said Eddie seriously. 'Never underestimate the Irish. It was a paddy taught me how to make letter bombs. And they love to get square.'

'Yeah, fair enough,' answered Les. 'But you know what I mean. There's about one chance in a million of anything going wrong. It's just a glorified holiday.'

'That's right,' said Price. 'And I'm bloody paying for it.'

Norton held up the envelope full of money and grinned. 'Right on. I reckon me and Peregrine'll give this five grand some hurry up. I hope there's a TAB and a massage parlour in this Tweed Valley. Any good restaurants up there, Eddie?'

'Hey,' said Price, emphasising the point with his finger. 'You just make sure you look after this rooster while you've got him up there. And while he's down here keep him very low profile; we don't want anyone to know he's in the country. It's more than likely nothing's going to happen. But like Eddie said, don't underestimate these people.'

'Yeah, fair enough,' said Les. 'I was only joking. I'll keep him under wraps at my place till Tuesday, then we'll be on our way.' Norton put down the money and picked up the photo of Peregrine and his friends. 'What sort of a bloke is he, anyway? You any idea? You said he was filthy rich.'

They sat there talking and drinking for a while longer. Price couldn't tell Les anymore than what O'Malley had told him. But he did reiterate that back in England, Peregrine was in a lot more bother than he had realised. At around four, they locked up the club and turned out the lights. Les said goodbye, telling Price he'd ring him as soon as he had Peregrine in his house. Then with his case of Fourex tucked up under his arm he and Billy walked up to their cars, and that was another week over at The Kelly Club, though, for Les, it was a little more interesting and ended up a better result than some others.

ALTHOUGH IT WAS quite sunny, Sunday still had a pronounced chill in the air. The sou'wester was keeping the temperature down but it was the kind of day that if you found a spot out of the wind it could be quite pleasant. Norton's kitchen wasn't too bad at all. The winter sun was streaming through the window where Warren, who had been up about half an hour before Les, had prepared a big breakfast of bacon and eggs and hash browns for them both. Now he was sitting back sipping coffee and listening avidly while Les told him about the house guest they would be having for the next couple of days. Being a man of good taste himself, Warren was more than looking forward to it.

'This Peregrine sounds like he might be a pretty interesting sort of a bloke,' said Warren, smearing another slice of toast with blackberry jam. 'Shit eh? To think we'll be having a member of the Royal Family staying at Maison Norton for two days. That is a turn up for the books.'

'Yeah,' nodded Les. 'I'll put him in the spare room. He'll be sweet in there and it's only for a couple of nights.'

'I don't know how Sir Peregrine Normanhurst is going to handle the spare room if he's been used to living in a castle. It is a bit grotty.'

'What do you mean? It's got a bed. There's a wardrobe.'

'Yeah. One you found in the street. What about the two ton of rubbish in there?'

'What about it? Half of it's yours.' Warren had to concede the point. 'Anyway, if he don't like it he can sleep on the lounge. Fuck him. What's he want for nothing? Unless you want to give him your room.'

'I couldn't give a stuff if it was Prince Charles himself. He's not getting my room.'

'Well, that settles that. 'Cause Peregrine sure as hell ain't gettin' the landlord's.' Norton got up from the table and went to the loaf of Vogels sitting next to the sink. 'You want another piece of toast?'

They finished breakfast, taking their time over another pot of fresh coffee, and by then it was almost one. Warren left Les to do the washing up, saying he was going round to some girl's place at Rose Bay and he'd see him and the house guest that evening. After he'd gone Les showered and changed into a pair of jeans and sat around reading the Sunday papers for a while. However, something Warren had mentioned earlier kept playing on his mind. He put the paper down and went into the spare room.

Warren hadn't been far out saying there was two ton of rubbish and it was a bit grotty. It looked like a rat's nest. There were magazines, posters, dirty clothes and other junk strewn or stacked around the floor. In the corner were car parts, batteries, the roof-racks off Warren's car plus a spare tyre, his boogie board and flippers. Rusting away in another corner were two spear-guns, half a push-bike and more junk. The wardrobe was still the same ghastly purple colour it was the day Norton found it in Lamrock Avenue, complete with the cracked mirror and the tattered Save The Rainforests stickers. The single bed had a pillow, two old grey blankets and nothing else. There was no curtain, just a single, white Holland blind. Travelodge the room wasn't. Norton surveyed the uninspiring scene for a moment then began stacking things and pushing others into the corners with his foot. He ran a carpet sweeper over the middle of the room and tidied the bed. Aah, bugger it, he thought. It's only for two nights. He looked at his watch. I'd better get going. His plane might be early.

Peregrine's plane was on time, but Les was late due to a truck overturning on Gardeners Road. Not that it made all that much difference because as usual at Sydney airport it took the passengers on flight 389 over an hour and a half to get through customs. Standing behind the throngs of people, squeezed against the barrier at the arrivals section, Norton was glad he'd brought the Sunday paper with him.

The remnants of the previous flight had trickled through, pushing their metal trolleys full of luggage or dragging suitcases on wheels to be greeted and led away by laughing and occasionally crying relatives and friends. There was a pause for a while then a murmur went through the crowd as the passengers from flight 389, looking noticeably more tired and dishevelled than the previous crowd, began to arrive. Norton studied them intently, not really sure what he was looking for; a blurred photograph of one man amongst about two hundred people. Norton watched their faces as they went past the barrier picking up the different accents; mainly English with some foreign and Australian. Suddenly a figure slowly pushing a metal trolley at the edge of the crowd caught Norton's eye. He was not quite as tall as Les, and was wearing a blue trench-coat and matching suede trilby. It was the figure's positive bearing that got Norton. A definite aloofness, as if he was trying to distance himself from the others around him.

From about twenty feet away, Norton studied the man in the trilby, as he removed his trench-coat and folded it neatly across an expensive leather suitcase in the trolley. The figure still seemed oblivious to the people around him, not looking for anybody, but exuding an insouciant confidence that whoever he was there to meet would soon come to him. Beneath the trench-coat, the figure was wearing a plain grey worsted suit cut in traditional English style: three-button front, ticket pocket and two splits in the back. A chalk-striped blue shirt, old school tie and brown suede shoes had Britain stamped all over them and considering whoever it was had just arrived from a thirty-hour flight, the only creases seemed to be in the blue handkerchief in the top pocket of his coat. Norton edged forward for a better look at his face. He had finely-chiselled features, high cheekbones and a straight nose over a strong mouth. His eyes were a hazel green and though Norton could see the graininess in them, the way they occasionally darted around suggested the person in question could at times have some sort of a sense of humour. He looked to be about twenty-two and definitely not the 'Hooray Henry' Les had been led to believe. Les stared at him till their eyes met then made a gesture and moved closer to the rail. The man in the grey suit moved closer also.

'Are you — Peregrine Normanhurst?' asked Les, a little

hesitantly. The man nodded his head briefly. 'Take your gear down there.' Norton nodded to the end of the barrier and moved down as Peregrine followed.

'I'm Les, anyway,' said Norton, as Peregrine brought his trolley to a halt. 'I'll be looking after you while you're out here.' They exchanged a brief but warm handshake.

'Pleased to meet you, Les.' Peregrine's voice was clipped but extremely well-modulated.

Les picked up the heavier of the two bags. 'Follow me. The car's just over here.' Peregrine picked up his overnight bag and trench-coat and followed Les out of the terminal, stopping momentarily to take a pair of sunglasses from his inside coat pocket and slip them on.

'How was the trip over?' asked Les.

'Absolutely ghastly,' replied Peregrine tightly.

'Yeah?' Norton was surprised. 'I thought they looked after you on British Airways.'

'Oh, the food and service was quite marvellous — as one would expect. But we hit this bloody turbulence nearly all the way. I don't think anyone got a wink of sleep.'

The way Peregrine hesitated, almost spluttering when he used the word bloody suggested to Les that this might be the absolute height of his vocabulary of swear words. He made a mental note to watch his Ps and Qs, for the time being anyway. 'Oh well. You'll get a good night's sleep tonight, anyway.' Peregrine didn't bother to reply.

They arrived at Norton's old Ford and Les opened the door. Peregrine looked at the old banger like he'd never seen anything like it before and stepped inside as if he expected something to jump out of the seat and bite him.

'You ever been to Sydney or Australia before?' asked Les, climbing behind the wheel after slinging Peregrine's bag on the back seat. Peregrine shook his head. 'Well, I live at Bondi. You'll be staying at my place for a couple of days then we'll be heading up the North Coast.'

Peregrine nodded disinterestedly. 'Are we going in this?' he asked.

'No. I'm getting the loan of another car on Monday. Tomorrow.'

Peregrine nodded again and stared indifferently out of the windscreen.

Figuring Peregrine was tired and a little testy after his long flight, Norton didn't bother him with any small talk on the way to Bondi. Referring to Les's limousine as 'in this' didn't go over too well, but he could understand the Englishman's irritability and reasoned he'd be okay once he was settled down and had a cup of coffee and a bit of a feed. They arrived at Norton's house in silence.

'Which is yours?' asked Peregrine dully, as he surveyed the row of semis once they were out of the car.

'This one,' smiled Les. 'Come on.'

If Peregrine Normanhurst's stiff upper lip was beginning to curl a little when he walked in the front door, it almost rolled up his face and over his head when he stepped into the spare room.

'Well, what do you reckon?' grinned Norton. 'It's nothing marvellous, but at least you'll be safe here.'

Peregrine surveyed the room like it was the scene of an axe murder. 'What do I reckon?' He had another look around the room then turned to Les. 'Do you know how to get to Kings Cross from here?' Norton nodded. 'Do you know the Sebel Town House?' Norton nodded again. 'Right. Then let's go.'

'You don't like this?' asked Les.

'It's rather nice actually,' replied Peregrine, his voice dripping with sarcasm. 'I'm just curious as to who lived here before me. The hunchback of Notre Dame? Or do you use it to breed some sort of animals for scientific purposes?' Without waiting for a reply, Peregrine picked up his bags and tramped back down the hallway. They were halfway up Old South Head Road before Norton found the heart to speak.

'Listen, Peregrine,' he said. 'I don't know what anybody told you before you left. But I'm not supposed to let you out of my sight the whole time you're here.'

'Then you can jolly well sleep on the floor of my room at the Sebel if you like,' replied Peregrine. 'But I am *not* staying in that . . . kip.'

'Okay. Suit yourself,' shrugged Norton.

In silence they arrived at the Sebel Town House. Les parked the car, picked up Peregrine's suitcase and followed him up the red-carpeted, marble steps of the Sebel into the rich brown carpeting and cedar panelling of arguably the finest hotel in Sydney.

'Yes, sir. May I help you?' asked the smiling young man at the reception desk.

'I'd like a room please,' said Peregrine, ignoring Les taking in the luxury and elegance of the surroundings.

'Certainly, sir. Anything in particular you have in mind?'

'Your best.'

'Well, sir. The Presidential Suite is taken. So is The Hardy Aimes Split Level and the Penthouse. The Sir Robert Helpmann is available at $700 a night.'

Peregrine pulled out his wallet and produced a Gold American express card. 'Tuesday morning we're going to this North Coast of yours, is it, Les?' Norton nodded blankly. 'Good.' Peregrine turned back to the desk clerk. 'Then I shall take the Sir Robert Helpmann for two nights.'

'Yes, sir. Certainly, sir. What name is it please?'

'Normanhurst. Sir Peregrine Normanhurst. The Third.'

Visibly impressed, the desk clerk began filling in the appropriate paperwork. Norton, also impressed, looked on in silence. Christ! he thought. Seven hundred bananas a night. This pommy cunt might be a snob but Jesus, he's sure got some style. Wouldn't Price love him?

The desk clerk summoned a porter who seemed to materialise out of thin air. 'Room 1012,' he said briefly.

The porter almost snapped to attention. 'This way, sir,' he said to Peregrine. Les went to say something but Peregrine cut him off. 'Now, Les,' he said, with icy politeness. 'I am going to my room. Alone, by myself, without you. I am going to have a light meal, a bottle of champers and in two hours I intend to have about fifteen hours sleep. Nothing will happen to me tonight. And I do not wish to be disturbed. May I suggest you do something similar and I shall see you on the morrow. Good day to you, sir.' Leaving Norton standing there, Sir Peregrine Normanhurst III followed the porter into the lift. He didn't look at Les as he waited for the doors to close.

Well, how about that, thought Norton as the lift doors swished shut leaving him standing in the foyer. And good day to you too, sir. You pommy prick. Still, he mused, if I had a bundle of dough and the choice between my place and staying here I think I know what I'd take. Then a more disturbing thought occurred to him. Shit! I'd better ring Price and let him know what's going on.

Price had his answering service on. He didn't leave a message but rang Eddie instead. Eddie's phone didn't answer, so Les rang Price again, leaving a message to say where Peregrine was and everything was sweet. Oh well, nothing much else I can do now and Peregrine should be all right here, surely to Christ. It's as safe as a bank and he's only been in the country five minutes. He looked at his watch. Just on six. Couple of beers'd go down well. He got in his car and headed home.

Instead of going straight home, however, Norton headed down to Woolloomooloo. The crowd spilling out onto the footpath in Cowper Wharf Drive and a thumping version of 'Pretty Woman' coming from the Woolloomooloo Hotel told Les The Eddys were revving up for another Sunday at the 'Loo'. Yeah, why not? There was a parking spot not far from the pub. Les pulled in and joined the crowd; in no time he'd found some people he knew and was in a shout. The hotel was rocking. The Eddys had the crowd dancing in the street and on the median-strip too and the Hahn on tap was delicious. It was a great evening, but after about eight middies Norton thought it might be best if he went home and tried to ring Price again. He bought another shout and left.

When Norton stepped through the door of his house, Warren was sitting in the lounge room drinking Jack Daniel's and Coke with three of the best sorts Les had ever seen: a brunette and two blondes in the tightest-fitting, crutch-hugging jeans imaginable. Norton thought for sure his luck was about to change but the first words Warren spoke, without even bothering to introduce Les, told him who the girls had come to see.

'Well,' said Warren, coming straight to the point. 'Where is he?'

'Where's who?' grinned Norton. 'I'm right here. What more do you want?'

'No, not you, Les,' sneered Warren. 'Peregrine. What have you done with him?'

'Yeah, where's this rich baronet?' trilled one of the blondes.

'He's at the Sebel Town House,' replied Norton.

'The Sebel Town House?' Warren rolled his eyes with mock disbelief. 'You mean to tell me the ignorant pommy bastard chose to stay at the Sebel rather than take the spare room? I don't believe it.'

'Neither do I,' replied Norton, avoiding Warren's stare.

'We could go up the Sebel and see him,' said the brunette.

'No.' Norton shook his head firmly. 'He's just come off a thirty-hour flight and he's buggered. He wants to go straight to bed.'

'Oh,' said the brunette.

'But not to worry,' said Norton brightly, giving his hands a rub. 'All's not lost. Why don't we have a little party here?'

The two blondes looked at Norton like he was something the police had just exhumed. 'Can you take us to the Sheaf?' they asked Warren, as the brunette rose from the lounge and zipped up her jacket.

'Sure.' Warren finished his Jack Daniel's and Coke. 'You want to come down the Sheaf, Les?'

Norton shook his head. 'No, mate. I got to make a few phone-calls and I want to have an early night. I got a fair bit to do tomorrow.'

'Okay. Well I'll see you when I get home.'

'See you then.'

Warren ushered the girls down the hallway. They didn't say goodbye to Les. Les didn't bother to say goodbye to them.

After throwing some chops under the griller Norton tried once more to ring Price and Eddie, but got the same answer as before. He finished his meal and after another couple of unsuccessful attempts settled back to watch a Chevvy Chase movie on TV. He was in bed by eleven. Warren came home alone about twenty minutes later.

By MONDAY THE weather was noticeably warmer. The sou-'wester had swung around to the north and although there was the odd bunch of grey clouds pushing across the sky there was more than enough sunshine. It was an ideal day for a run in Centennial Park. Norton did exactly that, plus some exercises after he got up at seven. Warren was still in bed when he left, but was up and finishing breakfast when a perspiration-streaked Les returned home at eight-thirty. In contrast to Norton's sweaty florid appearance Warren had the look of a cat that had just drunk all the cream and was almost whistling to himself when Les walked into the kitchen.

'Hello, Les,' he said airily, looking up from his coffee. 'How was the run?'

'Good,' replied Norton. 'You should get up and try it yourself one day.'

'I was going to, but the alarm never went off.'

Les opened the fridge and took out a bottle of spa-water. 'What happened with your three girlfriends last night? Friendly little trio, weren't they?'

'Yeah,' agreed Warren. 'They were a bit up themselves all right. I ended up leaving them at Baxters.'

'Lucky Baxters.'

The twinkle still in his eye, Warren continued to study Norton as he drank the spa-water straight from the bottle. 'You read this morning's paper?' he asked very matter-of-factly.

Les looked at the *Daily Telegraph* sitting on the kitchen table. 'Nahh. Why should I? Apart from the football results, there's never anything in it on Monday.' Saying that, he flipped it over to the back sports page. 'Hello. Wests beat Manly. 26-6. Shit! How about that?'

'Yes,' answered Warren, still smirking. 'Evidently one of the Manly players got sent off for head butting.'

'Yeah?' Norton shrugged. 'Oh well. Serves the prick right.'

Warren finished his coffee and headed towards the door. 'Anyway. I'd better get going. The advertising world is calling. I'll ah . . . leave you with the paper. Ta ta, mate,' he chirrupped.

'Yeah, righto, Woz. See you tonight.' Norton stared down the hallway for a moment after Warren had left. He's in a funny mood this morning, he thought. Maybe he got his end in last night and he's not telling me. Anyway, I'm going to have a shower and cook a bit of breakfast. Then I'd better go and check up on Lord Shitbags at the Sebel.

After he'd showered and changed into a tracksuit, Les made some toasted sandwiches and a pot of tea and settled down to enjoy them while he flicked through the morning paper.

The front page was the usual thing. More strikes. Another cocaine bust. The Prime Minister jumping up and down because America was poaching Australia's wheat market. Norton thumbed on heading towards the sports section till he came across Damien T'aime's column. T'aime was a pudding-faced journalist who wrote a full-page social cum gossip column. Not quite a social butterfly — more of a social cockroach — T'aime liked nothing better than to dig up dirt and dust and whatever he could to embarrass the glitterati and fringe dwellers of Sydney society. The column was always written in a breezy, high camp but acerbically witty style. Leading restauranteurs were referred to as noshmongers. Actors were mummers. First-nighters were the freebocracy. Parties were called knees ups and were always launched in either a sea of Fosters or a tidal wave of Moet amidst a crush of bouffants and bagels surrounded by fragrant women enveloped in a blizzard of lace and taffeta etc, etc. But it was an amusing enough column and if it didn't quite tip a bucket on the pompous Sydney social scene, it certainly tipped a well-deserved teacup or two, thanks to the information supplied by Damien's moles, as he always referred to his informants. Damien must have had a mole well and truly planted in The Sebel Town House because when Norton saw the banner across T'aime's column for Monday the fifteenth, his bulging eyes nearly rolled out of his head and plopped in his tea.

BOOZY BARONET BUTTS BLACK-CLAD BORE

howled the headline, and underneath it were two photos. One was of Peregrine waving a bottle of champagne in the bar of The Sebel Town House and the other was of a scowling radio announcer, Adam Pratt, who Norton recognised because he always wore black clothes and a black hat, being ordered from the premises by the hotel security.

'Jesus Christ!' wailed Norton in astonished disbelief. 'What the fuck's this?' He began reading the column.

My, my, my (T'aime's column miaowed) what *is* the Royal Family coming to? It appears mega-rich Brit and Baronet somewhere in the queue for the throne, Sir Peregrine Normanhurst III is implanted at The Sebel Town House. Pezza, it seems, was enjoying a quaff or three of champers in the Sebel bar when Bollinger Bolshie and airwaves bore Adam Pratt accosted him for an interview. One word led to another and I'm told the bolstered baronet nutted Pratt with an absolutely splendid head butt one would expect to find more amongst Liverpool dock-workers than the fun-loving Royal Family. No one knows who started the set-to at the Sebel, but on Sir Peregrine's request, ashen-faced staff were forced to remove Pratt. And seeing as Sir P. is gladly forking out $700 a night to stay in The Sir Robert Helpmann Suite at The Sebel, Pezza's request held a lot more sway than the black clad, media star who was flung out into the cold forthwith. Sebel staff are as usual tight-lipped about the whole affair, but be assured, gentle readers, your scribe will keep digging. Incidentally, that rattling sound you're hearing is Sir Robert Helpmann rolling over in his grave.

Norton quickly read it again then let out one word. 'Shit!!!' He dropped the paper and what he was eating and hurried to the phone dreading the thought of making the call. It rang just as he got there. Ohh Jesus, thought Les, his heart sinking, I'll bet this is him now. It was.

'Les! Have you seen this morning's paper?' howled Price.

'Yeah. I just read it.'

'Well, what bloody happened?'

'Didn't you get my message?' swallowed Les.

'Yes. And why wouldn't he stay at your place?'

'Dunno,' lied Norton. 'Me and Warren done the room up for him. Got new sheets for the bed. Even put some flowers in there. He just wanted to stay at the Sebel. I couldn't stop him. What was I gonna do? Put a headlock on him?'

'Christ! Wait till O'Malley sees this. He's going to have a stroke.' There was a pause on the line through which Les could hear Price's laboured breathing. 'What are you doing now?'

'Nothing,' replied Norton. 'I only just read the paper and I was about to call you.'

'Right. Well go straight up to the Sebel Town House and keep an eye on this prick. And don't let him out of your sight. I can't put my head into it, but ring me as soon as you get up there.'

'Righto, Price. See you then.'

Norton hung up and looked at the phone for a moment. I suppose I'd better ring Lord Beaverbrook up, tell him I'm on my way and make sure he waits for me. He began thumbing through the phone-book.

The receptionist at The Sebel was polite, but firm. Sir Peregrine had left strict instructions that he was not to be disturbed before twelve noon. No phone calls, nothing. Sorry, Mr Norton, but those are my orders. Thank you, sir. Shit! fumed Norton. He rang Price again who angrily debated whether Les should go up and kick the door in. But he figured that with the hotel security on the job Peregrine should be safe enough. He told Les not to worry, just be at The Sebel at twelve and go straight to Peregrine's room.

Norton hung up once more and looked at his watch; it was getting on for ten. What to do till twelve? Well, I can finish my breakfast for a start, he thought, moving back to the kitchen. Then start packing a bit of gear for the trip, and I'll pick up that car this afternoon. I'll take His Highness out with me. The tea was still warm, Les poured himself a cup and began flicking through the paper again, subconsciously turning to T'aime's column on page six. Somehow the sight of Pratt being flung out of the Sebel and the Hooray Henry waving the bottle of champagne in the air managed to take the flavour right out of Norton's toasted ham sandwiches.

THE ATTRACTIVE, WELL-GROOMED public relations lady at The Sebel had to be the most polite person Les had ever come across in his life. She introduced herself as Katherine, rang Peregrine's room and escorted Les up in the lift. By the time they'd reached the tenth floor Norton was sure she had a black belt in manners and a degree from Harvard in diplomacy. Norton felt a bit edgy about the whole scene, but Katherine soothingly assured him it was just one of those unfortunate incidents that do happen from time to time and Sir Peregrine definitely was not at fault. She took him to Peregrine's room, knocked, and then opened the door for him. Les thanked her and was told it was a pleasure.

Norton couldn't quite believe his eyes when he first stepped into Peregrine's suite. It was a huge white room surrounded by floor to ceiling mirrors reflecting the light from a number of crystal chandeliers hanging daintily from the ceiling. Where there were no mirrors, the walls were dotted with watercolours and other paintings. Powder blue carpet ran wall to wall, blending in perfectly with the turquoise lounge and other furnishings. A glass table and chairs sat in front of a bed which looked more like Bondi Baths with a doona thrown over it. The entire wall behind the bed was a beautifully tiled and painted al-fresco mural of the Mediterranean, which made the whole room look twice as big again and beyond the bed through a length of lace curtains Les could see a balcony with views across half of Sydney. Norton was checking out the contents of a bar to his right when he heard a voice trill out.

'Les, dear boy. Over here.'

Norton stepped in a little further and turned to his left. Sitting back in an immense spa-bath covered in foaming soap-suds and holding a glass of champagne, was Peregrine. Next to the gold plated taps behind his head was an ice-bucket holding a bottle of Cristal champagne and next to this was a tray containing the remnants of a dozen oysters, lobster and prawn terrine, caviar and some smoked salmon. From the way Peregrine's eyes were swimming around Norton tipped that the bottle of bubbly sitting in the ice-bucket wasn't the Englishman's first.

'Hello, old porpoise,' beamed Peregrine, holding up his glass. 'How goes it?'

The change in Peregrine from the serious-faced aristocrat who had arrived at Mascot, to the Hooray Henry guzzling champagne in the bubble bath took Norton by surprise. 'How goes it?' he parroted. 'Pretty good, I suppose. What about yourself?'

'Splendid. Absolutely splendid.' Peregrine took a large slurp of champagne, and smiled at Norton. 'Well, don't look so glum, old chum. Help yourself to a glass of champers. It's a jolly good drop this. It's Elton's favourite, you know.'

Norton stared at Peregrine as if he couldn't quite believe

what he was seeing or hearing. 'Have you seen this morning's paper?' he asked.

'Yes.' Peregrine motioned with his glass. 'It's on the bed. Bit of a beano that one, what? Not a bad photo,' he smiled. 'But I don't quite know if I like that hack's way with words. I know you Australians are a bit light on when it comes to protocol and manners. But referring to me as Pezz! I mean to say.' Peregrine screwed up his face and took another slurp of champagne.

'Do you know how many people read that T'aime's column?' asked Les incredulously.

Peregrine shrugged. 'I imagine about the same number who listen to that other oaf on the radio. Not very many at all.'

'Well, you're wrong. About half a bloody million a day.' Peregrine continued to look uninterested. 'Christ, mate,' said Les. 'We're trying to keep you under wraps, and now half of bloody Sydney knows you're here.'

'So?' shrugged Peregrine again.

'So! Jesus! Don't you realise the trouble you're in? And the trouble we're going to for you?' Norton shook his head in exasperation at the indifferent look on Peregrine's face. 'What happened, anyway?'

'It was all quite ridiculous, actually.' Peregrine reached behind him and topped up his glass with Cristal. 'You sure you won't have some?' Norton shook his head as Peregrine settled back into the bath. 'Well, I left you and came to my room. Had a bite to eat, got cleaned up and found I was a bit over-tired. So I thought I'd nip down to the bar and have a drink or two before retiring. Anyway, I'm in there, sipping a bottle of champers, minding my own business and admiring a photo of Carol Drinkwater on the wall, when this spoofer, all dressed in black with a ridiculous black hat on and some stupid medallion strung round his neck comes up, thrusts a microphone in my face and demands an interview. I told him to naff off and went back to the bar. So whoever he is, follows me over and starts pestering me again.'

Norton looked at Peregrine for a moment and shook his head. 'That doesn't sound like Pratt's style. He's generally pretty polite.'

'Well,' conceded Peregrine, 'I must admit I *was* rather drunk ... Anyway, he said he was an announcer for radio something or other. I looked at him in his black outfit with his boring, droning voice and told him I thought he looked more like an out-of-work magician. One word led to another and, I don't know, maybe I was tired, or maybe it was the champagne. So I conked him.'

'You what?' Norton had to blink.

'I nutted him. You know.' Peregrine slipped straight into a full on cockney accent like something out of Minder. 'I nutted the geezer — din't I guv. Your muvver got a sewing machine, squire? Well get that stitched. Oi!' Despite himself Norton couldn't help but smile. 'Anyway, I don't think anyone has ever laid a hand on this blithering bandersnatch before because he let out this most diabolical howl. It was despicable. So I kneed the bounder in the cods. And I might add, he went down like the jolly Titanic.' Norton stared and shook his head. 'The next thing I know, this other toad with a head like a soccer ball and a face like a bent smiley button, has appeared out of nowhere with some other wally and started taking photos. Then Security arrived. I insisted they throw the entire rabble out and retired to my room forthwith. Next thing I know it's morning. I'm enjoying my breakfast kipper and the whole thing's in one of your local bin-liners. It's all very boring really.'

Norton shook his head and rolled his eyes to the ceiling. 'I don't bloody well believe it,' he groaned.

'Believe what you like, old boy,' said Peregrine. 'But I absolutely insist on one thing. It wasn't my fault.'

Peregrine took a deep breath and submerged beneath the foam, leaving Norton staring at a skinny white arm holding a glass of champagne above the surface. Despite himself, a giant ripple of laughter shook his entire body. Peregrine might be an awful snob, but he was definitely a man after Les's heart. And where had Norton heard those words before? It wasn't my fault.

'Anyway, Peregrine,' said Les, when the Englishman surfaced for air. 'You're definitely going to have to lay low now, mate. No going out. And no leaving the room.'

'*Au contraire*, old boy,' insisted Peregrine. 'After all that sleep and a few tipples, I feel absolutely tip-top. So I'm off into the city and then it's out on the tiles tonight. Let's get something straight between us, Les.' Peregrine fixed Norton with an even look. 'I appreciate what you're doing, though I do think it's a great load of waffle all round. But I am not your prisoner. Okay? So I'm off into town. Because I know that tomorrow you're dragging me off to some remote part of this godforsaken wilderness for two weeks.' Peregrine drained his glass. 'Gad! It's all too ghastly to even contemplate.'

Norton's face began to scowl. 'Listen, Peregrine,' he said evenly. 'I think you'd better get something into your head.' Les was about to continue when the phone rang next to the bath.

Peregrine picked it up. 'Yes?' He listened intently for a moment then looked quizzingly at Les. 'It's for you. Someone called Saliva?'

Norton smiled and nodded. 'I know who it is. Tell him to come up.'

'Very good. Send him to my room,' answered Peregrine and hung up.

'You mind if I make myself a cup of coffee?' asked Les.

'Help yourself, old boy.'

Norton went to the bar and began fossicking around for a jug and some instant coffee while Peregrine continued to splash around in his bubble bath. After a minute or two there was a knock on the door. Les opened it and got an inquisitive smile from Katherine.

'G'day, Les. How's it going?' said the man next to her.

'All right Eddie. Come on in.' Les smiled back at Katherine and closed the door.

Wearing black jeans and a matching leather jacket, Eddie Salita walked into the suite, looked briefly around and stood at the end of the spa-bath.

'Peregrine,' said Norton. 'Here is someone I want you to meet. This is Eddie. Eddie's going to help look after you too.'

'Hello, Peregrine,' said Eddie, his face a solemn mask.

'Hi.' Peregrine nodded briefly and indifferently through the soapsuds.

'I'm just making a cup of coffee,' said Norton to Eddie. 'You want one?'

'Yeah, righto. It's fuckin' freezin' outside now.'

Norton moved back round to the bar and motioned with his head for Eddie to join him. While he was making their coffee, he quietly told Eddie more or less what Peregrine had told him and described his attitude to what was going on around him. Eddie listened and nodded grimly then they took their coffees back to the side of the spa-bath.

'Got your photo in this morning's paper, mate?' said Eddie, taking a sip of coffee.

Peregrine shrugged moodily from under the soapsuds without answering Eddie. It was bad enough Norton being there invading his privacy; now he had another stranger to contend with and he was making sure his feelings were known.

'Oh well,' continued Eddie. 'Doesn't matter all that much I suppose.' Then he turned to Norton. 'You may as well piss off, Les. You gotta pick up the car and pack your gear and that. I can look after things here.'

'Okay,' said Les, pleased in a way to be getting out of the place. He put his half finished cup of coffee in the sink. 'I'll see you later then, Peregrine. Don't forget, mate. We'll be leaving early in the morning. Probably around six-thirty.' Peregrine nodded but didn't reply. 'I'll see you after, Eddie.'

'Righto, Les. Give us a ring round six or so.'

'Okay. See you then.'

The door closed and Les was gone.

Eddie began walking around the Sir Robert Helpmann suite, sipping his coffee while he admired the furnishings. 'Nice place you picked to stay in,' he said nodding approvingly. 'Very nice indeed.'

'It's adequate,' sniffed Peregrine.

'Yeah, right. Adequate.'

Eddie gave a short laugh and moved towards the balcony. He hit a button and the electric curtains swished back to give a superb view over Sydney. Eddie opened the sliding glass door and stepped out onto the balcony. 'Nice view you got too,' he called back pleasantly to Peregrine while he sipped his coffee in the chilly sou'wester whipping across the balcony.

'I say! Would you mind closing the door?' Peregrine called back. 'There's quite a draught coming in here.'

Eddie smiled over at Peregrine and stepped back inside leaving the door open. Still slowly sipping his coffee he strolled to the end of the spa-bath.

'Les tells me you're thinking of going out for a bit of a drink tonight.'

'I'm not thinking of going out. I *am* going out. Till late. Very late.'

Eddie gave another little chuckle and sipped some more coffee. 'Yeah, well, why wouldn't you?' he smiled. 'You're young. You're rich. You're not a bad looking bloke. If I was in your shoes I'd probably be doing the same thing.'

'Exactly,' said Peregrine bluntly. 'Now would you mind closing that blessed door.'

Eddie smiled benevolently at Peregrine then finished his coffee and put the empty cup to the side of the bath. 'The door?' he said 'Oh yeah. I forgot the door.'

Like a snake striking, Eddie reached across the spa-bath and with his left hand, took Peregrine by the hair and yanked him out of the water making him yelp with shock and pain. With water dripping everywhere off his naked body, Eddie frog-marched Peregrine out onto the balcony and with a grip of iron forced him up over the edge. With his right hand, Eddie whipped a .38 revolver from a holster beneath his jacket and rammed the muzzle into Peregrine's date. It was bitterly cold out on the balcony. There was nothing under the Englishman's face but ten floors of thin air, he had the cold barrel of a Smith and Wesson wedged in his bum and a not too happy Eddie Salita holding him by the scruff of the neck like a dog with a rat. Sir Peregrine Normanhurst III was absolutely terrified and about twenty seconds away from shitting all over the barrel of Eddie's gun.

'Now you listen to me, you fuckin' pommy prick,' Eddie hissed right into Peregrine's ear. 'There's a lot of people going to a lot of trouble to look after your skinny fuckin' neck while you're out here. Me, I don't give a fuck about you one way or the other. I'd just as soon throw you over the edge and make it look like suicide, and save us all a lot of fucking about all round. You listening?' Peregrine gasped a reply and tried not to look at the pavement ten floors below. 'Now I don't know what sort of pricks you run around with in England. But out here, we ain't got time to be fucked around. So what d'you want to do, shithead? Behave yourself and have a nice two-week holiday in Australia? Or go hang-gliding au naturale, with your bowels blown up through the top of your head?' Eddie nudged the barrel of the .38 a little further into Peregrine's quoit. 'Make up your fuckin' mind, knackers. I ain't got all day and it's freezin' out here.'

'All right. All right. Whatever you say,' gasped Peregrine, choking back a tear.

'Good.'

Eddie pulled Peregrine back from the edge of the balcony and pushed him inside, sliding the door closed with his heel at the same time. He marched him back across to the spa-bath and lowered him into the water. 'Now,' smiled Eddie, putting the .38 back in its holster. He picked up a towel and began wiping the water from his leather jacket and jeans. 'Isn't it nice to know we've both got a perfect understanding?'

Peregrine's eyes were still bulging with fear. His face was flushed and a small tear trickled down his cheek. He flinched suddenly as Eddie reached for the ice-bucket behind his head.

'Well, well, well, what have we got here?' smiled Eddie, picking up the almost empty bottle. 'Cristal. My, you *have* got good taste, Peregrine. This is Elton's favourite, you know.' Eddie finished what was left and dropped the empty bottle back in the ice-bucket. 'I'll tell you what, old bean. Why don't we have another one?' He picked up the phone at the side of the bath. 'Hello. Room service? Yes. Could we have a bottle of '68 Cristal to room 1012 please.' The little hit man picked up a piece of smoked salmon from the tray and popped it in his mouth. 'And some smoked salmon too. And while you're there . . .'

ABOUT AN HOUR or so after leaving Eddie with Peregrine at the Sebel, Les had left his car at home and was in a taxi heading along the Princes Highway to Tempe. He had the slip of paper Price had given him and was trying to recollect who the car dealer was. Bill Kileen? Yeah, I know him now, not a bad style of a bloke. Loves a drink. He comes up the game every now and again; punts about fifty dollars and drinks about another five hundred's worth of bourbon. He must either owe Price a favour or Price is getting him back for all the free piss he's gone through. Oh well, Norton chuckled to himself. He's got a car yard and I've got the pick of the cars. There's got to be a Mercedes there, or, seeing as we're going up the bush, a nice new four-wheel-drive.

His train of thought was interrupted by the taxi driver. 'Hey, mate. Did you say this place was opposite the Tempe bus depot?'

'Yeah,' replied Norton, looking up from the slip of paper.

'Well, there's the bus depot,' said the cab driver, nodding out his window. 'That must be it on the corner.'

He stopped the taxi next to a car yard near a set of lights where a number of coloured plastic flags fluttered in the chilly sou'wester. Above the Australian flags was a white on black sign: Kileen's Prestige Kars.

'Yeah, this is it all right,' nodded Les. 'What do I owe you?' He paid the cabbie and got out.

If Norton was expecting Kileen's Prestige Kars to be the BMW or Bentley dealership at Tempe he was in for a bit of a surprise. The car yard, like its owner, had definitely seen better days. A black, wrought-iron fence, part of which was missing, housed about fifteen or so clean, but fairly nondescript cars. For some reason a sign saying *Free Firewood* was wired where the length of fence was missing. The cars — Holdens, Fords, Mazdas, Toyotas etc — all had the usual spiel pasted across the windscreens. *Make Me An Offer. Save $$$. Ready*

For Work. Four On The Floor. This Week's Special. The pièce de résistance appeared to be a yellow, Daihatsu Hi-Jet mounted on blocks at the front of the yard. There were no new, four-wheel drives and definitely no Mercedes. As Norton stood there surveying a very uninspiring scene, a slightly-built figure with straight brown hair and a wispy blonde moustache, shuffled from a white office at the rear to a small white caravan in a corner of the yard. Yeah, that's him all right. Killer Kileen. Hope he's sober. It's well after lunch. Norton waited till the figure in jeans and blue V-neck sweater shuffled from the caravan back to the office and went in after him. He gave the door a bit of a tap and before he had a chance to speak, Kileen jumped up from what he was doing and greeted Les like he was a long lost friend.

'Les! G'day mate. How are you goin'? How's things?' He had bright, inquisitive brown eyes and a cheerful but gruff voice that spoke of cigarettes, late nights and booze.

'Not too bad, Bill,' replied Les, with a brief handshake.

'You're out here to pick up that car, right?' Les nodded. 'Righto.' Kileen gestured to the yard. 'Help yourself. They're all the grouse, too, I might add.'

'Okay, thanks.'

As Les said that a phone rang in another room. 'I'll be back in a sec,' said Kileen and went to answer it.

Norton nodded a reply. He was about to go out into the yard when something near the table Kileen had been sitting at caught his eye. He moved over for a closer look. In a plastic kitchen-tidy were a dozen empty bottles of Jim Beam. Next to these in another kitchen-tidy was a solitary empty bottle of Diet Pepsi. Christ, thought Norton, this bloke *does* like a drink. If ever he dies they'd better not get him cremated — it'll take them six weeks to put the fire out. He shook his head and walked out to the yard.

It took Les five minutes of indifferent looking to narrow the field down to three cars: a red Holden sedan, a hotted-up green Torana or a white T-bar automatic Ford station wagon. He was checking to make sure the Ford had a stereo when Kileen appeared.

'That was my missus on the phone,' he said. 'She'd talk the leg off an iron-pot.' Norton tried to ignore him as he checked out the Ford station wagon. 'You picked one out yet?'

'Yeah,' nodded Les. 'I'll take the station wagon.'

'Good idea,' smiled Kileen, running a hand along the roof. 'Top car this. Eight months rego. New tyres. Motor's just been done up. A woman traded it. Had to sell it because she was pregnant. Her husband was a doctor. The car's never . . .'

Kileen was about to go into his full on, car dealer's spiel when Norton cut him off. 'Hey mate. I'm only borrowing it, remember. I don't want to buy it.'

'Yeah, right. Sure.' Kileen smiled and made a gesture with his hands. 'You know I am only lending this to Price for a couple of weeks 'cause I owe him a favour. So you won't . . . you know, flog the guts out of it will you, Les? I mean, I got to sell it when you bring it back. So look after it a bit, will you, mate?'

'Sure,' replied Les, in all honesty. 'I'll look after it. It's only to get me and another bloke up to this property and it'll be sitting there doing nothing. Apart from the drive up and back, I'll hardly be using it at all.'

'Sweet. Terrific. Good on you, Les. Just hold on a sec and I'll get you the keys and rego papers.'

Norton removed a sign from the windscreen saying *T-Bar Automatic* as Kileen came back and handed him the keys and rego papers. Kileen shook hands with him and wished him a good trip; Les thanked him and backed out into the yard. Kileen motioned him to a driveway at the side of the yard, Norton drove down it, gave the horn a toot then drove through the lights to make a U-turn and head back in the direction of Bondi.

By the time Les had passed Centennial Park, he'd put the two-year-old station wagon through its paces, without flogging it too much, and was pleased to see it went well. He was also pleased to see the stereo-radio worked okay and guessed the cassette did as well. Yeah, not a bad car at all, he thought happily. The trip up north is going to be a breeze. In fact when Norton had almost reached Bondi he liked the car that much he made a mental note to make Kileen an offer when he got back and update his old Ford sedan. Cruising along, he decided to go down the back of Bronte past Tamarama and have a look at the sea, which was always clear and blue and smooth during the offshore winds in winter.

He was rounding the bend at Tamarama slowly heading towards the surf club, when a familiar figure standing against the railing checking out the ocean caught his eye. The figure turned just as Les drew near and waved. It was Tony Nathan, the surf photographer. What the hell thought Norton, being in an extra good mood, I'll stop and have a mag. See what he's got to say for himself.

Tony was a medium-built fellow in his thirties with a mop of bushy black hair and a face that seemed to register a permanent, impassive patience. He was always broke and always had a story about some bastard who had just ripped him off. So to make ends meet, and to compensate for everyone dudding him with his photographs, he worked part time as a disc jockey in a bar at Randwick, where, because of his hair, someone nicknamed him 'Steelo' as in steel wool. Because of the music this got mishmashed into Steely Dan and somehow his nickname alternated between the two. Les got to know him when he occasionally left North Bondi for Tamarama where Tony lived, and often borrowed Tony's boogie board and flippers at the beach. But Tony was a popular, likeable bloke and was arguably, probably because of his endless patience, the best surfing photographer in Australia. Steelo's only fault, if there was one, was that nobody in Australia swore as much as him, not even Norton.

Les stopped the car, got out and crossed the road. 'Hello there, the Dan,' he said, leaning against the railing next to him. 'What are you up to, mate?'

'Not much,' answered Tony tightly. 'Just standing here freezing my fuckin' nuts off.'

Norton shifted his gaze to what Tony was looking at; about half a dozen surfers were getting stuck into a red-hot left breaking near the reef down from the surf club. A squat figure in a red and white steamer with corn blonde hair caught his eye. 'Hey, isn't that Cheyne Horan out there?'

'Yeah,' nodded Tony. 'I was thinking of getting a few photos of him, but it's starting to fill up.' They both watched as Cheyne took off and tore apart another left. 'No, fuck it,' said Tony. 'I'll save my film for Newcastle tomorrow.'

'Newcastle?' Norton registered his surprise. 'You going to Newcastle tomorrow?'

'Yeah,' grunted Tony. 'Got to take some photos of Mark Richards.' Then he went into one of his tirades. 'But I gotta catch the fuckin' train. I got no fuckin' car. Got no fuckin' money. And I hate catching fuckin' trains, the cunts of fuckin' things never run on time. Fuck it. It'd give you the fuckin' shits.'

'Hey, hang on a sec, Steelo,' smiled Les, remembering he owed Tony a few favours. 'I'm going up the North Coast first thing tomorrow. I can drop you off at Newcastle. What time you got to be there?'

'About nine-thirty.'

'Well, come up with us. We're leaving at six-thirty.'

'Fair dinkum?' Tony's eyes lit up. 'Unfuckin'real.'

'I got to pick a bloke up at the Cross at six-thirty, so I'll pick you up at six-fifteen. Where do you live?'

Tony pointed to a block of units just up the hill from the beach. 'Those units there. Flat four.'

'Okay. Be out the front at six-fifteen tomorrow.'

They stood there for a few more minutes watching the surfers but it started to get too cold for Les. Tony said he'd stay a while longer and he'd see Les in the morning. Norton said goodbye and emphasised to Tony not to be late.

Well, that's all right thought Les, as he cruised towards Bondi. At least I'll have someone to talk to for a while on the way up besides Lord Shitbags the Third. He'll probably be hungover and whingeing all the way up. Norton hadn't been given enough notice about the trip to get some tapes made up, but he called in to see his mate at Peach Music and bought a few new ones to listen to anyway. After perusing what was available, Les settled for some Divynls, Hunters and Collectors, Best of Richard Clapton, James Reyne and a few others. The cassette player in the car worked like a charm, and it was loud. Richard Clapton was thumping the daylights out of 'Getting To The Heart Of It' and the speakers were almost breaking loose from the interior when Norton pulled up outside his Bondi semi, groceries in the back and tank full of petrol, at around four-thirty.

By seven he had everything he needed packed for the trip and had found time to make a big feed of steak and kidney for dinner. Warren was home from the advertising agency eating it with him while Les told him his plans for the next two weeks.

'So, Woz, old buddy, old pal,' said Norton as they attacked the stew. 'I'd get into this while you got the chance if I were you. 'Cause it's the only decent meal you'll be getting till I get back. For the next two weeks it's back to McDonalds and the Pizza Hut for you, old son.'

Warren smiled as he ate. Loath as he was to admit it, Les was right. Warren hated cooking and the big Queenslander could certainly cook up a good home style feed when it came to it. 'Ohh, I dunno,' he said, forking up some more stew. 'That Tom Piper stuff in the tins tastes pretty much the same as this.'

'Good,' replied Les. 'Well, get yourself a couple of dozen cans first thing tomorrow. It's on special this week at Flemings. Right next to the dog food.'

Warren smiled and conceded the point. 'So, where are you going again?'

'Just the other side of Coffs Harbour — some bloke's property. But if anybody asks you where I've gone, you don't know. Okay?'

'Suit yourself,' shrugged Warren, adding a little more pepper and salt. 'But why all the secrecy with this bloke anyway? I mean, what's the point? He's just had his dial splattered all over the *Telegraph*. Unless you haven't noticed, wally.'

'I noticed it all right, you little shit. And don't think your cynical remarks and innuendoes at the breakfast table this morning didn't go unnoticed either.' Warren grinned straight at Les. 'No,' continued Norton, 'the poor bastard just had a nervous breakdown in England and I'm taking him up the bush for a bit of peace and quiet for a couple of weeks. Away from reporters and the rest of that shit.'

Warren's grin turned into a raucous laugh. 'Nervous bloody breakdown,' he guffawed, 'he looked all right in the paper this morning. I think the only nervous breakdown he had was when you showed him the spare room. I noticed you gave it a bit of a tidy up and took down my poster of Rodney Rude too.'

'Yes. I certainly did my best,' sighed Norton. 'I guess there's just no pleasing some cunts, is there?'

They finished dinner, then had a couple of cherry danishes Warren had brought home from one of his yuppie cake shops in Paddington. While Warren washed up, Les rang Eddie at the Sebel Town House and was surprised to hear that Peregrine had changed his mind about going out that night. Eddie would stay with him all night, Les needn't worry and he'd see him in the foyer at six-thirty sharp. What Norton didn't see, when he hung up, was Eddie sitting back on the turquoise lounge in the Sir Robert Helpmann suite, one eye on the TV down low, the other on the door with a chair propped under the handle and a third eye on Peregrine laying back on the bed eating a lobster, staring daggers at him and wanting desperately to go out somewhere, get drunk on champagne and do a bit of womanising. But Peregrine knew the only way he was going to get out that door was to go through Eddie, and he had more chance of getting through Turkish Customs with five kilos of hashish strapped to his head. Monday night in Sydney looked like being a very quiet one for Sir Peregrine Normanhurst III.

After the washing up, Les and Warren turned up the heater and watched a Clint Eastwood movie on Channel 10 in which

Dirty Harry once more swept the streets of San Francisco clean of machine gun-toting low life, armed only with a .357 Magnum and without wasting a single bullet. It was a freezing cold night, Les had to be up early, Warren was tired and they were both in bed before eleven. The last thing Norton did before he hit the sack was take the spark-plug leads out of his car, just in case there might be someone in Bondi desperate enough to want a '68 Ford sedan, the duco of which had never seen a chamois nor the interior a whisk-broom in the best part of a year.

TUESDAY MORNING WAS teeth-chatteringly cold when Norton got up at five-thirty and made some coffee and toasted sandwiches. There was no rain and not many clouds, but a bitter sou'wester was blowing — the kind that cracks your lips, freezes the back of your neck and makes your eyes and nose run. Thank Christ I'm getting out of this for a couple of weeks, he thought, as he tossed his gear in the back of the station wagon. He was out the front of Tony's flats at six-fifteen sharp, but no Tony. Then Norton remembered something. When it came to getting his arse into gear Tony Nathan moved about as fast as a tortoise towing a speedboat. He gave him a couple of minutes then started bipping the horn, little ones at first, then he just left his hand on it. Before long, windows were being flung open and a torrent of curses and abuse in about twenty different languages and accents was being directed at Norton. After a minute or two of this Steelo, wearing some sort of coloured Balinese jacket with his camera bag slung over his shoulder, came strolling nonchalantly down the side passage eating an apple. Acting as if he had all the time in the world, he ambled towards the car, quite oblivious to the avalanche of vituperation raining down from above and completely oblivious to Norton fuming in the station wagon.

'Come on, fuck you,' cursed Norton as he reached the door.

'Don't panic,' replied Tony casually. 'We'll get there.'

'Don't panic. Fair dinkum — you're like a fuckin' old moll. Get in the back too.'

Still taking his time, Steelo climbed in the back seat. He barely had time to find the seat belt, let alone put it on, before Norton spun the station wagon up Delview Street like he was doing a Le Mans start, sending Steelo, his camera gear and his apple sprawling all over the back seat.

'Jesus fuckin' Christ,' sputtered Steelo. 'What have you done? Just robbed a bank?'

'In your arse Steelo, you prick.'

Steelo managed to retrieve his Johnathon. He was still chewing on it when they rocked to a halt outside the Sebel.

'I TRUST YOUR brief stay with us was enjoyable, Sir Peregrine?' smiled the desk clerk as Peregrine settled his account.

'Yes, quite — thank you,' he answered with a thin smile, trying to ignore Eddie's stare and the smirk planted across the little hit man's face.

'And will there be a forwarding address, sir?'

'There'll be no forwarding address,' cut in Eddie quickly. 'After that unseemly incident in the bar, Sir Peregrine wants his privacy.'

'I understand perfectly, sir,' smiled the desk clerk. 'Well, enjoy your stay in Australia, Sir Peregrine.'

'He will,' answered Eddie, winking at Peregrine's scowl. 'I'll make sure of that.'

Eddie glanced at his watch: it was exactly six-thirty. At six-thirty and two seconds he was pleased to see Norton pull up out the front. He picked up the larger of Peregrine's bags and walked out of the foyer, motioning with his hand for Peregrine to stay where he was. After checking out the street like a fox sniffing the wind he nodded to Peregrine to join him.

'How's things, Les?' he said, tossing Peregrine's bag in the back of the station wagon.

'Good,' answered Les. He got out of the car and moved round to the back. 'What about yourself? Everything sweet here?'

'Good as gold,' winked Eddie. 'Couldn't be creamier.'

Norton turned his attention to a very sullen Peregrine, dressed in blue corduroy trousers, matching wide-shouldered jacket and the same trilby he had on at the airport. 'Hello, Peregrine,' he said. 'How are you, mate?'

'Fine,' replied the Englishman tightly. He climbed in the front seat without waiting for anyone to tell him what to do.

Les noticed Eddie eyeing Steelo in the back. 'He's all right. He's a mate of mine. I'm giving him a lift to Newcastle.'

The little hit man nodded an impassive approval. 'Just wait here for a minute, Les,' he said. Eddie jogged down to his Mercedes parked about a hundred metres down from The Sebel, opened the boot and took something out. He was back in an instant and handed Les a small overnight-bag.

'What's this?'

'A gun. It's an old 9mm Robinson. So don't lose it.' Norton accepted the bag reluctantly. 'Snooker it under the seat or in the tyre well. You probably won't need it; but take it just in case. Have a bit of target practice. There's two hundred rounds of ammo there too.'

'Yeah — all right.' Norton nodded without any expression.

'Well,' Eddie smiled and gave Les a quick handshake. 'Have a good time up north.'

'I'll ring you as soon as we get there,' said Les, getting behind the wheel of the car.

'Do that. See you later, Peregrine.' Eddie gave the Englishman a cheeky grin and tapped the roof of the car. 'Keep smiling.'

Peregrine returned Eddie's grin with a very sour, very quick, once up and down. Les gave the horn a toot and they were on their way.

'Peregrine. This is a mate of mine, Tony.'

'G'day Peregrine,' said Tony, offering his hand. 'How are you mate?'

'Fine, thank you,' replied the Englishman with a quick shake.

'I'm dropping Tony off at Newcastle, about an hour and a half's drive from here. Tony's a photographer.'

At the mention of the word photography, Peregrine's eyes lit up. He was also pleasantly surprised to meet someone who wasn't either a hit man or a heavy. 'You're a photographer, Tony?'

'Yeah,' replied the Dan, without a great deal of enthusiasm. 'Worst thing I ever done in me fuckin' life.'

'I dabble in photography,' said Peregrine. 'A close friend of the family back in England is quite a famous one.'

'Yeah. Who's that?'

'Lord Snowdon.'

'Lord Snowdon!' Steelo was visibly impressed. 'Shit! Is he a mate of yours?'

ABOUT HALF AN hour or so later Norton was on the other side of Hornsby heading towards the toll-gates at Mt. Colah and the start of the expressway; roughly the same time as the two English journalists introduced themselves to Katherine the PR lady at The Sebel Town House. They were handsome, dark-haired men, impeccably mannered with soft, rich, yet slightly strange English accents, and there was the hint of a smile in their inquisitive green eyes. They left their car just down from the hotel with a third journalist behind the wheel.

'Yes, Katherine,' smiled the journalist holding the camera-bag. 'We're with the *Manchester Guardian*. We're here to do a feature article on Sir Peregrine's visit to Australia.'

'Oh, what a shame,' said Katherine, returning their smiles with a sympathetic one. 'You've missed him by about half an hour.'

For a split second the smile in the two reporter's eyes turned to icy steel. 'We've missed him?' said the one on the left.

'Yes. He checked out at six-thirty.'

'Did he say where he was going?' asked the one with the camera.

'No,' Katherine shook her head. 'I'm afraid Sir Peregrine didn't leave a forwarding address.'

'Was he with anyone when he left?'

'There was a gentleman who stayed the night with him. But Sir Peregrine drove off with two other gentlemen. In a white Ford station wagon I think it was.'

'The two men he drove off with, were they English?'

'I don't know,' replied Katherine. 'But the gentleman who stayed with him last night was Australian.'

'And you've no idea where they went?'

'I'm sorry.'

The two reporters exchanged a brief glance. 'Okay, Katherine,' said the one holding the camera-bag. 'Thank you very much, anyway.'

'You're welcome, anytime,' smiled the PR lady.

Grim faced, the two journalists returned to their car, where the English accents quickly disappeared to be replaced by a much stronger brogue.

'Sonofabitch!' cursed the one with the camera-bag. 'We've missed the bastard by a half fockin' hour.'

'Christ!' said the one behind the wheel. 'It's enough to make you sick.'

They sat in silence for a moment staring moodily at each other. 'What do you think we should be doing?' asked the third.

'Drive back to the flat,' said the one with the camera-bag. 'Ring up. Tell them we've lost him — only for the fockin' time being, though.'

The driver looked at his watch. 'It'll be almost midnight

back there. Not the best time to be waking Liam with news like this.'

'Nor his mother.'

'Don't be worrying too much about old Mrs Frayne,' said the one with the camera. 'That woman is well used to this sort of thing by now.'

NORTON'S PLANS FOR an enjoyable trip, cruising along listening to his new music and having a bit of a chat to Tony and Peregrine were well and truly thwarted, much to his disdain. He'd had the radio on very low, listening to nothing in particular as they headed out of Sydney and intended dropping a cassette in as soon as they got onto the freeway. Peregrine and the Dan, however, had got into an engrossed conversation about photography. Peregrine the pupil, was listening intently, and Tony the expert was in his element. Norton was like the cocky on the biscuit-tin: not in it at all. He drove along in enforced silence and by the time they were at Berowra he was fed up to the gills with f/1.8 lenses, f/1.4 lenses, light-emitting diode displays, depths of field, aperture-preferred automatic metering, silicon photocells and more bullshit that went straight over his head. As soon as he dropped his sixty cents in the basket at Mt. Colah, he slipped on a Divynls cassette. The band had got through the first four bars when Peregrine gave him a look of sour and utter contempt.

'I say, Les,' he bristled, with frigid politeness. 'Would you mind turning that down, please? We're trying to have an intelligent conversation here.'

'Yeah, piss that fuckin' shit off,' barked Steelo. 'I got to listen to that disco fuckin' garbage four nights a week at the bar. I'm half deaf now from putting up with it — low fuckin' top-forty shit that it is. Stick it in your arse.'

Peregrine had to blink at Steelo's tirade. 'I wholeheartedly agree,' he nodded.

Norton reluctantly turned off the cassette and switched on the radio, but the local music was so bad and they made him keep it down so low he may as well have not had the thing on at all. He drove on fuming in silence. He was fuming so much he forgot he had to go through Newcastle and took the Wollombi turn off. Tony was so engrossed in bayonet-mounted lenses and four frames per second power winders with Peregrine he didn't notice where they were going either. Then it dawned on Les and he screeched to a halt just out of Hexham where they rejoined the Pacific Highway.

'Well, here you are, Steelo,' said Les cheerfully. 'Newcastle.'

Tony looked around him and screwed up his face in disbelief. 'Newcastle?' he howled. 'This isn't fuckin' Newcastle.'

'Yes it is. What's that sign say over there?' Norton pointed to a sign on the opposite side of the road: Newcastle 20 kms. Hexham 1km.

'I got to get to Bar Beach,' protested Tony.

'Well I'm not stopping you,' shrugged Norton. 'And I sure as hell ain't getting stuck in Newcastle traffic at eight o'clock in the morning.'

'Jesus fuckin' Christ!! How am I gonna get there?'

'Walk. Catch a bus. How do you think, you wombat?'

'I've got two bucks. That's got to get me my lunch and my fare back to fuckin' Sydney.'

Norton shrugged indifferently. 'Snip your surfie mate Mark Richards. He's the world champion. He should have plenty of money.'

'Ahh, Jesus fuckin' Christ!! Fuck it. Fuck, fuck, fuckin', fuck, fuck . . .' To an accompanying string of further profanities, Tony picked up his camera-bag and got out of the car.

'See you back in the old steak and kidney, Steelo,' grinned Norton.

Peregrine waved a quick goodbye just as Les bipped the horn and they were on their way again, Tony Nathan's curses still ringing vividly in their ears.

'I say,' said Peregrine. 'That was a bit unsporting of you, wasn't it? Leaving your friend stranded there without any money.'

'Steelo?' answered Norton. 'Mate. He wouldn't have it any other way.' Norton watched Tony disappearing in the rear-vision mirror for a second or two. 'Now Lord Normanhurst, warden of the cinque ports or whatever you are,' he chuckled, turning off the radio and replacing it with a cassette. 'I think it's well and truly time we got the Les and Pezz show on the road.' He pressed the cassette, hit the volume and immediately the Divynls began howling into 'Siren'.

'Oh my God.' Peregrine turned his face away in anguish. 'That's ghastly.'

'No,' grinned Norton, bopping away to the music. 'That's Christine Amphlett. She's grouse. You ought to see her in her school uniform.'

After they'd travelled about fifteen kilometres or so Norton felt he'd had enough fun and Peregrine had copped a good enough blast of rock 'n' roll, which he evidently didn't seem to be too keen on, so he turned the car stereo down. Considering he'd had an early night and not much to drink, the Englishman still seemed tired and edgy apart from the annoyance of the loud music, which had Norton a little curious as to why; although he did notice a definite bad vibe going in Eddie's direction when he cheerily bid Peregrine goodbye outside the Sebel at six-thirty.

'So how are you feeling now anyway, Peregrine?' asked Les, realising this was the first real start of any conversation he'd had with the Englishman since they'd left Sydney.

'I'm quite all right, thank you,' replied Peregrine shortly.

'That's good. How come you changed your mind about going out last night?'

'Your friend Eddie persuaded me that it might be better if I stayed inside for the evening.'

From the way Peregrine spoke Norton twigged something must have happened in the room. 'Yeah.' He turned and smiled at Peregrine. 'Eddie can be very persuasive at times, can't he?'

Peregrine ignored Les's stare. 'Yes. He has a certain way about him, hasn't he?'

A few more kilometres sped by in silence. 'You hungry?' asked Les. Peregrine shook his head. 'I had a good breakfast at the hotel.'

'Well, there's a place up ahead, Buladelah. I'm gonna stop and have a steak sandwich and make a couple of phone calls. You feel like a cup of coffee?'

'Yes. I suppose I could manage a cup of coffee.'

'Righto.'

They sped on through the Australian countryside in silence, apart from the music playing lightly in the background. Norton made a couple of half-hearted attempts at conversation but Peregrine virtually ignored him, preferring to stare out the windscreen in silence. Christ! I hope he's not going to be like this the whole trip, thought Les. This is going to be a real lot of fun. I may as well have a side of veal sitting there. Still, he's only been here barely two days, I suppose. What can you expect? But he sure needs livening up. Don't know how though. And I don't fancy sitting here watching him guzzle bottles of champagne, if that's what it takes to get his rocks off. Ah well, I suppose I'll think of something.

More countryside went past without anything being said.

70

The Divynls tape finished; Norton slipped on some Machinations. Before long they were in Buladelah. Norton swung the station wagon into the BP garage and restaurant parked to the side and switched off the motor.

'Come on, mate,' he winked. 'Let's have a cuppa.'

They walked into the restaurant and found an empty table amongst several truck drivers and a few other travellers. Les ordered, and told Peregrine he'd be back as soon as he made his phone calls. He returned and sat down just after their food and coffee arrived about five minutes later, the hint of a smile flickering in the corners of his dark brown eyes.

'Have to ring Eddie, did you?' enquired Peregrine, with more than a hint of sarcasm in his voice. 'Tell him I haven't tried to escape?'

'No, nothing like that,' replied Norton brightly. 'In fact I just tried to ring a mate of mine who lives near Coffs Harbour. Tell him I'd have dinner with him tonight. But there was no one home. I'll ring him again later. We'll stay at Coffs Harbour tonight. We're in no mad hurry. That way we'll get to where we're going in the daytime and feeling fresh. What do you reckon?'

Peregrine shrugged and took a sip of coffee. 'You're driving,' he said uninterestedly.

They sat in silence. Les polished off his steak sandwich while Peregrine checked out the surroundings and the heads on some of the truck drivers as he delicately sipped his coffee.

'I suppose this must be all pretty strange to you, Peregrine,' said Norton, washing down the last piece of crust with coffee. 'Out in the middle of nowhere, not knowing a soul?'

'I suppose one could say that.'

'It's all a bit strange to me, too. I've never been to this place we're going to in the Tweed Valley. And I don't know much about you or this whole set up either. All I know is your godfather's the Attorney General, you've got a lot of money and you're related to the Royal Family. And you're in some sort of trouble with the IRA. You want to tell me about it? I mean, what happened in Ireland that these people would want to go to all that trouble to kill you?' Norton gave a shrug. 'Apart from head butting that wombat at the Sebel, you've got to be one of the most inoffensive blokes I've ever met in my life.'

For a brief moment a little life seemed to come into Peregrine's eyes as he reflected into his coffee. 'There's not a great deal to tell, actually. And I'm not very good at explanations. It was just one of those spur of the moment things.' He stared evenly at Les. 'But if you insist . . .'

'Well . . . I wouldn't mind,' said Les.

'Very well, then.' Peregrine took a sip of coffee. 'I was with some friends in London. We were drinking and arguing about the Irish. One word led to another and I happened to mention my cousin Lewis, who's a captain in the Coldstream Guards stationed in Belfast, and if they didn't believe me about this thing we were arguing about, I'd drive up and ask him myself. And I'd bring back two pints of Guinness from a Belfast pub while I was there. Someone dared me. So we did.'

'We?'

'Stephanie Wingate. My current girlfriend. She came along for the ride.' Peregrine made a defensive gesture with his hands. 'It was also an excuse to run in a new Aston-Martin I'd just purchased.' Norton nodded still a little mystified. 'Anyway, Les, to make a long story short, we get to Liverpool, over to Ireland and arrive in Belfast. Stephanie is now driving and I'm giving directions as we head for the barracks where Lewis is stationed, when, bless my soul, if I don't see him sitting on a motorbike outside this pub talking to three fellows. I immediately tell Stephanie to pull up and jump out of the car waving a bottle of champagne. I . . . might add, I'd been drinking rather heavily the whole time. Lewis sees me and almost turns white. I didn't realise, I mean . . . well, I didn't know he was working undercover. The three men he was talking to immediately go for their guns. But Lewis, who I might tell you is the crack shot of his regiment, gets to his gun first, and shoots all three dead. It was an absolutely ghastly sight, Les. I can tell you that, when I look back at it.'

'I reckon it would be,' agreed Norton.

'Anyway, Stephanie starts screaming. We both turn around and as we do I accidentally knock the gun out of Lewis's hand with the bottle of champagne. You must remember, Les, I was quite drunk and this all happened so quickly.' Norton nodded. 'Next thing I know, Lewis is pushing me towards the car, screaming at me to clear off, then he gets on his motorbike and roars away. However, in my drunken state, instead of getting in the car, I pick up Lewis's gun and call out to him that he'd forgotten his gun. The mob came out of the pub at all the shooting and see me holding this gun, which luckily stops them for a moment. They regroup and are getting ready to tear me to pieces, when just in the nick of time, a British Army patrol arrives on the scene. This time I do get in the car and Stephanie takes off like jolly Sterling Moss. And we don't stop till we get back to London.'

'Not even for the two pints of Guinness?'

'Not even for a piddle.' Peregrine shook his head and reflected into his coffee. 'The stupid thing is some paddy got the number of my car. And my cousin and I are very similar in looks. Now they think I'm Lewis, and Lewis is me, and I shot the three men. And . . . oh God, Les, I don't know what the stupid buggers think. And in a way, I don't give a toss either, to be perfectly honest.'

Norton shook his head in amused amazement. 'It's a funny one all right. But still, I wouldn't be taking it too lightly, if I were you.'

'Well, I'm not really,' conceded Peregrine. 'That's why I agreed to come to Australia; while Lewis sorts all this rattle out back home.'

'Yeah, what's this Lewis's story? What's he got to do? Go in and shoot some brother, Frayne or something?'

'That's right,' nodded Peregrine. 'You know about the Frayne brothers do you?'

'More or less. My boss explained it all roughly to me. I'd just like you to fill in a few loose ends, that's all.'

'All right. Well, Liam is his name. He's the older brother of the two Lewis shot outside the pub. He's the one making all the noise and the one who's convinced I'm Lewis and vice versa. Cousin Lewis is sure, as is my father, that if he can kill this remaining Frayne brother and get a mistaken identity story run in Fleet Street press or some magazine or something, it should clear me. Then we can all live happily ever after.'

'It sure sounds all right,' shrugged Norton.

'Oh, if I was foolish enough to be seen in Belfast someone might take a pot-shot at me. But if I stay in England, to-ing and fro-ing the way I do, they're not going to worry much about me. To the Irish, Les, I'm small potatoes. And I don't mean that as a joke.'

'What if Lewis doesn't get this Liam Frayne?'

Peregrine shook his head adamantly. 'He will. Lewis is the best there is. Besides, they want to shoot him anyway. He's a suspected arms courier — he's supposed to bring them in from the Middle East and steal them from the British Army.'

'A suspected arms dealer? So what? They shoot him, then give him a fair trial afterwards?'

'That, unfortunately, Les,' smiled Peregrine, 'is how it works in Ireland these days.'

Norton shook his head almost in disbelief. 'Well, I'm glad I'm over here and not there,' he said sincerely.

'You and I both, old boy,' replied Peregrine, still smiling. 'Though I would much prefer to be back in England than here, I can assure you of that. Still, I promised father I'd stay here for two weeks and I shall.'

'And you don't think the Irish will follow you out here?'

Peregrine dismissed Les's question with a wave of his hand. 'No. They wouldn't bother coming all this way. Where would they find me?'

'What about that bloody thing all over yesterday's paper?'

The Englishman screwed up his face and dismissed this with a wave of his hand also. 'If you ask me, Les,' he said tiredly, 'this whole blessed thing has been blown out of all proportion. Me having to come all this way out here. In fact, I wouldn't be surprised if Lewis hasn't sorted it all out by now, to be quite honest.'

'Well, let's hope for your sake he has.' Norton drained his cup of coffee and looked evenly at Peregrine. 'Anyway, what do you reckon? We start making tracks?'

'Am I to take it that that means leave?'

'Words to that effect, in part, thereof — yes.'

'Then let's go.' Peregrine had a quick look around the cafe. 'The heads on some of these truck drivers in here remind one of something one would expect to find haunting a castle somewhere on the Cornish coast.'

Norton paid the bill, Peregrine bought a bar of chocolate and they walked back out to the car. Before they left, Les took the bag Eddie had given him from under the front seat and stuffed it in the tyre-well. Then they were on their way.

They continued their journey in silence, although Les felt he could distinguish a slight but unmistakeable change in Peregrine. The Englishman still wasn't saying much but he did seem noticeably cheerier and on several occasions Norton saw him tapping his feet lightly to the music coming through the speakers. It appeared that their brief conversation in the cafe had given Peregrine a chance to open up a little and maybe get one or two things off his chest. Les might not be a bosom buddy, but for an obviously rough man he was friendly and tried to show some understanding, quite unlike Eddie. And when it all boiled down, apart from his godfather miles away in Canberra, Peregrine didn't know a soul in Australia. There were definitely worse people he could be spending his two weeks in Australia with.

They zoomed on through the North Coast countryside: distant blue mountain ranges, uneven plains, hills thick with trees sloping up from the sides of the road. Every now and then they'd cross the odd river or stream or bump over some railway-crossing surrounded by tiny hamlets of a dozen or more houses. It was a clear blue day and even though they were barely 250 kilometres from Sydney both men could notice the chill leaving the air now and the further north they went the warmer and more pleasant it became. More countryside went past in silence, both men still preoccupied with their own thoughts when the Englishman undid his jacket and wound his window half way down.

'I say,' he muttered, a little unexpectedly. 'It's getting quite warm.'

'Warm?' Norton couldn't help but grin. 'Mate, this is the middle of winter.'

'Winter? God, what's it like out here in the summer?'

'In a word Peregrine, hot. Bloody hot. And millions of bloody flies.'

Peregrine loosened his collar and stared out the window. 'Phew!' he exclaimed. 'This would be quite a decent summer's day back home.'

A signpost whizzed past: Kempsey, 210 kms. They both saw it at the same time.

'We might stop there for a bit of lunch,' suggested Les.

'Sounds good,' smiled Peregrine.

About ten kilometres north of Nabiac Norton chuckled quietly to himself. The Machinations tape had stopped playing. He pulled it out and slipped on some Hoodoo Gurus.

'So,' he said, as 'Bittersweet' piped through the speakers. 'Where actually is home to you, Peregrine?'

'Home?' replied the Englishman. 'Well, I have an estate in West Sussex. But I also have a mews in Knightsbridge in London. I suppose my social life revolves mainly around there. The West End.'

Norton nodded. 'How do you get on with the cops?'

'I beg your pardon?'

'Coppers. How do you get on with them? What do you think of them?'

Peregrine looked quizzingly at Les. 'That's a rather unusual question isn't it?'

Norton shrugged and glanced up at the rear-vision mirror. 'Is it?'

'Well,' Peregrine seemed a little lost for words. 'I don't quite know how to answer that,' he said cautiously. 'I imagine my friends and I get on quite well with the police — or the bobbies, as we call them. We don't really bother them. And they don't really bother us. They have a job to do like anybody else I imagine — why?'

'Well, I hate the cunts myself,' grunted Norton sourly, making Peregrine blink at the bitterness creeping into his voice. 'They're fuckin' fleas, the lot of them.'

'Well, if that's the way you wish to think,' Peregrine had to blink again, 'then you're entitled to it. But personally, I have nothing against them at all.'

'Well, I reckon they're all cunts,' repeated Norton grimly. 'And there's one behind us right now.'

Without thinking, Peregrine spun straight around, and sure enough, barely ten metres behind them was a highway-patrol cop on a motorbike.

'I wonder what he wants?' said Peregrine.

'What do you think the cunt wants?' growled Norton. 'To pull me over for speeding. The prick.'

No sooner had Les said that than the cop on the motorbike flashed his lights and turned on his siren.

'Well, I suggest you pull over,' said Peregrine.

Norton looked at Peregrine and his lip curled. 'Pull over?' he hissed. 'Listen. I got shoved in gaol because of one of those arseholes on motorbikes. Fuck him. Let's make the cunt earn his money.'

Norton slammed his foot straight to the floor. The Ford station wagon immediately bucked into second gear, forcing them both back against the seats as they took off like something out of 'The Dukes of Hazzard', the needle on the speedometer climbing crazily like a thermometer gone berserk.

'My God, Les,' said Peregrine, wide-eyed. 'What do you think you're doing?'

Norton didn't answer. He just gritted his teeth and gave Peregrine a look of pure savagery.

Round the bends they hurtled, tyres screaming as Norton ignored the double yellow lines and overtook the other cars and semi-trailers as though they were standing still. Eyes bulging like tennis balls, Peregrine rocked from side to side straining against his seat belt while right behind them the highway-patrol cop stuck grimly to their tail, his siren wailing like a banshee through the peace and quiet of the North Coast countryside.

Terrified and trapped, Peregrine sat there clutching his seat belt in disbelief at what was going on around him and what had happened to him since he arrived in Australia. The previous day some cold-blooded killer had pulled a gun on him and threatened to throw him off the balcony of his hotel room. Now some other thug with a pathological hatred for the police, whom for a moment he had thought was half all right, had him involved in a high-speed car chase through the countryside trying to escape the highway-patrol. And these people were supposed to be looking after him.

After about another five kilometres of screeching, smoking tyres and wailing sirens Norton muttered something under his breath and began to slow down. With a look of utter contempt at the cop in the rear-vision mirror he finally pulled over to the side of the road and turned off the motor. The cop pulled up behind them. He sat there watching them for a moment then slowly got off his bike and walked warily towards them.

'Have a look at this prick,' snarled Norton. 'How would you like to get out and kick him right in the nuts?'

Still wide-eyed, Peregrine stared at Norton and shook his head.

The cop walked up to Norton's window. Les glared straight ahead, totally ignoring him. Peregrine sensed he could see the highway-patrol cop's eyes flash behind his sunglasses.

'Okay. Get out of the car,' said the cop.

'Get fucked,' replied Norton.

Peregrine gave a double blink, scarcely believing his ears.

'I said get out of the car,' repeated the cop, louder this time.

'And I said to get fucked,' replied Norton.

'Right. That's it.' The cop pulled out his service revolver and levelled it straight at Norton's big, red head. 'Now get out of the car.' He moved the barrel towards Peregrine. 'You too,' he barked.

Les and Peregrine exchanged looks. Finally Les undid his seat belt and they both got out, standing on either side of the car.

'Where's your driver's licence?' ordered the cop.

'In my arse,' replied Norton. 'Same place I reckon you keep your brains. You want to have a look?'

'Ohh, you're a real funny fellah, aren't you?' said the cop, moving a little towards the front of the car. 'Real funny.'

'Officer, I think there's some sort of misunderstanding here,' cut in Peregrine.

'You shut up,' answered the speed cop, moving the gun

towards the Englishman. 'And put your hands on top of the car. That goes for both of you.'

The cop's gun still on him, Peregrine placed his hands on the roof of the station wagon. Norton moved his hands towards the roof of the car also, but as he did he lunged to his right and, quick as a cat, brought his hand down across the speed cop's wrist. The gun flew from his hand and clattered onto the bonnet of the car. The cop made a clumsy attempt to retrieve it but Norton sent him sprawling onto the ground with a solid shove and picked up the gun himself.

'Now,' snarled the big red-headed Queenslander, levelling the pistol at the speed cop. 'Let's see how tough you are without your gun, you prick of a thing.' The cop looked up at the barrel of his own revolver; he swallowed hard but didn't say anything. 'Come on. On your feet, arsehole,' ordered Norton.

The cop got to his feet his hands held out at his side. Peregrine watched him with bulging eyes, not quite believing what he was seeing. 'Les . . .' he said tentatively.

'Shut up, Peregrine,' snapped Norton. 'Okay, you rotten copper cunt,' he snarled, thumbing back the hammer of the .38. 'Now I'm gonna blow your head right off your stinkin' copper shoulders.'

The cop swallowed hard again. Through his sunglasses and under his helmet Peregrine could still see the fear on his face. 'Les,' he almost stammered. 'You can't do this.' The Englishman was now just as scared as the speed cop.

'Pigs arse I can't,' replied Norton, his voice dripping malice. 'We'll shoot the bastard here and bury him in the bush along with his bike. No one'll ever find him. The perfect murder, Peregrine; and one less copper in the world.'

'No, Les. No,' begged Peregrine.

'Shut up.' Norton brought the gun up an inch. 'Okay, copper. Say your prayers.'

'Les, for God's sake, man,' pleaded Peregrine.

'All right,' cut in the speed cop. 'Shoot me, you cunt. I don't give a fuck. But at least let me die like a man.' He removed his helmet to reveal a crop of spiky red hair not unlike Norton's. Like a British spy asking for a last cigarette before facing the firing squad, he looked evenly at Peregrine then turned to Norton. 'You got any Fourex in the car?'

The look of bitter hatred on Les's face turned to one of understanding. Still holding the gun on the speed cop he went to the back of the station wagon, opened it and took a can of Fourex from a small esky behind the back seat. He returned to his original position and tossed it to the speed cop. 'Fair enough,' he nodded.

The ginger-haired cop ripped the ring pull off, flung it over his shoulder and held the can of Fourex proudly towards the surrounding bush. 'At least now I can die like an Australian.' He poured about half the can of beer down his throat in one go and looked defiantly at Norton. 'Okay, you bastard,' he belched. 'Do your best.'

'Eat lead, copper.' Norton brought the gun up and his finger tightened on the trigger.

Peregrine couldn't believe what was happening. It was the nightmare in Belfast all over again. 'No, Les, no!' he shrieked. 'You can't do it.'

Showing amazing courage and agility Peregrine leapt across the bonnet of the station wagon and grabbed Norton's arm. Norton appeared stunned at Peregrine's actions and somehow the Englishman was able to wrestle the gun from his hand. It fell to the ground just in front of the speed cop.

'Quick, get the gun,' yelled Peregrine, still wrestling with Norton. The highway-patrol cop ignored the Englishman and slowly took another swig of beer. 'I said get the gun!' yelled Peregrine again.

'I will,' said the cop impassively, giving his mouth a wipe at the same time. 'Just as soon as I finish me can of Fourex.'

Peregrine eased up in his struggle with Les, who for a big man and a so-called heavy seemed to be putting up very little resistance. He stared at the speed cop in disbelief. 'Are you mad or something?' The cop ignored Peregrine and continued to nonchalantly sip his beer. 'Oh, for God's sake, what sort of a man are you?' Peregrine let go of Norton's arm and picked up the gun. Still shaking and with one eye on Les he thrust it towards the cop. 'Here, quick. Take it.'

The cop nodded at Peregrine who was holding the gun like it was a burning stick of dynamite. 'Thanks, mate,' he said casually. 'Just stick it on the bonnet of the car. I'll get it in a minute.'

Peregrine stared at the cop slack-jawed. 'What the . . .?'

Without bothering to answer the red-headed cop took the gun from Peregrine and put it in his holster. 'Good thing it's got no bullets in it,' he said smiling at Norton. 'How are you, Les?'

'Pretty good, Carrots,' replied Norton. 'How's that beer?'
'Beautiful.'
'S'pose I'd better have one myself then.' Ignoring the dumb-

founded Peregrine, Les took another can of Fourex from the esky. He ripped off the ring-pull and shook hands with the young cop. 'Good to see you again, George.'

'You too, Les. Cheers.'

'Cheers, mate.'

They both took a healthy pull on their cans then Les turned to Peregrine. 'Peregrine, this is a mate of mine, George. George, this is Peregrine.'

The cop offered Peregrine his hand. Peregrine looked at it for a moment then shook his head. 'No,' he said. 'No. Ohh no. No! No!' Abruptly Peregrine spun on his heel and stormed off, stopping with his back turned and his fists clenched a few metres from the car. He turned around and pointed an accusing finger at Norton. 'That wasn't funny,' he fumed.

'Wasn't it?' Norton turned to his speed cop mate. 'Did you think that was funny, Carrots?'

'Funny? No, I didn't think it was funny,' said Carrots, his smile fast turning into a grin. 'I thought it was hilarious.' Then both he and Les started to crack up.

There was nothing Peregrine could do but stand there glaring at what to him, were two Australians with a very warped sense of humour rolling around and spilling beer all over the front of the car. He watched them in disgust for a while, then went and got in the front seat and continued glaring out of the windscreen in silence.

Les and Carrots regained most of their composure and finished their first can of beer. Norton made a move towards the esky in the back of the station wagon but Carrots shook his head.

'Remember I was telling you over the phone I couldn't stay long,' he said.

'Yeah,' replied Norton, a little disappointed. 'What's the strength of that? I was hoping to have a good mag to you.'

'There's been a bad murder,' said Carrots. 'Two young pricks from Maitland in a stolen car picked up a local girl hitch-hiking. They raped her then decided to have some fun with her.' Norton winced at the look on his mate's face and the tone in his voice. 'I won't go into details of what they did. But they ended up cutting her throat then dumped her on the side of the road.' Norton shook his head in disgust. 'You should have seen the body, Les. Poor little sheila. She was fifteen and about six stone dripping wet.'

'Fuckin' animals,' spat Norton.

'No. Not animals, Les. Animals wouldn't do what these two did.'

'Yeah, you're right, George.'

'Anyway, their car broke down the other side of Gloucester. We got a fair idea where they are. We'll go in and get them now.' Carrots gave Les a thin smile. 'Take them into custody. Do all the correct paperwork. Then see that they get a fair trial.'

'You never know,' said Les, returning Carrots thin smile. 'With a bit of luck they might try and shoot it out.'

'Hah! You're kidding, Les. Pricks like these are only good for killing sheilas and people that can't fight back. As soon as they see us they'll shit themselves.'

Norton shook his head. 'Maybe in cases like this,' he suggested, 'the parents should be allowed to visit them in their cells for a few minutes — alone.'

Carrots pointed his finger at Les. 'Now that's what I do call a deterrent.' He finished his can of beer and handed the empty to Les. 'Get rid of this for me, will you, mate? I got to get going.'

'Sure.' Norton took the empty can and gave Carrots a quick handshake at the same time. 'I'll call in and see you on the way back — same as last time.'

'See you then, Les.'

'See you, mate.'

As Carrots walked past the station wagon he waved and gave Peregrine a scurrilous grin. 'See you later Peregrine, old fellah. Nice to have met you.'

The Englishman turned towards him, caught his eye briefly then turned away without saying anything. Norton climbed into the car about the same time as Carrots roared off on his motorbike.

'So,' enquired Les, as he buckled up, 'how are you feeling, Peregrine?'

There was a frosty pause for a moment or two before Peregrine answered. 'How am I feeling?' he said tightly. 'How do you think I feel? You damn fool.'

'Now come on, Pezz, don't be like that, mate. It was only a joke.'

'Don't be like that. Oh good God. And I would appreciate it if you wouldn't refer to me as Pezz. My name happens to be Peregrine.' Tight-lipped, he fumed at Norton. 'And that stupid lark was your idea of a joke was it? Brilliant. What can I expect next? Exploding cigars? Flowers in your lapel which squirt water? Rubber snakes in my bed?'

'No, nothing as corny as that.' Norton was slightly admonished, though underneath he was doing everything he could to stop from cracking up again. 'But fair dinkum, Peregrine, it costs you nothing to laugh. And the look on your face after you performed that superhuman effort to wrestle the gun away from me, and Carrots told you to put it on the bonnet of the car. Mate, I hate to say this, but it was priceless.'

'Yes. Well that's . . . marvellous, Les. And I'm so pleased your friend and yourself got a good laugh.' Peregrine folded his arms and nodded towards the highway. 'Now just drive me to wherever it is we're going, would you?'

Norton started the car. 'Righto mate,' he smiled. 'Next stop Kempsey. You'll feel better after a bit to eat and a couple of beers.' As Les slipped the station wagon into drive he gave the Englishman a wink. 'Pezz.'

By the time they got to Kempsey and with a bit of gentle coaxing from Les, Peregrine was noticeably feeling a lot better. He was almost smiling. Norton was pleased to find the same two apple-cheeked old birds in the same old country hotel as last time still serving up huge, steaming plates of the same old country style food. There was no corn beef and parsley sauce on the menu this time, but instead a rich, creamy calves' liver and bacon casserole full of fresh onions and capsicums that had them both licking the plates. And the bread and butter custard was on again too. So by the time Norton had pumped Peregrine full of this, plus four sparkling middies of Tooheys New, the Englishman was feeling decidedly better indeed and agreeing with Norton that it wasn't such a bad joke after all that the big Queenslander had pulled on him, just somewhat unexpected and a bit of a shock to the system after what had recently happened in Belfast, that was all. Norton had to agree with Peregrine's point of view there. In fact by the time they got to Macksville and Les had played his Divynls tape again Peregrine was openly laughing about the whole silly incident and starting to think that Norton wasn't such a bad bloke after all and this two weeks in the Australian countryside might not be as unbearable as he had expected, although in no way comparable to flitting around Europe in a Bentley drinking Bollinger with a young lady from the nobility.

Norton, on the other hand, was pleased he had somehow managed to break the ice with Peregrine, even if it had been in such an outrageous fashion. It seemed that the Englishman had copped it sweet, although a couple of times Les could detect from the tone of his voice there might be a bit of a square up coming. One thing did go straight over Norton's head, though, when Peregrine said Les had done as much for his self-esteem as Charles Bukowski had done for the Californian Women's Liberation Movement. They took their time and were in Coffs Harbour well before three.

'Where were you thinking of staying, Les?' asked Peregrine as they stopped at a set of lights in Grafton Street.

'Dunno,' shrugged Les. 'I might just see if I can find us a decent motel.'

'What about this place?' Peregrine handed Norton a brochure from inside his jacket. 'I picked it up at that hotel in Kempsey.'

Norton studied the small, glossy pamphlet while he waited for the lights to change. 'Penguin Beach Resort?'

'Yes. According to that brochure it's on this main highway just on the other side of town.'

'Sure looks all right,' conceded Les. 'Yeah, righto,' he shrugged, as the lights changed to green. 'Why not?'

Five minutes later they came to a huge white sign on blue poles, next to an Italian seafood restaurant overlooking the ocean.

'Here it is,' said Les, and hit the blinker. 'Let's have a look.'

They turned off the highway down a neatly-tiled driveway dotted with palm trees, tropical fruit trees and native plants set in exquisitely landscaped gardens. The driveway circled a parking area; Les slowed up for a speed-hump as a green BMW pulled out and pulled in next to a maroon, Jaguar Sovereign.

'Christ!' exclaimed Norton. 'What about this joint? Very how's your father.' Peregrine said nothing but had to nod in agreement.

They took their bags from the car and walked across to a spacious, palm-dotted foyer where the door swished open automatically, leading them to a front desk with a statuette of a penguin sitting at one end.

The whole place reeked of spacious, opulent comfort. Indirect lighting bathed the walls and sunlight streamed down from the skylights high in the ceiling above onto the dozens of lush indoor plants. The decor was mainly soft blue and grey with touches of pink, except for the colourful patterns on the cane lounges placed around the walls, and the pastel tones of the murals and paintings hung above them. From the metal poles supporting the skylights hung swarms of beautifully painted balsawood parrots which scarcely moved in the air conditioned stillness. Les and Peregrine hardly had time to exchange approving glances before they were almost swamped by politely efficient staff in blue uniforms, the men in sweatshirts, the women in neat skirts and tops, all with a blue and gold penguin motif on the front.

Naturally enough Peregrine wanted the best rooms the resort had to offer. Unfortunately the ultra swish had been taken by a German industrialist and his entourage and a team of Texan zillionaires. Then Les remembered why he was there and who he was with and insisted on adjoining rooms. The management was expecting a convention in the following day and the only two adjoining rooms were two standard ones on the sixth floor; one floor above the front desk.

'That will do admirably,' said Les.

They signed the register then the staff picked up their bags and just about bore them into the lift and up to rooms 219 and 220 which were on an open hallway almost overlooking the front desk.

'Why don't we throw our stuff inside and check the place out?' said Les. 'Get changed later?'

'Jolly good idea,' replied Peregrine. 'My room's closest to the lift. Give me a tap in five minutes.'

Christ! thought Norton, after he'd thrown his bag on the Sealy posturepedic double bed. If this is a standard room, I wonder what those other ones were like? The room was large, bright and spotlessly clean, mainly blue and grey again with indoor plants and pastel-shaded murals around the beige walls. There was a colour TV, stereo, fridge and bar and behind the blue lounge the curtains swished back to where a sliding glass door opened onto a balcony giving a magnificent view of the beach and the small islands not far from the shore. Christ! thought Norton again, smiling to himself and pleased that Peregrine had found the place. I reckon we ought to spend the two weeks here. Then again he remembered why they were there. No, he sighed, one bloody night's gonna have to do. Five minutes later he and Peregrine were in the lift heading for the third floor.

They strolled along a wide corridor to another lift with a glass back which took them to the first floor and what seemed to be a solarium. The huge room was thick with lush plants and spaced with more comfortable cane lounges and chairs. Flocks of parrots hung suspended in the air and the whole area was bathed in the sunlight coming through an almost completely glass ceiling. A small indoor pool meandered around the blue-grey carpet and mauve walls to the sepia-toned tiles which led to the bistro and main dining room. After a quick check of the menu and wine list, Les and Peregrine strolled out to the pool area.

Neither man had to say anything as they followed the white scalloped pathway to the pool; the surroundings did it for them. An explosion of coloured flowers and tropical trees burst from more meticulous landscaping. A tiny stream bubbled through the rockeries and beneath wooden bridges to momentarily stop in a pool full of lilies and brightly-coloured carp. An attendant who was feeding the fish smiled and said hello as they walked past. Les opened a gate and they stepped through to where the sun was sparkling on a massive, irregular, man-made lagoon edged in parts with volcanic rock. Pink umbrellas and white banana-chairs surrounded the pool, the outdoor jacuzzi and the childrens' pool and playing area. Through the glass fence behind the pool they could see the blue waves crashing and hissing across the sand and they spotted the islands they had seen from their balconies. They strolled around the pool to the glassed-in spa-bath which joined the gymnasium. There didn't appear to be many people around — a dozen or so on the banana-chairs and one or two couples enjoying the heated pool. The only others were the blue uniformed staff who seemed to be forever sweeping, wiping or cleaning something.

'Well, what do you reckon, Pezz?' smiled Norton. 'Looks like something out of a James Bond movie, don't it?'

Peregrine the aristocrat couldn't help but agree. 'Simply marvellous. I also noticed the prices when we booked in; it's not at all expensive. Anything comparable to this in Europe, if you could find it, would cost you a fortune. Not that that would worry me at all, Les,' he added with a grin. 'I happen to have several.'

'Yes, so I believe,' chuckled Norton. 'So what do you want to do — seeing as you're our guest in this fine country?'

'Do?' Peregrine walked over to Les and actually placed a friendly hand on his shoulder. 'Well, I think the gentlemanly thing to do would be to get changed into something a little more appropriate for the occasion, dear boy, and spend what's left of the afternoon sitting by the edge of the pool sipping the best cocktails the establishment has to offer.'

'Peregrine,' winked Les. 'I think that is an absolutely splendid idea. Quite gentlemanly indeed.'

Twenty minutes later they had changed and were placing

their towels on two banana-chairs closest to a sign which said Ring For Service.

Norton had to suppress a bit of a chuckle as Peregrine set himself up at the pool's edge. It wasn't his complexion or build — for a to-and-from he wasn't chalky white and he was more wiry than skinny — it was the outfit. Les just had on thongs, shorts and a Mexican beer T-shirt Warren had given him, but Peregrine did frock up for the occasion. He had on a jade Pierre Cardin bathrobe and matching Gucci shorts, black Italian leather sandals, and a Yves St. Laurent sling wallet and sunglasses. This outfit was topped by a small white Panama. If Noel Coward could see this, he'd roll over in his grave, thought Les. But Peregrine was completely oblivious and so, it seemed, were the others seated around the pool.

'Well come on, old boy,' he said, moving to the side of the pool. 'Last one in's a rotten egg.' Then he dived in. He surfaced a few metres out and began swimming towards the middle with the worst style Norton had ever seen. His arms flayed madly at the water as his head swung from side to side and he made hardly any progress. He stopped and turned to Les.

'What's it like?' Norton called out.

'Absolutely marvellous, old boy.'

'Yeah? You sure?' Norton's tongue was planted firmly in his cheek.

'Of course. Come along! Don't be such a slacker. Ho! Here we go.' The Englishman duck-dived to the bottom of the pool while Norton watched laughing to himself. Peregrine was like a little child having the time of his life and thinking he was killing them. Les watched him for a little while then he dived in. Norton would never make the East German swimming team but he managed to get to the other side of the pool and back in about the same time it took Peregrine to make it from halfway.

'Yeah, it's not too bad, I suppose,' he said, holding the edge of the pool with one hand.

'Oh, come on now, Les. Where's your sense of adventure? This is absolutely beautiful. You know, I don't think you're as tough as you make out.' Flushed with his own wellbeing, Peregrine dragged himself out of the pool. 'Anyway, that's enough exercise for the day, I think. Time now for drinky-poos.'

'Yeah. Not a bad idea. I'm just about buggered myself after all that.' And wait till I get you out on this farm, Horatio Hornblower. I'll give you sense of adventure.

They towelled off and Peregrine ordered drinks: Fourex for Les, a nice long whisky sour for himself. These arrived promptly and Peregrine immediately ordered two more. And that was how they spent the afternoon, except that after his third whisky sour Peregrine switched to Tom Collins. By then it was getting on for five and the sun was starting to go down over the mountains and banana fields surrounding the resort. Les asked Peregrine what he wanted to do that night. Peregrine suggested dinner in the resort restaurant around seven-thirty then a trip into Coffs Harbour later that night. Norton replied that that didn't sound like a bad idea at all.

'But do we have to wait till half past seven before we eat?'

Peregrine gave Norton a look of disdain across the top of his Tom Collins. 'My dear boy — a gentleman never dines before seven.'

'What about a bloody hamburger?

Peregrine shook his head and finished his drink. 'Shall we leave?' he sniffed.

Norton spent the next couple of hours reading a magazine, getting changed, drinking one or two beers from his fridge and not doing a great deal at all except stand on his balcony and think how lucky he was to be there. At seven-thirty sharp he was in a clean pair of jeans and a brown Le Shirt knocking on Peregrine's door.

'Sorry I'm late, old chap,' said Peregrine, razor in one hand, shaving cream all over his face. 'I was reading a book and dozed off. Shan't be a tick.'

'That's all right, mate. Take your time.' Les closed the door. 'You had a shower yet?'

'Yes. Had a quick one about five minutes ago.'

'Yeah. I heard you poms are pretty quick when it comes to having a shower. I'm surprised you had one at all.'

'What was that, old boy?' came from the bathroom.

'Nothing, mate. Nothing at all.'

While Peregrine finished shaving, Les had a bit of a quick check of his clothes; there wasn't a real lot but what there was was top quality. He also made a mental note: 82 cm waist, size 8 shoes. Next to the bed were two books by Charles Bukowski: *Women* and *War All The Time*. There was also a small book of Shakespearean sonnets. He had a quick read and replaced them.

'So, how are you feeling?' he asked as Peregrine came from the bathroom.

'Absolutely first class. How about yourself?'

'Good. But I'm bloody hungry. I'd eat the maggoty arse out of a dead bandicoot.'

'Yes . . . well I don't know that I'm that hungry but I am rather peckish.' Before long Peregrine was in a pair of tan velvet trousers, cream silk shirt and a matching cravat. On Les it would have looked poncey. On Peregrine it looked as it should. Aristocratic.

'You ready, old boy?' he smiled.

'Reckon,' replied Les, rising from the lounge. 'Let's hit the toe.'

They took the lift to the restaurant.

The restaurant was tastefully furnished in blue and white and overlooked the pool area and the beach beyond. The bar area was to the left and in between sat a young bearded piano player in a tuxedo tinkling out the theme from *The Godfather* on a baby grand. He smiled around the room in his white tuxedo as his hands moved gracefully across the keys — it looked like something out of an old Humphrey Bogart movie. The restaurant was fairly large and appeared to be about half full. You couldn't miss the Texans and their wives down one end next to the windows. The women all had two hundred dollar hairdos, horrible loud dresses and enough jewellery to embarrass Marie Antoinette. The men wore customary calf-length boots, arrow-pocketed jackets and trousers and string ties with turquoise toggles. Not far away sat the Germans, all stiff and conservative, eating almost in unison. Sitting there straight-backed, silent and Teutonic, they looked as if they would all jump up from the table, click their heels and give a Nazi salute if someone had yelled out 'achtung'. Around them were families, couples and a girl of about twenty-eight with two other girls who were about eighteen. From behind a desk materialised the head waiter in a tuxedo.

'For two, is it, sir?' he said to Peregrine.

'Yes thank you.'

'Anywhere in particular you might wish to sit, gentlemen?'

Peregrine nodded to a cubicle next to the wall. 'Just there should do.'

'Certainly, sir.'

The head waiter ushered them to their table, placed the wine list and menus in front of them and vanished. As they studied the menu, the voices of the Texans carried across the room. Peregrine turned towards them momentarily then turned to Les.

'Do you know why American tourists talk so loud, Les?'

he asked. Norton shook his head. 'So they can hear themselves over their clothes.'

Norton gave a bit of a chuckle. 'Anyway, this food looks all right.'

'Yes, it certainly does. Have you made up your mind yet?'

'Yes,' nodded Norton. 'I'm going to have the Triton seafood cocktail in light raspberry sauce for starters. And . . . the lobster nouvelle with brandy cream and vegetables Julienne for the main. What about you, Pezz?'

Peregrine gave the menu one of those looks of grudging approval. 'Well, I might have the smoked goose Riverina with red currant and port wine sauce for an entree. And the Danish fillet of beef with blue vein cheese and port wine sauce again for the main. For dessert? I'll see how I feel after this.'

'Yeah, me too. What about wine?'

Peregrine looked at Les impassively. 'Les, please. I only ever drink French champagne.'

'You seen how much it is a bottle?'

'Yes, I noticed. And if I drink ten bottles a day for the next fifty years I still wouldn't make a dent in twelve months' interest.'

Norton studied the Englishman for a moment. 'Just how much money have you got?'

Peregrine shrugged. 'About twenty-four million.'

'Twenty-four million bucks! Shit!'

'Twenty-four million *pounds*, Les.'

'Pounds! Christ! That's about fifty million bucks. Fuckin' hell. What's it like to have fifty million dollars?'

Peregrine shrugged again. 'Hasn't everybody got fifty million dollars?'

Norton shook his head and they ordered. And for the next half hour or so they ate the most beautiful food imagineable and drank '71 Dom Perignon at $190 a bottle.

Two bottles of shampoo had them roaring a little so they decided they might have sweets. Both went for the Banana Coruba, which was caramelised bananas rolled in coconut and almonds then flambed in Jamaican rum at the table. It got them even drunker and went down extremely well, so well, in fact that Peregrine ordered another bottle of Dom which they had brought to them in the piano bar.

The piano bar was laid-back and tastefully decorated in shades of grey with matching cane chairs. The boys found a table beneath one of the smoked glass windows facing away from the pool. It wasn't very crowded, one or two couples, a well-dressed man with his two young daughters and one table away were the two young girls and the older one who were in the restaurant earlier. Norton began to notice them just as the waiter placed an ice-bucket with their champagne next to their table. The two younger girls were pretty in a snooty sort of way: plenty of dark eye makeup, short auburn hair shaved up high at the back and baggy black pants rolled up to their calves above shiny Dr Martens. Apart from being a bit young they definitely weren't Norton's type. The one with them was, though: tall with reddish blonde hair combed loosely but neatly down each side of her face, she had piercing blue eyes and a slightly square jaw which suggested she may have been of Nordic extraction. Unlike the other two, she was wearing a trim pink and grey Reebok tracksuit and white aerobic boots. Peregrine caught the two younger girls' eyes just as the waiter popped the bottle of champagne.

'Care to join us?' he asked politely, gesturing to the empty chairs next to him. 'You're more than welcome.'

The two younger girls looked at the one in the tracksuit. She shrugged a look of 'why not?' and the next thing the three of them were seated at the boys' table.

'I'm Peregrine, and this is my friend, Les.'

'Hello girls,' smiled Norton. 'How are you?'

'Fine, thank you,' was the general chorus as Peregrine ordered more champagne and the piano player began tinkling 'Stormy Weather' in the background.

The waiter poured the girls their drinks. There was a quick 'cheers' all around then it was bottoms up and the girls introduced themselves. The two younger ones were cousins, Kirsty and Josephine; Josephine at eighteen was a year older than Kirsty. They came from Armidale where they attended an exclusive young ladies' finishing school. Their fathers were graziers with stacks of money and had promised the girls a week at Penguin Resort if they did well in some exam; which they did. The older girl was a little more formal and gave her full name which was Ingersoll Ovstedal. She was Norwegian and was the girls' governess cum au pair girl sent along by daddy to keep an eye on them.

'It is lovely here to be sure,' said Ingersoll, sipping on her glass of bubbly. 'But sadly we have to leave at eight in the morning. The driver calls for us.'

'Yes,' nodded Peregrine. 'I could not agree with you more. It is absolutely delightful here. And sadly we too are only here the one night ourselves. So,' he raised his glass and smiled. 'Why don't we make this last night a good one?'

'Yeah, why not?' grinned Norton, glowing from all the champagne.

'Reckon,' chorused Kirsty and Josephine and tipped another glass of Dom down their sweet little throats. Ingersoll shrugged, smiled and drained her glass too.

Three bottles of Dom Perignon later, Tuesday night at Penguin Resort was beginning to shape up quite nicely. Josephine, seated next to Peregrine, was starting to get very heavy eyes for the young Englishman; his charm, well-modulated voice and impeccable manners almost had her in a spell. Generally with two Australian girls, if one meets a guy and fancies him a bit the other will run interference and do everything in her power to drive a wedge between them. In this particular case, however, Kirsty appeared to have the hots for Peregrine herself and was doing the exact opposite. Ingersoll, who was supposed to be keeping an eye on the two girls, was now beginning to get a bit fruity herself from all the Dom and appeared to be more intent on keeping an eye on Norton, steadily moving closer towards him on the seat. Norton knew one thing for sure. He wasn't going far. In the background the piano player tinkled from 'Ain't Misbehavin'' straight into 'Gimme the Moonlight, Gimme the Girl'. The man had magic in his fingers.

'I say,' exclaimed Peregrine. 'That chap's jolly good.' The others all agreed. 'Waiter!' he called out. The waiter appeared and Peregrine had a freshly opened bottle of Dom and the ice-bucket sent to the piano player. 'Tell the young gentleman, with our compliments. And we'll have another two bottles.'

'Certainly, sir.'

The piano player gave a double blink when the waiter placed the ice-bucket and champagne next to him. Wide-eyed he stared over to where the waiter was pointing then smiled appreciatively. All five smiled and waved back. Drunk or not, Sir Peregrine Normanhurst III had certainly added a new dimension to the term big spender.

'So, tomorrow you are leaving also, yes?' Ingersoll said to Les.

'Yeah. We're off to the Tweed Valley for a couple of weeks,' nodded Norton. 'A mate of mine's got a property up there. We're stopping on it while he's away.'

'I wish we didn't have to go tomorrow,' said Kirsty. 'I love it here.'

'Yes, me too,' added Josephine. 'It's so ... so romantic.' She gazed directly at Peregrine. 'Do you find it romantic here, Peregrine?'

Peregrine smiled softly at Josephine. 'Are you asking me, Josephine,' he said 'whether this resort and the evening bring out any romance in me?'

'Yes.'

Peregrine put his glass down for about the first time that evening, took Josephine by the hand and looked softly into her eyes. 'Take all my loves, my love, yea take them all,' he began.

> What hast thou then more than thou hadst before?
> No love, my love, that thou mayst true love call;
> All mine was thine before thou hadst this more.
> Then if for my love thou my love receivest,
> I cannot blame thee for my love thou usest;
> But yet be blamed, if thou thyself deceivest
> By wilful taste of what thyself refusest.
> I do forgive thy robbery, gentle thief,
> Although thou steal thee all my poverty;
> And yet, love knows, it is a greater grief
> To bear love's wrong than hate's known injury.
> Lascivious grace, in whom all ill well shows,
> Kill me with spites; yet we must not be foes.

Poor young Josephine didn't know what hit her. She sat there staring at Peregrine who was still holding her hand. 'What was that?' she blinked.

'That?' smiled Peregrine. 'Just a little Shakespeare I picked up at Harrow. And brought on by your beauty and the delights of the evening.'

Being good and drunk, most of the verse went straight over Les and Ingersoll's heads, but the way Peregrine recited it and really gave it the Richard Burton treatment, they had to be impressed none the less. Christ! thought Norton. Fifty million bucks or not, this boy's got style with a capital ST.

'Do you know any more?' asked Kirsty.

This time Peregrine took both their hands.

> Two loves I have of comfort and despair,
> Which like two spirits do suggest me still:
> The better angel is a man right fair,
> The worser spirit a woman colour'd ill.
> To win me soon to hell, my female evil
> Tempteth my better angel from my side,

And would corrupt my saint to be a devil,
Wooing his purity with her foul pride.
And whether that my angel be turn'd fiend
Suspect I may, yet not directly tell;
But being both from me, both to each friend,
I guess one angel in another's hell:
Yet this shall I ne'er know, but live in doubt,
Till my bad angel fire my good one out.

This left both Kirsty and Josephine starry-eyed and more than a bit wet in their pants. Peregrine was their Patrick Swayze, Tom Cruise and George Michael all rolled into one. Even Ingersoll was now starting to heave a little. She moved closer to Norton and undid the top of her tracksuit slightly giving Les a glimpse of something much more spectacular than the fjords around Folgefon.

'Nothing like a bit of the old bard,' hiccupped Peregrine, 'to add a drop of flavour to things. I only wish my tawdry voice could do the man justice.'

'Oh Peregrine, it does, it does,' chorused Josephine and Kirsty.

'You're both too kind,' smiled the Englishman.

They ordered and drank more champagne, then someone suggested they have a swim. Peregrine said this sounded like a jolly splendid idea and asked the head waiter if they could be served champagne out by the pool. The head waiter assured Peregrine that at $190 a bottle and the way he was throwing money around he would be served champagne if he wanted to jump off the roof with a candle stuck in his arse, singing 'A Star Fell From Heaven'. However, Ingersoll said that she'd been outside for a bit of fresh air earlier during an excursion to the loo and the wind was now well and truly up and even though a frolic around the pool would be a lot of fun, in the middle of August at ten-thirty at night it would be rather chilly to say the least, even for an Eskimo let alone a Norwegian.

'I know,' said Peregrine. 'I'll get that chap on the piano to play a request.'

He swayed to his feet, weaved clumsily across the room and whispered something in the piano player's ear. The piano player looked thoughtful for a moment then grinned and nodded. Peregrine returned to his seat, smiled at the curious looks on the others' faces and poured himself a fresh glass of Dom. He'd just raised it to his lips when the piano player switched gently from 'Am I Blue?' into 'Till The Lights Of London Shine Again'.

'Not a bad old song, this,' beamed Peregrine, crooning some of the words in a voice that wasn't too bad for a complete drunk. 'But the next one is considerably better.' He smiled directly at Josephine when he said this.

While Peregrine hummed some of the lyrics the others sat in silence watching him with the piano tinkling softly in the background. Then the piano player switched from that song straight into 'Only A Kid Named Joe'.

'This one is especially for you, Josephine, my dear,' said Peregrine, raising his glass. Once again it was another lovely old song and this time Peregrine hummed the lyrics directly at Josephine.

> She's only a kid named Joe,
> What's her last name, I don't know.
> But I buy the papers
> From a kid named Joe.

This was the final straw for the young schoolgirl from Armidale primed up with bottle after bottle of French champagne. Her eyes swam and her knickers began melting down her legs quicker than the flambéd caramel flavouring the boys had earlier on the banana Coruba. She was breathless, speechless and Kirsty wasn't far behind her.

'Any chance of some more Shakespeare?' sighed Kirsty, after Peregrine crooned another chorus and the song finished.

'Why don't we go somewhere quieter to hear it?' suggested Josephine, turning to Ingersoll. 'Do you think it would be all right if we went back to Peregrine's room while he read us some more sonnets?'

The way she said 'we' indicated she meant her and Kirsty and no one else. Paradoxically, this was music to Ingersoll's ears. She was dying for an excuse to get the red-haired Queenslander alone somewhere too, but being the girl's governess she had to appear worried or at least look a little concerned.

'I'll go along too,' panted Kirsty. 'So there'll be the two of us.'

'Well ... I suppose it will be satisfactory,' nodded the tall, sexy Norwegian, trying her best to look serious. 'But do not forget, girls. Eight o'clock we are leaving. Seven o'clock we must be up for the breakfast.'

'We will,' chorused the two schoolgirls, almost leaping to their feet and dragging Peregrine to his at the same time. 'Come on, Peregrine.'

'Well ... I ... Yes, that sounds like a splendid idea. Jolly good indeed.' He stood a little unsteadily on his feet. 'Just one moment,' he said, then lurched across to the bar where without so much as the blink of an eye he signed the tab for the best part of two grands' worth of food and drink. He returned to the table and extended a hand to Ingersoll. 'My dear lady. May I just say that this has been an absolute pleasure.'

'Likewise too I am sure,' smiled Ingersoll, giving his hand a polite squeeze.

'I shall see you in the morning, Les.'

'Yeah righto, mate,' winked Norton. 'Look after yourself. Night girls.'

'Goodnight, Les.'

That left Ingersoll and Norton alone with 'Fire Down Below' tinkling in the background and you didn't need to be a rocket scientist to know what was on both of their minds. But there was a certain amount of protocol to be observed and they would have to give the others at least five minutes start before they raced to Norton's room and started ripping each other's clothes off.

'Well, it's certainly been a funny old night,' said Norton. 'That Peregrine sure knows his Shakespeare.'

'He does for sure,' breathed Ingersoll, edging a little closer.

There was a pause for a moment.

'What would you like to do now?' asked Les.

'I don't really care.'

'Would you like to come back to my room? We could get some more champagne and there's a late night rock show on SKY Channel.'

'That sounds very good,' heaved Ingersoll, giving Les a good sight of her white bra and a pair of lovely big tits that had him drooling like Zeke Wolf over a lamb chop.

'Then let's go.'

Norton got to his feet and offered Ingersoll his hand. When she took it and almost pulled him face down onto the table, Les realised just how drunk he was. Christ! he thought, as the room spun slightly. You can shove that French shit in your arse. I'm stickin' to Fourex.

Drunk as he was, Norton still ordered another bottle of Dom Perignon from room service, which he charged to Peregrine, figuring he would have insisted on it anyway. It arrived about two minutes after they did. Previously Norton had dimmed the lights and turned the TV on low in the background. Some rock group that could have been INXS was playing. He popped the bottle of Dom and poured them both a glass.

'Well. Here's looking up your old address, Ingersoll.'

'And yours too,' giggled the tall Norwegian girl.

They moved across to the sliding glass door on the balcony. Les had drawn the curtains open earlier and there was a beautiful view across the resort to the beach, where the moon was turning the smooth darkness of the water into silver. The tiny islands were silhouettes in the distance and the waves licking gently at the water's edge were like crushings of white lace.

'It is very beautiful here,' said Ingersoll. 'The moon. The sea. Everything.'

'Yeah,' agreed Les. 'Like something out of a Mills and Boon novel, ain't it?'

Ingersoll didn't reply, she just looked across deeply into Norton's eyes. Les went to put his arm around her and managed to spill a little champagne down the front of her tracksuit.

'Ohh shit! I'm sorry,' he spluttered, and made a clumsy attempt to wipe it off with his free hand.

The attempt to wipe it off went on longer and longer and got slower and slower, with Les spreading more champagne into her top than he was wiping off. Ingersoll started to heave. She tilted her face slightly to one side and Les kissed her on what to him felt like the most lovely warm lips imaginable: firm and assertive, yet sweet and yielding. He took both their glasses and placed them on the table next to them, knocking one over in the process. Ingersoll wound her arms around his neck and began kissing Les more intently, her mouth widened and her tongue fervent and exquisite darted out to be met immediately by Les's. He unzipped the front of her tracksuit, slipped her bra-straps over her shoulders and eased her breasts out. They were firm and round like two big juicy rockmelons. Ingersoll sighed as under Norton's firm but gentle touch the nipples began to harden and colour. He ran his tongue around her ears, under her chin and throat and across her breasts. Ingersoll held his head into her as he kissed her nipples.

Norton felt like he was going to go mad. 'You know what I want to do?' he said. 'I want to pour champagne all over your set and lick it off.'

Ingersoll heaved noticeably. 'What is it you Australians say?' she breathed. 'Go for your life.'

Les moved her towards the bed and she slipped out of her tracksuit down to a pair of skimpy white knickers. Norton got down to his Speedos and turned off the lights and turned down the TV. With only the moonlight shining in from the balcony, Les could see that Ingersoll had a body that would make a chief Rabbi carve a swastika on the wall of a synagogue. She undid her bra and lay back on the bed. Norton poured some champagne into a glass then tipped a little over Ingersoll's breasts. She gave a tiny giggle which quickly turned into sighs and moans of delight as Les began slowly licking it off.

'What a way to drink champagne,' he grinned.

'What a way to serve it,' she smiled back.

While he was licking off the champagne, Les slipped his hand onto her ted and began stroking it under her knickers. Ingersoll spread her legs and started writhing on the mattress. Les kissed her lips, fondled and kissed her breasts and poured champagne into her navel and sucked it out. Ingersoll started going into a frenzy. Beneath his touch Les could feel her ted start to soften up like a big, juicy Bowen mango. Then Norton must have hit an erogenous zone or something because suddenly the Viking came out in Ingersoll.

With a growl like a panther she tore her knickers off and Norton's Speedos as well. She pushed Les onto his back as if he weighed nothing, stroked his cock a couple of times then climbed up on top of him arching her back and shaking her head from side to side as she eased him inside of her. Her ted was an absolute delight: not too big, not too small and as firm and warm as you'd like. Les fondled her breasts and stroked her shoulders; in the soft light he could see her face twisting and her eyelids fluttering as she began grinding away. He pulled her down to him and kissed her and felt her hair billow and sway across his face. His head spinning from all the champagne earlier, Les held back for as long as he could, but it was getting too good. He grabbed a pillow from behind him and slipped it under his backside for a bit more thrust. A shudder shook Ingersoll and she ground down faster and faster, harder and harder. Les couldn't last any longer. He grabbed her shoulders, forced her down and drove up at the same time. Ingersoll choked off a scream, Les couldn't help but let out a roar then exploded inside her just as Ingersoll threw her head from side to side in a flurry of reddish blonde hair and orgasmic delight.

MEANWHILE IN ROOM 220, Peregrine had set up pretty much the same scene. He'd ordered the champagne, dimmed the lights except for the bedlamp, tuned the radio to some soft rock station and drawn the curtains for an almost identical view to the one from Norton's room. He had his back to the girls and in his drunken state had clumsily opened the bottle of Dom and was pouring them a drink.

'Here you are, ladies,' he beamed, always the perfect gentleman. 'Cool champagne for your warm lips.' He turned round to the girls and his aristocratic eyes nearly fell out of his upper crust head. By the time Peregrine had opened the bottle and poured three glasses, Josephine and Kirsty had taken off their clothes and were down to their Kayser Perfects. Josephine's were a kind of shiny maroon, Kirsty's blush pink.

'I say,' spluttered Peregrine.

They both had top little bodies, nicely rounded boobs and slim waists. Their bikini lines were trimmed perfectly and the mounds under their knickers looked like the bonnets on two Volkswagens.

Peregrine's eyes were bulging and his jaw had dropped about a foot. 'I say,' he said again.

'What did you want to say?' smiled Josephine.

'I . . . I . . .' Peregrine didn't know what to say.

The two Armidale schoolgirls advanced on Peregrine and began undressing him; Kirsty undid his cravat and unbuttoned his shirt, Josephine began undoing his trousers. When they got him down to his Y-fronts, Josephine placed his hands on her breasts and Kirsty slipped her arms around his waist and started kissing his neck and ears. Poor Peregrine. It was yet another atrocity perpetrated on him since he'd arrived in Australia. He'd just got over all that trouble with Les and Eddie and now he looked like being pack-raped by two nubile schoolgirls. Peregrine may have been a bit of a lad with the debutantes around the West End, but nothing like this had ever happened in jolly old London. And what was that play he'd taken Stephanie Wingate to three weeks before he'd left? *No Sex Please, We're British.*

'I say, girls,' he stammered. 'This is most extraordinary, I must say.'

'You promised us more Shakespeare, Peregrine,' said Josephine, a little authority coming into her voice as she pushed him back onto the bed.

'Well yes . . . but . . .'

'Well, come on,' said Kirsty. 'Let's hear it, baby.'

Peregrine began reciting as Josephine and Kirsty got on either side of him and started kissing his chest, neck and ears.

'*Some say thy fault is youth, some wantonness,*' he gasped. '*Some say thy grace is youth and gentle sport.*'

'Mmmh! That's beautiful,' crooned Josephine. 'Keep going.'

'*As on the finger of a throned queen, the basest jewel will be well esteemed. So are those errors, that in thee are seen. So truths . . .* Oh good God!'

Peregrine took a quick glimpse down. Kirsty had his dick out, stroking it, then running her tongue up and down the sides.

'Come on, Peregrine,' ordered Josephine. 'More Shakespeare.'

'*The teeming autumn, big with rich increase, bearing the wanton burden of thy prime* . . . Oh my God.' Kirsty had her mouth around his knob now and was drawing on it, slowly and firmly. '*Yet this abundant issue seemed to me* . . . Oh Christ! *But hope of orphans and* . . . Oh dear! . . . *unfathered fruit. For* . . . Jesus! . . . *summer and his pleasure wait on thee, and, thou away* . . .'

That was as far as Peregrine got. His voice trailed away as Josephine slipped off her knickers, slewed around and lowered herself down on him; the Englishman now found it extremely difficult to recite Shakespearean sonnets with a juicy eighteen-year-old ted spread across his face. He gasped in some air then poked his tongue up; Josephine squealed, Kirsty kept mouthing him down below. The next thing Peregrine knew she'd straddled him and was forcing him inside her. He moaned into Josephine's ted as Kirsty began grinding away.

'Don't make him blow yet,' panted Josephine. 'I want some too.'

'All right,' gasped Kirsty.

After a few minutes Kirsty got off and so did Josephine. Peregrine brought his head up for a quick look around to find Josephine on her back next to him with her legs spread apart.

'Come on, Peregrine,' she heaved, and lasciviously ran her tongue over her lips. 'My turn.'

Peregrine rolled over and mounted Josephine; she gave a tiny scream as he pushed to get it in then squealed with joy as he began stroking. Behind him, Kirsty started running her tongue up and down his back, across his buttocks, into the cheeks of his backside and around his balls. Peregrine felt like a flock of magpies was about to fly out of his arse. He also felt like he should be ashamed to be in such a situation as this with two young schoolgirls he had liberally applied with champagne. Instead of feeling disgust though, Sir Peregrine began to thoroughly enjoy it and in a matter of seconds his behind was going up and down like Yehudi Menuhin's elbow. He drove it further into Josephine who screamed with delight;

behind him Kirsty kept running her tongue over his back while she gave herself a handjob as she began getting more and more turned on by the whole sordid scene. The champagne had dulled his senses a little, preventing him from going off too soon, but before long he was stroking like a steam-engine as he zoomed down the straight for a big finish, making every post a winner. With a roar like a lion he drove it up and poured himself into Josephine, who with Kirsty screamed as they both managed to come at the same time.

THE BREEZE COMING in from the ocean was rustling the curtains in Norton's room and in the soft darkness of the night you could see the moon shadows dancing from them across to the bed. The TV was still on very quietly and Ingersoll had on one of Les's T-shirts as they lay cuddling beneath the sheets.

'Normally, I am not ever like this,' she said, her head on Les's chest as she gazed up into his dark brown eyes. 'Especially because with the young ones around.'

'Same with me,' replied Norton. 'Usually I'm a good Catholic boy. I don't know how I let you bring me back here and seduce me. It must have been all that horrible bloody French champagne.'

'I seduced *you*?' protested Ingersoll.

'Of course you did, you wog bastard. You're an animal.'

'What!!? Why . . .'

Ingersoll gave Les a thump on the chest and got kissed lovingly for her trouble. The kiss seemed to last for some time then rolled into another one. Her tongue slipped out to be met once more by Norton's. There was a flurry of hand movements beneath the sheets plus a little moaning and groaning then Les rolled over and got between her legs.

'This time, Ingersoll,' he smiled, as he gently entered her. 'I'll do all the work if you like. You can take it easy.'

The second round of love-making was even better than the first and took a lot longer. However, on top of all the champagne it also took a lot out of Les. He only meant to close his eyes for a few moments when they finished, but instead found himself sliding deeper and deeper into the gentle darkness of unconsciousness. He didn't hear Ingersoll turn the TV off or see her smiling down at him in the moonlight; and he didn't feel her kiss him softly on the cheek or hear her whisper '*sov godt*' just before she left.

* * *

SOMEHOW OR OTHER, in his drunken state, Peregrine had made it rockily to his feet after his romp with Josephine and Kirsty and had poured the girls a glass of champagne. They were laying back on the bed, observing his nudity from beneath the sheets.

'I say, girls,' he said, raising his glass in a toast. 'Here's to a jolly splendid evening.'

'Oh yes. Rather,' mimicked Josephine. 'But it hasn't finished yet, has it?'

'Yes. What about a little more Shakespeare?' giggled Kirsty.

'Shakespeare!' snorted Peregrine. 'To hell with Shakespeare I say.' He put down his glass and jumped onto the bed. 'How about a bit of Lord Alfred Tennyson?' he said, and got beneath the sheets grabbing both Josephine and Kirsty on their teds.

> Into the valley of death rode the six hundred
> Fanny to the left of them,
> Fanny to the right of them,
> Fanny in front of them.
> Their's not to reason why,
> Their's but to screw or die.
> Into the valley of fanny rode the six hundred.

'Now,' he added with a grin. 'Who wishes to go first?'

Josephine did and it was almost a carbon copy of the first one, although it lasted a little longer. Peregrine swapped the girls over and gave it everything he had, but he was swimming a bit from all the champagne and once he'd emptied out he was a shot bird. He rolled off Kirsty, smiled at her briefly then went out like a light. He didn't hear the girls leave nor did he see them nick one of his cravats and two of his monogrammed silk handkerchiefs for a souvenir.

NORTON WOKE UP just before ten with a hangover from the champagne that would have brought a water buffalo to its knees: his throat was burning and his mouth felt like someone had cut his tongue out and sewn one of B.O. Plenty's socks in it. Outside it didn't look like too bad a day but at that particular moment Norton didn't want any part of it. He stumbled to the bathroom, remembering they had to be out of their rooms by ten-thirty. After soaking up about a gallon of cold water straight from the sink he rang Peregrine. Peregrine was in even worse condition, but at least he was still asleep.

'Urrnhhh?' he mumbled into the receiver.

'Peregrine,' croaked the voice at the other end. 'It's Les.'

'Urrnhhh?'

'We're supposed to be out of here in another half hour.'

'They rang me before.'

'What did you say?'

'We'd stay another night.'

'Righto. I'll ring you back about one.' He hung up.

That suited Les. If there was one thing he didn't feel like, it was packing his bags and driving for about five hours. He flopped back on the bed making a mental note to ring Eddie later and let him know where they were and what they were up to.

He did that when he finally surfaced around twelve-thirty. Eddie said that that was okay but best they got up to the farm by Thursday just to be on the safe side. Then Les rang the desk to see if there may have been a message from the Norwegian girl from Armidale. There wasn't. A car had called for them and they left just after eight o'clock. Sorry, Mr Norton, there was no forwarding address. Bummer, thought Les. He wouldn't have minded seeing Ingersoll again. She was more than all right. Oh well — you win some, you lose some. *C'est la vie*. Then he rang Peregrine again. This time the Englishman was awake. But only just.

'So how are you feeling, Peregrine?'

'Rather jaded, old chap. I can assure you of that.'

'I'm stuffed myself. You had any breakfast?'

'I've just ordered something to be sent to my room.'

'I'm gonna do the same thing. How about I meet you down by the pool in an hour or so?'

'Good idea. I'll see you then.'

After a steak sandwich, orange juice and freshly brewed coffee and apart from a rotten headache, Norton was in about as good a condition as he could be to face the day, so he threw on a pair of shorts and a T-shirt and headed for the pool. After a wallow in the spa and a swim he felt a little fresher so he propped in about the same position as the day before in amongst about the same number of guests. Peregrine arrived about twenty minutes later looking like Hercule Poirot in *Murder On The Nile*. He muttered a quick hello to Norton, dropped his things on the banana-chair next to him then plunged into the pool for another solid half lap in the same scintillating style that had amazed all the guests the day before. When he stood next to Les, towelling himself off, Norton lowered his sunglasses for a closer look at something on the Englishman. There were four or five love bites on his neck, and what looked like about two hundred on his back.

'Hey, Peregrine?' queried Les, 'what the fuck did you get up to last night? Have you seen your back?'

Peregrine paled. 'Oh dear. They're not on my back too, are they?' He shot a quick glance at the other guests then wrapped a towel around himself and lay back on his banana-chair. 'Oh really. How embarrassing.'

'Embarrassing,' snorted Norton. 'Disgusting'd be more like it. Those two poor little girls were still going to school. They'd be lucky if they were twelve years old.'

'They were more than jolly twelve,' retorted Peregrine. 'They were seventeen and eighteen. And if they went to school, there must be a version of St. Trinians in Australia.'

Norton gave Peregrine a very heavy, and also a slightly envious once up and down. 'So what happened?'

Peregrine thought for a moment. 'I don't know that I care to tell you,' he hesitated. 'However — if you insist . . .'

The Englishman gave Les what was almost a blow by blow description of the carryings on in the room the previous night, which had Norton more than a little envious and almost cracking up inside. When Peregrine had finished it was all Les could do to keep a straight face. He looked at Peregrine and shook his head.

'That has to be one of the most disgusting stories I've ever heard in my life. You should be thoroughly ashamed of yourself.'

'Ashamed?' sniffed Peregrine. 'I'm abhorred. Those two little beasts took advantage of me in my drunken state and attacked me. Literally raped me.'

'Ohh, yeah. Raped you, did they? I didn't hear you banging on my wall for help. Why didn't you call the hotel security if it was that bad?'

'Well . . . there was no need to go that far,' shrugged Peregrine, a slight smile beginning to flicker around the corners of his eyes.

'Fair dinkum, Peregrine. I don't know what to say. You're out here barely three days and you're head butting journalists in hotels, and having weird orgies with schoolgirls in the country. It doesn't sound very British to me.'

Peregrine looked away for a moment. 'Anyway, what happened to you after I left? I suppose you're going to tell me you and the au pair girl just sat there holding hands and listening to the best of George Gershwin? She was all over you like a cheap suit when I walked out the door.'

'Yes. We sat there for a while,' conceded Norton. 'Then we went back to my room for a cup of coffee and swapped recipes for strawberry jam.'

'Oh yes, of course, old boy. Now pull this one — it plays "Rule Brittania".'

'Well,' chuckled Norton. 'If you insist, old chap.'

Now it was Norton's turn to give a version of what happened in his room, including how it started by him spilling his drink down the front of Ingersoll's tracksuit. This had Peregrine laughing like a drain, both with amusement and relief at knowing he wasn't the only one who had been carrying on like a seasoned-up hyena the night before.

'And you didn't hear her when she departed either, Les?'

'No.' Norton shook his head. 'She just vanished without a trace. There one minute. Gone the next.'

'Then I suppose one could say,' chuckled Peregrine, 'there was quite a bit of coming and going in both our rooms last night.'

'By Jove, one certainly could, couldn't one?'

They both howled with laughter at Peregrine's corny joke then flopped back on their banana-chairs, oblivious to the looks they were getting from the other guests. After a while they settled down a bit.

'So what do you fancy doing for the rest of the day, Pezz old mate?'

'Well. I'm not actually feeling one hundred percent.'

'No, me either.'

'So why don't we just take it easy, it's quite lovely out here in the sun. Relax. Have a swim. Have another superb meal in that restaurant again tonight. And maybe take a drive into town afterwards. What do you say?'

'I reckon that sounds like a pretty good idea. But if we do have a meal, how about we go a bit easy on that French shampoo?'

'We'll see what happens.'

And that was how they spent the afternoon. Taking it fairly easy. The odd swim now and again. A flop around in the spa-pool. Talking about this and that. Les went for a bit of a stroll along the beach, but mostly they were just laying around, half asleep, half awake, and dozing off every now and again. It was the kind of lazy afternoon Les liked. Towards the later part of the day Norton took a sort of drowsy peek around him out of one eye, and noticed small groups of people come out of the resort, check out the pool, the spa and the gardens, gaze over the fence to the beach, gawk around in general for a while then go back inside. There were some men, but they were mainly women in their mid-twenties to early thirties with well-groomed, shiny hair. They were mostly dressed in designer jeans and all were wearing white sweat-shirts with some triangular motif on the front. Half-asleep, Les didn't take all that much notice, preferring to doze off. Before long it was four-thirty and the sun was starting to fade.

'Well, what do you reckon, Peregrine?' said Norton. 'The day's just about stuffed. We hit this on the head?'

Peregrine sat up and blinked his eyes a few times. 'Yes all right, then. I'm starting to feel a little peckish actually. And kindly don't bother to tell me how hungry you are, will you?'

They left the pool and walked back inside the resort. The solarium wasn't exactly a hive of activity, but there were a number of blue-uniformed staff putting up lights and setting up tables and two men were hanging a mirror ball from the ceiling. In amongst the workers were clusters of the same people Norton had noticed outside in the white sweat-shirts; some were seated drinking coffee, other were standing around talking and all appeared to be carrying clipboards and biros. His curiosity aroused, Norton turned to a blue-uniformed man standing at the bottom of the ladder; around his waist was a leather holster full of various shaped screwdrivers and a tape measure and it looked like he was an electrician and possibly the foreman.

'Hey, mate,' said Norton. 'What's goin' on?'

'We're setting up a disco,' was the reply.

'A disco?'

'Yeah. There's eighty sales reps for Zinkoff Hair Products having a convention here for three days. The management's puttin' on a disco for them.'

'Really?' said Peregrine.

'Yeah. Wish I could go,' added the electrician with a chuckle. 'Sixty of 'em are sheilas.'

Les and Peregrine turned to each other that quickly, their eyeballs almost clicked. 'Did you hear that?' said Les.

'I certainly did. And I don't think we shall bother going into Coffs Harbour tonight.'

'No way. Thanks, mate,' said Les, turning to the electrician.

'You're welcome.'

They shared the lift with, and nodded politely to, a couple of male sales representatives and Les got a closer look at the motif on the breast of their sweat-shirts. It said: 'Zinkoff, Reaching For The Future'. When they got out two of the staff walked past carrying a large banner saying the same thing. It was obvious the company had brought them all up there for a rev up and to write off a bit of taxation. Peregrine suggested they have dinner about seven-thirty then see what the Zinkoff disco had to offer. Les said this sounded like another splendid idea on Peregrine's behalf and he'd call for him then.

When Les turned on the SKY channel in his room he was delighted to find they were running an hour and a half of highlights from the Thomas Hearn's and Sugar Ray Leonard fights. Before he knew it, it was seven-thirty and he was dressed in his Levis and a white Hawaiian shirt and knocking on Peregrine's door. The Englishman was ready this time, sporting some kind of Italian jeans covered in pockets and seams and a pink silk shirt with a matching cravat to hide his lovebites.

There were tables covered in drinks and splits and on a railing above, a disc jockey was setting up his stand and whispering 'test — test' into the microphone when they walked into the solarium. The head waiter and the piano player in the restaurant recognised them from the previous night and there were polite smiles all round and they sat down in the same place as they had before. Around them were about the same number of diners, maybe a few more. This time Peregrine went for the smoked trout in horseradish sauce for an entree. Les had sweetbreads Calvados with apple brandy. For a main, Peregrine decided on the Veal Hongroise in cream, paprika and mushroom sauce. Les reckoned the Barramundi Breval with mushrooms and the chef's special sauce looked pretty good. Peregrine insisted on Dom Perignon again. Yeah, why not, agreed Les. The meal and the service was once again first class and so was the banana Coruba after. They drank two bottles of Dom, which immediately put a head on all the champagne they'd drunk the night before, so Les suggested they have a couple of coffees to settle them down a bit before they attacked the disco. The piano player was tinkling away sweetly in the background, but by now the steady bass from the disco was starting to pump in through the door. They finished their coffees, Peregrine settled the bill and they both decided it was time to get down and boogie.

The solarium was raging when they stepped inside. It had to finish by 11.45 and the Zinkoff reps were cramming everything into the three hours that were left. The mirror ball was spinning, music was pumping out of every corner and everybody was shukking and jiving, romping and stomping, twisting and shouting. Three of the resort staff were done up as astronauts serving free drinks and the reps were pouring it down their throats like they were expecting the world to end at midnight. The electrician was right about the odds: there would have been at least four women for every man and they were all shapes and sizes, mainly around thirty, carefully made-up and well-groomed in dresses of different colours, styles and lengths and all wearing the mandatory dark stockings. The men were about the same age with neat short hair, the odd moustache, conservative sports shirts and trousers. They were all out for a knees-up and a bit of hanky panky but even though they came from all over Australia, any stray tooling done in the firm would have to be kept very much on the discreet side. However, all the other guests had locked themselves in their rooms and there was an obvious man shortage which made Peregrine and Norton fresh meat for the table. Norton hadn't brushed up too bad in his Hawaiian shirt and from a distance Peregrine would have looked like a young David Bowie to the average thirty-year-old female sales rep with a few gin squashes under her belt. They weren't there long before they were getting plenty of once up and downs and even a few twice up and downs.

All the seats were gone but they managed to find a small table up against the wall where some potted palms were placed around the tiny indoor stream that ran towards the bistro. Peregrine had got into the waiter's ear as they left the restaurant and it wasn't long before he arrived with an ice-bucket, a bottle of Dom and four glasses.

'Well, what do you reckon, Peregrine?' said Norton, pouring himself a drink. 'The odds are certainly in our favour. You could have a head like an apple on a stick and still finish up with something here tonight.'

'Yes, I agree. There's no shortage of crumpet here, is there? But my hat. Some of them look old enough to be your aunty.'

'Yeah, you're right. They're nearly all diesels. Still, there's got to be something in there worth cutting out of the herd.'

'Mmmhh,' nodded Peregrine. 'I imagine we'll find a trade-in somewhere before the night is over.'

They stood against the wall, watching the dancers moving around in the smog from the smoke machine, finished the first bottle of champagne and ordered another. For some reason

Norton suddenly found he was bored. What should have been a smorgasbord of women was starting to look more like a big feed of stale cheese sandwiches and sausage rolls. The music was plain, bland disco, each song sounding the same as the one before, with the same monotonous bass line and beat from a drum machine. Either the disc jockey had never heard of Machinations or The Angels or Rose Tattoo, or if he had, he was keeping the Zinkoff team safe from them. After thirty minutes of boom-boom-boom-boom-bum-bum-bum-bum-one-two-three-four, Norton would have given his left nut for a bit of Spy Vs Spy. Then he noticed Peregrine had zeroed in on something like a point-setter.

A pretty little girl of about twenty-one, with short dark hair bobbed under an elfin face and pert lips was walking towards them holding a drink. She was wearing a blue lurex top tucked into stretch black tights and a wide black belt with a huge silver buckle hugged her tiny waist. Peregrine waited till she was almost on top of them, then he struck.

'Cynthia,' he beamed, bringing his hands up to his side. 'I say! Imagine running into you. And in here of all places.' The young girl looked at Peregrine quizzically as the Englishman drew back slightly. 'It *is* Cynthia isn't it? Cynthia Robards? Celeste's sister? You came to the studio with her the other week when she put down that demo tape?'

The young girl smiled and shook her head. 'My name's Heather. I'm a hairdresser. I come from Port Macquarie.'

'Oh dear me,' spluttered Peregrine. 'I am so sorry. I had you confused with someone else. My deepest apologies.'

'That's okay,' shrugged the girl. 'Don't worry about it.' She looked at Peregrine for a moment; something in his voice had her in. 'What did you mean — put down a demo tape?'

'My father owns EMI records in London. I'm out here on a business trip promoting Mick Jagger's new album. Celeste Robards was in the studio a week or so ago getting her new album together and she brought her young sister with her. They're both in Australia at the moment seeing some relatives and I thought it was you. The similarity is quite uncanny I must say. Quite.' The young hairdresser didn't really know what to say, but Peregrine had her in. And he was about the only guy there close to her age and his old man owned EMI records. That had to be a plus. 'Anyway,' continued Peregrine, still oozing charm. 'It is rather dark in here, and one can make a mistake. So may I offer you a glass of champagne to make up for me being such a prat?'

'Well . . . yes. Thank you. That'd be nice.'

Peregrine took her half-finished drink from her, handed her a glass from the ice-bucket and topped it up. 'I'd best get another bottle. That one's finito.' He nodded to the waiter standing by the restaurant door, who nodded back. 'Heather, is it?'

'Yes.'

'I'm Peregrine. And this is Les.'

'How are you, Heather?'

'Hi, Les.'

As Heather turned to Norton, Peregrine wiggled his eyebrows at him over her shoulder. Les smiled back but not too obviously. Well, chalk one up to you, Peregrine old son. The oldest dodge in the world: haven't I met you somewhere before? And he's pulled off a new variation of it. He edged away slightly to give Peregrine a chance to fill Heather full of Dom Perignon and piss in her pocket at the same time. Well, it's catch and kill your own in here. Now what about yours truly?

Norton let his eyes run around the disco in the solarium again and couldn't help but find his thoughts running back to Ingersoll in her pink and grey tracksuit. The women around him may have been clean and well-dressed, but there were definitely no Norwegian au pair girls. There had to be a possibility on the fringes though somehow. He was trying to fathom it out when he heard an over-polite voice to his right.

'Hi there. How are you?'

She was about thirty-five, blonde, in a white sweat-shirt and loose pants holding a drink and a cigarette. She had a big arse and no tits and the nicest thing you could say about her face, which supported several double chins, was that it was homely.

'Pretty good, thanks,' replied Les, then dodged around her with a side step Russell Fairfax would have clapped.

Someone sitting at the end of a lounge next to four other women had caught his eye earlier. She was no more than thirty. She had jet black hair combed in two neat bangs up under her chin, sexy dark eyes edged tastefully with mascara and long pink fingernails. A sleeveless black dress with Stiletto stencilled across the front in silver was wrapped around a whippy body emphasising the thin silver jewellery around her neck and wrists. Unlike the gushing women seated next to her she'd left her Zinkoff name-tag in her room and she had fox, written all over her in capital letters. Their eyes had met for a brief moment earlier and she had returned Norton's smile. After leaving 'fat arse' in his wake with a body swerve, Les squatted down next to the one in the black dress.

'You mind if I sit down here for a moment?' he said. 'There's a couple of poofs over there keep trying to get on to me.'

Black dress looked at him indifferently for a moment, except for the hint of a smile creasing the corners of her eyes. 'That wouldn't surprise me,' she said. 'It's probably the shirt.'

Norton had to give her a double blink. He'd tried to be a bit clever and she'd flattened him with a perfect squelch. 'Shirt? What's wrong with my shirt?'

'Nothing. Apart from looking like you just pulled it out of salad-dip, it looks terrific.' Black dress seemed to look foxier than ever when she could see she had the big Queenslander stuffed for a comeback.

'Lovely, isn't it?' said Les, shaking his head. 'I'm feeling all emotional and upset so I come to you for a bit of comfort and understanding. And all you do is insult me.' He reflected into his drink. 'I dunno. It's a tough old world and it's getting tougher.'

'I think you'll live with it, handsome.' She let her eyes run across to where Peregrine was still talking to Heather. 'I noticed you and your friend over there getting into that Dom Perignon like you own half of Bordeaux. Any chance of a glass?'

'You like a bit of French shampoo, do you?'

'I love it. But unfortunately it's not on the Zinkoff free list.'

'Say no more,' smiled Norton.

This was the moment Les had been waiting for. He looked across the dance floor, held up his hand and caught the head waiter's eye then made the appropriate gestures with his fingers. The head waiter understood perfectly. In roughly two minutes he was over with a fresh bottle in an ice-bucket and two glasses. Long enough for Les to find out Foxy's name was Margaret and to tell her his.

'Room 220, is it, sir?' said the head waiter.

'Of course,' replied Norton, winking over at Peregrine as he signed the bill and slipped the head waiter a twenty; not too flashily but enough to make sure Margaret could see. Norton figured it was worth the excruciating pain of having to extract a rock lobster from his kick to bridge up a bit and it was the first time he'd put his hand in his pocket since they'd arrived at the resort.

'Anyway, cheers,' said Les, after he'd topped up her glass.

'Yes, cheers. And thank you. This is lovely.'

'So where are you from, Margaret?' he asked.

'Melbourne. A place called Box Hill.'

'Melbourne!' Les took another look at her eyes. 'I might have guessed,' he smiled.

'Why's that?'

Norton was almost laughing. 'I was down there not so long ago.'

It turned out Margaret was originally a hairdresser but had been a sales rep for Zinkoff for the last nine years and was now the area manager for the district in Melbourne where she lived. The job didn't turn her on all that much but it was ten times easier than hairdressing, she now knew all the lurks and perks and all her clients and she'd be lucky if she worked three hours a day; so she'd be foolish to toss it in. She lived on her own after being married for four years to a builder who drank too much and was now divorced. Not being all that company motivated, the sales convention didn't turn her on much either. But it was a break from Melbourne and part of the job and things could definitely have been a lot worse than drinking champagne in Penguin Resort.

Les told Margaret he was a physiotherapist with a practice in Double Bay. Peregrine's brother was Mark Knopfler the guitarist in Dire Straits and was in Australia buying a property on the North Coast on behalf of his brother. Les had been the band's official masseur and physiotherapist the last time they toured Australia. Mark had kept in touch with him and had his brother contact him when he arrived in Australia to be his driver and advisor while he looked over various properties in NSW. It was all expenses paid and there was a good earn for Les at the end. How could I possibly think up a contrived load of horseshit like that? Les mused. It must be this bloody champagne. Still, it's better than telling her I'm a bouncer up the Cross and Peregrine is a pommy pisspot on the run from the IRA. But it went over all right with Margaret. She was impressed and even thought Les looked like he could have been a masseur because he had big strong-looking hands.

They began to get along famously. They knocked over one bottle of Dom and Les ordered another. She introduced him briefly to the women on her right who gave him polite but uninterested smiles, which suited Les because they were a boring, suburban-looking lot — their names went in one ear and out the other and he didn't feel like sharing any of his champagne with them. Starting to glow a little from the French fizz, Margaret suggested they have a dance. Why not? thought Norton and chivalrously helped her to her feet. As they moved on to the dance floor he noticed Peregrine was nowhere to be seen.

Margaret wasn't real bad on her feet, much better than Les, with lots of hand and hip movements as she spun in and out of the other dancers. To Norton's ear the music wasn't the best for dancing to but he jigged around, even did a bit of dirty dancing and found he was starting to enjoy Margaret's company. He also found he was enjoying the thought of getting into her pants. They had a few more dances then some real lemon came on so they sat down.

Some of the other women had gone when they returned to the table and the disco now seemed to be thinning out in general. Les sat down next to Margaret and figured this might be as good a time as any to make a move.

'Well, Margaret,' he said, pouring them the remainder of the second bottle. 'Looks like this'll be over soon. What are you thinking of doing then?'

'I don't really know, Les, not much I don't think. I have to be up reasonably early in the morning. We've got quite a few things on tomorrow.'

'Yeah, we're leaving ourselves tomorrow. But,' Norton shrugged. 'I was going to say, if you want to, you could come back to my room, we could have another bottle of champagne and I'll give your back a bit of a rub. I won't charge you Double Bay prices.'

Margaret smiled at him from across the top of her glass while she thought about it; and somehow seemed to look more like a fox than ever. 'All right, then,' she said. 'Just for a little while, though. But I won't walk out with you. I'll say goodnight to some people here and I'll meet you in your room in about twenty minutes.'

'Okay,' said Les, getting to his feet. 'It's room 219. See you then.'

'Bye, Les.'

Norton drifted off towards the lift whistling softly to himself. This could turn out to be all right, he thought. That sheila from Melbourne is a dead set horn. And I know where I'd like to give that little fox physiotherapy. Right on her beaver. He got to his room and rang for another bottle of Dom Perignon. While it was arriving he switched the TV on to more rock video on SKY channel and got changed into a tracksuit. Almost half an hour later Les was thinking she might have changed her mind when there was a light tap on the door.

'I'm a few minutes late,' said Margaret, as she stepped inside.

'It took a little longer to get away than I thought.'

'That's okay. I see you got changed too.' Les noticed she was wearing a blue and white, Ça Va tracksuit which clung to her willowy body in all the right places.

'Yes. This is much more comfortable. Besides, after three hours in that disco my dress smelt like a bag full of ham-hocks.'

'You don't smoke?' Margaret shook her head. 'No. Neither do I.'

'My husband used to and half the time it was like kissing an ashtray.'

Norton chuckled. 'Yeah. They're not the best are they? Anyway, I've got another nice bottle of shampoo chilling over there. Why don't we have a glass?'

'Wonderful. Thank you.'

Les poured them both a drink and they moved across to the sliding glass door. The view across the balcony was almost as beautiful as the one the night before, with possibly just a few more tufts of cloud drifting lazily across the night sky.

'You've certainly got a nice view from here, haven't you?'

'It's not bad, yeah. What's yours like?'

'All right, but we're on the other side.'

'We?'

'I'm sharing with another girl from Melbourne.'

'Where's she?'

'Asleep.'

'She doesn't know what she's missing, does she?' grinned Norton, raising his glass.

Margaret took another sip of champagne and gave Les another one of those foxy smiles from across the top of the glass that made his blood race a little.

'So what about my rub?'

'Sure. But we'll have to make do with some suntan oil. It's all I got.'

'No worries,' smiled Margaret. 'I brought this.' She produced a small bottle of baby oil from the front of her tracksuit and handed it to Norton.

'Good as gold,' he replied. 'That should do admirably. Here's what we'll do.'

Without waiting to be told, Margaret unzipped the front of her top, slipped it off and hung it over the nearest chair revealing a nicely rounded pair of boobs sitting comfortably in a delicate black bra, that was as much lace as it was brassiere. The half cup thrust them up slightly and pushed her two dainty pink nipples against the lace. Norton nearly crushed the bottle of baby oil in his hand and felt like kicking a hole through the sliding glass door.

'Righto,' he croaked. 'Okay . . . yeah.'

Norton put their glasses next to the ice-bucket sitting on the table and moved it a little closer to the bed then sat up one end of the bed with his back against the wall. Margaret got in between his legs and bent slightly forward, pushing her hair down on either side of her neck. With her knees up and facing the TV she fitted between Les's legs perfectly. Les tipped a little baby oil on his hands, rubbed them together till it was warm then sprinkled oil on her back and began slowly working it in.

'Mmmhh!' she murmured. 'That feels good already.'

He sprinkled more baby oil on her and began rubbing it around her shoulders and up and down her spine just using the strength of his fingers.

'Ohhhh! That feels so good,' she crooned.

'It'd want to,' said Norton. 'I get fifty bucks an hour for this in Double Bay.'

Margaret chuckled and lightly slapped him on the knee. Les rubbed more oil around the small of her back using the flat of his hands; Margaret sighed, reached across and finished her glass of champagne. Les stopped for a moment, finished his, then poured them both another glass. He worked more baby oil into her back and around her shoulder blades, held her head with one hand and rubbed oil into her slender neck with his fingers; first one side, then the other. Her skin was soft and supple and easy to rub. Margaret was crooning softly, loving every second of it. They stopped for a moment and drank some more champagne.

Norton slipped her bra-straps down and began working harder on her shoulders, kneading them with his fingers. Again without saying a word Margaret reached behind her, unclipped her bra and dropped it on the bed. A small tremor went through Norton and in about two seconds he had a horn that hard a cat couldn't scratch it. Margaret leant back into him, closed her eyes and sighed; out of the bra her boobs looked rounder and juicier than ever. Les sprinkled baby oil on them and began massaging it in, watching them glisten in the moonlight as the nipples rose and firmed. Against him he could feel Margaret's breath getting shorter as she started to come to the boil.

She opened her eyes for a moment and looked up at him;

they were two swirling pools of molten emerald inviting him down. Les cradled her shoulders with one arm and, still massaging her breasts, tilted his head down and kissed her. It was as if their lips were made for each other the way they melted together. Margaret snaked her arms around his neck and drew him down to her and her tongue, hot and sweet, played cunningly around his mouth.

Margaret's lips were made for kissing. They were a blend of softness and pure delight and the woman herself was brimful of sensuality and sex appeal. There was no stopping Les now. He slid his hand down the front of her tracksuit pants on to her ted, now damp and hot. He stroked it softly for a few moments as Margaret made tiny moaning sounds as she kissed him feverishly. He slipped her tracksuit pants and knickers off at the same time, then got up and stepped out of his. As he stood at the edge of the bed Margaret knelt up, reached over and took hold of his dick and slid her mouth over the end of it making moaning, sobbing sounds from deep inside her as she did. Norton's eyes fluttered and his knees buckled. Christ! he thought. Fancy wanting to go out drinking piss with your mates when you've got this at home. That builder in Melbourne must have had an empty biscuit tin for a head. He let her draw on it for a while then he had to stop or he would have spurted all over the place. He eased her back on the bed and entered her; she shuddered and let out a long low groan. Norton's old boy fed on it and got harder as he worked it in, deeper and deeper. Margaret wound her arms around his neck and back as she kissed him and rode with him, squealing all the time with delight. Ingersoll might have been strong and horny, but Margaret was sexuality plus: and all woman.

They got stuck into it as if they were expecting Fred Nile to come banging on the door saying he was going to pass a law in fifteen minutes that there was to be no more sex in New South Wales for twenty years. Margaret thrust herself up at Les, writhing on the bed and kicking her legs in the air while Norton drove down. Then Les felt it coming and he couldn't stop. He began to stroke faster, arching his back and stiffening his legs till finally he gripped the cheeks of Margaret's backside giving her every centimetre and poured himself into her as she howled and writhed around the bed with unrestrained rapture.

They lay together for a little while getting their breath back and their heads together. It had been more than just an ordinary roll in the hay. Norton cradled an arm around Margaret feeling more than a little pleased with himself. Not only because it had been an unreal screw. He really liked her. She had good looks, sexuality, a sense of humour and sophistication and above all, she was the complete sensuous woman in Norton's eyes. Whether it meant him going down to Melbourne or having to fly her up, he was going to make sure he saw plenty more of Margaret again, no matter what. Completely relaxed, he closed his eyes as he felt her get up and heard her use the bathroom. When he opened them again he saw she'd got dressed and was standing in front of the mirror tidying her hair. A small pang of disappointment went through him; he was hoping she may have stayed a while and maybe they could have gone off again.

'You going already?' he asked.

'Yes.'

'I was hoping you might have stayed for a while.'

'Well, I can't really stay.'

'No. Fair enough.'

He wrapped a towel around himself and stepped towards her as she headed towards the door. Les put his arm around her to hold her and give her a kiss goodnight and although she kissed him lightly back she didn't quite seem to melt into his arms.

'I'll see you in the morning before I leave,' he smiled.

Margaret returned his smile but didn't quite look him in the face when she did. 'Goodnight, Les. Thanks for the champagne.'

The door clicked and she was gone.

Norton cleaned his teeth and straightened the bed. He began to understand Margaret's feelings and why she left so abruptly. She's probably a little embarrassed going off like that first time up he thought. And you can bet your life she's never met anyone in Melbourne like the superscrew from Dirranbandi. Yes, I understand, he sighed. She's only a woman. He watched the silent TV for a little while then went to sleep. He was looking forward to seeing her again in the morning.

FROM THE TIME Peregrine left the disco, it had taken him approximately forty-five minutes to get into Heather's pants and about five minutes to empty out. She told him that by coincidence she was a singer and went back to her room to get her harmonica. Peregrine had to sit through at least half a dozen songs, including a rendition of 'Me And Bobby McGee', that would have had Janis Joplin rolling over in her grave. She had a nasally, screeching voice like a sulphur-crested cockatoo with a bad hernia, and a brain about the same size as well. This didn't stop Peregrine from promising her a two-year recording contract as soon as he got back to Sydney. Oddly enough though, Heather appealed to Peregrine. She was a half-baked, trendy dolly bird, totally naive and completely blasé to anything going on around her and she'd just turned twenty — it was almost a case of birds of a feather flocking together. Peregrine decided to take her to the farm with him for the two weeks.

Heather hadn't quite fallen head over heels in love with Peregrine, but no one had ever bought her French champagne before and none of the boys in Port Macquarie were multi-millionaires; his father owned a recording company so that had to be a plus. With his contacts and her voice, it would only be a matter of time before she was catapulted into stardom. She was on holidays so the two weeks off work would be no problem and you never know, the farm could be fun. There'd have to be a place somewhere she could hide if Peregrine got too punishing and she only had to sleep with him of a night. Whatever their feelings for each other they still managed to have another ordinary fuck before they went to sleep, and as Heather stayed the night, another one in the morning.

NORTON SLEPT LIKE a baby and woke up with a grin on his face just before eight. He had a shower, packed some clothes and rang Peregrine's room.

'Peregrine. It's Les. How are you mate?' he said brightly.

'Absolutely whizz bang, old boy. Yourself?'

'Terrific. You disappeared rather smartly last night. I went for a dance with that girl in the black dress, looked up and you were gone.'

Peregrine chuckled into the phone as he looked across the room at Heather, towelling herself off after a shower. She'd thrown her toothbrush and a spare pair of knickers in her bag when she went to get her harmonica the night before, so there was no need for her to go to her room first thing that morning.

'Yes. Well, young Heather and I decided to come back here for a drop of champers. What about yourself?'

'I finished up pretty much the same way,' laughed Les.

'Good show, old boy.'

'So what are you doing for breakfast?'

'Well, seeing as it's our last morning here, I wouldn't mind having a bit of something decent in that restaurant. What do you say?'

'I reckon that's a top idea, Pezz.' This suited Norton nicely. He felt like having a good breakfast before they left and it would give him a chance to see Margaret again or one of her friends from work and find out where she was. 'How about I call for you in say, fifteen minutes?'

'Splendid. See you then.'

Les packed the rest of his gear, made sure he looked all right for Margaret, then collected Peregrine.

He gave Heather a big smile when he first saw her, but it faded a bit when Peregrine told him going down in the lift that she would be joining them on the farm for the two weeks. And there wasn't a great deal he could do about it without making a real prick of himself. However, when he thought it over, if Peregrine had a bit of crumpet on the farm, he wouldn't be worrying about wanting to go out chasing after it. Maybe it was for the best.

The restaurant was fairly crowded when they walked in, but the staff soon found a table for The Great Gatsby from room 220, his red-headed offsider and their lady friend. It was a buffet style breakfast. A waitress set your table for you then you helped yourself to what was on. If you wanted your eggs Benedictine or poached or whatever, a chef would do that for you, and there was no shortage of choice food. They all settled for scrambled eggs, bacon, fresh fruit, croissants, and cereal, and got into it with great gusto. While they sat there eating and chatting away Les had a squizz around the restaurant, hoping to see Margaret. He finally spotted her blue and white tracksuit when they had almost finished, sitting with a table of six at the end of the buffet near the windows. He smiled and waited till she got up to get some more coffee. She had her back to him when he came up behind her.

'Hello good-looking,' he grinned. 'How are you?'

She turned, looked at him briefly and completely straight through him, then totally ignored him. Norton's eyebrows knitted and he gave her a double blink, thinking she might have been playing some sort of game.

'Margaret,' he said again. 'How are you?'

Again she totally ignored him. It was no game. She filled her cup with coffee and all Les got was a brief and icy 'Excuse me' as she reached over for a slice of toast. Having got that, she turned on her heel and rejoined her friends at the opposite end of the restaurant, leaving Norton standing there like a stale bottle of piss holding half a plate of sliced honeydew melon.

Norton couldn't believe his eyes. He was absolutely dumb-founded and hurt. He'd been given the complete and utter blurt, à la carte. It wasn't just a dent in his pride. Margaret had kicked every one of the panels in and the windscreen and headlights too. So much for his ideas of being seen around town with the sensuous, sophisticated woman from Melbourne. The dirty, poxy low moll, he fumed. Ignoring me like that. Fuckin' bitch. Then it dawned on him what had happened. Les had been used, screwed and abused. So much for his feelings. He was nothing more to Margaret than a one night stand. And you could bet she couldn't get down the pub fast enough and tell all her fuckin' mates either, the cunt. A burst of angry air snorted from his nostrils as he took his plate of honeydew melon back to his table. He didn't chew it as he glared towards the other end of the restaurant, he remorselessly ground it to a pulp. Heather was alone at the table when he sat down. Well one thing for fuckin' sure, thought Norton. If I can't get a sheila, Peregrine's not fuckin' gettin' one either. That's for sure.

'Where did Peter go?' he asked.

Heather looked at him for a moment. 'Peter?'

'Oh, well, I meant Peregrine.'

'He went to his room. To get his wallet, I think he said.'

Les glanced at his watch. 'Yes, he's probably forgotten to take his medication.'

'Medication?'

'Yes his tablets. Peter's not a well man.'

'Peter? What's this Peter? His name's Peregrine.'

'Yes, I forget sometimes. We're calling him that at the moment. Anything to keep him happy — and calm.' Heather gave Les a double blink as he leant across the table towards her. 'Just what did Peter . . . Peregrine, tell you last night?'

Heather hesitated for a few seconds. 'He said his father owned a recording company in England. He was out here promoting Mick Jagger's new album, then he was going up to the Tweed Valley to buy a property.'

'Oh yes, that one.' Les nodded sagely. 'And what did he tell you about me?'

'He said he'd hired you as a driver.'

'Oh dear. Tch tch. He said that?' Norton looked the young hairdresser right in the eye. 'Heather,' he said quietly. 'I'm not his driver. I'm a male nurse. Peter's a very sick man.'

'What?'

'He suffers from schizoid distrophobic homicidal melon syndrome.' Heather gave a treble blink. 'We've just released him from Morriset after two and a half years of constant therapy. He tried to kill his second wife with an axe.'

'Second wife?'

'Yes. He tried to stab his first wife and drown their two children in the bath.'

'First wife? Children? But he's only twenty-two.'

Les gave a worried laugh. 'That's part of the syndrome. They don't age. He's forty-six.'

'Oh my God!!'

'His parents are wealthy, yes, they own a smallgoods factory in Wollongong. They love him and even though his treatment costs a fortune, they'll do anything to keep him happy, which is why we're here. But I feel I should tell you, we're not going north to buy a property. We're going to a private sanitarium to give Peter injections of live sheep glands. It's a new Swedish treatment.'

'Oh shit!'

'But come along with us. It could help with Peter's treatment. Though I should warn you, there'll only be myself and Dr Fishbinder there. So be a bit careful.' Norton gave Heather a reassuring smile. 'Peter will be under medication most of the time and we'll give you a whistle to carry with you at all times, which you can blow if he should . . . if he should menace you at all. And we'll both be along pretty smartly to tranquilise him.' Heather's jaw had dropped noticeably; Les gave her hand a quick pat. 'But go along with our little charade and don't say I told you anything. And for God's sake, don't upset him. I'd hate to have to subdue him in front of all these people. It looks awful. Especially when he starts to foam at the mouth. Anyway, here he comes now. Just carry on like you know nothing.'

Peregrine was all smiles when he came back to the table; Les winked and smiled back at him. Heather was pretty cool about it all too. As soon as Peregrine's bum had hit his seat she jumped up and stared at him like he was the phantom of the opera.

'I'm not coming to the farm with you, Peregrine,' she blurted out. 'I'm staying here. Then I'm going back to Port Macquarie.'

Peregrine looked at her and blinked. 'Wh . . . what?'

'Ohh, that's a bit of a shame,' said Norton. 'I was looking forward to your company.'

'What made you change your mind?' asked Peregrine.

'I can't take the time off from work.'

'But you said . . .'

'Peregrine,' cut in Norton. 'If the young lady can't come, she can't come. Just take it easy.'

'I am taking it easy. I just don't understand.'

'Well, just keep your voice down a little. These people are having breakfast.'

'I am keeping my jolly voice down. And why don't you keep out of this? It doesn't concern you.'

Norton made a gesture with his hands and gave Heather a look of helplessness and worry.

'I have to go now,' she said quickly. 'I'm expecting a phone call. Goodbye, Peregrine. Goodbye, Les.' Heather turned and zoomed out of the restaurant so fast she almost left a vapour trail.

'Good Lord!' exclaimed Peregrine. 'What was that all about?'

'Buggered if I know,' replied Les. 'She was all right a minute ago.'

'What did you say to her while I was gone?' A hint of suspicion crept into Peregrine's voice.

'Nothing,' shrugged Norton. 'All I said to her was there was no TV on the farm, which is the truth. She reckoned that was no good 'cause she couldn't watch "Neighbours".'

' "Neighbours"?' Peregrine screwed up his face. 'That's the most wretched show I've ever seen.'

'Heather evidently doesn't think so. She never misses an episode. Thinks the sun shines out of Kylie Minogue's arse.'

'Oh God.'

'Yeah. Anyway, who gives a stuff? She was a bag, anyway.'

'Oh, I don't know. She wasn't all that bad.'

'Turn it up, Peregrine. She had a head on her like Daryl Somers' Ostrich.'

'Who?'

'Don't worry about it. Come on, let's finish our breakfast.'

'Yes, why not.' Peregrine took a sip of his coffee which was now cold. 'By Jove, they're strange creatures these Australian women, though.'

'Yeah,' nodded Norton, with just a little sourness in his voice. 'You can bloody well say that again.'

They finished eating and when they went over to sign the

tab, Les couldn't help his eyes from wandering to where Margaret was still sitting at the end of the buffet with her friends. He felt like walking down and telling her to get well and truly stuffed in front of everyone. But what would that have proved? There was nothing he could really do without making a prick of himself and embarrassing the woman. He'd been dumped on and that was that. They'd both had a good session in the sack: cop it sweet. However, there was something snide and cowardly he could do as a parting gesture.

He told Peregrine to wait for a moment while he walked back down to the buffet on the pretext of getting a piece of toast. Margaret had her back to him, the others didn't know who he was and took no notice as he stood not far away nonchalantly chewing on a piece of toast while he gazed out of the window. About three feet from Margaret and still nibbling on his piece of toast, Norton eased out a monstrous, musty, rancid fart. It had all the remnants of last night's rich food and four bottles of champagne in it and Les knew from the heat as it slid silently out of his arse it was going to be a bottler. He gave his backside a little shake to ensure Margaret and her friends got the lot, then still gnawing on a crust of toast, he rejoined Peregrine. As they started to leave, Les looked over his shoulder and his craggy face broke into a grin when he saw the upheaval he'd caused at Margaret's table. Two had raced to the open window knocking over their chairs in the stampede to get there; the others were blinking around the restaurant with looks of disbelief and shock as they rapidly waved their hands in front of their faces. Margaret had turned away and momentarily caught Norton's eye. He gave her a little wave and the sardonic grin on his face soon told her who was responsible. More than satisfied with the result of his reprehensible deed, Norton joined Peregrine and they left.

There were warm smiles all round when they checked out and lots of 'Come again sir' and 'It was a pleasure having you'. Norton produced the money Price had given him and offered to pay his half of the whack at least, but Peregrine signed and paid for it without a blink.

'We might just duck into Coffs Harbour for a sec,' said Les, when they had their bags in the station wagon. 'There's a couple of things I want to get.'

'Suits me. I wish to pick up a few odds and ends myself.'

They were there in about ten minutes and parked in Grafton Street not far from the city centre.

'Have a walk around,' said Les, as he locked the car. 'I'll see you back at the car in twenty minutes or so.'

'Okay, old boy.'

Les got part of what he wanted in a health food shop and put that in the car. Then he found an army-disposal store and got the rest. The owner packed that into two large plastic bags and Les put that in the station wagon as well. He was sitting in the front seat reading a copy of the *Coffs Harbour Advocate* when Peregrine climbed in with two small plastic bags.

'Get what you wanted, mate?' asked Les.

'Yes. And I sent a couple of postcards, too.'

'Is that a good idea?' frowned Norton. 'Letting people back home know where you are?'

'Well, we're not staying in Coffs Harbour, are we?'

'No, I s'pose not. What's in the bag?'

'Some Panadol and that. A couple of paperbacks and two tapes.'

Norton looked suspiciously at the bag containing the two tapes. 'They'd better not be bloody Boy George or some bunch of pommy hairdressers playing synthesisers.'

'No, they're not, you oafish great bounder. It's just an old Rod Stewart and some Pet Shop Boys. In fact how about slipping one on for me now?' Peregrine handed Les one of the tapes.

'All right. Seein' as you're an old mate.'

Norton put the tape in the cassette, fiddled with the controls for a moment then they started heading out of town going north. There were a few clouds around but it had warmed up noticeably and even though there was a bit of a sou'wester blowing it was quite a pleasant day to be travelling.

'Ohh, yeah,' smiled Les, nodding at the music coming from the speakers in the back. 'This isn't a bad track, this. "West End Girls".'

'It's good.'

The smile on Norton's craggy face turned into a bit of a grin. 'I don't think there'll be to many West End girls where we're going, Pezz.'

'No. Probably not.'

They left Coffs Harbour with the ocean on their right and travelled on listening to the music.

'So what happened with you and the lovely Heather last night, Peregrine?' enquired Les.

'That's funny,' smiled the Englishman. 'I was just going to ask you the same thing about the girl in the black dress.'

'Well, go on,' said Les. 'You go first.'

They laughed and talked about the previous night and one or two other things that had happened to them so far on the trip. Norton took his time driving, pointing out a few things of interest in the countryside to Peregrine. They stopped for a leak at Woodburn, a feed of fish and chips at Ballina and, still taking their time, were in Murwillumbah not long after three.

'So, this is Murwillumbah, is it, Les?' said Peregrine.

'Yep,' replied Norton. 'Beautiful downtown. Heart of the Tweed Coast.'

'Looks nice.' Peregrine gazed out his window at a long row of backyards full of washing flapping on sagging clothes lines. Opposite the dilapidated wooden houses built up on stilts was the railway line and an equally ancient and dusty railway terminus to their right. 'Reminds me of Brixton,' he added.

Norton turned left over a wide concrete bridge that spanned the Tweed River then hit the blinkers again and took the next on his right, a small street that ran into the main street in Murwillumbah. He cruised slowly down the street a short distance then pulled up outside some hotel.

'What are you looking for?' enquired Peregrine.

'That place there,' replied Norton, and switched off the motor.

Opposite them was a restaurant with flowers and rosellas painted all over the front: The Hard Cheese Wholemeal Cafe. Times must have been hard, along with the cheese, in the cafe because it was closed with a To Let sign in the window. Next door was a Real Estate Agency, The Tweed Valley Stock And Station Agents And Auctioneers.

'I've got to pick up the keys,' said Les. 'You can come in if you want but I'll only be a couple of minutes.'

'No. I'll wait here.'

Norton liked the dusty front window of the Stock and Station Agency with its dead flies, saddles, bridles, old photos and other bric-a-brac, it had that beaut country flavour to it. He could just imagine what the agent would look like: R.M. Williams boots, moleskins, woollen tie and an Akubra hat, probably smoking the makings. The last thing Les was expecting when he walked in the door was Benny Rabinski, his bald, five-foot-tall, Jewish ex-landlord from Bondi wearing blue trousers and a white shirt. Having done the transaction over a bad phone line, Benny was expecting a Mr Northam and the last person he was expecting was Les Norton, the 'goyim' who had brassed him for ten weeks rent and his brother Marvin for six several years ago in Sydney. They stared at each other in mutual disbelief.

'Benny Rabinski!?' said Les.

'Les Norton!?' said Benny.

'What are *you* doing here?' they both said together.

There was a pregnant pause for a few moments then Les spoke. 'I'm here to pick up the keys for Cedar Glen.'

'I was expecting a Mr Northam. Not you.'

'Well, looks like they made a blue don't it,' grinned Les. 'But isn't it a pleasant surprise?'

Benny seemed to shrink a little. 'Oi. Such a surprise.'

'Listen, Benny, if I told you once, I told you a thousand times. I put the money under your door. Somebody must have nicked it.'

'Marvin's too?'

Norton shrugged. 'You know what it's like around Bondi. Anyway that was years ago, Benny. You can't go on blaming me forever.'

Benny shook his head, then turned and took a set of keys from a hook on the wall. 'You know the position with the farm, Mr Norton,' he said, placing the keys on the desk. Norton nodded slowly. 'You've got the place for two weeks with an option to purchase. A Mr Brennan telegrammed the money through. $300 for rent. Plus a $500 bond. $800 all together.' He stared at Les as he pushed a form across to him to sign. 'Are you thinking of buying this property yourself?'

Les shook his head. 'No. But that bloke out in the car is. He's a rich Englishman.' Suddenly Les cursed himself for saying that.

Benny looked across at Peregrine. 'Why don't you bring him in?'

'He wants his privacy for the moment. But he'll see you if he decides to buy it.'

'I can call out.'

'Now come on, Benny. The gentleman doesn't want the hard sell at the moment. He just wants his privacy. To think.'

'All right then.'

'Anyway, what can we expect when we get out there?'

'There's no phone or TV. There's a fridge, hot water, cooking utensils, blankets. There's a caretaker, Ronnie Madden. He might be there today. If not, you'll always find him in the

Yurriki Hotel. You know how to get to Yurriki and the property from here?'

Les nodded. 'I got a map and directions in the car.'

Benny looked at Norton a little suspiciously as he handed him the keys. 'Doesn't your friend want to know how much it is?'

'Ohh yeah . . . how much is it?'

'Two point five million.' Benny's kindly Jewish face broke into a smile and he made an open-handed gesture. 'But you tell him to see me and we can negotiate.'

'And you with such an honest face too,' smiled Les, making the same open-handed gesture. He jiggled the keys and turned to leave. 'Hey, before I go — what are you doing in Murwillumbah, Benny?'

'My wife inherited some property up here. She likes it. So do my two fine boys. Plus,' Norton's old landlord looked him right in the eye, 'There were getting to be too many unscrupulous people living in Bondi.'

'I know exactly what you mean, Benny,' sympathised Norton. 'It can be a proper bastard living there at times. See you later, mate.'

'Jesus, talk about the ghost of Christmas past,' said Norton, when he got back in the car. 'You wouldn't believe who was running that estate agency. My old reffo landlord from Bondi.'

'Do tell.'

'Yeah. I took him and his brother to the cleaners for about a grand.'

'That's lovely, isn't it?' said Peregrine jokingly. 'Now everybody will know we're up here.'

Les missed Peregrine's humour. 'No, I think everything should be all right,' he said seriously, wishing he hadn't told Benny he had a rich Englishman with him. 'Anyway, let's head for Yurriki.'

They turned into the main street in Murwillumbah with its two or three pubs, police station and courthouse and rows of cars angle-parked to the curb, took a left and a right, found the Nimbin, Yurriki turn off and headed west. They crossed the Tweed River twice, one particularly noisy wooden bridge almost shaking the chassis out of the car, and followed the narrow, winding road as it led through the lush green valleys, small mountain ranges and the occasional homestead. One particular mountain to their right with an irregularly-shaped summit something like an ugly nose caught Norton's eye.

'You see that mountain over there?' he pointed. 'That's

Mount Warning, the first place in Australia to get the sun in the morning. The Aborigines reckon it's spiritual.'

'Yeah?'

'Yeah. It's also supposed to be some sort of power source.'

Les watched curiously as Peregrine bent his head down and started looking at the mountain side on. 'What are you doing?' he asked.

'I was just thinking,' laughed the Englishman. 'If you observe the top of that mountain from this angle, it looks like your nose.'

Norton looked back at Mount Warning, scowled, then looked back at Peregrine. 'Keep that sort of talk up, and it'll look like fuckin' yours.'

It wasn't long and they were in Yurriki.

'So this is beautiful downtown Yurriki is it?' said Peregrine, looking around at the few cars parked in the main street and fewer people. 'Looks nice. You ever been here before?'

'No.'

'Can't say I blame you.'

'Let's check it out anyway.'

Like all small country towns in Australia, Yurriki consisted of one main street. There was a tiny park with a War Memorial and a fairly busy public school to its left, opposite this was the local one-man butcher shop, what appeared to be a run-down community centre then a School of Arts, with a glass case full of posters and community notices out the front. Next was a supermarket, some more ancient wooden shops and the solitary phone box sitting outside the post office which, like the rest of the town, looked as if time had completely passed it by. A bit of a dip in the road brought them to a one-lane wooden bridge which spanned a picturesque little stream: Roland Creek. To the right of the bridge was another small park with an old steam engine sitting in it and opposite this was an old wooden, two-storey pub with the customary ver-andah running round the top floor. The Yurriki Hotel. A garage was a little further to their right and what appeared to be an old wooden church built off the main street, and that was it.

'Excitement City, isn't it,' said Peregrine.

'Las Vegas it ain't,' agreed Norton, stopping the car outside the hotel. 'Won't be a sec,' he said. He was back in a few minutes with a case of beer and two bottles of champagne.

'Fourex, eh?' said Peregrine. 'What's in the bag?'

'A couple of bottles of High Noon.'

'High Noon? What's jolly High Noon.'

'That's another great western. Isn't it, old chap?'

'Are you trying to say champagne?'

Norton winked. 'Gotta look after you, haven't we, mate?'

'I just hope I can get it down.'

'You'd better, 'cause that's all they got. And you ain't gettin' none of my Fourex.'

Les did a U-turn back through town and pulled up outside the post office. 'I'm just gonna make a quick phone call,' he said, getting some change from his pocket. 'I won't be a sec.'

He rang Eddie, who wasn't home, so he left a message with Lindy to say they'd arrived in Yurriki and were on their way to the farm and everything was sweet. There was no phone on the farm but he'd ring every time he came into Yurriki. When Les stepped out of the phone box he saw Peregrine was standing outside the School of Arts looking at the community message board. He strolled up alongside him and looked in the glass case.

'Well, what do you reckon, Peregrine?' he said. 'You gonna go for the psychic healing or the therapeutic massage?'

Peregrine studied the notice board for a moment. 'I don't know,' he replied. 'I was thinking of trying the rebirthing or the magnetic balancing. I don't see any ads for the local escort service in there.'

'In Yurriki? Mate, I reckon the only way you'd get a root in this town would be to dig up a gum tree. Come on. Let's go and see if we can find this farm.'

The turn off to Roland Creek road was behind the War Memorial. Following Eddie's map they headed further west towards Mt. Cudmore and Mt. Warning National Park till the bitumen ended just past the Nimbin turn off and they hit dirt road. They went down a dip and along a straight when round the next corner Les slowed down for what he first thought were two large sheets of blue plastic fluttering along the side of the road.

'Jesus, look at that,' he said excitedly, pulling the car up and pointing across Peregrine. 'Two bloody peacocks.'

The male's huge train with its blaze of blue and green feathers almost took Peregrine's breath away. 'God, they're absolutely magnificent,' he said.

'You're bloody lucky to ever see any, especially like that. Dogs get them, or feral cats. Or mugs take shots at them. I reckon they'd belong to someone.'

Peregrine watched the two birds frollicking just outside his door. 'People shoot them? You're joking, Les.'

'I wish I was, mate. But there's some loonies running around with guns. Sports shooters they're called, Peregrine.' They watched the two beautiful blue birds going through their mating ritual before they abruptly disappeared into the scrub. 'Come on, let's go,' said Norton.

They crossed another tiny arm of the creek. The road dipped, and rose again, then at a curve on the left was a metal gate with a wooden one next to it. Les stopped the car and had another look at the map.

'Yep. This is it,' he nodded. 'Cedar Glen.'

The metal gate was painted white and slung between two poles with another two poles above; a stained wooden letter box sat between it and the older wooden gate on the right. Les found the right key, opened the gate and rolled the car over the metal grill onto a concrete drive, then closed the gate behind him again. The concrete drive led through a huge open field on their right and a swampy looking one on their left. They followed the driveway to where it crossed a beautiful little creek full of ferns and trees and climbed several metres to another white metal gate set on poles. A billabong formed where the driveway crossed the creek and to the left of this was an old, rickety wooden bridge that had obviously been disused for some time. The second gate was open and they drove straight in for their first sight of the house.

It was two storeys high but the bottom storey had been built about a metre into the ground. It was all solid wooden beams and thick poles and looked more like a small fortress or a stockade than a house. Oddly-shaped windows faced everywhere and the entire house was surrounded by well-kept rockeries full of palm trees and native plants identical to the French colonial style of landscaping in Saigon during the thirties when that part of Asia was known as Indo-China. A hundred or so metres to their right was a set of stables in a fenced-off field where half a dozen horses watched them curiously as if they too seemed to be appreciating the strange beauty of this unique homestead set in the middle of nowhere. Les stopped the car in a covered driveway and they got out.

The rear of the house was identical to the front, more thick beams and poles, and looking around him Les could see they were in a valley surrounded by a high ridge of trees making the only access to the homestead through the front field and along the driveway. It was now crisply silent with the car engine off and the only sound was the sighing of the wind in the trees and the calling and whistling of countless birds.

'I say,' said Peregrine. 'This is certainly different from anything I've ever seen.'

'Yeah,' agreed Norton. 'It's not what I was expecting. It looks like someone's taken Fort Apache and put it in northern New South Wales.'

'Who did you say it belonged to?'

Norton shrugged. 'All Eddie told me was that some American colonel from the Vietnam war built it. He was a survivalist or something.'

Peregrine gazed around at the surrounding mountain range and the solidly built house. 'You could certainly survive here,' he said. 'Let's have a bit of a look around.'

They walked across to a brick-paved barbecue area trellised with vines, creepers and stag-horns. More huge poles supported these and there was a beautifully-crafted, solid rosewood bar area with a sink and an old fridge; a turn of the taps told Les there was no shortage of clear, clean water. There was an old table and chairs and hanging off a beam above this was a set of stereo speakers fastened back to back. Les smiled and pictured himself eating plenty of steaks and drinking plenty of Fourex out here over the next two weeks.

The bar area was built onto a small cabin or guest quarters; Les found the key and opened the double glass door. Inside was a double bed and blankets, a built-in wardrobe and an unusual en suite full of blue and grey slate tiles, old brass taps and great slabs of solid granite which even formed a seat in the shower. There were more wooden beams and crafted woodwork everywhere.

'Do you want to sleep in here?' asked Les.

As he said that, a rather healthy looking frog jumped out of the shower area, bounded across the en suite and splashed down the toilet bowl with a startled croak.

'Why don't we have a look at the rest of the place first?' replied Peregrine.

'Okay,' laughed Norton. 'We'll start at the top and work down.'

They strolled back to the driveway and up a set of thick wooden steps to where a small verandah led into the kitchen and the top part of the house. Inside was more polished wood from the floor to the ceiling. Huge beams supported the ceiling which in turn were supported by poles thicker than your waist that were nothing more than roughly hewn lengths of trees complete with twists and knots. The walls were red cedar shingles, the kitchen table was one huge slab of polished cedar with a table made from a solid slab of black marble next to it. None of the countless windows opened — instead, there were fly-screened vents alongside which opened to let the air either in or out. There was an old brown corduroy lounge and Les was happy to find that the porta-gas stove worked and there was a decent-sized fridge. A large bedroom full of more polished cedar and oak had an en suite almost as big. There was a study between it and the kitchen which opened onto another verandah at the front of the house. The view over the rockeries and gardens from above made the place look even more French colonial than ever; a tricolour fluttering in the breeze and French Foreign Legion band playing 'The Marseillaise' would not have looked out of place at all. When Les stepped back inside, Peregrine was coming out of the bedroom with a grin on his face.

'This bedroom will do me admirably, thank you,' he said.

Norton glanced over at the double bed sitting beneath a huge window. 'Go for your life,' he shrugged. 'I'm not fussy.'

Gazing around them they noticed another solidly-built verandah overlooking the barbecue area with a set of steps running down from it.

'I have to admit that this place is quite unique,' said Peregrine. 'All this wood and the craftmanship — the chap who built it must have owned a jolly sawmill.'

Norton ran his hand up and down one of the poles supporting the ceiling. 'What I reckon he's done is he's brought all his own timber down from those mountains. He'd want to,' he added, 'the wood in this joint'd cost you a million dollars.'

'It almost reminds you of the inside of an old sailing ship.'

'Yeah,' nodded Les absently. It reminded him of something else, but he couldn't quite think what it was. 'Come on. Let's have a look downstairs.'

A set of concrete steps took them a good metre below ground into the bottom of the house and into a bedroom even bigger than the one upstairs. It too was made of more polished and crafted wood: maple and cedar walls, a double bed, a desk, and huge built-in wardrobe. But it was the enormous open bathroom that brought a gleam to Norton's eye — it was pure decadence. The walls were a blaze of various shades of blue and gold tiles set like a mosaic to look like waves breaking and the sun rising on a beach. There were shiny brass taps and faucets but the pièce de résistance was a tiled, sunken bathtub big enough for six people. It looked like something out of Nero's palace in ancient Rome. Norton chuckled inwardly — he could definitely see himself flopping around in the bath full of Radox while he sucked on one cold can of Fourex after another.

'Well, I'm certainly glad we worked at those sleeping arrangements, Peregrine,' he grinned.

When he turned around Peregrine had opened another door which was an office with a long desk running along one wall with a computer on it which didn't appear to be working. They both had a tap on the keys then left it.

The bedroom led out past a laundry then back into another lounge room bigger than the one upstairs; this time the floor was made of brown ceramic tiles and the ceiling was much higher. There were more wooden beams and poles, double windows that didn't open with vents alongside, and a solid wooden ladder which led up to a small loft overlooking the front of the gardens. In one corner of the room was a potbelly stove with a Canadian brand name.

'Christ!' said Norton. 'Does this joint ever stop?'

'It's certainly amazing,' agreed Peregrine.

A side passage laid with the same brown tiles led from lounge room number two past more windows which didn't open but gave an uninterrupted view of the front gardens. The corridor ran the length of the house past another tiled en suite, a couple of bunks in another kind of room, then into another bedroom. This time the ceiling was a lot lower and the walls were made of split logs and timber which was stained a dark brown, giving it a definite rustic or American backwoods appearance. You almost expected to find Davy Crockett sitting on the double bed in his coonskins cleaning a muzzle loader. It was quite dark and Norton hit a switch on the wall for a fluorescent light. As he did a huge Huntsman spider scurried across the wall and disappeared into a built-in wardrobe.

'My God! What was that?' said Peregrine.

'Just an old Huntsman spider,' replied Norton. 'He won't hurt you.'

'I'll take your word for it. Well, shall we go back into that other room? It's . . . rather gloomy in here, wouldn't you agree?'

'Yeah, righto.' Norton switched off the light and went back into the bottom lounge room.

'Well, what do you reckon so far, Pezz?' said Norton, pretending to be warming his hands in front of the pot-bellied stove. 'It sure is different, ain't it?'

'It's certainly quite odd for Australia,' agreed Peregrine. 'It reminds one of a stockade, or something one would expect to find up in the Canadian rockies.'

'Yeah, right. It looks like fuckin' Fort Bravo or something. That yank colonel must've thought he was John Wayne. Look out those windows, Peregrine.' Les slipped into a Walter Brennan voice. 'Imagine if'n them Injuns tried to get us folk in here. We'd pick the pesky critters off afore'n they got past that there first row of trees. Heh heh!'

'I see what you mean,' nodded Peregrine, gazing out of the windows to the view across the grounds. 'Why don't we get up early tomorrow and have a jolly good game of Cowboys and Indians?'

'Okay,' replied Les brightly. 'But I bags being the goody.'

'Very well, old boy. Whatever turns you on.'

They went back out to the barbecue area, found a couple of glasses and had a drink of water while they took in the peace and quiet as the sun began to set; the only sound was the sighing of the wind and the continued calling of the birds in the trees and fields. Norton noticed a massive hole about seventy metres long and about five metres deep had been excavated a few metres out from the barbecue area.

'Looks like they were just about to put a pool in,' he surmised, as they walked over and gazed in. There was about half a metre of water in the bottom, some bullrushes and movement of what were probably frogs and crickets.

'Pity they didn't,' said Peregrine. 'Be nice to have somewhere to go for a bit of a dip.'

'I wouldn't worry. There's bound to be plenty of billabongs in that creek for a swim.' Norton kicked a rock into the hole and watched it splash on the bottom. 'Good place to hide a body though, ain't it?' he grinned. 'Eddie'd love something like that. Anyway, we've seen the house, let's get unpacked before it gets dark. We can check the rest of the place out tomorrow. We might have a bite to eat then I'll show you your present I got you.'

'A present?'

'Yeah,' winked Les. 'I'll show you after.'

Norton's first priority was to stack the beer and champagne in the fridge; the groceries he left sitting on the kitchen table. The beds had blankets but no sheets so it looked like the young English baronet would have to do it a bit tough for the first night, though Les did promise himself he'd drive into Murwillumbah first thing tomorrow and get a set of personally monogrammed silk ones for his guest. He put the Radox bath on hold, settling for a nice long shower instead. After he'd changed into his tracksuit, Les went upstairs with the bag he'd got from the disposal store in Coffs Harbour. Peregrine was sitting on the end of his bed; Les dropped it next to him.

'Here you are, mate,' he said cheerfully. 'Your present.'

Peregrine opened the bag and cautiously pulled out a pair of tiger stripe cammies, a webbing belt, a khaki army shirt, combat jungle boots, a black singlet and a forage cap.

'What the deuce is this?' he queried. 'I didn't come up here to join the SAS. And I'm absolutely positive Margaret Thatcher took back The Falklands. What . . .?'

'Suit yourself,' shrugged Les. 'But we're gonna be up here for two weeks. If you want to get around looking like Bryan Ferry that's your business. But we'll be tromping all over this place and there's ticks, leeches, snakes, spiders and Christ knows what else out there. I've got a set of the same gear, but you please yourself.'

Peregrine twisted the canvas and rubber boots in his hands. 'I suppose you're right,' he conceded. 'Okay. Thanks — it might even be a bit of fun.' Peregrine spread the army clothing out on the bed. 'So, what's for tea?'

'Chilli beans à la Norton.'

Les was now in the kitchen where he'd turned his ghetto-blaster to some local radio station playing hillbilly music. He'd unpacked two large tins of red kidney beans, chilli sauce, garlic, bread and other odds and ends and was frying some onions in a large pan he'd found in one of the cupboards. Peregrine came out to see what was going on.

'You like chilli beans, Pezz?'

'I don't mind. Do I have a choice though? I suppose it's either that or starve?'

'That's about the size of it, daddio.' Norton opened the two tins of beans and dumped them in the pan. 'To be honest mate, I didn't know what we'd find in Yurriki. But there's a supermarket and a butcher shop there, I'll get some steaks and all that tomorrow. You'll love my beans, though. Tomorrow it'll sound like a Salvation Army band tuning up in here.'

'Wonderful, Les. I can't wait.'

'The hills'll be alive,' laughed Norton. 'But it won't be with the sound of music.'

Peregrine walked over to the ghetto-blaster. 'Do you mind if I lose that radio station, Les? That music is practically intolerable.'

'Yeah, it is a bit punishing, isn't it? Put a tape on.'

Peregrine rummaged around in the cassette holder till he found one of the tapes he'd bought in Coffs Harbour. The next thing, Rod Stewart was rasping his way through 'Gasoline Alley'. Les opened a can of Fourex and suggested Peregrine do the same with a bottle of champagne then they settled into a bit of steady drinking while the beans bubbled away in the pan.

'Well, Peregrine,' said Norton. 'Looks like it's gonna be a pretty quiet old two weeks up here, mate. No TV, no phone, no sheilas, nothing.'

'It certainly looks that way,' agreed the Englishman.

'So why don't we just roll with the punches? Eat plenty of good tucker, get plenty of sleep. Go for nice long bush walks and just relax till your cousin sorts all this business out back in Ireland.'

'Yes. I think that's about the best thing we can do under the circumstances. Lewis will more than likely be on the case right now.'

'He might, too. Let's hope he is.'

'So here's to cousin Lewis.' Peregrine raised his glass and Les did the same with his can of Fourex. 'I say, this High Noon's not a bad drop.'

'You like it?'

'Mmmhh. It could do with just a smidgen of fresh orange juice.'

Les smiled and winked at the Englishman. 'I'll make sure I get a case first thing in the morning.'

TRAGICALLY, EVENTS BACK in Ireland weren't quite working out as well as Peregrine would have liked them to, as Laurie O'Malley was to find out when he picked up the phone in his Red Hill residence in Canberra. It was the third time he'd been on the phone that week about his godson, Peregrine. The first time was when Peregrine had rung him from the Sebel Town House to let him know he'd arrived safely in Sydney. The second time was the day after T'Aime's article in *The Telegraph* and O'Malley had to get in touch with Price to find out what was going on. Now this one from Peregrine's father in England. Peregrine's cousin, Captain Lewis Standfield's Land Rover had just tripped a remote-controlled mine in Lisnaskea, County Fermanagh. The driver had been killed outright and Lewis was in a military hospital in Belfast with two broken legs and multiple internal injuries and was not expected to pull through. Ironically, the bomb wasn't set specifically for him. He and his driver just happened to be another British patrol in Northern Ireland in the wrong place at the wrong time. It rated a paragraph in the *London Daily Mail* and a half a one in the *Evening Standard*.

Yvonne entered the study and couldn't help but notice the look on the Attorney General's face as he stared grimly out at the cold, bleak surroundings of Canberra.

'Bad news, sir?' she asked quietly.

O'Malley nodded solemnly. 'The worst.' He looked at her momentarily then decided to ring Price direct.

'Christ! What a bastard,' said Price, after O'Malley had told him what had happened in Ireland. 'What do you think is the best thing to do now?'

'Peregrine's father told me he'd been on the phone to Army Intelligence in Belfast and they're trying to organise another SAS unit to go in and get this last Frayne brother. So you might have to keep Peregrine up on that farm for a week or two longer.'

'That's no problem, Lozz. I've got a good man with him now, and I can always send Eddie up there if it comes to a pinch.'

'I still don't think anything will happen to him out here. I just didn't like that thing in the paper, that's all.'

'No. That was a bit unfortunate, all right. But he's as safe as a bank up where he is. I couldn't even find the place myself if I wanted to.'

'Yeah. Fair enough, Price.'

They talked a little longer with Price telling O'Malley not to be unduly concerned, things would work out all right. He wouldn't tell Les or Peregrine what had happened to Lewis for the time being and if need be he'd keep Peregrine on the farm for six months if they had to. He'd keep him posted every time Les rang up.

However O'Malley wasn't the only one who had been on the phone to Northern Ireland that week. The three English journalists had rung Belfast from their unit in the inner city suburb of Stanmore on Tuesday to tell a certain bereaved party that they had missed their quarry by thirty minutes, and two days later the trail was still well and truly cold. If only they had known that by sheer coincidence the man they should really have been after was almost dead in a Belfast hospital, they could have saved themselves a lot of trouble, aggravation and money in ISD calls. Unfortunately, that's often the way it is with the Irish.

Two men were sitting on the lounge in the unit looking at the third man after he had just hung up the phone. In the kitchen, two women with dark hair and green eyes were preparing coffee and sandwiches. On the wall behind the man who had just hung up the phone was the green, white and orange flag of the republic.

'What did he say this time, Patrick?' asked one of the men on the lounge.'

'He's not at all happy, I can assure you, Robert,' replied the man who had been on the phone, who then turned to the other man on the lounge. 'I think you might have gathered that from the way I was talking, Brendan.'

'I did,' replied the third man. 'And it surely puts a chill in the air when that man's got the hump.'

'Aye. It does indeed.' Patrick looked at the others for a moment. 'So he said to keep looking. Try that hotel again. Keep ringing those journalists we know. The bastard can't be too far away. I'd best be telling you also that if we don't find him, there's a good chance he'll be coming out here himself.'

'Oh, good Christ!' said Robert. 'That's all we need. There'll be bodies everywhere.'

'Aye,' agreed Brendan, 'Liam's always been known to shoot first and think about it later.'

Patrick fixed his two compatriots with an expressionless gaze. 'He also said that if he does come, he'll be bringing Logan Colbain and Tom Mooney with him.'

'Oh Christ!' said Robert again.

FRIDAY MORNING DAWNED bright and clear at Cedar Glen with the dew glistening on the leaves and the calling of countless birds. A few tufts of cloud were being scudded towards Mount Warning by the light sou'wester, but it was beautiful for August, with no sign of rain. Les was up around six-thirty. The previous night he'd found an old deck of cards and they had a few games of gin rummy while they talked and Peregrine demolished his two bottles of Great Western while Les made an awful mess of his case of Fourex. Consequently neither of them had much trouble sleeping, in fact the only thing Norton could remember about getting to bed at ten was the coolness and moisture in the air and an owl hooting in a tree close by when he came downstairs to his room.

Peregrine had his dressing gown on and was in the kitchen when he went upstairs.

'G'day, mate,' Norton said brightly. 'How are you feeling?'

'Not too bad, actually,' was the reply. 'I slept rather well.'

'That's good.'

'I don't know about your chilli beans though. They certainly keep one regular, and warm up the old date somewhat, as well.'

Norton laughed and walked over to the stove. 'That's how a Mexican knows when he's hungry, mate. When his arsehole stops burning. Anyway, there's still plenty left. I might warm 'em up for breakfast.'

'Oh God. Here we go again.'

Good or bad, Peregrine still had a large plateful plus coffee and toast while they listened to the radio. Les suggested that seeing it was such a peach of a day outside and they were both feeling so good they should get into their army clobber and check out the farm, then drive into Yurriki afterwards and get some food and more drink. Peregrine said why not, and he'd see Les downstairs in about twenty minutes.

'Sir,' snapped Norton, clicking his heels together and giving Peregrine a brisk salute as he walked into the barbecue area.

'As you were, corporal,' smiled the Englishman, returning Norton's salute.

Peregrine's army clothing fitted him perfectly, right down to the cammies tucked into his combat boots. His forage cap was at a slightly more rakish angle than Les's but both men looked identical, as if they'd just stepped off the cover of *Gung Ho* or *New Breed* magazine.

'How do I look?' asked Peregrine.

'Terrific. Like something straight out of the battle of Bala-clava. Your cousin Lewis would be proud of you.'

'Thank you, corporal.'

'You're welcome, sir.'

Peregrine gazed around the property in front of them then up to the mountain range behind them. 'Where do you want to start?'

'Well, according to that rough map Eddie gave me, there's a dam up there somewhere.' Les pointed slightly to their right then directly up behind them. 'But I reckon we ought to start at that gate there, and take that trail through the horse paddock and follow it up round that ridge. Might be a bit of a slog, but it won't do us any harm. Not in this air anyway.'

'Very well. You lead the way.'

Norton adjusted an army sheath knife on his webbing belt. 'Righto, mate. Let's go.'

They clambered over the gate and steadily began climbing, following an uphill trail. There was an old barbed wire fence choked with lantana on their left and the horse paddock fading away on their right. Les didn't put the speed on too much but kept up a steady pace; Peregrine didn't fall behind at all and even appeared to be enjoying the bit of a hit out.

After about fifteen minutes, Les looked back and could barely make out the property two kilometres or so below them. The trail levelled off at an old wire gate in a clearing then went left with a narrower, steeper one going right. They crawled through a gap in the old wire gate and took the left trail. The track got noticeably steeper for at least another kilometre. The bush was dense on either side of the trail and thick with eucalypt and gum trees, but it wasn't long before they began to notice dozens of huge stumps, most over ten feet tall and wide jutting up on either side of the trail like rows of rotten teeth.

'God! Look at the size of these stumps,' said Peregrine. 'They're enormous. What on earth are they?'

'Probably old cedar trees,' replied Les. 'Legacies from our so-called pioneering days, when we lost seventy-five percent of our rainforests and half our animals.'

Peregrine gave one of the stumps a kick and a great piece of rotted, rust-coloured wood broke away. 'Good Lord! What must have it been like up here years ago with all those huge trees?'

'Before they raped and pillaged it? Paradise, I imagine.' Norton shook his head at the aftermath of destruction around him. 'Between the Japanese and the sawmills, they're still doing their best to fuck what's left now. Come on.'

They continued to climb steadily till the ridge levelled off again into the clearing full of native shrubs and blackboys. Through a gap in the trees they stopped to take in the magnificent view over the valleys and mountains right across to Mt. Warning, blue in the distance. The strain of the climb, plus the chilli beans must have begun to tell on Peregrine. Not long after they stopped he broke wind with a crack that sounded twice as loud as it was in the silence of the surrounding bush. By sheer coincidence a flock of at least twenty Red

Crowned Cockatoos took off from a nearby gum tree at the same time. Norton turned to the young Englishman and gave him a look of utter contempt.

'You filthy disgusting pig,' he sneered. 'You just frightened away all those beautiful birds.'

Peregrine was completely flummoxed. 'I . . .'

'A bit of decorum, please, if you don't mind. You're not back in bloody England now.' Norton shook his head and sniffed disdainfully. 'Come on. And make sure you keep down wind.'

'I . . .' Red with embarrassment, Peregrine fell into step behind Les, firmly convinced it was his fart that had scared all the birds.

They followed the trail further till they came to another clearing on the ridge dotted on either side with dozens and dozens of blackboys of all sizes.

'I say, what are those things, Les?' asked Peregrine.

'Blackboys. They're all hundreds of years old, you know. Oddly enough they flourish in bushfires. Look great, don't they?'

'They certainly do. Look at that one there.' Peregrine pointed to a particularly tall one next to another one with two spears sticking up and a number of little ones around them. A flowering vine had taken root in the bushy green top of the tall one and from where they stood it resembled a wig woven with flowers. 'It looks like a skinny black woman with flowers in her hair.'

Les and Peregrine caught each other's eye and as if on cue they both started singing.

'Flowers in her hair. Flowers everywhere. I love a flower girl.'

Then they both burst out laughing.

'Come on,' said Les. 'You're carrying on like a bloody hippy.'

But as he looked back Norton could just picture how the Aborigines must have started their legends and tales. The tall, black native plant did look like an elegant woman with flowers decorating her hair and the one next to it could be the warrior with his two spears guarding the valley and the little ones around them were their children. Hippies, Aborigines, no matter what. It was still a lovely sight.

The trail rose then and they came to another clearing with a yellow mark carved into a tree with numbers on it and two arrows pointing in either direction. Les figured that must be the boundary. He also figured they'd come a good five kilometres and a glance at his watch said they'd been gone the best part of an hour. The trail leading on over the ridge was good but the one going back down towards the property narrowed into a mess of lantana; Les decided against it.

'Well, Pezz,' he said. 'We may as well head back the way we came. I don't fancy bashing my way through all that lantana.'

'Yes, it does look rather thick.'

Although Peregrine was puffing and sweating profusely his eyes were bright with excitement and even if he was doing it tough it was obvious he was enjoying every minute of it.

'How about this time you lead the way?' said Les.

'All right then,' replied Peregrine enthusiastically.

Seeing it was downhill, Peregrine clapped on the pace thinking he was running the legs off Norton. Les deliberately fell behind a little but he did have to keep his finger out to keep up; for a fellow less than half his size and one that didn't train at all, Peregrine was showing quite a bit of stamina. They double-timed past the clearings, the stumps and the blackboys, and in what seemed like no time were scrambling through the old wire gate from where Les could see the house and the property in the distance.

'Don't go straight to the house,' said Norton. 'Cut across that field down the bottom and we'll get onto that other trail and see if we can find the dam.'

'Righto, old boy.'

Near the bottom they helped each other through the barbed wire fence, crossed about a hundred metres of field, went through another barbed wire fence then down a steep slope onto a sloshy trail of mud that led back the way they'd come but nowhere near as steep. They followed the trail, thick with lantana and wild tobacco plants, for about half a kilometre when out of nowhere on their right loomed a huge shed made from logs and thick wooden beams; it had to be the best part of two hundred metres long. Inside it smelt of must and decay and flocks of tiny swallows flitted amongst the spider webs that encrusted the ceiling.

'I wonder what this could have been?' said Peregrine.

Les kicked the soil floor which was rich with fowl manure. 'Probably an old poultry shed I'd say, going by all this shit in the soil.'

They gave it a bit of a once-over then proceeded on their way.

The sound of water trickling over stones into a swampy area on their left told them they were at the dam before they actually came to it. The dam was an enormous natural lagoon over three hundred metres in diameter that backed onto the start of the mountain range; in the calm stillness of the morning sun it shone like a huge, dark green mirror. Crickets and frogs startled by their presence dived into the water amongst growths of lilies spread around an old wooden pontoon running about five metres out from the muddy shore. Set in metal grills around the edges were numerous citrus trees full of fruit not quite ripe enough to eat. Before long the sounds of countless birds started up again, echoing off the surrounding hills and across the smooth calm water. Peregrine cautiously edged out onto the pontoon but soon changed his mind as it began to sink in amongst the water lilies.

'I wouldn't fancy falling in,' said Norton. 'There could be any bloody thing in there.'

'Quite right,' agreed Peregrine, scrambling back to shore. 'It looks jolly deep too.'

They hung around a while longer while they listened to the birds and had a drink of water. Les cut a lemon from one of the trees and gave half to Peregrine; one bite was enough to have them grimacing and spitting juice onto the ground. They washed their mouths out and started back towards the house.

Not far past the shed they noticed another muddy trail churned up with tyre marks leading off to the right.

'May as well check this out, see where it goes,' said Les. 'What do you reckon?' Peregrine nodded in agreement.

The trail led though more scrub then into a clearing that was obviously the farm tip. Two scooped-out holes were about a quarter full of bottles, beer cans, bursting plastic garbage bags and other junk. To the side an old yellow, box-trailer was rusting silently away in the bush. There weren't all that many flies, but enough for mid-August.

'Jesus! Be nice here in the summer,' mused Les. Through the bush he spotted another shed on another trail. 'Let's see what's down there.'

The shed was nothing more than a galvanised iron roof covering some rusty wire mesh nailed to a dozen or so poles. It was choked with weeds and scrub and was probably another holding pen for poultry. Not far away was another shed almost as big as the first one they'd found. As they approached it, a flapping sound almost as loud as a helicopter taking off in the surrounding silence filled the air. To their amazement two huge scrub turkeys flew out of the shed and over their heads in a squawking gobble of feathers and dust.

'Suffering cats!' said Peregrine. 'What was that?'

'Couple of scrub turkeys,' smiled Les. 'See the size of their backsides? They must be doing all right up here.'

They stepped inside the shed and more swallows and wrens startled by both them and the fleeing scrub turkeys started chirruping around the cobwebs and rusting fluorescent lights hanging from the ceiling. Les gave the floor another kick.

'More bloody poultry,' he muttered.

They gave the shed an indifferent once-over and headed back to the house.

The trail led away from the house and around; a few metres from the shed another small trail led off to the right.

'Want to have a look what's up there?' said Norton.

'We're here now,' shrugged Peregrine, 'why not?'

This particular trail was steep and muddy and bogged them underfoot. It climbed almost half a kilometre through scrub and gum trees before opening out into a perfect circle about twenty metres across ringed with gun-barrel straight white cedars, their delicate green tops towering over fifty feet above their heads. It was oppressively hot and still in the middle of the clearing, around which was a riot of tropical plants — part of a rainforest which pushed up against the ridge above. The sides of the clearing had been packed flat and when they walked over they found dozens of logs beneath the undergrowth stapled together with stainless steel bolts to form a kind of wall.

'Wonder what the bloody hell this was here for?' queried Les.

'Reminds you of a bunker or something, wouldn't you say?' said Peregrine.

Norton shook his head in amazement. 'Buggered if I know.'

They strolled around the mysterious clearing for a while, then began walking back the way they had come.

The trail brought them to the bottom corner of the property with the house about three hundred metres away and another two sheds between. They were about to head towards them when the sound of running water to their right made them walk in that direction. The creek running around the property split to form a tiny island of pebbles and ran into one of the prettiest little billabongs Les had ever seen in his life. It was about fifty metres across, crystal clear and the sound of the water flowing over the rocks was like music. A tiny bridge of flat-laid logs joined the island to the shore and as they approached several unseen animals plopped into the green coolness, leaving only a trail of bubbles to mark their presence. After the heat, sweat, flies, mud and mosquitoes of their three-hour walk it was just a bit too much for Peregrine and Les. They exchanged a brief look and, fully clothed, leapt straight in after the animals.

The water flowing down from the mountains was freezing cold but clean and refreshing. Both men let out a roar of shock when they surfaced.

'Whoa! It's a bit bloody brisk!' spluttered Norton.

'Yes. But not all that bad,' said Peregrine, ducking under again.

They wallowed and splashed around for a while then got out dripping water, grinning like two silly big kids.

'Fair dinkum, you're a nice dill,' said Norton. 'Fancy going swimming in all your clothes.'

'What about your jolly self?'

'Yeah, but I'm an Australian. You'd expect an Australian to do something stupid like that. Not the English, though — and especially not the Royal Family. Come on.'

Dripping and spitting water they sloshed their way back towards the house deciding to check out the last two remaining sheds and that would be it.

The one nearest the billabong was a concrete and wood building about the same size as an average house with a loading dock out the front; the double aluminium door was unlocked so they sloshed inside. From the smell, the number of sinks, old paper towel containers and other paraphernalia left laying around it wasn't hard to tell what it had been used for.

'This has been an old slaughterhouse,' said Les. 'That's what those other sheds were. They must have had some sort of a chicken farm or something out here at one stage.'

'Phew! It smells like it,' grimaced Peregrine.

They slopped around the abandoned slaughterhouse, leaving trails of wet footprints on the dusty concrete floor.

'Well, this is all very interesting,' said Peregrine. 'But I think I'd prefer to be somewhere else.'

'Yeah. It does nothing for me. Less for the chickens, though, I'd say.'

They left the way they entered.

Between the slaughterhouse and the farm was a wooden tool shed about the same size as a four-car garage. The windows were covered in dust and the door was locked but through the wire grill Les could see wooden benches, vices, shelves stacked with tins of rusty nails and screws, old fan-belts, petrol tins and other assorted junk one would expect to find in a typical tool shed on an Australian farm. It was even less interesting than the slaughterhouse and Peregrine by now was looking completely stuffed so after a cursory look they left it, walked back to the barbecue area and flopped down in two chairs with a glass of water each.

'Well, that was the farm, Pezz,' said Norton, starting to undo his boots. 'What did you think?'

Peregrine slumped in his chair almost too exhausted to talk, let alone move. 'Fascinating, I have to admit. Completely different from anything back home.'

'Yeah. There's still the stables and that fenced-off area down towards the road, but bugger it. We'll have a look at that some other day.' Peregrine barely nodded his head in agreement and Les could understand his feelings; it wasn't a bad hike for a slightly-built fellow who wasn't at all used to this kind of heat and conditions. 'I'd get out of all that wet gear if I was you,' said Norton, starting to remove his boots and trousers.

'I will in a minute, Les.'

'Okay. Suit yourself.'

Peregrine slumped back and closed his eyes for a moment. He opened them with a start when he suddenly heard Les cursing.

'Fuckin' rotten little bastards!' he fumed. 'Look at the cunts of fuckin' things.'

Peregrine stared at Norton who was frantically plucking something from his ankles which were wet and shiny with blood. He flung them on the ground where they squirmed around like two live black jelly beans.

'Good heavens. What on earth are they?'

'Fuckin' leeches,' cursed Norton, giving them each a whack with the heel of one of his boots; which seemed to make absolutely no difference at all to the two squirming little bloodsuckers. 'That's why I was telling you to get all your gear off.'

'I haven't got any on me,' said Peregrine, with half a smile. 'I'd certainly know if I did.'

'You think so?'

Norton gave the two leeches another thumping with his boot then began wringing his clothes out and draping them over the chairs in the barbecue area. Les had his back turned to Peregrine when he heard the Englishman scream; he smiled as he turned around, knowing exactly what to expect. Peregrine had his boots and trousers off and his ankles and socks were also thick with blood. There were six leeches: three on each leg.

'Oh, Jesus Christ!!' Peregrine was almost hysterical as he began tearing the leeches from his legs. Les picked the remainder off and couldn't help but burst out laughing as Peregrine began wildly smashing at the bloodsuckers with one of his boots. Like Norton's efforts, it seemed to make no difference to them at all. 'Good God! How do you kill the bloody things?' howled Peregrine, continuing to flail away with his boot. 'They're like creatures from outer space.'

'Stay there a minute,' chuckled Norton.

He went up to the kitchen and returned with a container of salt, which he poured all over the leeches. It wasn't long before they were squirming black balls, spewing up all the blood they'd sucked out.

'Let's have a look and see just what colour your blood is, Pezz,' said Norton. He looked closely at the leeches then shook his head, very disappointed. 'No. Red, same as mine. You sure you're in line to the Royal Family, mate? You could be a ring-in. A lousy bloody commoner.'

Peregrine shuddered and gingerly peeled away the rest of his clothes. When he wiped the blood from his legs there were six deep black holes, neat enough to look as though they'd been bored in with a drill.

'Jolly, rotten little sods,' he spluttered. 'I didn't feel a blessed thing.'

'No. They got their own local anaesthetic. Clever little buggers, aren't they?'

Peregrine shuddered and made a gesture with his hands. 'That's the end of walks in the Australian bush — thank you very much.'

Norton chuckled and gave the Englishman a reassuring pat on the shoulder. 'You'll be right, mate. Come on, get cleaned up and I've got some iodine and band-aids in my room. Then we'll go into town.'

They showered, changed, had a cup of coffee and about an hour later were driving into Yurriki. Peregrine was a lot brighter, but he was still definitely unimpressed by the attack of the killer leeches from outer space.

First stop was Yurriki's one-man butcher shop opposite the War Memorial. The butcher was about thirty and balding, with his hair combed into a smother. He had quick brown eyes and a face and paunch that said I love schooners. Bustling around behind the blocks he had a brusque, take-it-or-leave-it attitude that he probably got away with because he was the only butcher in town. Helping him in the shop was his wife. She had thick brown hair, hazel eyes and a backside that said I love pork chops and sausages. Norton ordered ten T-bones, two kilograms of sausages and a dozen cutlets. The butcher told him bluntly to come back in half an hour and he might have it ready.

From there it was only a short stroll to the supermarket. Peregrine said he'd like to walk around and take a few photographs; that suited Les and he said he'd meet him back at the car. He also said he wished Peregrine had produced his camera earlier as he would have liked to have got some photos of him locked in combat with the killer leeches. The Englishman gave him a thin smile as he walked away.

At the supermarket Les got enough fruit, vegetables and groceries to send an expedition up Mt. Everest; he also shouted Peregrine a pair of blue stubbies, a plain cotton shirt and some thongs. Les had an ice-block, rang Eddie, and once again had to leave a message with Lindy, picked up the meat, which was unbelievably cheap, then met Peregrine back at the station wagon.

'How did you go? You get a few photos?'

'Yes. That rather large building is an old butter factory and there's quite a lot of wild flowers and lizards and things running around out the back.'

'Yeah? That's good.'

'They're also having a fete there this weekend. I saw a poster saying "Yurriki Buttery Bazaar, Sunday 21st". What say we come down and have a look?'

Norton imagined what the local bazaar would be like. Wall-to-wall hippies selling everything from organic wild fruit jam to crystals guaranteed to metaphysically transport you into the fourth dimension. 'Yeah, why not?' he shrugged. 'Might be a bit of fun. What else did you do while I was working me guts out getting the shopping?'

'Nothing much. Strolled around, looked in the shops, sent a couple of postcards.'

'You sent a couple of postcards? Shit! You didn't tell anyone where we're staying, did you?'

'Oh, Les, the cards had a photo of Mt. Warning on them, that's all. And crumbs, I had to think of father and mother, and Stephanie. Besides, the way the mail moves out of this country, I'll be home a week before the blessed things get there.'

Norton thought about it, but somehow he just wasn't happy. 'Yeah I s'pose you're right,' he said. 'Anyway, you feel like a beer?'

'Yes, I do actually — after all that jolly walking this morning, a cold glass of pilsener would go down rather well.'

Les gave Peregrine a wink as they got in the car. 'Or as we say in Australia, mate, the first one won't even touch the bloody sides.'

What Peregrine didn't tell Les on the short drive to the hotel was that he'd had quite an interesting conversation with the postmaster. It appeared he was filling in for his father who was in hospital having an operation to remove some varicose veins; he usually ran a courier service from Murwillumbah to Sydney and Brisbane. When Peregrine casually asked how long it would take for the cards to reach England, he was told that for the right price they could be couriered to Brisbane and would fly out on Saturday. Sunday was a holiday at each end, but they'd link up with the courier service in London and be at their English address by Wednesday or Thursday at the latest. Peregrine certainly had no trouble finding the right price. He sent his parents and Stephanie a card each and also sent half a dozen to some of his fellow Sloane Rangers in London.

The interior of the Yurriki Hotel was pretty much what you would expect to find in a one-pub, Australian bush timber town. High wooden ceilings with thick beams and polished wooden walls covered by old photos of local rugby league teams, bullock wagons hauling giant logs and other memorabilia. Cheap brown curtains hung over the windows and tatty brown carpet covered the floor, on which were scattered several beat-up chairs and tables. There was the mandatory pool table with a few video poker machines close by and a jukebox next to a red phone in one corner. Opposite this was a snack bar and brick fireplace near a passageway that led to the toilets out the back. A sign above the bar, next to a photo of some mongrel-headed local alderman with a haircut to match, said '*We shoot every third salesman. The second one just left*'. A double-door led to a fairly extensive beer-garden full of chunky wooden chairs and tables. The bottle shop was next to the front door. In an alcove between it and the bar, several rough-headed locals were quietly drinking their beers when Les and Peregrine walked in.

They had a bit of a look around while they got a slow, silent once up and down from the locals and the publican.

'Well, what do you reckon, mate?' smiled Les.

Peregrine had another look around him and briefly returned the stare of one local wearing a battered Akubra, who had a lop-sided jaw and teeth like a fruit bat. 'What do I reckon?' he sniffed. 'I reckon even the beer in here would have two heads, wouldn't it?'

Norton caught what Peregrine was looking at. 'Yeah, I see what you mean. All we need is Burt Reynolds with his bow and arrow out the back, and a bloke playing a banjo out the front. Anyway, what are you gonna have?'

The Englishman peered into a glass-doored double fridge behind the bar filled with cans and bottles. 'I'll have a Heineken, thanks.'

The tall, skinny barman, looking more like a council clerk in his horn-rimmed glasses, shorts and long socks appeared in front of them. 'A bottle of Heineken and a middy of New,' said Norton. The barman served them then went back to the regulars in the corner.

The beer wasn't too bad, and nice and cold. They finished their first ones fairly smartly so Les ordered the same again.

'Hey, mate,' he said to the barman as he got their beers. 'You wouldn't happen to know if a Ronnie Madden drinks in here, would you?'

The barman nodded slowly. 'Yeah,' he drawled. 'Ronnie's a regular. Comes in most nights for a few. And always on a Friday.'

'What's he look like?'

The barman thought for a moment. 'Little bloke, gettin' on for forty. Long black hair, always wears an old brown hat. Got a gold stud with a ruby in it in his left ear.'

'Righto, mate. Thanks.' Les paid for the beers and the barman once again returned to his regulars.

'Who's Ronnie Madden?' enquired Peregrine.

'He's the caretaker where we're staying. Eddie knows him somehow. I'd like to have a yarn with him about the property.'

Peregrine shrugged and sipped his beer. Something on the wall near the pool table caught his eye. He walked over to it, had a closer look, laughed and came back to the bar.

'See that sign over there?' he said to Les.

Norton looked over to where Peregrine was pointing with his beer. It was a poster with an old negro minstrel on the front. It said: *Yurriki Humdinger Boogie Woogie Ball. Dogs And Guests Welcome*. 'Yeah. What about it?' said Les.

'It's on Saturday week. We should go to that too.'

Norton took another look at the poster and shrugged a 'Yeah, why not?'

Peregrine took a good slug on his Heineken and slapped Les on the shoulder. 'And you reckon there's nothing doing up here? My dear boy. We have this fine establishment to drink in. The Buttery Bazaar this Sunday. And the Humdinger Boogie Woogie Ball next weekend. This could be the entertainment capital of Australia.'

'Yeah,' nodded Les. 'Looks like the place pumps non stop.'

They had one more beer each, which really started to put an edge on their appetites, so Les suggested they go home and get the barbecue going. Peregrine agreed wholeheartedly. On the way out Norton got two cases of Fourex, six bottles of Great Western and two of Jacobs Creek.

Back at Cedar Glen, Peregrine gave Les a hand to unpack the groceries, but had to admit he couldn't help him with the barbecue. Back in England they had cooks, butlers and all manner of servants to attend to that and when it came to cooking, he was flat out lighting a stove. Les said not to worry. When it came to getting a barbecue going, no man or woman in Australia was a match for him. Just slip into those shorts and thongs and look and learn.

Norton made a big tossed salad and boiled some rice which they took down to the barbecue area along with the plates and other odds and ends. The old fridge was working okay so they crammed that with booze, which they attacked while Les got the fire going. Before long they were both well and truly in the mood, Les had the steaks and sausages on the barby and had fried the rice up on the hot-plate with some diced onion. There was an Otto-Bin next to the barbecue. Les went to put some rubbish in it and found it was absolutely packed to the gunwhales with empty Victoria Bitter cans. Hundreds of them.

'Jesus! Someone out here sure likes a fuckin' drink,' he said. After a look into the Otto-Bin, Peregrine had to agree.

The local butcher might have had a brusque, take-it-or-leave-it manner, but he could afford to. His meat was unbelievable. The T-bones were so soft you could have eaten them with a spoon, and his sausages had so much flavour they practically glowed in your mouth.

'Christ! How good are these steaks?' said Norton, gnawing on the bone like a hungry cattle-dog.

'Absolutely melts in your mouth,' agreed Peregrine, doing much the same thing.

'Reckon you could go another one?'

The country air and the exercise, plus the beers and the two bottles of Jacobs Creek and half a bottle of Great Western must have started to bring out the bulldog in the conservative English aristocrat. He jumped up from the table in his stubbies and thongs and grabbed a can of Fourex.

'Yeah, righto, cobber,' he drawled, not making a bad fist of an Australian accent. 'Shove another couple on. And bung a few snags on too, digger.'

Norton shook his head and went to the fridge. 'Isn't this gonna be lovely? Stuck out here for two weeks with you.'

They stuffed themselves with more steak, sausages and salad and sat back listening to the radio while the sun set over the farm and the valleys. The birds had stopped singing so Les turned the outside lights on as the crickets and frogs started up. After about an hour or so Les couldn't have fitted another beer in to save his life and suggested they take a stroll down to the front gate and back and walk some of the food off. Even though Peregrine was well into his second bottle of Great Western he said that didn't sound like a bad idea. Les got a torch from his room.

They crunched down the driveway stopping momentarily where it crossed the stream that ran around the property not far from the house. It bubbled and sang as it flowed beneath them in the moonlight and when Les shone the torch into the two crystal clear ponds on either side of them, several big yabbies scrambled amongst the rocks on the muddy bottom.

'Les, have you noticed anything about the way this driveway has been laid?' Norton shone the torch around and shrugged. 'The way the opening is bigger on one side forcing the water through when it comes out the other?' Norton shrugged again. 'And the way those rocks are squared off around the opening? You could set a turbine up just there and generate electricity.'

'Have like, your own little hydro-electric scheme?'

'Exactly.'

'So?'

'Nothing,' shrugged Peregrine. 'Just thought I'd point it out to you. That's all.'

Les nodded and they followed the torch beam along the concrete part of the driveway to the front gate.

The air was absolutely thick with dew coming down in the moonlight and a dense mist had settled on the two large fields on either side of them giving them an eerie, appearance.

'Shit! Have a look at that,' said Norton, flashing the torch around. 'Reminds you of that movie *Werewolves Of London* don't it? You're not a bloody werewolf are you, Peregrine?'

The Englishman shook his head. 'No. No werewolves in the Normanhurst family. Though I believe great-great-grandfather Augustus was a vampire.'

They reached the front gate and Les checked the lock. 'Perimeter's secured, sir,' he said, adding a quick salute.

'Very good, corporal. Now let's get back to the champers.'

They crossed the two ponds and were crunching along the gravel not far from the house when in a row of trees to their left Norton heard a movement and felt as if someone was watching them. He flashed the torch up into the trees to find three huge brown owls staring down at them; one was much bigger than the others and with their saucer like, orange eyes you couldn't miss them.

Peregrine suddenly roared laughing. 'Hello,' he cackled. 'It's Bunter. What are you doing up there Bunter, you blithering bloater?'

Norton looked at Peregrine like he was mad. 'What the fuck are you goin' on about?'

'In the tree,' giggled Peregrine. 'It's Billy Bunter, the fat owl of Greyfriars. Don't you recognise the piffling, pernicious porker?' Peregrine shook his fist at the completely baffled owl who thought the Englishman was madder than Les did. 'Get down from there at once Bunter, you fat, frabjous, foozling, frowsy owl! And report to Mr Quelch's study this instant.' Peregrine was now roaring at his own private joke.

To Les he was speaking a completely different language, and a nutty one at that. 'Fair dinkum,' he muttered. 'Two more weeks of this and I'll end up in the rathouse.'

Back at the barbecue area Norton still didn't feel like drinking any more beer. The Jacobs Creek now tasted like vinegar and he wasn't all that rapt in champagne at the best of times. What he should have got at the hotel earlier was a couple of bottles of bourbon. He watched indifferently as Peregrine slopped into another glass of Great Western with a squeeze of fresh orange.

'Hey, Peregrine.' The Englishman looked up from his glass. 'You want to come for a run into town while I get a couple of bottles of bourbon? We might even have a couple at the pub while we're there. What do you reckon?'

'Capital idea, old boy. Friday night in beautiful downtown Yurriki. There could be painted women and dancing in the street.'

'I doubt that. But I should be able to get a bottle of Jackys.'

Half an hour later they were cleaned up, changed into their jeans and heading into town.

There wasn't quite dancing in the street in Yurriki, but there were several drunks weaving around the front of the hotel, the worst of whom was the local butcher. He was in a pair of stubbies and a dirty blue T-shirt, down on his hands and knees completely muled out and looking like he was getting ready to have a laugh at the footpath.

'Recognise our local butcher, Peregrine?' said Les.

'My God. He didn't make those sausages, did he?'

Before they went inside, Les bought two bottles of Jim Beam Green Label and put them in the car with some Coca Cola.

Inside, the pub was honking along reasonably well. At the front end of the bar near the door were the older locals: RSL haircuts, thick necks, big ears and cardigans. Next to them were what looked like timber workers or stockmen in their R.M. Williams boots and jeans, oilskins and broken noses under battered Akubras. The rest seemed made up of battlers or 'alternates' with long hair and beards wearing mainly faded jeans, army pants, sleeveless tops, leather hats and wrist bands. There were a few children running about and a number of women. Most of them too had long hair, some plaited, sporting either jeans or gingham dresses with rough made, leather jackets or fake fur or animal skins over the top, Apache boots, and the odd pair of John Lennon glasses. Double Bay or Toorak it wasn't, but the children were all clean and well-behaved.

Les and Peregrine had a quick peruse of the situation and found a spot where the bar curved round near the jukebox, which was cranking out 'The Murwillumbah Bank Job' by The Bullamakankas. There were two women behind the bar now, not bad sorts wearing corduroy jeans and jumpers. Norton caught the eye of one and ordered a double Jack Daniel's and Coke for himself and a brandy and soda for Peregrine.

'Well, what do you reckon, bloke?' he smiled, looking around as he took a refreshing pull on his drink. 'Friday night in Yurriki. Boogie city, ain't it?'

'Wonderful,' replied Peregrine. 'Bad luck I'm only here for two weeks.'

They sipped their drinks while the hubbub of noise, smoke and clicking pool balls swirled around them. Peregrine said he was going to see what records were on the jukebox. While he was gone Les started checking out the punters a little more intently. The person he was looking for was wearing jeans and a brown Crestknit T-shirt in a half-hearted conversation with one of the stockmen near the front door. He was as short as the publican had said earlier, with long black hair under a battered brown hat, and even from where Norton was standing you couldn't miss the glint of the gold stud in his left ear. He also had a wispy goatee beard and a world-weary face with eyes that seemed permanently set in a tired smile. Norton waited till Peregrine came back.

'Find anything worth playing?'

'The music selection is absolutely abysmal. I've never even heard of half of the records. But there's an old Manfred Mann and "Come Back Suzanne" by Bill Wyman. And,' Peregrine's face lit up a little, ' "Living Doll" by The Young Ones. Do you like The Young Ones, Les?'

'Peregrine! How dare you ask me that? You utter, utter bastard!' Les dropped some money on the bar. 'Anyway, order another couple of drinks will you? I'll be back in a minute.'

Norton walked to the end of the bar and stood next to the short man with the stud in his ear. 'Excuse me, mate,' he said. 'Are you Ronnie Madden?'

The little bloke gave Les an odd smile, as if he already knew him from somewhere. 'Yeah,' he said shortly. Not 'Yeah, that's me' or 'Yeah, what can I do for you?' Just a blunt 'Yeah'.

'My name's Les. I'm staying at Cedar Glen. The estate agent told me you're the caretaker.'

'That's right.'

Norton offered his hand. Ronnie's was hard and calloused and for a small man he had a grip like a vice. 'If you've got a minute, I've got a mate down there. Do you want to meet him and we could shout you a drink?'

'Okay.' Madden turned to the others around him. 'I'll be back in a minute.' Then he followed Les to the other end of the bar.

'Peregrine. This is Ronnie, the caretaker.' Les smiled when he saw Peregrine stiffen at Ronnie's grip. 'What are you drinking, Ron?'

'Can of VB'll do.'

Norton ordered, waited till Ronnie got his drink and there was a quick 'cheers' between the three of them. 'You know a mate of mine in Sydney, Ron. Eddie Salita.'

'Yeah,' replied Madden.

'Where do you know Eddie from?'

'I . . . ah . . . knew him from when I lived in Sydney.' The caretaker had an already nervous, twitchy nature, but now he noticeably avoided Norton's eye when he answered his question.

'What? Did you work with him?'

'I . . . used to live down the road from him.'

'In Edgecliff?'

'Ahh . . . yeah. It could have been there. I'm not sure.'

Norton picked up on Madden's evasiveness when he spoke of Eddie. But that was understandable. A lot of people were evasive when they spoke about Eddie Salita.

'How long have you lived up here, Ron?' asked Peregrine.

'About ten years or so.'

'You must like it?'

'I do, Peregrine. It's good. Nice and quiet. Not many people.' Madden went for his pocket. 'What are you blokes drinking?'

'No, you're right, Ron,' said Norton. 'Finish these first. I'll get them.'

The caretaker didn't say anything. He just crushed his empty VB can as if it were an eggshell and dropped it in the butt tray running beneath the bar. Peregrine and Les exchanged a quick glance. Madden would have been flat out being with them half a minute and he'd downed his beer like it was a spoonful of cough medicine. They both suddenly realised where all the empty VB cans in the Otto-Bin back at Cedar Glen had come from.

Norton caught the barmaid's eye. 'Same again for us, love. And another . . . two cans of VB thanks. Take it out of that.'

The drinks arrived. Les sculled his first bourbon to keep up with Madden. 'How often do you do the caretaking on the farm, Ron?'

'Two or three times a week. That estate agent doesn't pay all that much.'

'Benny Rabinski?' chuckled Norton. 'That'd be about right.'

'But he pays for all me piss.'

That'd be enough, thought Norton, as the little caretaker downed the first can of VB, got rid of the can and immediately attacked the next one.

'Whereabouts around here do you live?' asked Peregrine.

'Not far from you. Next valley before the National Park.'

'On your own?'

'With a couple of mates.'

'You'll have to call round before we go back, Ron,' said Les. 'Have a bit of a drink and a barby.'

'All right.'

'Pity my girlfriend's father isn't out here,' said Peregrine. 'He owns a brewery back in England. I'm sure he'd like to meet you.'

Norton gave the Englishman a steely look.

'Anyway,' said Ronnie, downing can number three. 'I'm in a shout back there, I'd better get back. Nice to meet you fellahs, I'll see you again. Thanks for the drink.'

'You're welcome, Ron,' smiled Norton. 'See you after, mate.' Ronnie gave them a quick wink and returned to his friends at the end of the bar. 'Christ! Did you see that?' Norton's face was quite flushed from having to down a double Jack Daniel's and Coke. 'Could that little cunt put 'em away or what?'

Peregrine was already half pissed from drinking champagne back at the farm and the two double brandies had now topped him right off. 'I meant it when I said Stephanie's father would like to see him, Les. Believe me he would. I also know a couple of Harley Street specialists that would like to see Baldric's liver and kidneys too.'

'Baldric?' queried Les. 'What's this Baldric?'

'Don't you think he looks like that fellow out of "The Black Adder"?'

'His manservant?' Norton looked along the bar at the little caretaker who was turned side on to them and a ripple of laughter went through his body. 'Yeah, you're not wrong, Pezz.'

They stood there watching the crowd while they drank, when another familiar face loomed up at the bar next to Peregrine. Les recognised her and smiled briefly; she smiled a pissy smile back. It was the butcher's wife. She'd changed into her Friday night 'kill 'em' gear, a tight black knitted tank top and a black leather mini that her fat backside just squeezed into. Peregrine smiled at her as well, just as one of his songs came on the jukebox. The Young Ones murdering 'Living Doll'.

'I say, my dear,' he said to the butcher's wife, who looked just as drunk as he was. 'Would you care for a dance?'

It was for sure no one had ever approached the butcher's wife like that before, not in Yurriki anyway. 'Yeah, righto,' she cackled. 'Why bloody not.'

Peregrine and the butcher's wife started boogalooing around in front of the jukebox, much to the amusement of several of the patrons and Les. The butcher's wife probably hadn't cracked it for too many dances lately and was giving it everything she had and having the time of her life. Peregrine was having a good time too — because he was pissed out of his brain. They stopped boogalooing and got into a bit of dirty dancing. Peregrine was no Patrick Swayze and the butcher's wife no Jennifer Grey but what they lacked in technique they more than made up for in drunken enthusiasm. Peregrine spun her around and she threw her arms up. One tit fell out of her top and the crowd roared. She kicked her legs up, the crowd got a flash of red knickers and roared again. Norton nearly cracked up. Peregrine pouted and arched his back, whirled her around and around as the song finished, finally spinning her up against the bar next to Les with one of her legs on his shoulder. She was a bit starry-eyed and didn't know quite what to do when Peregrine kissed the back of her hand.

'My dear,' he said, 'that was absolutely delightful. Allow me the pleasure of buying you a drink.'

The butcher's wife was about to say yes, when a drunken voice close by roared out, 'Hey! That's my bloody missus you're mauling, you bastard.' Wobbling around like a jellyfish, his eyes bulging and his smother all over his head, was the local butcher.

Peregrine gave him a withering once up and down from over his shoulder. 'I'm terribly sorry, sir,' he sniffed. 'I thought she was your mother.'

This didn't go over too well with either the butcher or his wife. 'Oh, a bloody smart bastard, eh?' slobbered the butcher. 'We'll soon see how smart you are, mug.'

He made a drunken lunge at Peregrine, who instinctively brought his hand up and pushed the butcher in the chest. The butcher was that drunk he was flat out staying on his feet and reeled back towards the pool table just as a big red-headed bloke with a bushy red beard brought his pool cue up for a cushion shot. It hit the butcher smack on the temple and knocked him flatter than a blob of cowshit. From the crowd's point of view it looked as though Peregrine had thrown the best straight left since Muhammed Ali.

The butcher's wife let out a wail and rushed to her stricken husband snoring peacefully beside the pool table. She pointed an accusing finger at Peregrine. 'That rotten bastard just jobbed me husband!'

Dumbfounded, Peregrine looked at Norton, who for a split second closed his eyes. Friday night in a bush pub, the mob's full of piss and two strangers are in town starting fights and trying to steal their wives . . . Here we go again, thought Les. Next thing it was on.

Some big bloke in a Levis jacket lunged at Peregrine. Whether he just wanted to grab him or throw a punch Norton didn't know but he wasn't taking any chances. He blocked the bloke's arm with his left and slammed a short right into his ribs. The mug barely had time to gasp before Les slammed his right fist down the side of his head mashing his ear like banana. He gasped this time and hit the floor at Peregrine's feet, out like a light. A punter with a beard jumped forward, flush into a straight left from Les that splattered his nose right across his face. As he dropped his hands Norton kicked him right in the balls then when he sagged, grabbed him by the hair and ran him head first into the bar. He slumped into the butt tray, blood pouring out of his nose and forehead all over Ronnie Madden's crushed VB cans.

That was two down plus the local butcher. The mob stopped for a moment then some other hero threw a big left hook at Les. Les ducked under it and banged a right into the mug's ribs and another over the top into his jaw, breaking it in about five places. He too got grabbed by the hair and slammed head first into the bar to land face up next to his mate, blood oozing out of his mouth and scalp. Norton was a little off balance now, with his back to the mob, and he just had time to see another big goose try to take him from behind. It was time for a bit of fancy stuff.

When it came to straight out rough-and-tumble street fighting and boxing there weren't many better than Les or Billy Dunne. However, with all these new styles of fighting going round and after their own experiences at work, they both decided that it wouldn't hurt to know a bit of this Oriental stuff. And the bloke they got to teach them was George Osvaldo, a half Portuguese, half Korean who used to run Kung Fu classes in a hall near Coogee when Martial Arts movies were all the go and everybody wanted to be Bruce Lee. George worked at another casino in Rozelle so they got to be mates and they started training with him at Clovelly Surf Club early on Tuesdays and Wednesdays when nobody else was around. George taught them a style of fighting that was a cross between Hapkido and Thai Boxing. It didn't look quite as spectacular as the stuff on the screen, but if you did plenty of leg stretches it sure worked.

Norton grabbed at the bar for support and fired a snap side kick with his left foot straight into the fourth mug's chest just near his heart and felt the ribs crack under his heel. The mug clutched at his chest, sagged a little, and Les spun a crescent kick with his right foot onto his jaw, smashing it down one side. He bounced back off the mob and as he wasn't quite standing up Norton was able to get him with a hook kick, his right heel smashing the other side of his jaw, and he hit the deck. There was a solid bloke in front of Les wearing an old army shirt; Les sunk the toes of his left foot into his solar plexus, then grabbed him by the shoulder with his left hand and smashed his right elbow into his temple, splitting his eyebrow like a tomato. Les held him up and, with all his shoulder behind it, drove a straight right into his face, cannoning him through a gap in the mob and off the big red-headed bloke with the beard who had accidentally started the fracas in the first place, onto the pool table. Blood spurted out of his mouth, he gave a cough of pain and several teeth plopped out, adding a nice touch of white and red to the green felt table, before he too collapsed on the floor.

By now the mob had begun to realise that the red-headed stranger in their midst was, to say the least, horrifyingly efficient in the fighting department. There were battered and bleeding bodies lying everywhere and it was obvious that trying to get one in on Les was fast becoming a no result, so they dropped off. The jukebox had stopped playing and a couple of kids were crying as Les stood there, still tense, and exchanged glances with Peregrine. It looked like it was all over when the butcher's wife, who had missed nearly all the action, tending her husband, dropped her husband's head, jumped up and went for Peregrine.

'You dirty low bastard,' she shrieked. 'Bash my husband, will you?'

'Oh, you stupid woman,' protested Peregrine. 'I did no such bloody thing.'

'Bullshit!!'

She lurched forward tripping slightly over one of the bodies on the floor. Peregrine turned to Les and tried to get out of her way and he too stumbled over a body at his feet. His head went forward and the butcher's wife walked straight into it. From the mob's point of view it now looked as if Peregrine had head butted her. She screamed and, with a trickle of blood running out of her eyebrow, fell back into a woman wearing a white Levis jacket. As she held up the butcher's wife, blood went all over the sleeve.

'Look what the animal's just done!' shouted the woman in the white jacket. 'He's hit a woman.'

The mood of the mob turned sour. They angrily surged forward. There was just too many of them.

'Fuck this,' said Norton and he grabbed Peregrine by the collar and propelled him towards the door; by the time the mob had worked out who was going to be brave enough to lead the charge at Les, he and Peregrine were on their way to the car. As they went through the front door, Les heard a voice call out.

'See you, Les. Thanks again for the drink.' It was the caretaker.

Norton caught his strange, almost knowing look. 'Yeah. See you later, Ronnie,' he said tightly. The next thing he and Peregrine were burning rubber back towards Cedar Glen.

They reached the Nimbin turnoff before Peregrine, still trying to get into his seat belt, spoke.

'Good Lord,' he gasped. 'What was all that about?'

'What was all that about?' recoiled Norton. 'What do you *think* it was about, you fuckin' ratbag? You king-hit the local butcher and then you head butted his wife. Jesus! We're lucky we got out of the place alive.'

'I swear to you, Les,' pleaded Peregrine. 'I hardly did a thing. He fell over and she bumped into me.'

'Bullshit! You started it. And no wonder the poor bloke got the shits. You just about tried to root his missus on the dance floor.'

'We were only dancing. Having a bit of fun.'

'Bollocks, Peregrine. You're a sex-crazed mad dog. You'll end up getting us hung. No wonder the IRA want to kill you.'

Les gave poor Peregrine the rounds of the kitchen all the way back to the farm. But underneath, it was all he could do to keep from cracking up. He'd seen exactly what had happened and knew it wasn't really Peregrine's fault. It was also one of the funniest things he'd seen and one of the best fights he'd ever been in. Blokes went everywhere — only the mugs who deserved it got hurt and Les never got a scratch on him. It was just as much fun, though, making Peregrine sweat.

Back at the barbecue area, the Englishman was still in despair and no amount of pleading could convince Norton that it wasn't entirely his fault. Les opened a bottle of Jim Beam, got some ice together and poured them both a stiff bourbon and Coke.

'Here you are, Henry Cooper,' he said. 'Get that into you.'

'Les, please. You're going on like I'm some sort of nutter. I swear to you it was an accident.'

Norton watched as Peregrine took a gulp on his drink. 'Yeah, all right. I'll give you the benefit of the doubt with the butcher. But if you're gonna run round getting into fights, you don't want to go head butting sheilas. It doesn't go over too well out here.'

'Oh Good God, Les, how many times do I have to tell you? I didn't touch the wretched woman.'

'I dunno,' said Norton, shaking his head. 'But I'll take your word for it.'

Peregrine took a mouthful of bourbon and gave Norton a baleful look. 'Anyway, you needn't talk,' he spluttered. 'You looked like you were having the time of your life back there thumping into those unfortunate fellows. You must have done for about ten of them. God! I've never seen so much blood in my life.'

'What?!! Ohh, turn it up, Peregrine. I got a few lucky shots in on about four drunks — that's all. Anyway, what did you expect me to do? Stand back and let a bloodthirsty mob tear apart the man whose life my boss made me vow I would lay down my own to protect?'

Peregrine thought on it for a moment. 'Yes,' he conceded. 'I suppose you're right. I didn't think of that. But really, was there any need to just about kick one chap's head off? And almost put another's through the bar?'

Norton rattled the ice in his glass. 'Better their heads than yours, Peregrine.'

'Yes,' sighed Peregrine again. 'I guess you're right.'

They had a few more drinks and discussed the merits and demerits of the fight, with Norton still adamant that it was all Peregrine's fault. In the inky background the dew thickened the air and the calling of the nightbirds echoed around the farm. It had been a big day: the long walk in the morning, a huge meal, a bit too much to drink, topped with an all-in brawl. Before long both men were yawning into their drinks. Finally Les turned the radio off along with the outside lights and they went to bed. In the cool, clean night air, both of them slept like logs.

SATURDAY DAWNED BRIGHT and clear with maybe just the odd cloud or two being pushed through the sky by the light sou'wester. Norton rose just before seven and had a coffee with honey; Peregrine was still sleeping so he left him there. Les decided to do some stretches and other exercises and then go for a brisk walk around the property. He put on his army gear and did just that.

Norton headed for the corner of the farm they'd missed the previous day Whistling happily, he splashed along the creek bed even though it was over his knees and at times flowed around his waist; above his head, dead branches and other debris stuck in the branches of trees showed evidence of earlier flooding. The creek wound round the property for a kilometre, bubbled over a little set of rapids then near a small, circular field which was almost hidden from view, the bush opened up into another billabong three times as big and even more beautiful than the one they had found the day before. A number of large lizards and some other unseen animals scuttled away at Norton's approach.

After an hour of brisk walking in the increasing sunshine, Les was once again hot, dusty and sweaty. 'Don't worry, fellahs,' he grinned at the now vanished animals. 'I'm coming, too.' Fully clothed, he splashed in after them like a noisy water buffalo.

The water was cold, clean and refreshing. Norton wallowed around, duck-diving, spurting water and making stupid noises, then self-consciously he looked around him as if he expected someone to be watching. His face lit up in a grin when he realised there probably wasn't a soul for miles. He splashed around a while longer then decided to head back to the farm; as he climbed out of the billabong, the odd circular clearing caught his eye, so he thought he may as well check that out too.

The clearing was about fifty metres across; over the ground were scattered a number of thick poles, which appeared to have just been left there, and a number of others embedded into the ground in a large, haphazard circle. At one end were three pits about two metres across and two deep; rotting away in the bottom were more pieces of wood and what looked like small stumps. What the clearing and the holes were built for, Les couldn't guess, but there was definitely something odd and almost sinister about it all. He shrugged it off and began walking back to the house.

When he reached the driveway he noticed an old pushbike leaning against one of the rockeries. Wonder who that belongs to, he mused? He took off his wet clothes, hung them over the chairs in the barbecue area and, after checking himself for leeches, went up to the kitchen. Peregrine was in his dressing gown having a cup of coffee and reading an old newspaper.

'Sir Peregrine Normanhurst III,' said Les brightly. 'And how are you this morning?'

'Quite well, thank you, Les,' replied the Englishman just as brightly. 'Water's still hot if you want a cup of char.'

'Yeah, I wouldn't mind.' Norton moved to the kitchen. 'Who owns the old pushbike?'

'Baldric arrived to do some more gardening.'

Les had to think for a second. 'Oh yeah, Ronnie. What did he have to say?'

'Not much. Just asked if it was okay if he had a cup of coffee. He asked where you were. I said I didn't know. Then he was off to work. I must say, he does look decidedly shakey on it. And his breath, if you'll excuse the expression, smells like he's been using dogshit for toothpaste.'

'That figures. He probably drank every can of VB in the Tweed Valley last night.'

'I'd hazard a guess that he went close.'

Norton took his coffee out on to the front verandah. Ronnie was working on one of the rockeries with his back turned. Les watched him for a moment or two then went back inside.

'You had any breakfast yet, Peregrine?'

'No. Just coffee.'

'You feel like some bacon and eggs?'

'Yes, that would be splendid. This country air certainly puts an edge on one's appetite.'

'Okay. I'll get cleaned up and cook a bit of brekky.'

Peregrine wasn't joking about his appetite. He managed to polish off three eggs, plenty of bacon and tomato, plus a stack of toast and two mugs of coffee. Norton asked him what he intended to do for the rest of the day? Peregrine said he didn't want to do much at all, but bushwalking was definitely out; a swim in the little billabong and a prop there reading for the day would do him. Les told him about the new billabong he'd found earlier and Peregrine was keen to go and have a look. Right after he had done the dishes, insisted Les. Peregrine's minder he might be. His butler he definitely was not. But it wasn't hard: the two big grey things near the kitchen window were sinks, the green stuff in the plastic bottle was detergent. Mix it with warm water and it formed soapsuds. The plastic and rubber things were devices for cleaning mess from plates and cooking utensils. It was easy, insisted Norton. Peregrine would love it. While the young aristocrat was experiencing a whole new way of life in the kitchen, Les made another mug of coffee and took it out to Ronnie, tipping him to be a milk and two sugars man.

Wearing baggy King Gees, a blue singlet and the same hat he had on in the pub, the little caretaker was on his haunches pulling weeds from one of the rockeries when Norton approached. He turned at Les's footsteps and dangling from the corner of his mouth was a dead 'roll-your-own'.

'Hello, Ronnie,' said Les. 'I brought you a cup of coffee.'

'Oh thanks, Les,' replied the caretaker. 'Good on you, mate.'

Madden stood up and accepted the coffee gratefully. Norton studied him for a while and noticed the amount of sweat pouring from his face and arms. If you caught it all in a bucket it would probably still have a head on it.

'So how are you feeling, Ron?'

'Ohh, not too bad,' replied the caretaker, adding a wheezy, rattling laugh. 'We ended up having a few last night, though.'

'How many's a few? A dozen or so?'

'In the pub? Easy. Then we got into it back home.'

A dozen cans plus — not a bad drinker for a little bloke, thought Les, continuing to study the gardener as he sipped his coffee. He noticed Madden didn't mention anything about the fight and there was no way he could have missed it. That suited Norton. He didn't particularly want to bring the subject up himself. But there was something else about the little caretaker and the way he acted that didn't seem to gel to Les. Was it eyes or his manner? For the moment Norton couldn't quite work it out.

'So, how long will you work for today, Ron?'

Madden tilted his head towards the sky and took another sip of coffee. 'Another three or four hours or so. I'll finish this weeding then I'll mow down by the sides of the toolshed. I'll knock off 'bout two o'clock.'

'I'm gonna light the barby about then. You want to join us? Have a steak? There's plenty of piss there.'

Steak didn't get a great reaction, but the word 'piss' brought a gleam to the caretaker's eyes. 'Righto, Les. That'd be good.'

'We're going for a swim down in that billabong at the front. We'll see you when we get back.'

'Okay, Les. See you then.'

Les collected Peregrine plus a couple of blankets and some towels. He borrowed one of his books, which he threw into an overnight bag along with some fruit and other odds and ends, then took him down to the pool. Seeing they had to wade across the creek Peregrine wore his fatigues and boots like Norton, just to be on the safe side.

'I say,' said the Englishman, slipping his camera from his shoulder as they splashed up to the billabong. 'This is a beautiful spot.'

'I told you it was better than the other one.'

Norton spread the blankets out in a cleared, level spot close by, while Peregrine clicked off a few photos. Then he took him to the circular clearing and showed him the timber and the mysterious holes in the ground.

'What do you make of that?' he asked.

Peregrine shook his head. 'Blowed if I know,' he said. 'Blowed if I know, indeed. Unless they're wells?'

'With a billabong that big right next to them?'

'Yes, you're right. Could this be some sort of stockade? Are they tiger traps or something?'

'There's no bloody tigers in Australia, Peregrine.'

'Well, I couldn't tell you what it is,' replied Peregrine snapping off two quick photos. 'Anyway, old boy. Let's have a swim.'

They spent the next few hours in the warm sun, swimming, reading, watching the countless beautiful birds zipping in and out of the trees and doing one of Norton's favourite pastimes: sweet bugger all. Les found Peregrine's book, *Women* by Charles Bukowski, one of the raunchiest and filthiest books he'd ever come across; it was also one of the funniest and easiest to read. Peregrine was getting into a biography of Peter Sellers, which he appeared to be enjoying immensely as well. Before Les knew it, it was half past one. He was a bit on the peckish side and fanging for a can of Fourex, so they packed up and headed back to the house.

A pleasant thought struck Norton as he was wading across the creek. Having no TV and not seeing a Sydney newspaper for days, he'd forgotten the semi-finals were on. What a top way to spend the afternoon — drinking beer, eating steaks and listening to the footy. Who was it today, Balmain and Manly? Wouldn't matter. It would still be a good game. Ahh yes, how sweet it is, thought the big Queenslander as they splashed back to the house.

Ronnie Madden was cleaned up and sitting patiently in the barbecue area when they got there. 'How was the swim?' he coughed through the haze of his roll-your-own.

'Excellent,' replied Peregrine, as he and Les started climbing out of their wet fatigues and boots. 'Certainly gives one an appetite. Les tells me you're going to join us for a bit of nosh.'

'Yeah. You don't mind do you?'

'No. By all means, be our guest. And I might add that my manservant there is quite a dab hand at a barbecue too.'

'I'll give you bloody manservant in a minute,' growled Norton, draping his cammies over a chair.

'Hey . . . ah did you say there was a beer in the fridge?' said Madden, rubbing his hands together. 'All right if I have one?'

'Yeah. Go for your life,' answered Les. 'There's about three and a half dozen there. Just leave me a couple for tonight. I don't feel like driving into the pub.'

'Will do,' replied the caretaker, heading towards the barbecue fridge like a heat-seeking missile.

'Do you think we'll ever get back in the hotel after last night's performance?' asked Peregrine.

Madden laughed as he handed them each a cold Fourex. 'I dunno. They see a few stinks in there now and again. But Jesus! That was a ball-tearer you blokes put on last night.'

'You like that did you, Ronald?' asked Peregrine.

'It wasn't a baddy. They took a lot of sick boys into Murwillumbah hospital last night.' Madden turned to Norton. 'You sure know how to put 'em together, don't you mate?'

Les nodded his head towards Peregrine. 'He started it.'

'Yeah, I saw that,' said Ron.

'Ohh God, no. Not again,' wailed Peregrine.

Norton left them, had a quick wash then went upstairs to boil some rice and make the salad. Peregrine came up shortly and got changed, but he didn't give Norton a hand, which suited Les because he would have only got in the road anyway. When he came downstairs, Peregrine had almost finished his first can and Ron was into his third, but the little caretaker had gathered enough wood for the fire.

It didn't take long for Les to have the rice and onions frying and the meat sizzling. It was pretty much the same fare as the previous day, the only variation was some lamb cutlets which Norton squeezed fresh grapefruit juice all over from a tree near the second gate. While Madden was watching him, Les decided he might try and pump him for a bit of information.

'So you knew the bloke that built this joint, did you, Ron? The Yank colonel.'

'Daniel J? Yeah I knew him.'

'Was that his name?' asked Peregrine.

'Daniel J. Harcourt. Colonel, US Rangers. Brilliant soldier. Probably one of the best men to ever shoulder a rifle. Never knew what the 'J' stood for.'

'Where did you get to know him?' asked Les.

'I . . .' Madden hesitated for a moment. 'I did a bit of work for him when he had the duck farm.'

'Ahh, so it was a duck farm, eh?' smiled Norton.

'Yep. Biggest, plumpest ducks in the valley. Couldn't breed enough of 'em.'

'Where is he now?'

Ronnie shrugged. 'Don't know for sure. He's been gone about four or five months. Left sudden. I got an idea he went back to South East Asia.'

Madden got another beer, Les turned the sausages and squeezed more grapefruit juice over the cutlets.

'What made him build a place like this out here?' asked Peregrine. 'Almost in the middle of nowhere.'

The little caretaker took a huge drink of beer and seemed to smile inwardly. 'I guess he just liked it. Plus this is the safest place on earth.'

The others exchanged a quizzical look. 'Safest place on earth!!?' they chorused.

'Latitude 28 degrees south, longitude 153 degrees east. Safest place on the planet. If ever there's another war, the air currents coming off these mountains'll keep the fallout away from here. This is the safest place on earth. You can survive here.'

Les and Peregrine looked at Ronnie curiously. Then the little caretaker's expression altered and he abruptly changed the subject as if he regretted what he had just said.

'Good weather up here for winter, ain't it fellahs?'

'Yes, yes. Much better than back home,' agreed Peregrine.

'Well, I reckon these steaks are about done,' said Norton, giving one of them a squeeze with the barbecue tongs.

'Yeah. I'll say one thing for our butcher,' said Ronnie. 'He sure sells grouse meat.'

'Yeah. I reckon I can handle being barred from the local pub,' said Les. 'But I sure hope the butcher hasn't brushed us.'

'I was in town this morning,' chuckled Madden. 'He looks okay. But his wife's got a black eye and three stitches in her cheekbone.'

'That's what I mean,' said Les, motioning at Peregrine with his can of beer. 'He gets a few drinks in him and throws punches all over the place.'

'Yeah, I saw that too,' said Ronnie, breaking into one of his wheezy laughs.

'Oh, for God's sake,' pleaded Peregrine. 'Will you give me a break?'

Again the meat was cooked to perfection and so was the rice. The salad was crisp and Les had even managed to make a kind of garlic toast with the bread. They had an enjoyable afternoon eating and talking with Ronnie polishing off cans of Fourex at the rate of five for Norton's two. Les switched the radio onto the football about the same time as Peregrine switched to champagne and orange. Ronnie didn't seem all that interested in the football and after thanking them both, he left around three-thirty. This left Peregrine and Les sitting in the sun getting drunker and drunker. By the time Balmain had gone down to Manly by two points the sun had started to go down behind the mountains. By six-thirty the air was once again thick with dew and the nightbirds had started calling to each other across the valley. Les switched the outside lights on and stoked up the fire.

'Well, Sir Peregrine Normanhurst III,' he yawned, as he sat back down. 'It looks like being a very quiet old Saturday night in Cedar Glen.'

'Yes, it certainly does, old chap,' replied Peregrine, returning Norton's yawn. 'And just quietly, that suits me. I'm almost too choofed to move.'

'Yeah, me too.' Norton was surprised at just how tired he was. Normally at this time he'd be getting ready to go to work and finish around four. 'I reckon I might even be in bed before nine.'

'And I won't be far behind you. Curiously enough, I have absolutely no trouble sleeping up here.'

'No. Me either.'

Then Peregrine's eyes lit up. 'I know what I might do. I might go and feed Bunter.'

'Who?'

'Bunter. The owl. I'll give him one of those sausages.'

Norton had to laugh. 'Go for your life. In fact I might join you.'

They were about to get up when something flashing in the half light about twenty metres out from the barbecue caught Norton's eye.

'Hey, don't move, Peregrine,' said Norton urgently. 'Stay where you are. And keep quiet.'

Keeping stock-still, Peregrine followed the direction of Norton's eyes. The two, small lights flashed again, then moved slightly. After a moment or two they could see what they were.

It was a feral cat, a big one. Even in the faint light Les and Peregrine could make out the length of its thick, grey-black body with its massive scarred head, the two glittering green eyes watching them from the darkness, showing caution but absolutely no fear.

'Jesus! Look at that,' said Norton quietly. 'A bloody feral cat.'

'A cat? Jiminy! It's as a big as a dog.'

'Yeah. All that meat cooking's brought the bastard round.'

'What a repulsive looking creature.'

Norton stared at the huge cat watching them from the darkness, and thought of the destruction they and wild dogs do to the environment and wished he had a gun. A gun? Shit! He had a gun, all right, that bloody thing Eddie gave him when they were leaving. He'd stowed it under his bed and forgotten about it.

'Peregrine,' he whispered. 'Stay here and keep an eye on that moggie. I'll be back in a second.'

As quietly as he could, considering his drunkenness, Les went to his room, got the blue overnight bag and placed it on the bed. The gun was wrapped in an old red towel along with two boxes of bullets and two fully-loaded magazines.

It was an odd-looking weapon, very similar to an American Colt .45 Automatic, only the barrel extended about seven centimetres out to the front, with a distinctive thread running around it like a drill bit. It wouldn't have weighed much more than a kilo and had a comfortable grip and easy balance in Norton's hand. He clicked a magazine up into the butt, thumbed the safety back and with the gun down by his side walked back out to the barbecue area.

'I say,' said Peregrine. 'What have you got there?'

'It's a pistol Eddie gave me in Sydney. That cat still there?'

'Yes. He hasn't moved.'

'Good.'

Norton spotted the two lights still watching them, thumbed the safety forward and slowly brought the gun up. 'Watch this, Peregrine. I'll put one right between its rotten fuckin' eyes.' Les gripped his right wrist with his left hand and carefully took aim. 'Here, kitty kitty,' he whispered, as he curled his finger round the trigger. 'Make my day.'

Les squeezed the trigger, expecting one bullet to hit the feral cat. Instead, there was a vibrating flash of orange flame and a hammering roar that echoed across the valley. Eight shells rattled onto the barbecue table and the cat disappeared in a crimson spray of blood, fur, bone splinters and entrails. After the roar of the pistol the silence seemed more pronounced, broken only by the frenzied screeching of the startled nightbirds.

'I say,' said Peregrine. 'Jolly good shot.'

'Jolly good shot my arse!' exclaimed Norton, staring at the

pistol still smoking in his hand. 'What sort of a fuckin' gun *is* this?'

What Les didn't know was that Eddie had given him a Robinson S.R. Model II Constant Reaction Machine Pistol. Built in Australia during World War II, it had a unique rotating barrel and a precompressed recoil spring giving it virtually no kick, which was why, even at 600 rpm Norton was able to ring eight bullets into the cat.

Les and Peregrine walked over to where the cat had been. All that remained was a bit of its head, a shoulder, part of the tail and a few patches of grey fur on the blood-splattered grass.

'Bloody hell!' exclaimed Norton. 'Poor old puss. He never had a fuckin' chance.'

'Indeed no. What sort of gun did you say that was Les?'

'I think Eddie called it a Robinson.'

'Any bullets left?'

'I think so.'

'How about a shot?'

Les looked suspiciously at Peregrine. 'Well . . . all right. But aim the bloody thing up in the air a bit.'

Les carefully handed Peregrine the Robinson. The Englishman held it out in front of him and squeezed the trigger. There was another burst of orange flame accompanied by a hammering bang; six more shells flew out of the side and the magazine ejected at his feet.

'Jolly good!' said Peregrine. 'There's no recoil at all.'

'No, it's a ripper, isn't it?' Norton took back the weapon and picked up the magazine. 'Anyway, Dirty Harry, I reckon that's enough fireworks for tonight. I'm gonna put this thing away. It's a bit dangerous to be playing around with it, in our condition.'

'Yes, I agree.'

Les put the machine pistol back under his bed and they resumed their positions in the barbecue area over some bourbon and Coke, laughing drunkenly about some of the events so far. Peregrine decided it would be useless trying to feed Bunter now, after all that racket there would hardly be a bird left in the valley. But both agreed it was a good thing Les had nailed the feral cat. After their second bourbon both men were yawning like caverns; Les switched off the radio and the outside lights and they called it a night.

* * *

FOR THE MIDDLE of winter, Sunday was quite hot. There was hardly a cloud in the sky, the sou'wester had dropped off and even at six-thirty in the morning the sun was beating down into the valley. Yeah, well who needs an ozone layer anyway, thought Norton as he stood outside his bedroom. Peregrine was awake but not out of bed when Les went into the kitchen for a cup of coffee. With a bit of pressure Norton was able to get the Englishman up and was even able to coerce him into getting some exercise before breakfast, guaranteeing Peregrine that if he sat around stuffing himself with steak, guzzling bottles of champagne and getting all sleep and no exercise, he'd leave Cedar Glen after two weeks looking like Meatloaf. The Englishman reluctantly agreed and by seven-thirty was in his fatigues and boots joining Les for a brisk walk around the property and a swim in the billabong at the front of the house. Norton even got him to do fifty sit-ups.

Relaxing in the barbecue area after another big feed, Peregrine had to admit that it was the best he'd felt in months. Les promised him that another week of this and he'd be able to beat any woman in the Tweed Valley under five feet two. They hung around reading and soaking up the sun for the rest of the morning, then at about twelve-thirty they slipped into their jeans and T-shirts and headed for the Yurriki Buttery Bazaar.

There were quite a number of cars parked in the streets around town when they got there so Les guessed that the Bazaar must be quite an event on the Yurriki social calendar. They found a spot behind the school, crossed the street and under a huge banner strung between two trees, saying 'Yurriki Buttery Bazaar This Sunday' they propped in front of the old butter factory to get their bearings. After a quick exchange of bemused looks Peregrine threw his hands up in the air and rolled his eyes in mock terror.

'My God, Spock,' he said. 'Scotty's beamed us back to 1960.'

Norton returned Peregrine's look of horror. 'You're not wrong, captain,' he replied.

The bazaar consisted of rows and rows of stalls on either side of a dusty gravel path running around the old butter factory. There were crowds of people walking around and most of them were hippies or alternative lifestyle people of some description and they all looked like they'd come out of a time warp. The men nearly all had beards and long hair either plaited or growing anywhere. They wore batik sarongs, multi-coloured baggy pants and shirts, hats with feathers or flowers in them, sling bags over their shoulders, scarves round their waists. There were little vests with mirrors on the front, and even a number of flared jeans. They wore earrings and all sorts of things hanging around their necks; most were barefoot although there was the occasional capitalist who could afford a pair of tai-chi slippers.

The women, a lot of whom were carrying kids in backpacks, had hair much like the men: long or plaited, tumbling out from under men's hats or from gypsy scarves tied in the corners or under their chins. They wore patchwork tops, Tibetan tops, Arab tops and multi-coloured ones that could have been made out of anything. There were long dresses, short dresses, red stockings, blue stockings; some were barefoot, others had on moccasins or old granny boots to go with their granny glasses. A lot had flowers in their hair or coloured feathers dangling from pierced ears. One girl walked past in a Levis jacket that was more patches than material, with *Good News — Not All Of Us Are Under Control* stitched onto the back next to a peace symbol. Another went by in a green fez, another in an orange sombrero.

'Well, what do you reckon, Peregrine?' laughed Norton.

The Englishman shook his head. 'I wonder what happened to the local dry-cleaner. I'll bet he starved to death.'

'Yeah. I reckon some of those shirts haven't seen an ironing board since the battle of Hastings. Anyway, let's have a look around.'

They followed the path through the people and checked out the stalls, which were mainly food, old and new clothing, second hand junk or cheap jewellery. The stall-keepers ran from Hari Krishnas to freaks to people who wouldn't have looked out of place in the Queensland National party. There was an Atomic Coffee Stand, another selling tempura, one selling Granny's Homemade Ice Cream. The junk was anything from old sewing-machines to axe-heads, even empty jars and biscuit tins. Les ran his hand through a box of records and shook his head. Music From Big Pink. Richie Havens Stonehenge. The James Gang. Chain. Iron Butterfly. In Sydney you couldn't have given the stuff away, let alone sold it. Someone was selling ducks and drakes in a cage, another was flogging bulk raw muesli next to a stall selling macrobiotic jams, pickles and sauces. A bloke who looked like John Belushi was playing a guitar, with his wife on drums and their two kids both singing excruciatingly out of tune. Round the corner some other bloke with a beard was wailing into Bob Dylan on a guitar at the side of the butter factory. Behind the stalls was a blow-up castle for the kids to play on. The whole atmosphere was friendly and laid-back and most of the people there seemed to know each other. Their clothes may have been a bit scruffy, but the people themselves were clean and so were the kids. It was obvious they were nearly all just battlers or 'alternates' with no desire to live in the cities, doing their best to turn a dollar. And even if they were living in the past a little they added a bit of colour to the surroundings and certainly weren't doing anybody any harm, except maybe avaricious property developers, saw-mill owners and redneck members of The National Party who like to get drunk and go out shooting small animals.

At a small caravan, run by a Muslim couple dressed in light blue, Les and Peregrine stopped for a cup of coffee. The coffee was thick, strong and tasty. Les went for a piece of carrot and walnut cake. Peregrine opted for the chocolate wholemeal with coconut and date. Like the coffee, the cake was excellent too. The Muslim and his wife were friendly people and gave them a brochure on Islam to read while they enjoyed their snack.

'See anything you want to buy?' joked Les.

'As a matter of fact, I have,' replied Peregrine.

'Yeah?'

'Yes. What about yourself?'

'Well, oddly enough, there's a couple of things over at that Peace Stall that will come in very handy back on the farm.'

'Okay. Well, what say we finish this, walk around and sample a bit more of the local cuisine, then make our purchases?'

'That sounds like a good idea, Pezz.'

They strolled back through the crowd to where they'd come in. At the Hari Krishna stand was a sign saying: *Try Lord Krishna's Maha Basadams and Spiritual Food Bliss Balls.* They tasted okay but Les reckoned you'd have to eat six hundred to fill you up. These were washed down with fresh passionfruit juice from a stall run by two old people who looked like they could have been in The National Party. It was delicious, however, so they ordered two more. Next was a watermelon and pawpaw ice cream each from Granny's Homemade. These didn't go down too bad either on a hot day. Next to a stall selling free-range eggs some child of the rainbow was flogging Green Jungle Juice from a big glass cooler: wheat grain, mint, parsley and unsweetened pine juice. It looked like frogshit but was chilled and also quite delicious. Strolling around all these different and exotic food stalls Les and Peregrine noticed that the one doing the most business was two old country women selling steak sandwiches and sausages on a roll; around it, the lean, hungry flower children were about six deep.

The boys decided that there had been enough eating and drinking for the time being and it was time to buy what they had their eye on. Les led them back to the Peace Stall. Back behind the old sandshoes, magazines, rake heads and other junk were two banana-chairs in reasonable condition. The poor hippy wanted twenty dollars for the two. Les got him down to fifteen just to be a cunt.

'These will go very well down by that billabong, Pezz,' he said, tucking them up under each arm. 'I'll put them straight in the car and meet you back here.'

'Meet me back at Yasser Arafat's coffee stand.'

'Righto.'

When Norton returned, Peregrine was sipping coffee at the Muslim's caravan and staring intently in front of him where the stalls cornered around heading back towards the main road.

'So what's doing, mate?' he asked.

'What's doing?' Peregrine motioned with his cup. 'That's what's doing.'

He pointed towards a stall on the corner that was six bamboo poles with a green tarpaulin stretched over the top. Hanging on racks inside were rows of some of the strangest women's clothes Les had ever seen in his life. Minis, maxis, bum-huggers, tights, button-down tops, collarless, V-necks, some with shoulder pads, some with epaulettes; and all in the wierdest, most exotic colours imagineable. Where the designer had run out of ideas for colour, he or she had inserted feathers or strips of fake animal skin or fur. Fossicking around amongst the rows of clothing were two women who appeared to be in their mid-twenties. One had scraggly, ginger-black hair, the other brown with touches of orange. They both had sexy, pouting faces, heavily made-up with the emphasis on eye shadow, small, thick lips and squat bosomy figures something like Bette Midler's. The one with the darker hair had on a tight-fitting, one piece black, red and silver outfit which resembled a court jester's costume, pinned in the middle by a huge red belt with a silver buckle. The other was wearing a black and gold tank-top, leopard-skin tights and pixie boots; beneath a small, white Panama glinted a pair of orange-tinted, John Lennon glasses.

'Well. What do you think?' asked Peregrine.

'What do I think?' replied Norton. 'Nice. It's a pity they don't celebrate Halloween in Australia.'

'I had another look at their clothes while you were away.

They call themselves Mata Hari's Waterbed.'

'They look like they ought to be shot like Mata Hari too. You wouldn't wear any of that stuff to a shit fight. You're not thinking of buying some are you?'

'As a matter of fact, Les, I'm thinking of buying the lot.' Peregrine ignored Norton's double blink and replaced his coffee cup. 'Come on.'

Les followed Peregrine across to the girl's stall. The one in the Panama smiled when she saw the Englishman. 'Back again,' she said pleasantly. 'See something you like?'

'Actually,' replied Peregrine. 'I like it all. It's quite unique.'

'Thank you,' said the one in the court jester outfit. 'You're obviously a man of good taste.'

Peregrine smiled graciously, adding a polite nod. 'Ladies, allow me to introduce myself. I'm Peregrine Normanhurst. And this is my associate Les Norton.'

'I'm Marita,' said the one in the court jester gear. 'And this is Coco.'

'Pleased to meet you, girls,' smiled Norton, still mystified as to what Peregrine was on about.

Peregrine motioned his hand across the surrounding clothes. 'Ladies,' he said 'I'll get straight to the point. How many items of apparel would you have in here?' Coco screwed up her face. 'Your entire stock, ladies. How much is here?'

The proprietors of Mata Hari's Waterbed exchanged a quick look. 'Well,' said Marita a little hesitantly. 'There's fifty tops there. Twenty pairs of tights. Forty dresses. What's that? A hundred and ten . . . items.'

'And how much would you want for your entire range?'

'What!!?' chorused the two hippy women.

'I'd like to purchase the contents of your boutique. How much would you be willing to sell it for? Cash.'

Marita and Coco were completely flummoxed. It would normally take them at least six to twelve months to flog their rubbish, yet here was some bloke who spoke like Richard Burton and must have been eating Gold-Tops wanting to buy the lot in one go. He obviously had more money than sense so why not try to get top dollar? He could only come down.

'Four thousand dollars,' blurted Marita.

'Yeah. And don't forget they're all hand sewn,' said Coco anxiously.

'Done,' said Peregrine, with a quick gesture. 'And quite reasonable too, I might add.' From the back pocket of his designer jeans he produced twenty crisp, one hundred dollar bills. 'There's two thousand dollars there,' he said, placing the money in Marita's hand. She stood there and stared at it like it was something from outer space. 'How about I call around to your factory, or premises, tonight, and pay you the remainder? Plus some more, because I want you to ship the lot to an address in London, England. Is that satisfactory?'

'Sure. Anything you like,' said Marita.

'No worries Mr Normanhurst . . . Peregrine,' panted Coco.

'Excellent. Now if you would be so kind as to write down your address, or give me your business card.'

Coco started scratching away with a marking pencil on a piece of paper. It was a phone number and an address at Stokers Siding. 'Do you know how to get to Stokers Siding?' she asked. Peregrine looked at Les who nodded back. 'What time would you like to come out?'

Peregrine gave a quick shrug. 'Oh . . . say, six-thirty, seven.'

'Would you like to have dinner?' asked Marita.

The boys exchanged a quick look, figuring that Marita's and Coco's cooking would probably be as weird as their clothing.

'No, that's all right thank you,' replied Peregrine. 'But I may bring a bottle of champers to clinch the deal. Yes?'

'Okay, fine,' said Coco.

'Very well then, ladies.' Peregrine shook both their hands. 'May I say it has been an absolute pleasure doing business with you. And I'm looking forward to seeing you again this evening.'

'Us too. Goodbye, Peregrine. Goodbye, Les. See you tonight.'

The boys had barely made it to the front of the bazaar before Marita and Coco were kicking down the bamboo poles and stuffing their weird clothing into whatever it was they'd brought it out in.

The boys stopped not far from where they had walked in earlier. Peregrine seemed very pleased with himself, Les was almost dumbfounded.

'Fair dinkum, Peregrine,' he said, shaking his head. 'I don't believe you. Four grand for that load of shit. You've gotta have a pumpkin for a head.'

Peregrine chuckled out loud. 'That is precisely where you're wrong dear boy. That load of shit, as you call it, will be worth a fortune back in London.'

'What?'

'My girlfriend, Stephanie, owns a boutique in The Kings

176

Road. We'll flog that tatt in there for at least thirty times what I just paid for it.'

'You're kidding?'

'Not at all, dear boy. Remember what that girl Coco, said. Everything was hand sewn.'

'Yeah. Only because they wouldn't have the money to buy a sewing-machine.'

'Well, that's what the trendies in London with more money than brains are looking for. Handmade, Australian originals. Even the name, Mata Hari's Waterbed. That's a selling point.' Peregrine slipped into his cockney 'Minder' voice. 'See, that's wot the whole thing's all about, Terry. I give the punters wot they want, and pick myself up a nice little earner at the same time.' He slipped an arm around Norton's shoulders. 'And you never know, Tell. Keep schtoom. Say nuffink to no one. And there might even be a bit of wedge in it for you — know what I mean?'

Norton shook his head again. 'Good on you, Arfur. But I still don't believe it.'

'Les, my boy,' chuckled Peregrine. 'I only inherited a measly five million. This turned it into fifty,' he added, tapping himself on the forehead.

Norton stared into the crowd still milling around in the heat. 'Fair enough,' he nodded. 'Anyway, after all that wheeling and dealing, I feel like a drink.'

'Yes, me too. Do you think we can get back into the pub?'

'I hope so. That bloody Ronnie put an awful hole in my supply of Fourex. Oh well, if they boot us out we'll just have to drive into Murwillumbah.'

As they walked back to the car, Peregrine gave Les another pat on the shoulder. 'When you stop to consider it, Les,' he smiled. 'It hasn't been a bad day all round. You managed to rob some poor hippy of five dollars. And I've pulled in a lazy hundred and twenty grand. But you're learning, Les. You're learning.'

Norton found a parking spot opposite the hotel and told Peregrine to wait in the car while he went in and sussed things out. One of the girls who had been working on Friday night was in the bottle shop; she looked at Les indifferently. The publican was standing in the doorway to the public-bar. He turned around but didn't say anything either. They've probably forgotten what I looked like, shrugged Les. I'm not a regular, it all happened fairly quickly and we left pretty smartly. Oh well, good one. He bought two cases of Fourex, six bottles of Great Western, two more Jacobs Creek and two more bottles of Jim Beam plus some Coke.

'What did they say?' asked Peregrine, opening the back of the station-wagon when Les came back laden down with the booze.

'Nothing. I don't think they recognised me. Come on, let's go and have a drink.'

Because of the bazaar, the hotel was a little busier than usual for a Sunday. There was a fair crowd sitting and standing around out the front and quite a few in the bar, but nearly everybody seemed to be out in the beer garden. Nobody said anything as they walked through the mob of drinkers on the footpath, but when they got to the bar Norton distinctly felt a few eyes on him and noticed a couple of whispered conversations. Nobody said or did anything, and the publican was waiting in front of them, so Les ordered a middy of New for himself and a gin and tonic for Peregrine. These barely lasted two minutes so Les ordered the same again.

They'd just got their second drink when the bloke playing pool, who had accidentally started the fight in the first place, stepped up to the bar next to Les and ordered two schooners. He was a big man, taller than Les, with a mop of thick red hair and a bushy beard that made him look bigger again. But he had a soft voice and a pleasant if slightly brisk manner.

'G'day, mate,' he said to Les. 'How are you?'

'Not too bad,' replied Norton. 'How's yourself?'

'Good. Hey . . . ah, I saw what happened here on Friday night. That was half my fault.'

'Yeah I know. Bad luck it just got a bit out of hand.'

Redbeard laughed. 'I suppose that's one way of putting it.' He held out a hand. 'I'm Alan, anyway.'

Norton took his firm grip. 'I'm Les. This is Peregrine.' There was another quick handshake.

'I'm running the dance on Saturday night. You fellahs thinking of coming?'

'Yeah, we were, to tell you the truth.'

'It'll be a bottler. I got a good local band, plus The Bachelors From Cracow. They were putting down an album in a studio in Byron Bay and I've got them to come up and do a gig.'

'I've heard of them,' nodded Les. 'They're pretty good.'

'Yeah, it'll be a good night. Five bucks in, bring your own piss.'

'Sounds good.'

'Okay. Well, if I don't see you around before, I'll see you Saturday.'

'A big chance, Alan,' winked Norton.

As Alan picked up his beers and turned to walk away, he stopped and moved a little closer to Norton. 'If you're thinking of hanging around here this arvo, keep your eyes open. One of the blokes you belted has brought his brother down.'

'Should I be worried?'

'When you see Gorgo I think you might be. Anyway, I'll see you later, Les. You too, Peregrine.'

'See you, Alan. And thanks, mate.'

Les and Peregrine watched Alan join another bearded man sitting at a table near the snack bar.

'What was all that about?' asked Peregrine.

'Dunno for sure,' shrugged Norton. 'But if we hang around long enough I reckon we'll find out.'

They were facing away from the bar, taking their time over their second drink and talking about what time they were going to light the barby before they drove out to Stokers Siding when Les heard a voice to his right. It was a tight, strained voice, sounding as if it was coming through clenched teeth.

'Fancy yourself as a tough guy, do you?'

Norton turned slowly around. Standing next to him was a bearded man wearing a khaki army shirt. He had two black eyes, stitches in his face and his jaw was wired up. Behind him stood a tall, skinny bloke with an earring and a black T-shirt trying to look tough. Les gave the beard a quick once up and down. 'You talking to me, matey?'

'Yeah. Because of you I've got ten stitches in my face and a broken jaw.'

Peregrine looked edgy. Les continued to sip his beer. 'It could have been a lot worse,' he said casually.

'Worse?'

'Yeah. At least you didn't get your good shirt ripped.'

Beard sucked in a breath. 'Listen, tough guy . . .'

'Hey, hold on with this tough guy, shitbags,' cut in Norton. 'You and your pals were all keen to have a shot at my mate here — who's half your size. I just thought I'd step in and even things up a bit. Bad luck you got in the way.'

'Okay. Well, listen, tough guy. If you fancy yourself, my brother's out in the beer garden. He'd like to see you, if you're game.'

Norton took another sip of beer and shrugged. 'I'm not going far.'

'Good.'

The beard and his mate gave Les a last dirty look and walked off. As they were leaving, Les blew the one in the black T-shirt a kiss.

'I heard part of that,' said a worried Peregrine. 'What's going on now?'

'I'd say that must be the bloke who's brought his brother down.'

'What do you intend to do?'

'Finish this drink, then I'll probably have another one. Then I might go and see what's worrying this chap in the beer garden.'

'Oh forget it, Les. Why don't we just finish these and go?'

Norton gave the Englishman a strange smile. 'Peregrine, I'd rather let them carry me out of here toes up, than crawl out on my belly. We'll have another drink.' He motioned to the publican.

'Same again, mate?'

'No. A gin and tonic for him. And I'll have a double OP rum and Coke. Plenty of ice.'

Peregrine timorously sipped his gin and tonic. Norton knocked off his OP rum in about four swallows, swirled the ice around in the glass for the last few drops, then placed it on the bar.

'Okay, Peregrine,' he said, slipping his watch off into the back pocket of his jeans. 'I'm gonna go out and see what's up with the local rocket scientists. You'd better go and wait in the car.'

The Englishman shook his head and finished his drink. 'No. I'll come with you.'

'Okay. But don't you get involved. This is my doing.'

There was a bit of a hush when they stepped out into the beer garden. Les noticed a couple more of his opponents from Friday night scowling at him from behind more bandages than an Egyptian mummy. The beard was at a table of about a dozen men and women to his right. Seated next to him was his skinny mate in the black T-shirt. On the other side of the table however, was the biggest bloke Norton had ever seen in his life; even sitting down he was head and shoulders above the others and would have had to have been at least twenty stone. He had short, scrubby black hair and a stubble of black whiskers across a puddingy, baby-face. His mouth was a snarl of crooked, twisted teeth and Les could tell by the way his beady eyes blinked slowly as they focused on different things about him that he was either a simpleton or an inbred brought down from the surrounding mountains to fight him. So, you're Gorgo eh? mused Norton. I'll bet a week's wages you read the Melbourne *Truth*.

Norton's eyes ran around the table of faces then riveted on the beard's. 'All right, whiskers,' he said. 'I'm here. What do you want?'

'I'd like you to meet my brother, Emmett,' he replied, nodding to the monster sitting next to him. 'But we call him Gorgo.'

Norton turned to the big inbred. 'Hello Emmett,' he smiled. 'How are you, mate?'

Gorgo blinked at Norton a couple of times. 'Y . . . you hurt my brother,' he said.

Les nodded slowly. 'Well, maybe I did, Emmett. But it was just a fight in a pub. And he'll live.'

'W...well you shouldn't have done it. And n . . . now you're gonna have to fight me.'

The hesitant manner in Gorgo's voice and the way his eyes kept avoiding Norton's when he spoke indicated to Les the big inbred was mostly bluff, this was a gee-up and he wasn't all that keen to fight anybody. There could be a way out of this.

'Well, if that's the way you want it, Emmett. But I haven't got any argument with you, mate.'

'Yeah, you're not so tough now, are you?' said the beard.

Norton glared at Gorgo's brother and felt like giving him a quick backhander and opening up a few stitches again. If he ever spotted him somewhere on his own he just might too.

'W . . . what did you do it for?'

'Like I said, Emmett, it was just a fight in a pub. And if anyone got hurt I'm sorry.' The crowd was hooing and hahhing a bit around him but Norton could see this was fast developing into a Mexican standoff between himself and Emmett. May as well go along with the bullshit and save them both a lot of torn clothing and aggravation.

'W . . . well s . . . say you're sorry to my brother.'

Norton turned to the beard and although he almost choked on the words, somehow he managed to get them out. 'Sorry . . . mate. Now is it all right if I go back inside and finish my drink, Emmett?'

Gorgo was about to say something when Peregrine, who had been keeping a very nervous silence so far, decided to put his head in.

'Why you blithering bunch of country dunderheads,' he blurted out. 'My man here could go through the lot of you with a balloon on a stick. And as for you,' he said, turning to Gorgo, 'you preposterous, pie faced, piecan. He'd roll you in flour, dunk you in hot oil and serve you up with chips and peas, you unspeakable, fat spoofer.'

Norton shot Peregrine a look as if to say 'Shut up you dopey fuckin' idiot,' but it was too late.

The beard jumped to his feet. 'Emmett! Did you hear what he just said?' he shouted out.

'Yeah,' thundered the massive inbred, lumbering to his feet. He pointed a huge, dirt-caked finger at Les. 'Come on. Outside.'

'Yeah, give it to him, Gorgo,' came a voice from the crowd.

'Smash the bastard!' yelled another.

Norton sized up the hulking inbred standing in front of him; there was only one way to fight a monster like that: kick out his knee-caps or get him in the balls, throat-slash him, or gouge his eyes. If it came to the worst, smash a chair across his temple or jab a broken glass in his jugular vein. Fuck any of that fair go shit. This was now street survival: kill or be killed. But in all reality Emmett was just a simpleton, nothing more than an overgrown child and to seriously maim a poor unfortunate like that would be no better than bashing up a drunk or shooting a poor, defenceless animal. On the other hand, the sheer size of Emmett indicated that he would have enormous strength and if he grabbed hold of Les he could possibly crush him or break his back with his sheer bulk. There was one way of beating Gorgo without hurting him too much. If Les pulled it off properly, the only ones who would get hurt would be the mugs looking on and the bastards who brought poor Emmett down there to fight Les in the first place. It was time for a bit more fancy stuff, or as Bugs Bunny would say, 'Time to use a little "stradgity".'

Another fighter who used to train privately with George Osvaldo was a nuggety Scotsman called Mick McTigue. Mick's training was unfortunately curtailed when he finished up a guest of her majesty in Goulburn for a Clayton's crime; conspiracy to conspire to be a conspirator to something or other — the crime you commit when you're not committing a crime. But before Mick came to Australia he was Middleweight Judo Champion of Scotland and runner up in the Commonwealth. He and George taught the boys plenty. Being a boxer and quick on his feet, Billy took to judo like a duck to water. Norton wasn't quite as quick as Billy, but what he lacked in speed he more than made up for with strength and sheer tenacity. One thing Norton knew, as he watched the massive inbred getting to his feet, he was a lot faster than Gorgo.

'All right, Emmett, I'll fight you,' said Norton, having a quick look around him. There was a clearing amongst the chairs and tables, a bandaged face at a table to his left, another at a table behind him and the beard was to his right. The rest was a circle of drunken onlookers. 'But fuck going outside anywhere. We'll get into it right here, in front of all your mates. You game?'

Gorgo blinked at Les then around the crowd in the beer-garden. This suited him better still, his brother and all his mates behind him.

'Yeah. Let's go.'

The crowd moved back, Les exchanged a quick glance with Peregrine and stood facing Gorgo, hands open out in front of him and rocking slightly on the balls of his feet. The inbred shaped up awkwardly and let go with another cumbersome right haymaker. It was just as Norton expected, plenty of weight behind it and powerful enough to take your head off if it landed — even the breeze as it went past was strong enough to give you pneumonia. But it was that slow coming you could have knitted a pullover by the time it went past. Norton laughed to himself as he ducked under it. Now should come a big left. It did, and Norton easily slipped under that too. Gorgo bunched his fists and blinked at Les. His shoulder went back and he fired out another cumbersome straight right. This was the one Norton was waiting for. He took Gorgo's arm by the wrist, twisted it up as he stepped inside, turned and pulled it over his right shoulder, then gave it one good yank and bent over. Gravity and Gorgo's momentum did the rest, and twenty stone of inbred flew over Norton's shoulder in a simple shoulder throw.

There was a roar from the crowd as Gorgo slammed down onto a table of drunks, splintering it to matchwood. Glasses smashed and drinks went everywhere as his flailing arms and legs flattened four of the crowd and his right heel caught one of Les's opponents from Friday night across his bandaged head. He screamed with pain as the stitches were ripped out and blood started spurting down his face.

Through the beer, blood and confusion Gorgo hauled himself to his feet. He blinked at Les wondering what had happened; Les again rocked on his toes, evenly eyeing the big inbred.

This time, Gorgo threw a big left hook. It rattled past Norton's face like an express train, leaving him right in position for Gorgo's right. As it looped towards him Les blocked it with his left arm, stepped inside Gorgo again, wrapped his right arm around his waist and tucked his hip into his stomach. He pulled Gorgo's arm down, bending over at the same time, and got the startled inbred in an almost perfect hip throw. Les gave a little extra flick with his hip and let go of Gorgo's arm. Gorgo's legs flipped up over Les's head and he crashed down onto his brother's table, smashing it to pieces and flattening three or four drinkers, including black-shirt. His brother managed to duck out of the way, but a piece of table flew up and hit him in the mouth, knocking out a couple of teeth and ripping the wiring out of his jaw. He howled in agony and threw his hands up to his face trying to hold it all back together again.

Gorgo knocked several more people over and stood on their hands and heads as he rumbled to his feet again. His face was a twisted mask of confusion as he blinked at Norton standing in front of him, still rocking gently on his feet. Les almost felt sorry for him, but he had an idea what Gorgo's next move would be. He snatched a quick look behind him to make sure there was no broken glass on the ground and enough room; it would be a bit tight but he could do it.

Les was right. Gorgo gave a little snort of anger and charged at him like a wild bull. Les let him get to him then grabbed him firmly by the front of his T-shirt. He stepped back with him a pace before jumping up and planting his feet into Gorgo's chest then fell back, and as Gorgo came down with him, Les kicked out with his legs. It was a little clumsy, but effective enough for a stomach toss. Norton let go of the T-shirt and Gorgo barrelled through the crowd, smashing outdoor furniture and scattering the drinkers as if they were ten-pins.

By now the back of the hotel was starting to look as if a tornado had hit it. Gorgo may not have managed to hurt Les but he'd almost wrecked the beer garden and flattened at least fifteen drinkers. But the strain was starting to tell and it was a very tired, bruised and confused Gorgo who staggered to his feet to face Norton from about five metres away. I reckon one more ought to just about do it, thought Les, as Gorgo slowly lumbered towards him once again.

Gorgo blinked at Norton waiting in front of him, sized up where his head should be and threw out another looping right. It was even slower than the others. With all the time in the world Les stepped beneath it, grabbed him by the shoulder of his T-shirt and bent down, hooking his right arm under Gorgo's crutch, then taking the inbred's huge body over his shoulder, he straightened up as he pulled forward, and flipped him over his shoulder with a spinning wheel or fireman's throw. Gorgo gave a yell and crashed through another table landing on his back amongst the debris, his legs up against the barbecue pit. The fight should have ended there with Emmett winded but not too badly hurt. But a big, fat woman who had got up on a table for a better look, overbalanced as he sailed past and fell on her ample backside onto one of Emmett's legs. It broke behind the knee with a horrible crack that was heard all through the beer garden. This wasn't what Les intended and he felt sick in his stomach when he heard it.

Gorgo let out a howl of pain. He grabbed at his broken leg and started sobbing like a baby, tears streaming down his face.

'Jesus Christ!' cursed Norton. He quickly went over to Gorgo and cradled his massive head in his arm. 'You okay, Emmett?'

Gorgo howled and reached up pitifully for Les. 'Help me,' he sobbed. 'It hurts.'

Norton glared up at the crowd staring down at them. 'Well, don't just stand there like a bunch of fuckin' sheep,' he snarled. 'Give him a hand. He's broken his fuckin' leg.'

The fat woman took over as Les stood up. 'There, there, Emmett,' she said soothingly. 'Don't worry. You'll be all right.'

Norton took a last look down at Gorgo as Peregrine came up next to him. 'Come on,' he said. 'Let's get out of here.'

The crowd parted as they turned and walked through the smashed and overturned tables and broken glass towards the door. Standing in front of them ashen-faced was the publican.

'I remember you two, now,' he shouted. 'You're the ones that started all the trouble in here on Friday night. Get out — and don't ever come back. You're both barred.'

Norton gave him a quick once up and down and they went past. 'Suits me,' he said. 'It's a fuckin' shithouse anyway — and your beer's off.'

Peregrine gave the publican a quick once up and down too. 'I wholeheartedly agree,' he sniffed. 'Damn your impertinence! And you needn't worry, my good man. We've been thrown out of much better establishments than this.'

'I say,' said Peregrine, as they got onto the road out of town. 'I don't think I've ever seen anything quite like that. You almost wrecked the back of that hotel. There were bodies lying everywhere.'

'Yeah, terrific,' grunted Les.

'And as for that Gorgo, or whatever they called him, you

tossed him around like he was a bag of onions.' Peregrine shook his head. 'Where did you learn that? And then that fat woman fell on his leg. Poor Gorgo — he's gorgonzola now.'

'The poor bastard didn't really deserve that, Peregrine.'

'Well, maybe. But God, he was a giant.'

'And if you'd have kept your mouth shut, you dopey prick, nothing would have happened.'

'Oh come on now, Les. They were a bunch of twits. And I saw the look on your face when you had to apologise to that oaf with the beard.'

'Yeah, fair enough,' conceded Norton. 'But I still didn't like seeing that poor, simple goose get hurt like that.'

Peregrine smiled at Les in admiration. 'I don't know a great deal about you, Les. But you would have to be the best fighter I've ever come across. How would you like to come back to England with me for a while? I'll pay for everything, and give you a wage.'

'Peregrine,' replied Norton. 'How would you like to get well and truly fucked. You're bad news. Every time I go out with you, you get me into a fight. And now we're barred from the fuckin' pub. Christ! It's a good thing I bought all the piss before we went in.' Norton shook his head emphatically. 'No, that's fuckin' it, Peregrine. Get used to life on the farm, pal, 'cause we're not leaving it again until it's time for you to go back to England. And that's final.'

'What if you run out of Fourex?'

'That's different.'

'What about the dance on Saturday night?'

'Fuck the dance on Saturday night.'

They drove on in silence. But by the time they got to the front gates of Cedar Glen Norton had lightened up a little and had to agree with Peregrine that apart from Emmett breaking his leg it was a funny afternoon, especially the look on the publican's face. They got cleaned up and Les got the barbecue going. After a couple of cans of Fourex he was in a better frame of mind again. After a steak and half a bottle of Jacobs Creek he was laughing out loud.

'So what time did you tell those two witches you were coming out to settle for that horrible clobber?'

'About seven.'

'We might leave around six-thirty. I've got to ring Sydney and see if there's any messages. And let them know that you're all right. Hah! That's a fuckin' joke.'

Peregrine glanced at his watch. 'Well, we've plenty of time. It's not yet five o'clock.'

'Yeah. I might make some coffee.'

The bazaar had well and truly finished and Yurriki was as quiet as a cemetery when Les pulled up outside the town's one phone-box. He rattled the coins into the slot: this time Eddie was home.

'Les,' he said brightly. 'How's it going, mate?'

'Good, Eddie. Life in the country's not too bad at all.'

'How's His Royal Highness?'

'Safe as a bank. I think he's getting used to it, too. Any news from England?'

'No. Nothing yet,' lied Eddie. He figured what Les didn't know wouldn't hurt him. And there was no real point in upsetting Peregrine. With any luck this could still be over by the end of the week. He'd tell Les then no matter what. 'But I'll let you know as soon as there is.'

'Okay.'

'So what are you both doing?'

'Actually we're on our way out to a couple of sheilas' house.'

Les gave Eddie a bit of a rundown about Peregrine buying the clothes at the bazaar. He didn't mention the fight. They chatted for a while and then Les hung up, saying he'd ring again on Wednesday.

'Still no news from England, Peregrine,' he said, getting back into the car.

'That's understandable. There probably won't be any until Lewis gets it all sorted out.'

'Probably. Anyway, next stop Stokers Siding. We'll get that rattle sorted out then get back home. I wouldn't mind getting pissed tonight.'

They didn't have to drive as far as Stokers Siding; the instructions Coco had given Peregrine were to drive about fifteen kilometres out of Yurriki, cross two little bridges next to each other and two kilometres past them, opposite the saw-mill, there was a red house on the right. Les couldn't miss their house, not even at night: it was a brilliant, boiling red with a red roof. Built high up off the road, it was like one of those old wooden, Federation houses you still see in parts of Sydney, but with a lot more character. A vine and pot plant covered verandah surrounded the old house, there was a white picket fence at the front and what appeared to be cow sheds at the side. Les went up a steep driveway and parked behind an old green Kombi covered in mainly environmental stickers. A small set of steps ran up to the front door, which was open with the fly-screen shut. Peregrine gave it a quick 'shave and a haircut, two bits'.

Coco came to the door wearing a smile and a dark blue tracksuit. 'Hello,' she said. 'You found the place all right?'

'No trouble at all.'

'Come on in.'

She creaked open the fly-screen and they followed her down a threadbare, brown-carpeted hallway. Inside it was a typical old country house: wood panelling, high ceilings, brass light switches and floorboards that creaked under your feet. Marita was in a nicely appointed kitchen wearing a mustard coloured tracksuit like Coco's.

'Hello,' she said pleasantly.

There were more greetings and smiles all round. Peregrine handed Marita two bottles of Great Western which she put in the fridge. They exchanged pleasantries while the girls made them coffee. Then Coco asked Peregrine if he'd like to come out to the cutting room and see what he'd purchased.

The old cow sheds Norton had seen from the road turned out to be their work room. Marita hit a switch near the door and about half a dozen fluorescent lights suspended over two long cutting tables lit up the room. Sitting on the table, neatly folded next to two large packing cases was what Peregrine was getting for his four thousand dollars.

'Well, there it all is,' said Marita. 'You want to have another look at it?'

'If you wouldn't mind,' replied Peregrine. He had a bit of a browse through the weird array of dresses, tops and tights. 'Excellent,' he smiled. 'Excellent. Now here's what I'd like you to do.'

Peregrine took a piece of cardboard and a texta colour and wrote down the address of Stephanie's boutique in The Kings Road. He gave Marita the remaining two thousand dollars plus another thousand which would be more than enough to ship the clothing to England. He said not to worry about a receipt. He gave the girls his business card and told them they could rob him if they wished, but if they did the right thing and the dresses sold they could both be on a nice little earner for years to come. From the surprised, slightly hurt looks on the girls faces when Peregrine spoke about robbing him Les didn't think there was much chance of that.

'So, that's about it, ladies,' smiled Peregrine. 'I think you'll agree that's a reasonably fair way to do business?'

'I couldn't agree with you more,' replied Marita, blinking at the wad of money in her hand.

'Now what do you say to a glass of champers to cement the deal? Then my associate and myself will be on our way.'

'Okay, fine.'

Marita switched off the lights and they followed the girls back into the lounge room. While Coco was getting the champagne Les settled back on an old blue Chesterfield and had a bit of a look around. There was the usual women's bric-a-brac on the walls and sideboards plus a Picasso and a couple of Monet prints. A TV and a fairly modern stereo sat against one wall and in a corner an old lampstand threw muted light over a poster of Mae West. Coco returned with the champagne and four glasses, poured them all a drink and there was a quick 'cheers' all round.

It turned out the girls had lived in the Tweed Valley for seven years and owned the house which was once an old dairy. They originally came from Narooma on the South Coast, but had worked in Sydney for a while before moving north. At the mention of the words 'work in Sydney' Coco and Marita seemed to exchange fleeting smiles of amusement. They each had five-year-old daughters who were presently with their fathers and grandparents in Byron Bay. But that was another story. They hated city life and found the Yurriki area one of the last places left with a village atmosphere that the politicians and the Alan Bonds of the world hadn't yet managed to stuff up. Mata Hari's Waterbed was ticking over slowly, especially now thanks to Peregrine, and here they would remain until they were old and grey.

'I can't say I blame you,' said Peregrine. 'It's certainly a delightful area around here.'

'It sure is,' nodded Marita.

'Gee, this champagne's nice, Peregrine,' said Coco, draining the last of her glass. 'Okay if I open that other bottle?'

'Of course. That's what I brought it for.'

While Coco was in the kitchen, Marita reached towards a small, carved wooden box sitting on an old coffee table in front of her.

'You guys fancy a smoke?' she asked.

'What . . . pot?' said Norton.

'Yeah.'

'Sure. What about you Peregrine? You have a smoke, do you?'

'Well . . . I've had a bit of hash in London now and again.'

'Wait till you try this,' said Marita. 'This is our own Yurriki yippee grass. This'll really clear your woofers and your tweeters.'

Les and Peregrine watched intently as Marita pulled some very dark, very sticky looking marijuana from a plastic bag, mulled it with a little tobacco and began rolling a couple of joints.

'Could you sell us some of that?' asked Les. Drinking Fourex back at the farm was pretty good, but a little number at the same time would make it heaps better.

'I'll give you some.'

'No, I'll pay you. In fact, can we buy a bag somewhere? We're gonna be here for another week.'

'Puff's pretty hard to get now, Les.'

'Up here? You're kidding.'

'I wish I was. They used to grow a bit up here once. But it's too hard now. They've got helicopters going over every day. Pricks riding 'round on trail bikes. You've only got to have a Save The Rainforests sticker on your window and they pull you over and search your car.'

'Shit!'

'Are we talking about our heroes in the drug offensive, are we?' asked Coco, walking back into the lounge room.

'Yeah,' laughed Marita. 'I was just telling Les what it's like up here.'

Coco refilled their glasses. 'You guys have got to see it to believe it. There's squads of these idiots running around in full combat gear. Fatigues, boots, flak jackets, peaked caps. Armed with machine guns, shotguns, pistols, Christ only knows what, trying to bust a few hippies with a bit of pot. They must spend half their lives watching Sylvester Stallone movies on TV.'

'What about that day out at Raewyn's, Coco? This friend of ours has got an eight-year-old daughter and a fifteen-year-old mentally retarded son. Fifteen cops in combat gear hit her house one day. Kicked her door in, poked loaded guns in their faces. Nearly frightened poor Matthew to death. Half-wrecked her house, and got nothing. Fifteen would-be Rambos.'

'They're idiots running around with guns,' said Coco. 'They raided some people's farm we know near Nimbin. Couldn't find anything so they shot up the house and machine-gunned their water tank. This is after some other idiot's gone about two feet over the house in a helicopter and killed all their Angora goats. But these people were a bit smart. They sued the police department and finished up with half a million dollars. It took a while, but they got it.'

Even Peregrine had to laugh at this. 'What about that cop that gets on TV?' said Norton. 'He looks like a director of some bush RSL. I think he's a superintendent. He reckons they're growing pot up here to finance heroin deals.'

The girls both shook their heads in disbelief. 'If you want to see some millionaire heroin dealers,' said Marita, 'come to the dance this Saturday night. You won't find a car there worth more than five hundred dollars. If a pickpocket went through the place all he'd get would be exercise. Heroin dealers! I don't believe it.'

'There used to be a heroin dealer in Yurriki,' said Coco seriously. 'They burnt his car twice. Then told him to piss off or the next time they'd burn him in it.'

'It's all politics and corruption, Les,' said Marita. 'Come down hard on anyone with a bit of pot so they look like they're doing something while there's tons of rotten heroin and cocaine out on the streets.'

'Yeah. Haven't you seen the T-shirts?' said Coco. '*Support your local MP — Buy a gram of heroin today*. That's one you should take back to England with you, Peregrine.'

'Yes I'll get one for Uncle Henry. He could wear it into the House of Lords. I'm sure they'd be impressed.'

'So we figure if they're going to give free Methadone and syringes to smack freaks, we can grow a couple of plants down by the saw-mill. Anyway,' Marita gave the boys a wink, 'these are ready.'

Marita lit one of the joints and handed it to Les who nodded for Coco to go first. She took a toke, so did Les then it went on to Peregrine. Sure tastes all right, thought Norton, almost sweet. Not at all hard to smoke. It had been a while since Les had had a smoke and by the time the first joint was finished he'd begun to mellow out a bit. Peregrine eased back in his chair, a little glassy-eyed and blinked. Marita lit joint number two. It finished about the same time as half of the second bottle of Great Western and by now Norton was beginning to feel very mellow indeed. He too eased back further in his chair and a big, cheesy grin spread over his face. Marita and Coco were smiling back at him from the lounge. Peregrine was beginning to chuckle to himself.

'Get a buzz out of that, did you, Les?' asked Marita.

'Reckon,' replied Norton.

'What about you, Peregrine?'

191

'My word. It's quite exceptional.'

'Quite exceptional,' laughed Coco. 'I like that.'

Coco turned the stereo on very softly. It sounded like a local radio station; some country and western song. Whatever it was it certainly sounded all right.

'So, this is life out in the Australian countryside, eh, Coco?' said Peregrine.

'Yep. Out with the flowers and the animals. It's slow and it's corny, but it beats the hell out of a home unit in the city.'

'I could imagine.'

'What do you do in England besides sell clothes?' asked Marita.

'I . . . own property. I get an income from that. Which is why I'm out here. I . . . may invest in some more.'

'Oh. What about you, Les? What do you do?'

'I work up the Cross.'

'The Cross!' chorused the girls. They looked at each other then burst into laughter.

'Yeah. At a casino. I work on the door.'

Coco and Marita's laughter subsided and they sat smiling at the boys. It was starting to come together what they were. Peregrine, articulate and sophisticated with scads of money to throw around, the big bloke who kept in the background, polite but menacing. He was obviously taking care of the Englishman while he was out here buying land or whatever else it was he was up to. It was for sure they weren't dealers or anything to do with the police.

'We used to work up the Cross,' giggled Coco.

'Yeah?'

'Yes. When we first came to Sydney. We were flat motherless broke. We worked at a place called The Golden Delicious.'

'The Golden Delicious?' Norton thought for a moment then grinned. 'Hey, I've heard of that.'

'Yes,' laughed Marita. 'The House of Domination and Bondage. Just off William Street.'

'House of Domination and Bondage.' Peregrine blinked slowly. 'Good Lord, Marita. What ever did you do there?'

'Get dressed up in school uniforms, then tie up old judges and barristers and rich stockbrokers and whip the shit out of the stupid old bastards.'

Coco and Marita went into a fit of the giggles which cracked Les and Peregrine up as well, causing Peregrine to spill champagne all down the front of his trousers.

'My God,' he spluttered. 'I don't believe it.'

'That's what some of these stupid old pricks used to say too, when we'd finished with them,' laughed Marita.

Norton was starting to blink a little himself now. 'How long did you work there?' he asked.

'About six months.'

'What? Did you just get sick of it?'

'Sort of,' replied Coco.

'Yeah. Not being addicts we made a fair bit of money,' said Marita, 'which is how we bought this place.' She and Coco exchanged a quick laugh. 'But it was being too good at our job that brought us undone. Me anyway.'

'How do you mean?'

'Well, Les. You see . . . our specialty was blow jobs.'

'That sounds all right,' said Norton.

'Ohh, don't worry,' said Coco. 'We were the best in the business. Those old dills, and plenty of young ones too, used to come from miles around to get us to knock the top off it.'

'We gave the best polishes in Sydney,' winked Marita.

'Would these hot lips lie?' Coco winked and pursed her lips at Peregrine.

'So what happened?' asked Les.

'Well,' said Marita. 'I did a little job on the outside. I met this politician at a hotel near The Quay. It turned out he wasn't a bad old bloke. So I really gave him his two hundred and fifty dollars worth. I worked him over; I drained him, man. I gave the old bugger head like he'd never had before. Anyway, it must have been too much for him. 'Cause just as the old bastard was about to get his rocks off, he had a heart attack and turned his toes up. I bloody near shit myself.'

Norton and Peregrine both roared laughing again. Then something dawned on Les. 'I remember seeing something about that in the papers. That wasn't . . .?'

'Yeah, bloody oath. That's who it was.'

'His dick wasn't the only thing you left stiff in the room, was it love?' laughed Coco.

'Too right. They reckon it took them an hour to pull the bed sheets out of his arse. Anyway, I just left him there and split. But being a bigwig the papers got hold of it. Then the cops started investigating. We were both getting sick of the whole bloody scene, so we got out of town before they figured out who it was and I either had an accident or they found something to charge me with.'

'Could they charge you with murder by blow job?' queried Peregrine.

'Dunno.' Marita shook her head. 'But they'd probably try.'

'How about wilful desuction,' giggled Coco.

'They definitely would have got you for being an accessory after the fat,' roared Norton.

'I disagree,' chortled Peregrine. 'The evidence would never have stood up in court.'

Stoned and with a couple of champagnes under their belts Les and Peregrine started rolling around on their chairs, roaring like tigers. Norton couldn't ever remember laughing so much — there was no doubt it was a bloody good smoke the girls had. Marita and Coco weren't far behind them. It was a ripper of a story and one the girls obviously didn't tell too many people, not around Stokers Siding anyway. They probably liked to get it off their chests. But even without the pot or the champagne it was still turning out to be a very funny evening.

Norton regained his composure and through the mellow, peaceful haze of the marijuana noticed the girls grinning at them as if they had something on their minds. Or maybe they had thought of something else that was amusing.

'I'll tell you what,' said Coco. 'Seeing as you're not bad blokes, how would you like one for the road yourselves?'

'What . . .?' blinked Norton, still stoned off his head.

'A blow job,' smiled Marita. 'How would you like one on the house? No screwing. Just a nice polish.'

'Well . . . okay. Why not?'

'What about you Peregrine?' grinned Coco. 'It's the least we can do. You shouted us champagne. Bought all our clothes. Paid us cash. You want one too?'

Peregrine blinked as if he didn't quite believe it. 'I . . . I mean, well, yes. Why . . . not?'

'Okay. Come on.'

Coco took Peregrine and led him to a bedroom down the hallway. Marita motioned to Les. When he climbed to his feet and rocked a little, he again realised just how good the girls' pot was.

'This way,' she grinned.

Norton followed her to a bedroom a little closer. It was softly lit by a small table lamp next to a double bed with a mosquito net folded over the top. Norton could make out some posters and small paintings on the walls and above the bed were two fairly large speakers.

'Get on the bed and take your jeans off,' said Marita. 'I'll be back in a second.'

Norton did exactly that. Then as he lay there with the pillows under his head he began to wonder what was going on. Were these two women for real? Were they murderers? Maybe they were going to castrate him and Peregrine. Weird thoughts and colours and ideas were swirling through his mind. Marita materialised back into the room and removed her tracksuit. She had a solid, full-breasted figure and watching her in her white knickers and bra Norton couldn't help but feel a stirring in his loins. She sat on the bed next to him, bent down and gave him the lightest tongue kiss. As she did Les heard the speakers above his head scratch into life.

'Just relax,' she said softly, and ran her hand down to his loins.

Norton eased back onto the pillows and began thinking this wasn't too bad after all no matter what. These pillows were definitely the softest he'd ever felt and the bed had to be the most comfortable he'd ever been on. Smiling at him in her knickers and bra Marita was starting to look like Miss Universe. Norton couldn't ever remember feeling better or more relaxed in his life. Suddenly the speakers above his head roared into life and a haunting melodic voice filled the room.

'When I was back there in seminary school, there was a person there who put forth the proposition that you can petition the Lord with prayer.'

'Jesus Christ!' Norton jerked his head up from the pillows. 'What the bloody hell was that?'

'Relax,' said Marita. 'It's only the record.'

Norton settled down and the voice went on.

'Petition the lord with prayer. Petition the Lord with prayer.' There was a pause for a few seconds then the voice seemed to scream from every corner of the room. *'YOU CANNOT PETITION THE LORD WITH PRAYER!'*

'Bloody hell,' said Norton again. 'What's going on?'

'Relax,' said Marita. 'It's just a record. That's all.'

Les settled back into the pillows once more and the sounds of a beautiful harpsichord playing filled the room, accompanying that same haunting, lilting voice.

'Can you give me sanctuary? I must find a place to hide. A place for me to hide.'

The music was wonderful, the voice rich and resonant. Who could possibly sing like that? Norton was trying to concentrate on the music as Marita's gentle hand stroked him softly. Before long the swelling in his loins was a howling, pumping erection.

'Ooh!' he heard her say. 'That is a hard one, isn't it?'

The harpsichord and the voice went on. Les was lost in

a dream of colours and sound. It was fantastic. Marita continued to stroke him. The harpsichord paused and the music switched to a bouncing, heavy bass line of fast, trembling guitar and rattling maracas. At that precise moment Marita's mouth found him.

A shudder convulsed Norton's body. Never had he experienced anything as good as this. Marita's mouth was pure ecstasy. She drew on him as he writhed gently on the bed. New sensations. Weird music. Even weirder lyrics.

'Peppermint mini-skirts. Chocolate candy. Champion sax and a girl named Sandy.'

What the fuck is happening to me? thought Les. Marita went on. Her wild, hot tongue flicked up and down and across his dick and balls. She was teasing Les into a frenzy with her tongue. Then the music changed again to light jazz on an electric piano; the drummer had switched to a brush. Marita was driving him mad with her tongue. The words got crazier.

'Catacombs. Nursery bones. Winter women growing stones. Carrying babies to the river.'

Norton writhed on the bed and ran his tongue across his lips. Shit! What's happening?

'Streets and shoes. Avenues. Leather riders selling news.'

Norton's mind was racing. Marita had him that horny he didn't know which way was up; she was driving him insane. He couldn't last any longer. He wanted to roll her over, rip her underwear off and drive himself into her. He was seriously thinking of doing that when the voice called out.

'The monk bought lunch.' A laughing voice answered. *'He bought a little...?'* The voice replied. *'Yes he did.'*

The easy, skipping jazz abruptly changed into a pounding conga beat with a screaming electric organ and pumping bass riff. The strange, haunting voice called out again.

'This is the best part of the trip. This is the trip... The best part... I really like.'

At that instant Marita dived and her mouth seemed to take all of Les. The congas thumped and Marita went to work, her head going up and down. She drew harder and harder. Her tongue slithered. Her teeth nibbled gently. Norton now knew he was going to go insane. He clawed at the pillows behind his head, writhed around on the bed and screwed his face up with pain as Marita tortured him so exquisitely.

'Successful hills are here to stay. Everything must be this way. Gentle street where people play. Welcome to the soft parade.'

Norton moaned and groaned as stars exploded in his head. Rainbows tumbled and crashed into each other. Suns rose and set. Marita drew on. Then Norton could feel the itch starting to go through his whole body — Marita's mouth was the only thing in the entire world that could scratch it. His head thrashed from side to side. What was she doing to him? Voices filled the room.

'The lights are getting brighter . . . The radio is moaning . . . Calling to the dogs.'

Ohh Jesus. Norton's whole body stiffened. He knew it wouldn't be long now.

'There are still a few animals, left out in the yard. But it's getting harder . . . To describe . . . Sailors . . . To the underfed.'

What the fuck? The words were just a blur now coming from everywhere, the music a pounding barrage of strange, beautiful sounds. Norton could feel the torrent welling up in him. Marita was going for it, she had magic in her tongue and she wasn't stopping; no wonder that old politician kicked the bucket. Norton prayed his heart would hold out too. Then it started and it felt like every drop of blood was being sucked out of his body. Norton arched his back and held the pillows, he wanted to scream but forced his face into the pillows, and as tears trickled from the corners of his eyes, he literally exploded into Marita's mouth. The last thing he remembered before flopping back on the bed like a burst water bag was the voice as the song started to fade.

'When all else fails, we can whip the horses' eyes. And make them sleep. And cry.'

The music stopped. There was a deafening silence. Then a very upper class British howl came from down the hallway.

'Aaaarrrggghheeoowwoerarrgh-ow-ow-aaaahhhherrggh!!!'

MARITA AND COCO led Les and Peregrine down the front steps to the station wagon as though they were two patients coming out of a surgery after a heavy valium sedation. Thanks for calling out fellahs, and thanks for the champagne. After they had freighted Peregrine's clothing away to England first thing tomorrow they were off to Byron Bay to pick up the kids and have a bit of a celebration, they probably wouldn't be back till the end of the week. But they'd see them at the dance on Saturday night. You know how to get home from here? Of course you do. Goodbye, Peregrine. Goodbye, Les.

197

Still stoned off his face and a completely shot bird, Norton backed the car down the driveway, stopped and turned to Peregrine.

'Do you know where the fuck we are?'

Peregrine was in an even sorrier state than Les. 'I wouldn't have a clue,' he blinked. 'Australia?'

'I think we go to the right.'

'You sure?'

'No. But we can always turn around and come back. We got plenty of petrol.'

'Whatever. You're driving.'

They drove slowly up the road. Eventually they came to the two little bridges and the saw-mill.

'Yeah. We're right now,' said Les.

They drove along the deserted country road with nothing around them but the trees, the quiet and a brilliant canopy of stars above. After what seemed like ages, Les spoke.

'Well, Peregrine, old mate, what did you think of that?'

The Englishman shook his head. 'I don't know what to think, Les. I've never experienced anything quite like that. That Coco . . .'

'If she was just half as good as Marita, she'd still be a sensation. I am absolutely rooted.'

'I feel like I've been hit by a bus.'

They travelled on a bit further; creaking down the road at around fifteen kilometres an hour. Two small grey wallabies bounded in front of them then stopped at the side of the road blinking at the headlights going past.

'You know, Peregrine,' said Norton. 'They weren't a couple of bad sorts, those two girls.'

'Yes, I agree with you. They were both quite attractive.'

'In fact if they took off a little weight, I reckon they'd both be an eleven.'

'An eleven? What's an eleven, Les?'

'A ten that swallows.'

MONDAY MORNING AGAIN dawned bright and clear: Les was up around seven. He didn't remember much about getting to bed. The drive home seemed to take forever, they had one drink then flopped around like two old molls for an hour gutsing themselves on Promite sandwiches before collapsing into bed to sleep and dream.

Peregrine was wide awake when Les went up for a cup of

coffee and without much trouble he was able to get him out of bed for a brisk walk around the property and a few exercises; Peregrine even seemed to enjoy it, asking Norton to show him some of those fighting tricks he knew. Les showed him a couple then suggested he stick to head butting. But even in the brief week the young Englishman had been in Australia Les thought he could notice a definite change in Peregrine. His skin had tanned up noticeably, he looked a little harder and Norton's barbecued steaks seemed to be putting on weight in the right places. Peregrine was an intelligent, educated man, there was no doubting that, but now he seemed to be showing a definite maturity as well. Watching him ripping into his bacon and eggs at breakfast, Norton decided he liked young Sir Peregrine Normanhurst III. Les would even go so far as to give Peregrine the ultimate accolade an Australian can give an Englishman: not a bad bloke — for a pom.

They took their time over breakfast then gathered up some books and fruit, and with a banana-chair each, headed for the large billabong. Norton's two banana-chairs turned out to be a very good investment indeed. They spent the day reading, swimming, getting tanned up, and just plain relaxing. It beat the hell out of a day behind a lathe in some factory or the night shift down an asbestos mine.

Around two-thirty Les started getting the barbecue together and they both started to get drunk. Before they knew it they'd eaten, drunk and laughed their way though a stack of food and drink, it was almost seven and they were both on the nod.

'I don't believe this,' said Norton, yawning, stretching and shaking his head. 'But I'm just about ready for bed.'

'I know just how you feel,' replied Peregrine, returning Norton's yawn. 'A bit of a read for a while and I'll be out like a light. But there is one thing I'm going to do before I go to bed tonight.'

'What's that?'

'I'm going down to feed Bunter.'

Norton gave a laugh. 'I'll come with you.'

Peregrine gathered up some scraps of meat then he and Les walked around to the first gate with their drinks. It took them a while but they eventually found Bunter sitting on the branch of a pine tree watching them intently. This time he had two other owls with him.

'Hello,' said Les. 'He's brought a couple of mates with him.'

Peregrine studied the group of owls for a moment. 'Yes.

I'd say that was Harry Wharton and Hurree Jamset Ram Singh,' laughed Peregrine.

'Who?'

'A couple of his chums from the Greyfriars Reserve, Les, you unparalelled brigand.'

'Whatever.'

Peregrine spread the scraps of meat down and they stood back. The fat, brown owls watched them intently for a few moments with their wide, almost humorous orange eyes then, sensing Les and Peregrine meant them no harm, they swooped down, picked up the scraps and returned to their tree.

'Typical Bunter,' said Peregrine. 'Snooped the tuck and didn't even say gratters. Wait till Mr Squelch hears of this.'

'I might put some fruit out tomorrow night,' said Les, 'and see if I can get a few possums around. You ever seen possums, Peregrine?'

'No. Can't say that I have.'

'They're funny little bastards. Shit everywhere. But they make you laugh.'

They watched the owls for a while then Norton started yawning again.

'Jesus! I can't believe how tired I am. It must be this country air. It couldn't possibly be the piss.'

TUESDAY MORNING WAS pretty much the same as Monday, sunny and warm with the odd cloud being pushed through by a light sou'wester. Les was up at six. Peregrine was still asleep when Norton quietly made a cup of coffee so he decided to go for a run. He put on his Brooks and shorts, did a few stretches then loped off.

He jogged to the front gate, turned right and headed along the dirt road for about three kilometres then turned back. The undulating road ran next to a little stream full of birds calling to each other in the crisp, dawn light. A few farmhouses were built in off the road and now and again the sound of a dog barking would echo in the distance. He sprinted from the front gate back to the house, did a hundred sit-ups and push-ups and thought that might do it. Peregrine was sipping coffee when Les walked into the kitchen for a glass of cold water. 'Where have you been?' he asked, seeing Les in his shorts and running shoes, dripping with sweat.

'I was up early so I decided to go for a run.'

'Oh.' Peregrine sounded disappointed. 'Then you won't want to go for a walk this morning?'

'I'll still go for a walk with you. Come on. Get your boots on and I'll see you downstairs.'

'Oh, jolly good. And when we get back I'll cook breakfast.'

'Eggs Benedictine?'

'Don't know about that. But I can scramble them — I think.'

Norton climbed out of his shorts and into his fatigues and they had a brisk walk around the property. Peregrine was striding out now, really enjoying his early morning exercise. He also appeared to be taking an interest in things too, asking Les the names of all kinds of birds as well as a few plants and trees. When they got back to the house, Peregrine was true to his word and cooked breakfast. With a little supervision from Les he managed to make enough bacon and scrambled eggs with shallots for two, and enough mess in the kitchen for twenty.

'Well, how is it?' asked Peregrine, feeling quite proud of himself.

'Not too bad,' replied Les, ripping into it. 'You did good.' After two hours of exercise Norton would have eaten a greyhound and chased the mechanical hare. His eyes drifted across to the pile of mess in the kitchen. 'But I might do it tomorrow. Give you a break.'

'Whatever.' Peregrine stabbed at another piece of bacon. 'I'd quite like to go down to that smaller billabong today. The one in the corner near the duck shed. What do you say?'

'Righto,' shrugged Norton. 'Be a bit of a change, I s'pose. What I might do though, seeing as I'm doing the cleaning, is to give the whole place a bit of a sweep and that. So I'll see you down there.'

'Good show.'

They finished breakfast. Peregrine got his book and a banana-chair and headed for the billabong. Les got the detergent and a pot-scourer and headed for the kitchen. After finally finishing the dishes he got a broom and swept out the top half of the house. It was amazing just how much dust and grit the polished wooden floors gathered and it took him some time. The barbecue area was in need of a good clean too; there were grease stains and shit everywhere. But it wasn't too unpleasant a task out in the open with the radio going and the birds bobbing around on the grass. S'pose I may as well do my room too, he thought, while I'm on the job.

He cleaned out the shower and remembered that if he wanted to have that Radox bath he'd have to take a trip into Murwillumbah; there was no chemist in Yurriki. He flicked the broom across the floor and through the built-in-wardrobes. He pulled the bed out and got the broom in against the maple and cedar panelled walls. A movement under the bed caught his eye.

'Hello,' said Norton. 'A rotten fuckin' cockroach. The bastard must've followed me up from Bondi.'

Swinging the broom like a golf club, Norton whacked the bug up against the wall that he'd just pulled the bed away from. Stunned, it lay on its back, legs and feelers going everywhere.

'Now. One right in the ribs cocky, from old Uncle Les.'

Norton swung his foot back and kicked the cockroach against the wall. The cockroach crunched, there was a loud click and about a square metre of maple and cedar panelling swung in and up from the floor a couple of inches. 'What the . . .?'

Les swept the cockroach aside and knelt down for a better look. It was obviously a hiding place with a secret panel. Under closer inspection he found one of the knots in the wood had an indentation in it big enough to fit your finger, though if you didn't know it was there you'd be flat out to notice it. Les hooked his finger in and pushed. Once opened, the panel swung in quite easily but obviously you had to give it a decent thump to get it open. There was something inside. Les reached in and pulled out two Manilla envelopes and an oil painting. He looked to see if there was anything else. There wasn't, so he placed them on the bed.

The painting was about two feet by three feet, a head and shoulders portrait of an old Chinaman or an Asian. It was a brilliant portrait but at the same time done in great swirls of intense colours; reds, greens, orange, purple, yellow, yet not so bright or garish as to distract the viewer from the subject. A closer look showed the artist had even painted in a reflection of the subject in a kind of shadow. Norton was no art buff and this particular painting wasn't the kind he'd wish to hang on his wall, but he could tell just by looking, that whoever the artist was he certainly had a unique talent. In one corner were the artist's initials ENT. Les turned it over and on the back was another old painting indistinguishable because it had been painted over. In one of the other corners Les could faintly make out the name Reid. He gave it another once-over, shrugged and placed it on the bed.

He gave the smaller of the two Manilla envelopes a shake, opened it and tipped the contents onto the bed next to the painting. It contained four medals. On two the ribbon was yellow with three red stripes in the middle. Both medals were silver, one had an elephant on it, the other was embossed with what looked like the head of an old emperor in a funny kind of headdress. Both said 'For Bravery. Republic of South Vietnam'. The ribbon on the other two was red, white and blue. The medals were simply inscribed with Asian writing which appeared to be Japanese, but in the middle was R.O.K. R.O.K.? Norton snapped his fingers. Republic of Korea. Norton gave the envelope another shake and out fluttered a receipt. *Outback Bill's Second Hand Shop, Murwillumbah. One painting of Chinaman. $30:00.*

'Well, what do you know,' smiled Norton. 'I've got four medals for bravery and a painting of a dingbat. Heh heh! Not hard to tell who they belonged to.'

The remaining envelope was sealed; Norton slit it open with his finger. All it contained was several sheets of foolscap paper: photocopies of two interviews. One was with *Playboy* magazine, the other with some TV station in America. The person being interviewed was Daniel J. Harcourt, US Army.

'Holy bloody shit!' said Norton, and sat down on the bed. 'This is that bloody colonel.'

The *Playboy* interview was headed: *Daniel J. Harcourt, America's most decorated war hero tells why he quit the military and became a peacenik in New South Wales.* At the bottom of the page were three head shots of an average-looking, fair-haired man in his forties or fifties. Full-faced and expressive but with a noticeable twinkle of humour in his eyes. The sort of easygoing face you would see in TV commercials having a drink with the boys or driving a Holden utility.

Bugger the cleaning, thought Les. He closed the wall panel and pushed the bed back up against it, then went upstairs to read the two interviews over a cup of coffee.

The *Playboy* interview was laid-back and chatty but Norton could hardly believe some of the things he was reading about Harcourt. He'd been awarded 110 medals. Personally killed almost 10,000 men. One battalion he commanded in Vietnam killed 2,600 Vietcong and suffered only twenty-five losses. In one particular action in Korea, although shot in the head, Harcourt refused to leave the battlefield, charged five machine gun nests, killed 100 Chinese single-handed, rallied his troops and turned probable defeat into victory. He led his men into battle on crutches or with his arm in plaster or his leg wired up. He was totally devoted to his men; soldiers fought to be under his command, knowing their chances of survival with Harcourt were eminently better than under any West Point career officer who went by the book. He adopted guerrilla tactics and took on the VC at their own game. He wrote manuals on guerrilla warfare, designed weapons and equipment. He was the complete patriot, swearing allegiance to his country right or wrong. Then the same man did an about face in the middle of the Vietnam War, went public on TV and said the US military was run by a bunch of martini-drinking morons and the CIA was no more than an organisation of crooks out to subvert the world. He told Westmoreland and Haig to stick their war in their arse and their best officer resigned his commission.

The US military tried unsuccessfully to disgrace him, but when he got wind of a CIA plot for him to have an 'accident' or be 'terminated with extreme prejudice' he migrated to Australia in the early seventies. There was much more to the article than that. Talks of megaton overkill. How the character Kurtz in *Apocalypse Now* was based on him to a certain extent. His reference to war as 'an insane garbage disposal unit that churns out little white crosses'. Norton didn't stop till he came to the end then made a second cup of coffee and turned to the next article.

The other interview was a lot tighter. Harcourt had flown back to America and it was between himself, a small TV station in Montana and the editor of a US survivalist magazine called *Civilian Commando*. Harcourt was asked about his experiences in Korea and Vietnam and various questions on post nuclear survival and guerrilla tactics. But the interview boiled down to Harcourt saying he was convinced an atomic war was inevitable and he had found the safest place on earth somewhere in Australia. 'I have constructed a fully self-sufficient stockade in a valley,' he is quoted as saying. 'It is impregnable from the rear and sides. The only open space is to the west. But I have a defence perimeter and fields of fire from the house to the road. I will shoot them as they come down the road or try to cross my creek. I cannot be taken there. I will survive.'

'Well, I'll be fucked.' Norton took a sip of coffee and found that it was now cold. Then as he put the cup down the whole thing started to come together. Cedar Glen wasn't just a duck farm and a country house. It was a modern day survivalist fortress. You could tell from the way it was built, sunk into the ground almost like a bunker. The solid wooden foundations, the huge logs for beams and supports, the extra thick walls. The odd windows. The vegetable and fruit patches. Even the way the little billabong at the front was concreted so you could run a generator off it. And the view across the paddocks. Fields of fire. Defence perimeters. That pit down by the far billabong: pig's arse it was for tigers. That was a bloody mantrap. The strange circle of wooden beams up from the duck sheds, was a machine gun post or an artillery bunker. Harcourt was convinced there was going to be a nuclear holocaust and he was probably seeing people in black pyjamas carrying AK-47s in his sleep. And if an atomic war did break out it would be survival of the fittest. There'd be a complete breakdown of law and order. And what did Harcourt say? 'They will not take me here. I will survive.' Colonel Daniel J. Harcourt was the supreme survivalist.

Norton looked at the expressive face smiling at him from the bottom of the *Playboy* interview. Harcourt, he mused, you're either as nutty as a fruitcake, or one of the smartest men who ever walked on this earth. He drummed his fingers on the table and looked around at the solidly built interior of the house. I'd say it would have to be the latter.

Peregrine was laying back in his banana-chair on the little island in the billabong with his shirt off engrossed in his book about Peter Sellers when he heard Les approaching.

'Hello, old sausage,' he said, as Norton splashed across to him. 'How goes it?'

'Good, mate. Got all the housework done.' Norton opened his banana-chair and spread a towel over it. 'Jesus, it's nice here, isn't it.'

'Absolutely beautiful.'

When he was settled, Les handed Peregrine the two articles from his overnight bag. 'Have a look at these. This is the bloke who built this joint.'

Peregrine looked at the photocopies. 'Where did you get these?' he asked.

'In an old cupboard in my room.'

'I say.'

'It makes interesting reading, I can tell you.'

'I'm sure it would. So this is the American fellow who built the property?'

Norton nodded. 'I also found a painting and some medals as well.'

'A painting?' said Peregrine absently.

'Yeah — *Portrait of a Chinaman,* by Eric Norman Toejam.'

'Who?'

'Dunno really,' chuckled Les. 'But those were the initials in the corner.'

'Mmhh.' Peregrine continued to study the photocopies. 'I might read these now.'

'Go for your life. I'll get into a bit more of this Bukowski bloke.'

Peregrine put his book away and began flicking avidly through the pages. Norton was well into tales of sex, drugs and degradation in Los Angeles and laughing away when Peregrine spoke again.

'Well, I'll be blowed,' he heard the Englishman say.

'What was that?'

'This Colonel Harcourt. He's the most amazing fellow.'

'He was certainly different all right,' agreed Norton.

'He was absolutely convinced there was going to be an atomic war.'

'Yep. And this was the place he was going to fall back to.'

'Absolutely astonishing.'

'It all makes sense now, doesn't it? The way the place is built, those holes in the ground and that.'

'In a macabre sense — yes.'

'And what about his war record?'

'A hundred and ten medals. Almost unbelievable.'

'So just think, Pezz. If war breaks out in Europe while you're away, you're sweet here.'

'Oh my God! Don't even mention it. Imagine being stuck out here with you for the rest of my life!'

'Yeah. And nothing to drink either. We're both barred from the local pub.'

Peregrine flicked through the pages again. 'I wonder what on earth happened to him?'

'Dunno,' shrugged Les. 'The CIA might've got him.'

'That's a distinct possibility.' Peregrine returned the papers to Norton's bag. 'I might read that again tonight.'

Absolutely delightful would be as good a way as any to describe the afternoon at the little billabong. The August sun beat down, the water running around the tiny island rippled and sang and the sounds of the birds calling to each other rang across the still green water and echoed off the riverbanks. Before they knew it, it was almost three and both Les and Peregrine were starting to get a bit hungry. It was Peregrine who suggested they go back and see about getting the barbecue together. They packed up and began marching across the field past the duck slaughterhouse; as they approached the homestead a movement amongst the rockeries caught their eye.

'Hello,' said Peregrine. 'Baldric's here.'

Down on his haunches and deeply involved in his work, the little caretaker didn't notice them approaching.

'Hello, Ronnie,' said Les. 'At it again, mate?'

'Huh?' Madden spun around. Again he was covered in sweat and the customary half-inch of dead roll-your-own was dangling from the corner of his mouth! 'Ohh, hello fellahs,' he said, without getting up. 'Yeah, I couldn't get out here yesterday. And I got held up this morning. I wanted to make sure this fertilizer isn't too strong for these creepers I put in.'

Norton nodded. 'How long you been here?'

'About two hours.'

'We're just about to start lunch,' said Peregrine. 'Would you care to join us?'

'Well, I'm a bit strapped for time . . .'

'There's a drink there,' said Norton, winking at Peregrine.

'Well . . . I suppose. You got enough food?'

'Heaps. See you in about an hour.'

'Okay, Les. Thanks.'

Ronnie continued working. Les and Peregrine walked to the house.

'You want to have a look at that painting?'

'I'll get changed first then I'll come down.'

'Righto.'

Norton was in the en suite having a shave when Peregrine tapped lightly and walked into his room about thirty minutes later.

'I feel good after a shower,' he said. 'Quite hungry though.'

'Yeah, me too. I'm dyin' for a beer.'

'So where's this masterpiece you've unearthed?'

'On the bed.'

Les was engrossed in the final strokes of his shave when he heard Peregrine cry out.

'My God!'

'What was that?'

'My God!' repeated Peregrine. 'This painting. Where did you say you got it?'

'I found it in a cupboard. Along with those papers I showed you and those medals sitting on the bed.' Les splashed some water on himself and walked out wiping his face with a towel. 'Why?'

Peregrine was holding the painting out in front of him and his eyes were bulging. 'This is unbelievable.' He ran his hands over the frame and turned it over. 'There's another painting on the other side.'

'Yeah. By a bloke named Reid.'

'Reid?'

'Yeah.' Les took the painting and showed Peregrine the name on the back. Then he turned it over and pointed out to him the initials ENT. 'See, the famous Australian artist — Eric Norman Toejam.'

Peregrine continued to stare at the painting shaking his head as if he couldn't quite believe what he was seeing. 'This is absolutely incredible. I don't believe it.'

'Don't believe what, Peregrine?' queried Norton. His eyes narrowed slightly and a look of suspicion crossed his face. 'What's so different about this painting, Peregrine?'

'Huh? Oh . . . oh, it's nothing really.' replied the Englishman dryly. 'It's just that ah . . . I . . . ah, I have a Chinese family who do some gardening for me on my estate at West Sussex. And the resemblance to the grandfather is absolutely uncanny.' Peregrine looked at the painting and shook his head. 'Yes, that's old . . . Joe Wong all right. Right down to the wispy grey beard. By golly. Unbelievable.'

'Yeah?' shrugged Norton, climbing into his tracksuit. 'Hard to tell one from the other. Especially when they get old.'

'Were there any papers or anything with it when you found it?'

Les opened up the smaller Manilla envelope. 'Here you are. One receipt. Thirty dollars.'

Peregrine looked at the receipt then sat down on the bed and started to laugh. 'Thirty dollars. My God! I don't believe it.'

'No, neither do I,' said Les. 'I wouldn't give you thirty bob for the fuckin' thing.'

'So, what do you intend to do with it?'

Norton shrugged. 'I don't know. I don't want it.'

'All right if I keep it in my room?'

'Do what you like with it.'

'I wouldn't mind taking it back to England with me. I'd like to show it to old Joe. He'd be astounded.'

'Go for your life.'

'Thank you . . . Les.' Peregrine took the painting and the receipt and went to his room. When he came back down Les was in the barbecue area breaking up pieces of wood.

'Well,' he beamed. 'I think I might have a glass of champagne.'

'Yeah. I just opened a can of beer myself.'

Peregrine took a bottle of Great Western from the fridge and poured himself an overflowing glass. He grinned at Norton and winked. 'Cheers, Les.'

'Yeah. Cheers, mate,' replied Les, taking a mouthful of beer. 'I'm going up to get the rice and salad.'

'Would you like a hand?'

'No. She'll be right.'

When Les returned about twenty minutes later Peregrine had finished the bottle. Ronnie was sitting next to him smoking a roll-your-own. His tongue looked like it was about to ignite and his eyes kept darting towards the fridge as if he'd just sat through six screenings of Lawrence of Arabia.

'How you feeling, Ron?' asked Les, smiling to himself.

'Ohh, not too bad, mate,' replied the caretaker.

'Get all your gardening done?'

'Ahh . . . yeah.'

'S'pose you're a bit hungry?'

'A . . . bit.'

'It's been warm today all right.'

'It has, yeah.'

Christ! Why be a sadist? thought Les. 'You feel like a beer?' Madden nodded quickly. 'Help yourself.'

In the time it took Les to place the salad on the table Madden almost tore the door off the fridge, ripped the top off a can and poured most of it down his throat. By the time Les took the meat and rice across to the barbecue, he'd finished that and was halfway through another.

'I got something I want to show you, Ron,' said Les. He went to his room and came back with the Harcourt interviews; the caretaker had finished can number two and was well into number three. 'Have a look at these.'

While Les got the fire going, Ronnie flicked through the pages. 'Yeah, that's him all right. Old Daniel J. Funny bloke.'

'And this was where he was going to fight World War III from?' said Les.

'Yeah,' replied Ronnie. 'I guess that's what he had in mind.'

'They would have had some fun getting him out of here, Ron,' said Peregrine.

'Yeah,' replied the little caretaker, absently flicking through the photocopies. 'And they'd have lost a lot of good men before they did. Then I reckon he would've retreated up into the hills and picked them off one at a time. Even if it took him twenty years.'

Les and Peregrine stared at Madden curiously from across their drinks. As if he was suddenly conscious of their stares he stood up from the table and let out a wheezy laugh. 'But he's gone now and I'm the caretaker.' He drained his can of Fourex. 'You gonna have another beer, Les?'

'Yeah righto.'

'Hey, I heard you were down the pub again on Sunday.'

'Ohh, yeah. We had a bit of another set to in the joint.'

'That's not what I heard.' Ronnie handed Les a can. 'I heard you just about wrecked the place.'

'Yeah. We didn't do it much good. We're barred too.' Norton gestured towards Peregrine with his can. 'It was his nibs' fault again. He bloody caused it.'

The caretaker let go another wheezy laugh. 'Yeah, I heard that too.'

'Oh God!' cried Peregrine. 'Not this again.'

Once again the steaks and rice were cooked to perfection and the three of them proceeded to get full of food and drink. Ronnie wobbled off on his pushbike around six leaving Les and Peregrine to continue drinking. Les started to attack the bourbon around seven-thirty and at eight they went down to feed Bunter. Peregrine was roaring with laughter at the antics of the three owls, though somehow he seemed to be drinking and roaring with laughter more than usual all night. Buggered if I know, hiccupped Les. At nine o'clock they both literally crawled into bed.

PEREGRINE WAS AWAKE but not up when Les walked into the kitchen around seven the following morning. Laying back against the pillows, his hands behind his head, he was gazing at the painting of the old Chinaman now on the wall at the foot of his bed.

'Good morning, Les. How are you?' he called cheerily.

'All right. A bit seedy though,' replied Norton. 'Christ! We ended up putting a few away last night!'

'Yes. I'm a bit that way myself. It's that Ronnie — I think he's a bad influence.'

'You still want to go for a walk?'

'My word.'

Norton made his coffee then walked to the door. 'I'll see you downstairs.'

Peregrine made some coffee himself then wearing his fatigues and boots joined Les in the barbecue area. Norton was leaning against the fridge, a very worried look on his face. He stared at Peregrine without saying a word. The Englishman could sense something was definitely amiss.

'Something wrong is there, Les?' he asked.

Norton stared impassively at Peregrine. 'We're out of Fourex.'

'What was that?'

'Ronnie's drank every can of piss in the joint. We're out of Fourex.'

'Oh my God!' Peregrine screwed up his face and wrenched at his hair. 'Did you say — out of Fourex?' He fell to his knees and cried out to the surrounding hills. 'Did you hear that, Lord? Did you? We're out of Fourex. Oh God! How could you let this happen?'

'Hey. Don't joke, mate,' intoned Norton. 'This is serious.'

'Joke? How could you joke about something like this? This is a disaster of Orwellian proportions.'

'And we're barred from the local pub too.'

'Out of Fourex and barred from the pub too! Oh God!' shrieked Peregrine. 'Is there no end to this man's suffering?'

'So, I've been thinking,' said Les firmly. 'It looks like we take a trip into Murwillumbah. In fact this could be a very nice day for you, Sir Peregrine Normanhurst III. How would you like to see a living, breathing Australian beach?'

'How do you mean?'

'I'll tell you about it while we're walking.'

While they were striding out around Cedar Glen Les explained to Peregrine that according to his map in the car, about forty kilometres or so on the other side of Murwillumbah was the coast. There were literally miles of beaches but handiest for them were Pottsville, Hastings Point and Cabarita or Kingscliffe. There would have to be a pub or a good restaurant somewhere; they could make a day of it and it would be a break from the farm. Peregrine couldn't get into any trouble sitting on a beach. They could pick up the booze on the way back and Les could ring Sydney. Peregrine replied that sounded like an absolutely splendid idea. he had heard about the Australian beaches, it was a lovely day and he was more than keen.

They finished their walk, did some exercises and topped them off with a swim in the front billabong, then Les cooked them another monster breakfast. By around ten-thirty they'd cleaned up, tossed the two banana-chairs and a few other things in the station wagon and with Peregrine's Pet Shop Boys tape playing, were on their way to the coast.

It didn't take long to get through Murwillumbah, where Les turned south following the highway as it rose and fell through the hills, canefields and small banana farms built up on either side of the road.

'We turn off here,' said Norton, as they came into the small town of Mooball. He swung the car left at the railway crossing and over Burringbar Creek.

Peregrine pointed to the old country hotel behind them. 'I like the name of the pub,' he said. 'The Victory. That was the name of Nelson's flagship when we went in and sorted out the smelly French — for about the umpteenth time.'

'Whatever,' replied Les.

Another twenty kilometres or so on bitumen and they were in Pottsville.

Pottsville was a few motels, a garage, some houses and a couple of shops nestled around where the shallow creek ran into a granite breakwater built out into the ocean. It wasn't all that impressive and Les was about to give it a big miss when Peregrine started pointing excitedly.

'Quick, Les,' he said. 'Stop the car.'

Norton looked around thinking the Englishman must have spotted a couple of hot sorts in bikinis. 'What's . . .?'

'There's an antique shop just there. Let's have a look.'

Norton pulled up outside a milkbar. By the time he'd got out of the car Peregrine was across the road and inside the Pottsville Antiques and Art Gallery. A buzzer sounded when Les entered and he found himself in two or three rooms full of old butter churners, cedar chairs and tables, porcelain wash basins and other old bric-a-brac and old paintings. Peregrine was studying a black and white watercolour of an old battleship when Les caught up with him.

'I thought we were going to the beach?' he said.

'We are, dear boy,' replied Peregrine. 'I'd just like to have a browse around for a few minutes — that's all. Sometimes these out of the way galleries can be quite interesting.'

Les had another quick glance around. 'Yeah, terrific,' he muttered. 'I'll see you back at the car. I'm gonna get an orange juice.'

'As you wish.'

Sitting on the bonnet of the car, Les had finished his orange juice and was halfway through a Cornetto when Peregrine came walking across the street.

'You didn't buy anything?'

Peregrine shook his head. 'No. Nothing in there really worth purchasing.'

'What were you hoping to find? A Ming vase?'

The Englishman's face suddenly lit up. 'Sometimes Les, you never know what you might find. You just never know.'

'Yeah, righto.' Les finished his ice cream. 'Anyway, there's another beach further up, Hastings Point. Let's go and have a look.'

Hastings Point was pretty much like Pottsville. The same number of houses, shops and motels only with a nicer headland and a couple of tiny islands where Cudgera Creek emptied into the ocean. But still no pub.

'What do you reckon, Pezz?' said Norton, as they rattled over the narrow wooden bridge.

'It looks nice. Do you wish to stop?'

Norton screwed up his face. 'No, let's go further up. See what Cabarita's got to offer.'

'You're the driver.'

They travelled on another twenty or so kilometres along the coast road; unfortunately the beach was hidden by a strip of thick scrub. Les spotted a bush track, pulled up, did a quick U-turn and stopped in front of it.

'What are you doing?' asked Peregrine.

'Let's have a quick look at the beach. Come on.'

They followed the trail about twenty metres where it came out onto a deserted stretch of white beach with a small swell rolling in from the clear, blue Pacific Ocean. To their right the beach curved into a headland so far in the distance it was barely discernible. To the left it did the same; you could just make out the pine trees and high-rises of Tweed Heads. There was a light offshore breeze blowing and not a soul around for miles.

'I say,' said Peregrine. 'This is really lovely.'

'I told you, didn't I?'

'And what about this sand? It's so white.' Peregrine scooped up a handful and let it run through his fingers.

'Yeah,' nodded Les. 'The local council digs it up twice a year and has it all steam-cleaned.'

'Really?'

'Yeah. Bastard of a job. But it's worth it.'

213

'I say. It must take them ages.'

'They only do the top couple of feet.'

'Oh.'

'Come on. Let's see what else there is.'

They found what they were looking for a few kilometres further up the highway. The road rose up beside a rocky point overlooking a smallish white beach with a stream running into it. Further on, a smaller point started an expanse of white sand that ran all the way up to Kingscliff and Tweed Heads. Les swung the car into a parking area above the first beach. It was about the same size as Bronte except for the two uneven granite headlands dotted with stunted palm trees and clumps of jagged granite rocks strewn across the beach. A nice even swell was rolling in — about half a dozen surfboard riders were taking advantage of it. It was all very picturesque but what Les was looking for was built onto the beach not far past the smaller headland. The Cabarita Hotel Motel. A couple of minutes later he pulled up right outside the TAB next door.

'What do you reckon, Peregrine? This might do us, old mate.'

'I couldn't agree more. Why don't we have a look around?'

The large hotel was quite modern and clean with a bistro at the rear full of open-air furniture next to a park leading down to the beach. There were maybe a couple of dozen people seated around drinking and eating, seemingly oblivious to a number of birds picking at the scraps on the tables. There was a surf club on the opposite side of the road built over some old shops. The boys walked over and through a corner window Les could see a gym with a heavy bag, speedball and weights. At the rear, a couple of fair-haired clubbies were patching up some racing skis; Les gave them a wink and a smile and he and Peregrine got a couple of friendly 'G'days' in return. There was the standard Estate Agency, a fish shop and several more shops plus a garage called the Boganbar Auto Centre. The scene was very touristy and laid-back. Several cars swished past and a number of elderly people wearing straw hats came and went taking their own sweet time as they did.

'Do we need to go any further?' asked Norton.

Peregrine shook his head. 'This suits me admirably. It's beautiful.'

They found a table with an umbrella in the beer garden and Les got two middies of New. Carole King singing 'Far Away' was playing on the pub radio system and it wasn't long before they'd sunk four middies sitting there watching the ocean on the balmy August day.

'You hungry, Pezz?' asked Les.

'Those few beers have put a bit of an edge on my appetite.'

'Let's check the bistro out then.'

The menu was fairly extensive, mainly seafood. Peregrine went for the calamari and bream fillets; Les decided on the seafood basket. He got their tickets plus another two middies. They finished those just as the girl called their number; they collected their food plus two more middies. The food was delicious: nice crisp chips, fresh coleslaw and plenty of lemon wedges. By the time they'd got through that they each had six middies under their belts plus a stack of food and both Les and Peregrine were bloated.

'How are you feeling?' smiled Norton.

'Full as a boot,' replied Peregrine. 'And a little sozzled.'

'Yeah, me too. Those six beers sure hit the spot. I've got Tasmanian scallops and chips coming out my ears.'

'I wouldn't mind a walk.'

'Not a bad idea,' agreed Les. 'I might just duck into the TAB and put a couple of bets on first. You want to have a flutter?'

'No. I'll wait here.'

Norton strolled into the TAB five minutes before the third at Warwick Farm. He couldn't see any of Price's horses in the race, but he knew a horse from Wyong called Malley Boy had to be a good thing at 12/1. Les had twenty dollars each way. Some horse cast a plate at the barrier so the race was held up. However Malley Boy, even after a check in the straight, still managed to fall into third place and pay $3.50. Norton was thirty dollars in front. While he was listening to the race he didn't notice Peregrine go to the car and get his towel.

There was a race on at Mornington in ten minutes. Willets was the only Melbourne jockey at the meeting. What was a city hoop doing in the bush? And the horse's name was Cedar Rose. Cedar Rose? Cedar Glen? Yeah, why not? Norton had thirty on the nose.

When he walked back to the beer garden, Peregrine was gone. Les had a glance along the beach and thought he could see him walking towards the river mouth at the south end. He'll be all right, thought Les. I'll catch up with him in a few minutes. He went back to the TAB and studied the form while he waited for his race to come on.

Cedar Rose didn't look like losing and won by four lengths paying $9.60. Norton was now about three hundred in front for an initial outlay of forty dollars. You're a dead set genius, you big, red-headed spunk, Les chuckled to himself. Now for the big one — a hundred each way. On what?

Norton was intently studying the race forms pinned to the wall when out the corner of his eye he noticed a young girl run up to the two clubbies patching the skis at the rear of the surf club and point excitedly towards the beach. The two clubbies exchanged a brief look, dropped what they were doing and sprinted towards the ocean. Wonder what that was all about? thought Norton. He went back to studying the form. But somehow the horses and jockeys didn't seem to be registering.

'I wonder,' he said out loud. 'I just fuckin' wonder.' Next thing Norton was also sprinting for the beach.

CALAMARI AND BREAM fillets weren't the only thing Peregrine was full of as he strolled down to the beach. After six cold middies he was also full of Dutch courage and keen to do a bit of swimming. And why not? The sky was blue, the surf was gently rolling in, the board riders had gone and Peregrine had the beach to himself. With a towel around his waist he hiccupped his way into his English bathers and began breast-stroking through the surf. When he got sick of breaststroking he switched to the Mediterranean crawl, a style perfected by about ten thousand Greeks and Italians who have been rescued off Bondi and Bronte. It works beautifully in the calm waters around Sicily or Skorpios, but in Australia, where almost every beach is treacherous with rips, undertows and collapsing sand-banks, it's about as much use as a Violet Crumble Bar in a knife fight.

Peregrine couldn't believe how well he was going, one arm after the other, kicking gently with his feet, till he turned around to swim in. Along with his swimming style, Peregrine's luck immediately took a turn for the worse. Every ten strokes he did towards the shore took him another ten metres out to sea. Then the first wave hit him and he swallowed his first mouthful of water. Then the six middies and the calamari started coming up. Then the panic set in.

Peregrine floundered and thrashed at the water before finally throwing his hands up in the air in desperation. 'Help me!' he screamed. 'Help! Oh God! Help me! Help!'

When Norton got to the park overlooking the beach the two clubbies were almost across the sand. He could see Peregrine about two hundred metres offshore being tossed around in the white water like a piece of rag.

'Shit!' he cursed, and started galloping down to the beach. By the time he had his T-shirt off and was at the water's edge the two clubbies had reached Peregrine, who was going down for the third time and firmly convinced he was about to die. There wasn't a happier pom on God's earth when he felt two strong pairs of hands take him under the shoulders and chin. Norton put his T-shirt back on. Oh well, he thought. They don't need me now — besides, that's what lifesavers aren't being paid for, anyway.

The two lifesavers expertly swam Peregrine out with the rip, followed it along and began bringing him in about fifty metres further down the beach. Norton could have applauded — volunteers or not, there was going to be a good drink in it for the two clubbies. They were going well until they reached shallow water where a freakish shorebreak hit Peregrine in the back. One of the clubbies lost his grip and as Peregrine got tossed over, he too was swept across a clump of jagged rocks. The other clubbie got Peregrine onto the beach; Les ran to assist and noticed the water around the one now limping from the rocks was stained red.

'Shit!' said Norton.

The clubbie with Peregrine dragged him coughing and sputtering onto the wet sand; water was pouring out of his nose and mouth and he looked awful, but at least he was alive. Les went over to the other lifesaver who was sitting on his backside holding his leg; there was a bad gash running from his ankle up to his calf muscle and blood was oozing out over his hands.

'Jesus! Are you all right, mate?' asked Les.

The lifesaver gritted his teeth. 'Yeah, I think so,' was the stoic reply.

The clubbie with Peregrine had him on his stomach pumping seawater, calamari and Tooheys New out of him. On the park in front of the hotel Norton could see a small crowd starting to gather. Shit! This is all I need, he thought. Lifesaver hero saves visiting member of the Royal Family. This could make the local paper. Les took off his good Hard Rock Cafe New Orleans T-shirt, ripped it in half and wrapped it around the lifesaver's leg.

'Leave him,' he said to the one with Peregrine. 'He'll be okay. I'll look after him. See to your mate.' He took two hundred dollars from the pocket of his jeans. 'Here, this'll pay for your doctor's bill.'

The clubbie took the money and looked at Les. 'All right. Thanks mate.'

Norton wrapped one of Peregrine's arms around his shoulders and started half walking, half dragging him up the beach. He spotted his clothes laid out neatly on the sand, picked them up and draped the white cotton jacket over Peregrine's shoulders.

'Come on, Dawn Fraser,' he said. 'I think I'd better get you home.'

Peregrine lay on the front seat of the car and moaned, coughed, threw up and spluttered all the way to Yurriki. Worrying about whether he should get the ashen-faced Englishman to a doctor or not, Les was at Cedar Glen before he realised he'd forgotten the beer.

'Shit!' he cursed, as he got out to open the front gate.

Well, I reckon it'll just be dinner for one tonight, thought Les, as he put some dry clothes on Peregrine and placed him in his bed. The Englishman moaned something, rolled his eyes and began heaving. He was still pretty sick, but it appeared to be shock as much as anything else. Les placed a bucket beside the bed and watched him for a while then went down to clean the vomit from the front seat of the car.

Norton couldn't help but feel more than a bit nervous now. It had been a bloody close shave. Christ! Imagine if he'd have drowned. Price would have hung me. That's after Eddie had finished with me. Eddie! Jesus! I've still got to ring him yet. No that's bloody it. I'm going to have to keep the stupid bastard on the farm and watch him twenty-four bloody hours a day. It's just too risky. Norton was still thinking that when he drove into Yurriki later on to ring Eddie and tell him Wednesday had been just another day on the farm.

IT MIGHT HAVE been eight o'clock on a balmy August night in the Tweed Valley, but outside Churchill Court in St. Albans Road, South Kensington, London not far from Kensington Gardens, it was around ten-thirty on a cool, misty, English morning. The apple-cheeked courier driver was almost finished his round. He was five doors down the street when a dark-haired young man got out of the blue Land Rover parked across the road, took a small metal object from his black leather jacket and opened Unit 15's letter box. He ignored the two letters, but wrote down everything on the postcard, wiped it clean, replaced it, closed the letter box and strolled back to the car. He motioned to the driver and the Land Rover moved down to a phone-box on the corner. The young man in the leather jacket rattled some coins into the slot. It only took a few seconds to get through to Belfast.

PEREGRINE WAS STILL in bed sleeping soundly when Les went up for a cup of coffee around seven the following morning. He watched him snoring softly for a while, figured he looked all right and decided to leave him where he was and have a run. An hour or so later when a sweaty Les walked back into the kitchen Peregrine was sitting in his dressing gown sipping coffee, but looking quite green around the gills and very subdued.

'Hello, mate,' smiled Norton. 'How are you feeling?'

'I'm ... quite all right now, thanks Les,' said Peregrine quietly. 'A little weak.'

'Yeah, fair enough.'

Peregrine stared into his coffee and shook his head. 'My God!' he said. 'I can't ever remember being so frightened in my entire life. I honestly thought I was going to drown.'

'Yeah, well what do you expect, you stupid prick? Fancy going swimming out there with a gut full of beer and food. You deserved to drown.'

Peregrine's cheeks coloured. 'Well, I don't know about that.' He frowned up at Les from his cup of coffee. 'Anyway, where were you?'

'Where was I? In the TAB. And on a roll I might add. I should have won a bundle. Instead, your silly bloody caper cost me two hundred bucks and a bloody good T-shirt.'

'What do you mean?' said Peregrine, screwing up his face.

'The clubbie who cut his leg. I had to wrap my T-shirt around it, and I gave his mate two hundred bucks for his doctor's bill. Didn't you see any of that?'

The Englishman shook his head. 'I ... don't remember much at all. I remember swimming out and getting into trouble. Being sick in the car. And vaguely you putting me to bed. I must have been in shock.' Peregrine shrugged his shoulders. 'Why, what happened?'

Norton looked at Peregrine, shook his head, smiled and got a bottle of mineral water from the fridge. He explained everything that happened to Peregrine. By the end of the story

Peregrine's face was a mixture of disbelief and remorse.

'And that chap cut his leg quite badly?'

'Bloody oath,' nodded Les. 'A good ten stitches, easy.'

'Oh dear,' Peregrine had to look away. 'I feel such a fool.'

'You're bloody lucky those blokes were around, mate. Or you'd be dead. D-E-A-D. I wouldn't have got to you as quick as them.'

'Good Lord.' Peregrine ran his hands over his face and through his hair. He looked quite grief stricken. 'That's awful. The poor chap.'

'Yeah.'

Norton couldn't help but feel a little sorry for Peregrine now. He was no doubt feeling quite bad about making a mug of himself and getting the lifesaver injured because of his foolishness. But he had obviously learnt a lesson. Why leave him wallowing in misery? Best to get him out of it.

'Anyway, don't worry about it, mate. You're alive, and that's the main thing. You feel up to a bit of a walk?'

Peregrine thought for a moment. 'Yes. Yes, that would be good.'

'Okay.' Les dropped his empty drink bottle in the bin. 'I'll see you downstairs.'

As well as being quite stiff during the walk Peregrine was very quiet as well, which was understandable. But Les could see he was doing a lot of thinking and more than likely a bit of soul-searching as well. It isn't often you brush death so closely and so unexpectedly as that. When they got back to the barbecue area he got a glass of water and turned to Norton.

'Les,' he said firmly, 'I insist that you take me back to Cabarita some time today. I wish to personally thank those two young fellows who rescued me.'

Les wasn't too keen and shook his head. 'Ohh look, I wouldn't worry about it.'

'No.' Peregrine shook his head defiantly. 'I'm afraid I must insist. I wish to go to Murwillumbah first and do some business, which shouldn't take me more than twenty, thirty minutes. Then back to that beach. I'll see those two chaps for a moment or two. Then straight back home.'

Norton drummed his fingers on the fridge. He swore he'd keep Peregrine safely on the farm from now on. But they were out of steaks. And more importantly, still out of piss. What would it take? Two hours all up?

'Yeah, all right,' he nodded slowly, trying to sound reluctant. 'But straight in and straight back out. No mucking around.'

Peregrine seemed to brighten up a little. 'Splendid.'

'Okay. We'll have a bit of breakfast and get cleaned up.'

AT ABOUT TEN-THIRTY, the same time that Peregrine and Les were driving into Murwillumbah, Patrick, Brendan and Robert were sitting in their Stanmore unit wondering what their course of action was going to be that day. Calls to the British Embassy, to journalists, asking everywhere, other contacts, everything had struck out. Peregrine Normanhurst was nowhere to be found. The phone rang in the middle of their sometimes heated conversation. Patrick answered it. He paused, frowned into the receiver, cupped his hand over the mouthpiece and turned earnestly to the others.

'It's himself.'

Patrick listened intently for a few moments then reached for a notebook and biro. He wrote carefully, listened attentively, saying very few words before hanging up. He went through what he had just written and turned impassively to the others.

'That was Liam. They've found out where the English bastard is.'

'How?' asked Brendan.

'The dopey bastard had a postcard couriered to that Wingate woman in London. Listen to this. *My dearest Stephanie. How goes it, old pip? I'm here in this godforsaken wilderness stuck in a town called Yurriki near Murwillumbah just underneath Mt. Warning. Can you believe these names? One almost needs an interpreter to understand these colonials. I'm on a property called Cedar Glen which is rather nice, but with an Australian which is rather boring. He's a complete wally. If I survive this I shall write shortly. Pray for me, old pip. Fondest regards, Peregrine.* Well, there it is, lads. We know where the sonofabitch is. Now all we have to do is find him.'

'That shouldn't be too difficult,' said Robert, reaching for a map of New South Wales. He spread it out on the coffee table. 'Murwillumbah, did you say Patrick? Was there anything else?'

'There was one more thing.' Patrick let his eyes fall back to the notepad. 'They get here eight-thirty Saturday morning, British Airways flight 438. And they'll be bringing the Guinness.'

Robert and Brendan exchanged glances.

'Did you say they'll be bringing the Guinness?' said Brendan.

'That I did,' replied Patrick.

'Then it's surely on.'

'Aye,' nodded Patrick. 'It surely is indeed.'

LES CALLED INTO the Yurriki butcher shop on the way to Murwillumbah. The local butcher either didn't recognise him or didn't want to. Norton was able to order twenty T-bones, sausages, cutlets and some pork chops. He told the butcher he'd call back in a couple of hours or so. The local butcher said that suited him, he'd see him then. In Murwillumbah Les found a parking spot opposite the police station outside a tiny coffee shop next to a hotel. Peregrine appeared to have tidied up for the occasion; silk shirt, cravat, tailored brown tweed trousers and expensive shoes plus an alligator skin sling wallet. Les walked to the ANZ bank with him. The Englishman said he might be a good half hour or so, Les could come in and wait if he wished. Norton said he'd see him back at the car.

He got a Sydney paper and went to the little coffee shop; which sold good coffee and excellent pumpkin scones with jam and cream. Les caught up on the football while he waited for Peregrine. There was a pub next door and he could have got the beer while he waited but Les thought he'd get it on the way back — that way it would be colder when they got home. Forty minutes later he saw Peregrine get into the front seat of the station wagon. Les drained his second cup of coffee and joined him.

'Get everything done?' he asked, climbing behind the wheel.

'Yes. Everything.'

'What did you have to do, anyway?'

'Oh, a little bit of this, a little bit of that. Nothing really.'

'Fair enough.' Les slipped on his seat belt and started the engine. 'Okay, next stop Cabarita.'

'If you would be so kind.'

Norton pulled up in almost the same parking spot as the day before. The TAB had just opened but there didn't seem to be as many people about as on Wednesday. The two surf-skis were back on the grass at the rear of the surf club but as Les and Peregrine crossed the street they could only see one clubbie working on them; the shorter, fair-haired one who helped to save Peregrine. Engrossed in his work and with his back turned he didn't notice the boys until Les spoke.

'G'day, mate. How are you goin' there?'

The clubbie turned around and with a hand shading his eyes looked up at Les. It took him a moment or two to recognise who it was.

'Ohh, G'day mate,' he answered. 'How's things?'

'Not too bad. Remember my mate here?'

The clubbie nodded at Peregrine. 'Yeah. How are you feeling now, mate?'

Peregrine stared at the clubbie. 'How am I feeling? I feel fine. Only because of you and your friend.'

The clubbie shrugged a noncommittal reply and continued sanding the surf-ski.

'Where is your mate, anyway?' asked Les.

'At home. The doctor at the hospital told him to stay off his leg for a few days.'

'How bad is it?'

'They ended up putting twenty stitches in it.'

'Twenty stitches!' Peregrine had to look away for a moment. 'You mean to tell me, that my . . . my stupidity cost your friend twenty stitches in his leg?'

'Yeah, and his job. He just got a start last week at the pub as a cleaner. He couldn't turn up this morning so the boss put another bloke on.' The clubbie smiled at the look on Peregrine's face. 'But don't worry about it, mate. That's just the way things go.'

Peregrine stared at the clubbie who ignored him as he continued to sandpaper the surf-ski.

'What's your name?' asked Peregrine.

'Mine? Geoff,' replied the lifesaver.

'No. Your full name.'

'Geoffrey. Geoffrey Nottage.'

'And your friend's?'

'Brian — Byrne.'

'Excellent. Thank you, Geoffrey.'

Peregrine stepped into the surf club garage cum storeroom and found an old table covered in lifesaving equipment. He placed his sling wallet on top, removed some papers and took a gold Parker from his shirt pocket. The clubbie watched him indifferently for a moment or two then went on sandpapering the surf-ski.

'Not working yourself?' asked Norton.

'No. Things are pretty tough round here at the moment. I'm on the fuckin' jam-roll. It's enough to give you the shits.'

'Yeah. I know what you mean,' nodded Les.

'You up here on holidays, are you?'

'Yeah. Sort of.'

The clubbie finished one side of the ski, got up and went round to the other. 'Hey, thanks for that two hundred bucks, too, mate. That'll come in handy.'

'That's okay,' shrugged Les. 'It's the least I can do.'

Peregrine came out of the garage holding two small pieces of paper. He folded them together, walked around Les and handed them to the clubbie.

'Do you know what those are, Geoffrey?' he asked. The clubbie looked at them as if he wasn't quite sure. 'They're bank cheques. One for yourself. And one for your friend.'

The lifesaver opened the cheques, blinked then frowned at Peregrine in disbelief. 'Hey, these are made out for a hundred thousand dollars each.'

'That's right,' said Peregrine expressionlessly. 'One for you and one for your friend Brian. Take them to the ANZ Bank in Murwillumbah, with some identification, and that amount will be forwarded into both your accounts.'

Still blinking in disbelief the simple clubbie turned to Les. 'Is he fair dinkum?'

Norton was more than a bit taken aback himself. But he had seen Peregrine's generosity before. 'I reckon he might be, matey,' he grinned.

Peregrine turned to Norton. 'What does he mean Les? Is he doubting my sincerity? Geoffrey would you like us to drive you to the bank?'

'No. No that's all right,' said the absolutely dumbfounded lifesaver. 'It's just . . . shit! Christ! Bloody hell — a hundred thousand bucks! Jesus!'

'You see, Geoffrey, sometimes it pays to rescue a pom,' smiled Peregrine.

'You can bloody say that again,' said the totally amazed clubbie. 'Better than the one we pulled in weekend before last.'

'He didn't shout you a drink?' said Les.

'No, all he left was a ring round the beach.'

Norton tried not to laugh, but when he caught Peregrine's eye he couldn't help it.

'I . . . suppose I deserved that.' Peregrine extended a hand to the lifesaver. 'Thank you Geoffrey,' he said sincerely.

'Thank you too . . .' The lifesaver had to look at the cheque, 'Peregrine.'

The clubbie was miles away staring at the two cheques. Les and Peregrine left him where he was and walked back to the car. A few minutes later they were motoring down the coastway towards the Pottsville turnoff. They had gone some distance before Les spoke.

'Hey, that wasn't a bad effort, Peregrine. A hundred thousand each for those clubbies.'

'Two hundred thousand dollars to save your life, Les?' Peregrine dismissed it with a wave of his hand. 'If anything, they deserved more.'

'Whatever. But it was still a good effort. They were just a couple of battlers. I'm proud of you.'

'I must admit, I do feel a lot better. Now, there's one more thing I insist you do, Les.'

'Yeah? What's that?'

'Back at Murwillumbah I noticed a liquor store selling imported champagne and beer. Pull up outside and open the back of the car. While I'm in a good mood I'm going to educate your drinking habits.'

'What do you mean? Educate my drinking habits?' growled Norton.

Peregrine pointed an accusing finger at Les. 'I still claim that half the reason I almost drowned out there was because you had me almost full of that dreadful Tooheys New, or whatever you call it. It's ghastly. If I had been drinking something civilised like Heineken or Carlsberg, I probably would have been all right.'

'Ohh, don't give me the shits.'

'And as for that vile concoction you drink in the yellow cans. Fourex. I wouldn't give that to a dog. In fact, it tastes as though dogs have been swimming in it. Amongst other things.'

'What!?' Norton was almost going to stop the car. 'Listen. You're starting to take a few liberties, old fellah. I'm from Queensland and we soak our bread in it up there.'

'I think some of you have been soaking your heads in it. No, I admit English beer can be pretty ordinary. But don't try to tell me Australian beer's all it's cracked up to be. It's . . . it's rebarbative.' Peregrine baulked at the look on Norton's face. 'What are you stopping the car for?'

'I'm going back to Cabarita to belt those two clubbies. They should have let you drown.'

Thursday afternoon in Murwillumbah was like Thursday afternoon in any small Australian country town and Les was able to find a parking spot almost outside the bottle shop Peregrine had noticed earlier. He opened the back of the station wagon and followed the Englishman inside.

The shop was quite large with an extensive selection of wines and spirits. Arranged neatly on shelves, on either side of a double self-serve fridge, were around thirty different brands of beer. Behind the counter opposite was a cheery, country-looking woman in a plain cotton dress.

'Yes? What can I do for you?' she asked.

'Do you take American Express?' enquired Peregrine.

'We sure do.'

'Excellent.' Peregrine turned to the imported beers and let his eyes run over them. 'Mmhh,' he mused happily. 'Not a bad selection. Not bad at all. Okay, I'll start with a dozen bottles of Becks. And a dozen Stella Artois, Kronenbourg, and Gosser. A dozen Lowenbrau and the same of Heineken.'

The woman began stacking the six-packs on the counter and tapping the prices onto a calculator.

'Hello,' said Peregrine. 'I see you have Corona I'd better take three dozen of those. You wouldn't happen to have any limes?'

'I can get you some.'

'Good. Throw half a dozen in.'

'What the . . .?' said Norton.

'Quiet, Les,' commanded Peregrine. 'You might just learn something here. Now, a dozen Carlsberg, not the Elephant beer, the other one. And a dozen Tuborg. Oh! And just in case Lothar here starts to break out in carbuncles, throw in half a dozen cans of Fourex.'

'Make that a dozen.'

'Very well. A dozen. And keep them separate from the others.'

'I'm sorry these aren't all cold,' said the woman. 'I normally wouldn't sell this much imported stuff in a month.'

'That's quite all right. And I'll take a dozen bottles of Moet and a dozen bottles of Veuve Clicquot. You wouldn't happen to have any Cristal?' The woman shook her head. 'And six bottles of Beaujolais.' Peregrine turned to Norton. 'Well, come on, Les. Don't stand there like a Harrods dummy. Start putting them in the car. Now madam, how much do I owe you?'

'Just what the fuck are you trying to prove, Peregrine?' said Norton, as they turned left at the roundabout on the way out to Yurriki. He had a quick look in the rear-vision mirror. In the back of the station wagon were eleven dozen bottles of imported beer, a dozen Fourex, two dozen bottles of French champagne and a half dozen imported wines.

'I'm not trying to prove anything, dear boy,' replied Peregrine quietly. 'I'm just shouting you a few beers because I think you're such a wonderful chap.'

Les gave the Englishman a baleful look. 'Now piss in this one. It's waterproof. Christ! It'll take us six months to drink it.'

'Not if Baldric finds out it's there.'

'Shit! That's a thought.'

The butcher had their meat waiting back at Yurriki. Les didn't bother to check it; if it was just half as good as the last lot it would still be sensational. Shortly after they were back at Cedar Glen cramming as much beer and champagne into the two fridges as they could. What wouldn't fit was stacked in the cupboards downstairs.

'I wouldn't mind attacking some of this right now,' said Norton.

'If you wish,' replied Peregrine. 'But why don't we wait until it's all nice and chilled and get into it over the barbecue? We'll be really hungry then.'

'Okay,' agreed Les. 'What are you going to do?'

'I might have a read for a while.'

'I'll go for a walk.'

'Very well. I'll see you when you get back.'

Les spent the next couple of hours strolling around the property trying to picture the place through the eyes of Colonel Daniel J. Harcourt. It took on an entirely new dimension: the mantraps, fields of fire, the gun emplacement beyond the old duck sheds. In the evening sun he sat on a rail of the rickety old wooden bridge for a commanding view of practically the entire lower part of the farm. Yes, thought Norton, Cedar Glen sure is something else. Wish I had the money, I'd buy it myself. When he returned to the house and got cleaned up he found Peregrine laying on his bed with his hands behind his back staring at *Portrait Of A Chinaman* by Ernest Norman Toejam.

'How are you feeling now, mate?' he asked. 'You hungry?'

'Yes, rather,' replied the Englishman. 'I say, why don't we have some of those pork chops tonight? I watched you unwrapping them and they looked absolutely scrumptious.'

'Okey-doke. Pork chops, cutlets and sausages it is.'

Les boiled the rice. Peregrine made the salad. Next thing they were in the barbecue area and Norton had the fridge door open trying to work out what to drink first.

'Well, while you're making your mind up,' said Peregrine,

'I'm going to have a nice chilled bottle of '78 Veuve Clicquot.'

'Go for your life. I might try a bottle of this Stella Artois. I like the label.'

Les liked the label. He also liked the beer; two went down in less than ten minutes, then a Tuborg and a Gosser. Then he discovered the Becks.

'I'll tell you what,' said Norton, on his second bottle of Becks. 'You're right about this overseas piss. It's the grouse.'

'I told you, didn't I? Better than that wretched Fourex.'

'Ohh, I dunno about that,' said Les, feeling a bit of a traitor to mother Queensland. 'But it is good.'

Peregrine had to smile at the look on Norton's face. He was tearing into the imported beers like there was going to be no tomorrow, but loath to admit that he was loving it.

'Come here,' said Peregrine. 'I'll show you something.'

When Norton finished his second bottle of Becks, Peregrine took a bottle of Corona from the fridge, knocked the top off then cut a slice from one of the limes and jammed it in the neck.

'There you go, Les,' he grinned. 'Try that.'

Les took a tentative sip which turned into one great slurp. 'Ohh yeah,' he belched. 'How good's this?'

'I told you, didn't I? Les Norton, I'll make a yuppie out of you yet.'

'You might even do that,' laughed Les, taking another swig of Corona. 'I'll get a Mercedes and a car-phone. Next thing I'll be drinking at The Four In Hand.'

'You'll what?'

'Just a joke, Peregrine,' said Les. 'Just a private joke.'

The pork chops were as good as the T-bones and by six they'd finished their barbecue over a chilled bottle of Beaujolais. By seven Peregrine was into his third bottle of Veuve Clicquot and Les had knocked over an unknown number of imported beers including four more Coronas. By eight there were empty bottles everywhere, the ghetto-blaster was blaring and Les and Peregrine were both howling, screaming and baying at the moon, mule drunk.

Peregrine focused on Norton across a table of empties and other debris. 'Les,' he slurred. 'Les. I am so drunk I cannot believe it.'

Norton shook his head. 'No,' he blinked. 'Not a chance. No one, I repeat, no one could possibly be as drunk as me. No one in the world.'

'I would have to disagree there . . . I'm afraid. Have to.'

They sat blinking drunkenly at each other and into space when a look of suspicion crept across Peregrine's face.

'Les,' he hiccupped. 'Have you got a feeling someone's watching us?'

'Huh?'

Norton's drunken gaze shifted from the barbecue area to the grass surrounding them. At the edge of the darkness countless tiny pairs of light seemed to be winking at them. When Norton's eyes adjusted to the darkness he could see what they were.

'Hey, look at that, Peregrine,' he leered. 'It's the possums. I put some fruit out last night and they've come back.'

There were at least twenty grey possums watching them intently through big, sad-looking brown eyes, their soft pink noses twitching from side to side as they sniffed tentatively at the air. Some had babies clinging precariously to their backs, several had tiny black tails poking out of their pouches. One or two would come in for a closer look then turn around and scurry back, tails dragging behind them, bums up in the air. Others would rise up on their haunches and paw at the air as they sniffed in the boys' direction.

'Good Lord!' said Peregrine. 'I've never seen the like. They're absolutely marvellous. What on earth are they?'

'Brushtail possums. Cute little bludgers, aren't they?' Norton rose from the table and the possums withdrew into the darkness. 'If I can make it up the stairs, I'll go to the kitchen and get some more fruit.'

Like a bull in a china shop, Norton lurched up the stairs and clambered back down with half a dozen apples. He chopped some up on the table and scattered the pieces out onto the grass. The possums could sense that neither Peregrine or Les meant them any harm and before long had the pieces of apple in their paws munching and crunching away with delight.

'I say,' said Peregrine. 'Those shrub tail possums, or whatever you call them, are about the cutest little blighters I've ever seen.'

'Yeah. They're all right, aren't they?' Norton grinned at the little animals enjoying the pieces of fruit then sadness with a touch of anger crossed his face. 'You know, it's a shame really, Peregrine. Rotten fuckin' greyhound owners use them to blood greyhounds.'

'Oh no.'

'Yeah. Tie them to lures and let the dogs rip them to pieces. Nice people aren't they?'

'Oh God!'

'And some fuckin' idiot in Tasmania, wants to trap thousands of them, kill them and sell them to the Japanese as aphrodisiacs.'

'I could believe that,' said Peregrine. 'The bloody Japanese would eat *us* if they thought they could get off on it.'

'Poor bloody wildlife. It doesn't stand much of a chance these days.' Norton's gaze suddenly went from the animals to Peregrine. 'Hey. I just thought of something. You know what Murwillumbah means in Australian Aboriginal?' Peregrine shook his head. 'Place of many possums. I noticed it on a T-shirt in town today.'

'Really?' Then Peregrine's eyes lit up. 'I just thought of something too. You've got your friends, I've got mine. I'm going round to feed Bunter.'

'Good on you,' mumbled Norton. 'I'll stay here with the possums.'

Peregrine gathered up some scraps of meat and weaved his way round to the other side of the house. The three owls were in their customary positions in the trees, huge orange eyes beaming down.

'I say, chaps,' hiccupped Peregrine, placing the meat scraps on the ground. 'This is becoming almost intolerable. I've a jolly good mind to call Mr Squelch and have you bunked from Greyfriars. Especially you, Bunter, you piffling pernicious porker.'

Showing no fear now, the three owls swooped down and picked up the pieces of meat almost at Peregrine's feet then returned to their trees.

'Do help yourselves, you young smudges.'

Peregrine watched the owls drunkenly for a while then swayed back round to the barbecue area.

'They there?' asked Les.

'Certainly were,' answered Peregrine. 'And as hungry as ever.'

'Couldn't be any worse than these little bludgers.'

One possum was now on its haunches leaning against Norton's leg with one paw and grasping for a piece of apple Les was holding with the other. Peregrine laughed at its antics then poured himself a fresh glass of champagne. He raised his glass.

'The owl and the possum went to sea,' he hiccupped. 'In a beautiful pea green boat.'

'What the fuck are you talking about, Peregrine?'

'Just a joke, Les. Just a private joke.'

Norton raised his bottle of Kronenbourgh. 'I'll drink to that,' he belched.

UNDERSTANDABLY LES AND Peregrine were just a little bit seedy the following morning, but they still managed a brisk walk around the property and a good breakfast afterwards. But the best part of the day was definitely the time spent down at the smaller billabong with their books and banana-chairs laughing now about the events that had happened during their first week at Cedar Glen.

By around two-thirty Les had finished *Women* and Peregrine had got through his book on Peter Sellers. They had a final swim and decided to pack up and start getting their now habitual afternoon barbecue together. They were just at the rockeries by the rear of the house when a rumbling, rattling sound started coming up the front driveway. Norton wasn't quite sure what to do when Ronnie came into view behind the wheel of a blue tractor, with a metal tray on the back and a scoop at the front. He gave them a wave then parked it beside the tool shed. Les and Peregrine were in the barbecue area having a bottle of mineral water when he walked over.

'What's doing with the tractor, Ron?' said Les. 'You gonna do a bit of excavating?'

The little caretaker looked at them for a moment then sat down. 'Well, to tell you the truth,' he said, remorse spreading over his already anguished face. 'It belongs to the farm. I just borrowed it for a couple of days to do a bit of work around my joint.'

'Couple of days?' said Peregrine. 'We've been here over a week and it's the first time I've seen it.'

Ronnie squeezed his hands together. 'Yeah, fair enough. But do us a favour will you? Don't tell the estate agent I had it.'

'Jesus, I don't know, Ronnie,' said Les. 'Benny Rabinski's an old mate of mine. What do you reckon, Peregrine?'

The Englishman shook his head. 'Ohh, I wouldn't like to say. It's up to you, Les. The lease is in your name.'

Norton also shook his head then thought for a moment. 'All right Ronnie, I won't say anything this time. On one condition.'

'Okay. What's that?'

'You have a drink and a barby with us this afternoon.'

'Ohh, Christ, fellahs,' protested Ronnie. 'You blokes have had me round here nearly every day, and I haven't weighed in a zac yet.'

'So?' shrugged Peregrine.

'Well it just don't seem right.'

'Okay. Suit yourself, Ron,' said Les. 'But it's either that or I call copper on you to Rabinski.'

The little caretaker licked his lips and his eyes darted towards the fridge behind Norton; then he gave out one of his wheezy laughs. 'All right. It looks like you blokes have made me an offer I can't refuse.'

'You got it, Baldric,' said Peregrine.

After getting cleaned up, Les cooked steaks and sausages and speared Ronnie straight into the dozen cans of Fourex, then topped him up with Tuborg and Heineken but kept him away from the Corona, Becks and Gosser. Les liked the little caretaker, but in the state he was in and the way he was pouring beer down his throat Norton figured that letting him amongst those would be like giving strawberries to a pig.

'So what do you think of those imported beers, Ron?' asked Les.

'Ahh, they're all right,' shrugged Madden. 'We used to . . . I've drank them before.' The little caretaker drained his fifth bottle of Tuborg and tossed the empty into the Otto-bin. 'Piss is piss to me.'

'Yeah, I figured that,' nodded Les.

Baldric wobbled off around six-thirty. He knocked back the offer of a lift, saying he'd take a short cut that went past the Cedar Glen stables and down across the creek back to his place. This left Les and Peregrine to get drunk again.

By ten o'clock they'd fed the possums and the owls, the evening mist was filling the valley and apart from the ghetto blaster playing softly, the only sound was the nightbirds calling to each other and the crickets and frogs in the big hole near the barbecue area. Both Les and Peregrine had champagne and beer running out of their ears so they decided to have a goodnight bottle of beaujolais before they hit the sack. The bottle of beaujolais was almost gone and the boys were drunk and tired enough to be at the stage where they were now starting to tell each other what good blokes they were.

'Yeah. I've got to hand it to you, Peregrine,' said Norton. 'When it comes to a quid, you've got a heart of gold, mate.'

'You think so, Les?'

'Reckon. Those two lifesavers. The girls from Stokers Siding. Me. Are you this generous back home?'

'What? With the villagers on my estate? Of course. My word.' Peregrine took a slurp of wine. 'Why, only last week young Melville Spencer the village cripple came up to me, asked me for some money to study music in London. Said he wanted to be a conductor.'

'Yeah? So what did you do?'

'Had my groundsman nail him to the chimney. Then there was old Mrs Scrillitch. She kept complaining about a huge hole full of water right out the front of her house.'

'What did you do for her?'

'Gave her half a dozen ducks. I've only really ever had one bit of trouble: Old Bert. Ex-beefeater. Ninety years of age. Absolute pain in the neck. Took me to court. Claimed the walls in his cottage were too thin. I ended up having to repatriate him.'

'How come?'

'Well what could one do? I took the sheriff round to have a look. Opened the oven and there was the bloke next door dipping bread in old Bert's gravy.'

'So I s'pose you settled out of court.' Norton drained his glass. 'Yeah. You are a good bloke Peregrine, no doubt about it.'

BRITISH AIRWAYS FLIGHT 438 was almost on time when it touched down at Kingsford Smith Airport on Saturday morning, but it was closer to eleven o'clock when the three English soccer officials made it through customs. The three neatly-dressed men in overcoats didn't look at all like your average sixty-year-old, balding, overweight soccer official. These men were lean and hard and closer to forty. Their faces were a little gaunt but also handsome in a rugged sort of way. In fact, with their loosely parted dark hair and piercing green eyes, they didn't look unlike the three men waiting for them on the other side of the barrier. If the three soccer officials were tired and jaded after their trip like their fellow travellers they didn't show it and could not have been more pleasant as they opened their suitcases and presented their passports at separate counters.

'And the purpose of your visit, Mr Berkley, is to possibly recruit some Australian soccer players?' said the customs officer.

'Yes. Queens Park Rangers,' replied the dark haired man with the intense twinkling eyes.

'Hoping to find another Craig Johnston?'

'We'd certainly like to.'

The customs officer looked at the passport in front of him for a moment then brought his stamp down. 'Righto. A three month visa ought to be enough. Enjoy your stay in Australia.'

'I will,' smiled the soccer official. 'Thank you so much.'

The three men in the blue overcoats regrouped then joined the three men waiting for them outside the customs hall. They didn't make a great song and dance about seeing each other. The greetings and handshakes, though warm and sincere, were quick, almost inconspicuous. The six men quietly moved off into the bitter sou'wester whipping around Mascot to the two white Holden sedans waiting in the parking area.

'Did you have a good trip then, Liam?' asked Patrick.

'It was,' replied the gaunt-faced Irishman, answering for the others. 'But most of the time we spent working out the best way to go about this.'

'And have you come up with something?' asked Robert.

'We have. And we'll discuss it with you back at your flat. But first we have to go here.' Liam took a piece of paper from his pocket and handed it to Patrick.

'Botany?'

'Is that far from here?'

Patrick shook his head. 'Just down the road.'

'Good. Well then, Robert, why don't you take Logan and Tom back to the flat and we'll see you there after we pick up the doings. They came in on Lufthansa at seven am. So they'll be there waiting for us.'

Every para-military or criminal organisation, be it Tamil Tigers, Basque Separatists, the PLO, or a drug smuggling ring, all have their own ways of getting things in and out of countries undetected. The IRA were not different, and were probably better at it than anyone else. When Liam, Patrick and Brendan backed into the loading dock of a bond store off the main street in Botany, the trunk was waiting for them. They couldn't miss it. It was painted black with a red and white stripe around it and the words 'Queens Park Rangers Sponsored By Guinness' painted in white. They manhandled the weighty trunk into the boot of the Holden and drove off. The Saturday traffic wasn't too bad and in less than half an hour they were with the others in the Stanmore unit. The two women made strong coffee with something a little stronger added, there was another round of greetings then it was straight down to business.

Tom Mooney took a key from inside his coat pocket and opened the locks on the metal trunk. Inside were seven objects wrapped in white cloth; he took one out, removed the cloth and handed it to Patrick.

'Are you familiar with these, Patrick?' he asked.

Patrick turned the odd-looking weapon over in his hand. It had an unusual AUSAT sighting arrangement like a telescopic lens sitting on top, and the even more unusual idea of having the magazine behind the trigger mechanism.

'SA-80 Bullpups?' he said. 'No. I can't say I am. AK-47s or M-16s are more what I'm used to.'

'They're a present from Maggie Thatcher's Grenadier Guards in London. We got thirty of them three months ago before the saps even missed them,' said Logan.

'I won't go into a great ordnance discussion with you now,' said Tom. 'But they take thirty rounds and the clip goes in here.' He banged an empty clip into the bullpup then handed one each to the others. 'We'll sight them in and let off a few rounds when we get out into the countryside.'

'There's six thousand rounds of ammo there,' said Liam. 'But if that's not enough, we've got this.'

He took another object from the trunk, unwrapped it and placed it on the floor. He took three turnip-shaped shells from the trunk and placed them next to it.

'My God,' said Robert. 'A rocket-propelled grenade launcher.'

'Aye,' nodded Liam. 'An RPG-7. Made in Czechoslovakia, but a present from some friends of ours in Lebanon.'

'If we can't shoot the bastard out,' said Logan, 'we'll blow him out.'

'Saints preserve us,' said Brendan. 'You've certainly come prepared.'

'That we have,' agreed Liam. 'And with a bit of luck we hope to be away by Monday. Now here's what we intend to do . . .' He opened the map of New South Wales which Robert had placed on the table for him. 'Going by that postcard he sent to his bitch in London, he's only staying with one other — some Australian. Now I would say this place they're staying at in Yurriki, Cedar Glen, would be rented. It may even be up for sale. And it would be the only place around that area with that name. Agreed?'

Tom and Logan looked at Patrick, Robert and Brendan who nodded slowly.

'Now,' continued Liam, 'we've had some lads make some inquiries at Australia House in London and it appears this Yurriki is just a one-horse town, if that. So we go to Murwillumbah. Get there Sunday morning and go to every estate agent in the town and tell them we're English investors and we heard this Cedar Glen is up for sale and we'd like to buy it. One of them will surely have heard of it and give us the address. We'll go and check it out and if it looks to be all right we'll go in that night. And like I said, with a bit of luck we can fly back out on Monday.' Liam Frayne eased back in his chair and took a sip of coffee. 'Well that's about it, lads. If we leave around midnight tonight, even taking our time, we should be there by ten on Sunday. What do you think?'

The three younger Irishmen exchanged a quick glance. 'Sounds fine, Liam,' said Patrick.

'Dead easy,' agreed Brendan.

'Aye,' said Liam. 'Just this British bastard and one Australian. Too bad about the Australian. I don't mind them at all.'

'They're good people,' nodded Robert.

'And so were my two brothers and Huen McGine,' said Liam, through a thin smile. 'Now as you can imagine, Logan, Thomas and myself are quite tired from our journey. So we'd like a few pints, a good meal and then some sleep before we leave. May I suggest you lads do the same.'

AROUND THE SAME time the Irish were heading out for a pint and a steak, Les and Peregrine had finished their morning walk, got through another good breakfast and were down at the smaller billabong reading and enjoying the sun; Peregrine was into a Jack Higgins, Les had decided to re-read parts of *Women*. The August sun was streaming down gloriously and Norton had stripped to the waist. Peregrine however, had opted to leave his T-shirt on, saying his neck and shoulders were getting a bit sore. Which was understandable. The Australian sun, even in winter, can be quite cruel if you're not used to it; though Peregrine had appeared to be tanning up fairly well over the last week. Early in the afternoon he put down his book and turned to Norton.

'So what are we doing tonight, Les?' he said.

Norton was miles away. 'Huh? What was that?'

'Tonight. Saturday night. What's happening? Are we going to that dance in Yurriki?'

Norton shook his head and continued reading. 'No, fuck the dance. Stay home and feed the possums.'

'Oh, come on, Les. Don't be such a slacker. It could be good.'

Norton closed his book. 'Look Peregrine, every time I go out somewhere with you, you either get me into a fight or try to kill yourself. Stay home and talk to your owls.'

'If I stay on this farm any longer I'll end up looking like a jolly owl.'

'Good. I'll cook you a mouse.'

'Marita and Coco will be at the dance.'

'Bugger Marita and Coco.'

'You didn't say that last Sunday night.'

Norton went to open his book and closed it again. Peregrine was right. During the daytime the farm was absolutely beautiful. But at night, with no TV, phone or newspapers there weren't enough b's in boring to describe it. And the novelty of getting blind drunk every night was starting to wear a bit thin, imported beers or not. Yeah, thought Les. Another week of this and I'll end up looking like an owl myself. Only my ears'll start to droop and I'll grow another toe on each foot. The dance could be all right. There might even be a few stray babes there. All he had to do was not get too out of it and keep an eye on Lord Snowdon. And that Alan who was running the show didn't seem like a bad bloke either.

'All right, Peregrine,' he said, trying to sound as unenthusiastic as possible. 'Anything to fuckin' keep you happy. But if we go, it's on one condition.'

'Very well. What's that?'

'You gotta behave yourself. No starting any fights.'

'Les, I do not start fights. They were just two unfortunate incidents.'

'Yeah. What about when you head butted the butcher's wife?'

'Oh goodness gracious. I did no such jolly thing.'

Norton couldn't help but chuckle to himself. 'Anyway, don't worry about it. But if she's there, Patrick Swayze, you keep away from her.'

'I promise, I shall give her the widest berth imagineable,' said Peregrine emphatically.

'Good. Now I'll tell you what we'll do. We'll prop here for another hour or so. Then have a feed and a few beers, then put our heads down for a couple of hours. If we're gonna go Saturday night boogalooing in beautiful, downtown Yurriki, we may as well go fresh.'

'A very timely suggestion, Les,' nodded Peregrine. 'Absolutely spiffing.'

Later in the afternoon, when they'd finished reading and had enough sun, Norton was still in his fatigues and boots getting the barbecue together over the football and a bottle of Gosser. He'd finished that and was into a bottle of Stella Artois when Peregrine came down the steps from the verandah overlooking the sundeck. He too was still in his fatigues, with a smile on his face and something in his hand.

'I say, Les. This beano tonight is fancy dress, isn't it?'

'Yeah. I think so.'

'Well, what do you fancy going as?'

Norton shrugged. 'I dunno. I might go as a whip. Crack it a couple of times and come home.'

'What's wrong with this?'

On the table, Peregrine placed two red-checked tea towels and an old dark blue T-shirt he'd found in the laundry. With the barbecue knife he cut two circles of cloth from the bottom of the T-shirt, placed the tea towel on his head and bound it in place with the strips of T-shirt. For all the world it looked like a keffiyeh — an Arab headress. On top of his fatigues and combat boots Peregrine wouldn't have looked out of place running around some back street in West Beirut with an AK-47.

'Well, what do you think, Les?' he grinned.

'What do I think? Christ! Benny Rabinski wouldn't want to walk up the drive — he'd have a stroke.'

Peregrine cut off another strip of T-shirt, got the remaining tea towel and did the same to Norton then dragged him in front of the mirror in Norton's bedroom.

'What do you say, Les? We'll go to the dance as Arab terrorists. Those poor peace-loving hippies won't know what to think.'

Norton couldn't help but stare at the two tanned reflections staring back at him in the mirror. Peregrine was right. They did look like members of the PLO. All that was missing were sidearms and sunglasses.

'Jesus! I don't know, Peregrine. The way trouble seems to find you, some reffo'll be in there and take a shot at us.'

'Not a chance,' laughed Peregrine, and gave Les a slap on the back. 'What is it you Australians like to say? She'll be sweet, mate.'

* * *

IT WAS ALMOST seven when Les woke up from his afternoon nap. Peregrine was still in bed with the light on when Les went upstairs to make a cup of coffee. He got a brew together, gave Peregrine a few minutes then went into the bedroom and shook him lightly on the shoulder.

'Come on, mate, time to wake up. It's after seven o'clock.'

The Englishman blinked his eyes open. 'Huh? What? Oh it's you, Les.'

'Yeah. Did you get a bit of sleep?'

'Yes. Mmhh.' Peregrine yawned and blinked. 'God, I'm tired though.'

'You'll be okay once you have a shower. I'll see you when I come back up.'

Les finished his coffee downstairs then took his time in the shower and having a shave. Feeling like a million dollars now he got back into his fatigues and army boots, adjusted the red tea towel on his head and stood in front of the mirror.

'Les Norton, lion of the desert,' he grinned. 'You are truly the chosen one. Now, jewel of the cosmos, what are we going to take to drink?'

There was a small, red plastic garbage-bin with a clip-on lid in the laundry. He took that out to the barbecue area, put in a dozen bottles of Corona and some limes, plus a dozen assorted other beers, and six bottles of French champagne for Peregrine. They would more than likely end up shouting someone else there a drink; they could bring home what was left over. There was enough ice in the fridge to keep what drink there was chilled until he could get some more at the pub. If he couldn't get served he'd sling someone a couple of bucks to get it for him. When he went back upstairs Peregrine was showered and dressed, except for the tea towel and was sitting on the edge of the bed staring at the floor. He didn't look up when Les came in.

'How are you feeling, mate?' asked Norton. 'Ready for a big one?'

'I don't know,' replied Peregrine. 'I feel so tired. And I'm getting a darned headache.'

'Yeah?'

'Yes.' Peregrine rubbed at his shoulder. 'And somehow I've got this pain in the back.'

'You might be getting your period, Pezz.' The Englishman shook his head and continued to stare at the floor. 'I'll make you a cup of coffee. You got any Panadol?' Peregrine mumbled a reply as Les went to the kitchen. 'You'll be all right once you get to the dance,' he called out, as he switched on the electric kettle. 'Couple of bottles of that French shampoo'll fix you up.'

'I hope you're right,' answered Peregrine.

SOME NEW BARMAID was working in the bottle shop at the hotel so Norton was able to get two bags of crushed ice without any trouble. He parked the car behind the school and packed it into the plastic garbage-bin. Peregrine had brushed up considerably, but he was still noticeably stiff and stifling yawns as he got out of the car. Norton hoisted the garbage-bin up onto his shoulder, gave Peregrine a pat on the back and they crossed the street to the dance.

There were small groups of people walking around or standing outside the front of the hall. Alan was on the door and he had to blink a couple of times before he realised who the two Libyan terrorists were. Peregrine and Les had to blink a couple of times to recognise Alan. He was wearing black leotards, black ballet slippers and a cummerbund, a black coat, black shirt, white tie and a silver frosted, ten-gallon hat. He looked like a cross between Rudolph Nureyev, Buffalo Bill and Frank Nitti.

'Hello, fellahs,' he said pleasantly. 'You got here. Good to see you.'

'Wouldn't have missed it for the world, Alan,' grinned Les, paying for the tickets.

'I've got to organise a few things out here,' said Alan. 'Find a spot inside, and I'll come and have a beer with you.'

'Righto,' replied Les.

The big old wooden building was a typical country hall forgotten by time. High ceilings, timber floors and tongue-and-groove timber walls painted white with brown seating running around the bottom. There was an alcove near the front door, a kitchen to the right, behind that was a sort of dining room and the band was on stage at the rear. There would have been about three hundred people in the hall, but there still seemed to be no shortage of room. You were flat out telling one from the other, in fancy dress, though Les and Peregrine still managed to get quite a few once up and downs as they walked in wearing their cammies.

1920s flappers were dancing with cowboys and pirates. Spanish senoritas were dancing with spacemen and French apache dancers. Swarming amongst them were the hippies looking much the same as they did at the bazaar. Tie-died jeans, coloured vests, floppy hats with patches or flowers on them and sling bags. Tai chi slippers and sandals and no shortage of bare feet. Straggly beards, straggly hair and pigtails on the men. Long hair and plaits on a lot of the women. There were people of all ages and types and, to Les's and Peregrine's delight, a number of girls on their own. Playing amongst the grown-ups were clusters of spotlessly clean, well-behaved children. Some were dressed as fairies with wigs and tiny wings on their backs; the way they laughed and giggled as they played and danced they could have passed for tiny angels. Nearly everybody seemed to know each other and it was like one big village get-together or knees-up. Most had a beer or a drink in their hand but nobody was outrageously drunk. Toes were tapping and bare feet were slapping on the floor. Everybody was smiling and happy and if you were looking for trouble you'd come to the wrong place.

'Well, what do you reckon, Peregrine?' said Les, placing the garbage-bin to one side of the alcove near the kitchen. 'We may as well prop here.'

'Suits me,' replied the Englishman.

Norton popped a bottle of Moet for Peregrine and a Corona with a slice of lime for himself. They took a decent slurp each, then stepped around the other side of the alcove to get a better look at the band. It was a five piece with a fat, happy-looking girl on bass and lead vocals and a guy dressed like a French sailor on saxophone. Across the bass drum it said The Hemsemmiches.

Peregrine looked at Norton. 'Les,' he said. 'What's a hemsemmich?'

'I don't know,' replied Les. 'About a dollar twenty with mustard?'

The music was a kind of country and western, blues rock and not too bad. A lot of people were up dancing and most were listening or getting into it. To the right of the stage a DJ console sat in front of two turntables and behind these a tall, skinny guy in a floral shirt was rummaging through three or four milk-crates full of records.

'Hey this could be all right here, Peregrine,' said Norton, tapping away to The Hemsemmiche's version of 'Poor Poor Pitiful Me'.

'Yes, it certainly could,' replied the Englishman.

'All these peace-loving folk. I don't think even you could start a fight in here.'

'Thanks, Les.'

They returned to the alcove for fresh drinks and to watch the hippies and have a bit of a perv on the local girls while they listened to the band. Peregrine said his headache wasn't getting any better and swallowed another two Panadols. After a while Alan joined them. He offered them a beer, but Les took the top off the garbage-bin and said to take one of theirs. Alan gladly accepted a Lowenbrau.

'So how's it going?' said Alan. 'You having a good time?'

'Yes, quite good, actually,' replied Peregrine.

'I like the band,' said Les.

'The Sangers? Yeah, they're not bad, are they,' agreed Alan. 'The DJ's good too. And I told you The Bachelors From Cracow are on later didn't I?'

'You sure did,' nodded Les, raising his Corona.

'Yep, it's gonna be a good night,' smiled Alan. 'Anyway,' he drained his Lowenbrau, 'I've got some other people to say hello to. I'll catch up with you later.'

'See you, Alan,' chorused Les and Peregrine.

The band finished their last number of the bracket with the usual, 'We'd like to take a little break now and hand you over to our disc jockey for the evening — Tony.'

'Thank you The Sangers,' said the DJ. 'Okay, we've got some more good boppin' music for a while before The Sangers come back. And don't forget, later on our special guests all the way from Melbourne, The Bachelors From Cracow.'

Alan wasn't kidding about the disc jockey. He wasn't just good, he was a boogieing fiend from rock 'n' roll hell. For a taste he hit the punters with Hunters And Collectors — 'Relief'. This went into The Fabulous Thunderbirds — 'Powerful Stuff' straight into The Hippos — 'Dark Dark Age'. Then The Johnnys — 'Motorbiking'. By the time he got to James Reyne — 'Fall of Rome' the crowd was in a foaming-at-the-mouth dancing frenzy, you could hardly fit another bum onto the dance floor and Norton could take no more.

'Ohh, fuck this, Peregrine,' he said, downing over half a bottle of Corona in a swallow. 'I gotta get down, baby. And I don't give a stuff if I never get back up again.'

There was a happy-faced woman in a white top with dark hair and glasses tapping her feet to the music at the edge of the alcove. Les asked her for a dance. She said yes and they joined the bouncing, seething mass on the floor for a bit of slippin' and slidin' and reelin' and rockin'. The disc jockey kept the pressure up, flogging the punters unmercifully for the best part of an hour; Spy Vs Spy, Omar And The Howlers, Machinations, and even some old Jerry Lee Lewis and Gary Glitter. Les and his partner thumped and bumped around sticking as close to each other as possible, but half the time you didn't know who you were dancing with. It was just one big rage.

The woman in glasses lasted about forty minutes before throwing in the towel. Les thanked her and offered her a drink. She said she had to find her daughter somewhere and she'd probably come back. Peregrine was sitting down having a glass of champagne when Les plucked a Becks from the ice and just about swallowed the lot in one go.

'I have to hand it to you, Les,' said Peregrine. 'When it comes to dancing, you have a Dionysiac style all of your own.'

'Mate, I can't wait to get back out there,' Les winked and swallowed the rest of the Becks. 'Michael Jackson, eat your heart out.'

'Yes. All that's missing is the glove.'

The DJ stopped, the band came back on and the crowd settled down a little to listen to a bit of blues-rock. Les was getting into the Coronas when he noticed Peregrine smiling at something over his shoulder. Les turned around and there was Marita and Coco. Hello, our luck's in, thought the big Queenslander, but with them were two blonde-haired guys of about thirty and two pretty little girls. Bringing up the rear was an attractive girl of about twenty wearing a white blouse, tartan dress and a tartan string bow-tie.

'Hello, Peregrine. Hello, Les,' said Marita and Coco.

'Hey, hello girls,' chorused the boys. 'Good to see you.'

'You got here,' said Coco.

'Yes,' replied Peregrine. 'It's quite a night.'

'We saw Les dancing,' said Marita. 'Not that you could miss him. So we thought we'd come over.'

'Excellent,' smiled Peregrine, and nodded towards the garbage-bin. 'You'll have to join us for a drink.'

'Okay. Thanks.'

The girls introduced the two boys, Roy and Steve, who were the two little girls' fathers. They had smiles in their eyes and good warm handshakes. The two little girls were Crystal and Tessa; immediately upon hearing their names they took hold of their mother's dresses and buried their faces in the folds, giggling shyly. They saved the girl in the tartan dress till last. Her name was Colleen, and Colleen got a very heavy introduction to Peregrine.

'Colleen's into fashion designing, too,' said Coco.

'Is that right?' beamed Peregrine.

'Yes,' replied Colleen. 'I work from Byron Bay. But I come up and give the girls a hand every now and again.'

'Splendid.'

Norton couldn't help but chuckle to himself at the way Colleen was being given the big sell. It was obvious she'd been brought over as an offering for Peregrine. Be nice, do the right thing, and you never know, the rich pom might buy some of your clobber too. Half your luck, Pezz, thought Norton. She's not a bad little sort.

Like a true gentleman Peregrine poured the girls a glass of champagne and Roy and Steve had a Tuborg each. They weren't bad blokes and it turned out they shaped surfboards at Byron Bay. Norton had tipped them to be surfies of some description: the unkempt blonde hair looked very offshore on the tanned faces and if that wasn't enough, the 100% Mambo T-shirts and the Bad Billy cotton pants were a dead give away. They had another couple of beers from the garbage-bin then the two surfies went and got some of their own. The girls knocked over one bottle of Moet while they discussed fashions, assuring Peregrine the clothes he'd bought went to England on schedule, then they popped a bottle of Veuve Clicquot. All in all the night was going along famously. The band took another break and the DJ started up again so they all got up for a dance. All except Les. He was left to keep an eye on the two anklebiters. But they weren't bad little kids and Norton didn't mind them sitting on his knees and crawling all over him and blowing spit bubbles in his face while he tried to drink his Corona. And Crystal and Tessa didn't think Uncle Les was too bad for a grown-up either. After a few dances the others trooped back from the dance floor. As they did, Colleen was hanging all over Peregrine like a garage sale dressing gown. Peregrine Normanhurst III, thought Norton, you've done it again, buggered and all as you look. Now I wonder if there's something out there for Uncle Les?

Les was wondering what his chances were when the DJ announced that the next record would be the last before The Bachelors From Cracow. He grabbed a fresh Corona and moved to the edge of the alcove for a better look.

He got there just in time to see some bloke with jet black hair swept straight back over a pale, vampirish face pull the cover from a mixer just a metre or two away. At his side stood two girls with equally pale faces and spiky dark hair wearing men's double-breasted suits, T-shirts and Julius Marlow shoes.

'And now,' honked the DJ, 'let's give a big warm Tweed Valley welcome to our special guests for the evening, The Bachelors From Cracow.'

The crowd applauded and surged forward as the band walked out on stage carrying their instruments. They were a seven piece group — young with fifties-style flat-top haircuts and had intense, interesting faces. They nearly all wore cheap, dark suits and ties and had that hip city-boy look about them. The saxophone player was a swap for Max Headroom and the guy on electric piano had to be nearly seven feet tall with a big lantern jaw like Gomez Addams's butler. The trumpet player looked like a young James Cagney in a black bolero jacket. The best of the lot was the lead singer, he was about four feet tall with short black hair cut into a long scraggly fringe at the front that wisped across a nose big enough to double as a bus shelter. He looked like Tiny Tim after someone had shoved him in a wool-press.

No matter what they looked like, The Bachelors From Cracow could really wail. It was slick, cool, fast-lane jazz, so full of energy you'd think there were twenty on stage, not seven. To top it all, the reptilian lead singer had one of those smoky, crackling, tone-perfect voices ideal for singing jazz. If the band was the cake, he was definitely the icing. The music wasn't exactly Norton's cup of tea and the crowd obviously preferred rock 'n' roll. But every number they did was that tight and full of power no one could fail to be impressed. Peregrine was absolutely rapt and for a while seemed to have snapped out of his earlier lethargy.

'I say,' he spluttered. 'Those chaps are just... just sensational.'

'I like them too,' said Colleen, gripping his sleeve.

The Bachelors From Cracow did every track from their new album to an enthusiastic, appreciative audience. They got a big ovation, then came back for an unexpected but howling version of James Brown's 'So Good', after which they faded off stage into the arms of their girlfriends in the Julius Marlows.

The DJ returned, Norton finished another Corona then went for a leak. When he returned the others had gone except for Peregrine, who was seated with Colleen next to him. He motioned for Les to sit down on the other side.

'Les,' he said. 'I hate to be a slacker. But this headache is getting worse and I feel quite ill. I'm afraid I'm going to have to go home.'

'Yeah? Oh, that's no good.'

'Colleen has a car and she's offered to drive me.'

'Yes. I know how to get to where you're staying from here.'

'No, I'd better take you home,' said Les.

'No, it's all right,' insisted Colleen. 'I can do it.'

The way Colleen was insisting told Les that she wanted to get rich, young Peregrine on his own and talk a bit of fashion with him, among other things. However Les wasn't too keen on letting Peregrine go off with a complete stranger. He also wasn't too keen on leaving the dance. Still, Colleen wasn't really a complete stranger. She was a good friend of Coco and Marita who were now more or less business partners with Peregrine. Les thought about it for a moment. He'd walk up to her car with them and check things out.

'Okay,' he nodded. 'I'll walk up to the car with you.'

This brought a smile to Colleen's face and they started for the door. Les told Alan he was going for a few minutes and to keep an eye on the piss. No worries, Alan assured him.

Colleen drove a yellow, Cortina station wagon. As Peregrine climbed in the front seat he apologised once more for being a party-pooper, but he did feel decidedly ill. No sweat, winked Les, probably just a reaction to what happened on Wednesday. After making sure they got safely away, everything was in order and Colleen was of good character, Norton walked back to the dance.

Well, I've got about a dozen bottles of beer and two bottles of Moet left, thought Les. Enough to keep me going, anyway. He opened another Corona as the DJ ripped into some more rock 'n' roll. The place was still jumping and Les was figuring out which way to move when he noticed a young girl standing near the kitchen door eating some sort of a vegetarian curry roll. She was a pretty little thing, straight brown hair, wide, dreamy brown eyes and the sweetest crimson slash of a mouth Norton had seen in ages. Wearing stone-washed jeans and some sort of a double-breasted, blue-checked shirt, she didn't look like a hippy and was definitely no more than nineteen. Norton watched her chewing gingerly at the curry roll. He could smell it ten feet away and tipped whoever cooked it put plenty of curry in it.

'How's the roll?' he asked her.

'Bloody hot,' replied the girl quickly.

'Would you like a cold beer?'

She looked at Les for a moment. 'Yeah, okay. Thanks.'

Les got her a bottle of Stella Artois. She checked out the label then took a healthy swig.

'Ooh! That's really nice,' she said, and took another drink.

Norton smiled as he watched her demolish the rest of the curry roll and the beer in what seemed like a matter of seconds.

'Jesus, you can sure put it away for a little girl,' he said.

'All that dancing. I'm dried out,' she replied, with a polite belch.

'Yeah. He's a larrikin, that disc jockey.'

'Is he what.'

'Would you like another beer?'

The young girl thought for a moment. 'All right,' she smiled. 'Thanks.'

Les got her a bottle of Corona and a fresh one for himself. He didn't bother trying to impress her with the slice of lime. 'Cheers,' he said, and clinked her bottle.

'Yes, cheers,' she replied, giving Les a once up and down, her smile now slow and relaxed.

'What's your name?' asked Norton.

'Alison.'

'Not Alison Wonderland?'

'No. Alison Brisbane. But you can call me Al. Everybody else does.'

'Well, I'm Les. How are you doin', Al?'

'Pretty good, Les,' replied Alison. Then she grinned and gave Norton a friendly punch in the chest. 'How's yourself?'

'All right,' winced Norton. 'Till you broke two of my ribs.'

'You can take it.' Alison took a huge swig of beer. 'Hey, what happened to the other Arab? Did he go back to Mecca?'

'He felt crook and went home.'

'Bullshit!' said Alison. 'Your mother wanted the tea towels back.'

Alison was as cheeky as she was pretty and the more beer she drank the cheekier she got. Norton couldn't help but like her. It turned out she worked part time as a waitress in Brisbane and had come down to Murwillumbah for the weekend to visit her girlfriend. Her girlfriend had had an enormous fight with her parents and had stormed out in a huff and naturally she had to join her. They'd come to the dance to meet a friend of her girlfriend's and stay at his place for the night. His place turned out to be a caravan about the same size as a biscuit tin with no running water or toilet on five acres of ground going back towards Murwillumbah. She wasn't at all keen on sleeping on the floor of the caravan and still had her gear in an overnight bag in the friend's car. Alison gave someone on the dance floor a quick wave. It had to be her girlfriend and the friend. The girlfriend was a dumpy brunette wearing a cheap blue dress and an imitation leather jacket. The friend was in his thirties going a bit thin on top and the way he was dancing with the girlfriend it wasn't hard to tell what he had in mind. They stopped groping each other momentarily to wave back then continued as they were. The germ of a wonderful, beautiful idea was beginning to form in Norton's booze-affected mind when the disc jockey threw on Separate Tables — 'Change Your Sex'.

'Hey, can you dance Les?' asked Alison.

'Can a hoot owl hoot? Come on!'

They joined the other dancers and away they went. Alison's style of dancing was a bit like herself: cheeky. She'd dip her body and head at Les, bounce around him, move up close like she was teasing him then spin away and appear behind him. Norton's style was pretty much as Peregrine had described: Dionysiac without stomping on anybody's feet. But whatever, he was going great guns with the little cutie from Brisbane.

After about six dances they returned to the alcove for a couple of fresh Coronas. Alison took hers and said she was just going to see her girlfriend for a minute and find out what was going on. Les watched them talking for a few moments and noticed when Alison walked back she had a disappointed look on her face.

'Well, Les,' she sighed. 'It looks like I'm going to have to go.'

'Yeah? Why's that?'

'Paul wants to get going and that's my lift.' Alison screwed up her face. 'Jesus, I'm not looking forward to sleeping on the floor of that caravan. With Paul groping Jane right next to my head all night.'

Norton thought for a moment. His earlier idea seemed better than ever. But he was going to have to be quick. 'You don't have to, you know,' he said.

'How do you mean?'

'You could come back to my place. I'm staying on this huge farm. There's tons of room.'

Alison gave Norton a suspicious smile. 'Could I trust you, though?'

Les did his best to look hurt. 'Alison . . .'

The girl thought for a moment. 'All right,' she said, then

wagged a finger at Les. 'I'll come back on two conditions.'

'Sure,' shrugged Les.

'One, you behave yourself. And two, you drive me into Murwillumbah on Sunday to catch the two o'clock train.'

'Good as gold.'

'Okay. I'll go and get my bag out of the car.'

She went back to her friends who were getting ready to leave. They gave Les a brief smile as they walked past.

'I won't be a minute,' said Alison.

Well, I'll be buggered, thought Les, as he watched them walk out the door. This has turned out the grouse. She's like a little doll. And she's all my way. No need to monster her — just having her back later for a few drinks'll be a million laughs. And if something should eventuate, all the better.

Norton couldn't help but feel pleased with himself as he stood back and sipped his beer while he watched the hippies and the alternatives dancing away, drinking, smoking the odd joint and having the time of their lives in an old, dusty run-down School of Arts hall. Since he'd left Sydney he'd stayed at the grouse and ate and drank the best food and wines available. Now he was at a simple bush dance full of simple bush people and he felt this was the best yet. Millionaire dope dealers, Norton laughed to himself — half these people here would be lucky to own a colour TV and a car less than ten years old. All the millionaire drug dealers were too busy building resorts and high-rises all over what's left of the coastline of Australia. Destroying peoples' lives with heroin and cocaine and laundering their money by destroying the environment; aided and abetted by so-called developers, crooked councilmen and arguably the most corrupt politicians on the face of God's earth. And the only thing standing in their way were the hippies and the greenies — the ones trying to save the environment. The ones who the politicians, and their sycophants on certain radio stations try to shitpot all the time to cover their own smelly, slimy tracks. Norton's mind suddenly flicked back to the huge stumps of those old Cedar trees at Cedar Glen and the roots left rotting in the ground. Christ! When you thought about it simplistically, the only things keeping the planet together were the greenies and the roots of the trees. It was a fact.

Les was standing there awash in the virtue of his own karma, when he felt a tap on his shoulder. It was Alison, holding a battered K-Mart overnight-bag.

'I got my suitcase. Where'll I put it?'

Norton gave it a quick eyeball. 'Is there an incinerator down the back?' He put it down next to the garbage-bin, went to get a couple of beers and held up a bottle of Moet. 'You fancy a glass of champagne?'

Alison looked at it for a moment. 'Why don't we drink it back at your place? I just feel like one of those beers.'

'Okey doke,' said Les, and popped another two Coronas.

The DJ stopped and The Hemsemmiches came back on with, of all things, a reggae/rock version of 'Goin' Up The Country'. Alison dragged Les out onto the dance floor for a bit more slippin' and slidin', dippin' and teasin'.

And that was how they spent the next hour or two, drinking beer, laughing and dancing. Apart from Alan, Les didn't know a soul at the dance and neither did Alison. So they were stuck with each other for a bit of company. Alison was now starting to catch up with Les in being a drunken, laughing wombat. Now and again she'd hold his hand or take his arm, and sometimes when they sat down she'd rest her head on his shoulder. What a way to be stuck with someone, thought Les. He felt like the king of the world.

They were down to one bottle of Gosser when the DJ threw on James Reyne's 'Hammerhead'. They slow danced to that and the next track then finished the last beer. The dance was beginning to wind down a little.

'Do you want to go now, Al?' said Les. 'Have a drink and listen to a bit of music back at the farm?'

Alison moved her head slightly on Norton's shoulder. 'Okay,' she smiled.

Propped in the doorway after saying goodnight, Alan couldn't help but be impressed as he watched Norton strolling off down the street, the garbage-bin esky under one arm and Alison on the other. I wonder just who that red-headed bloke is? he mused. He's come into town out of nowhere, flattened six of the best fighters in Yurriki plus the biggest bloke in the Valley. Then he arrives at my dance in an army uniform drinking French champagne and imported beer like it's going out of style. And ups and leaves with the best young sort in the joint. Alan shook his head. Don't know who he is. But he's not bloody bad.

Norton was a little surprised to find the house completely in darkness and Colleen's car gone when he and Alison pulled up in the driveway at Cedar Glen. He switched off the engine and turned to Alison.

'Just wait here for a sec,' he said cautiously.

Norton let himself into the kitchen and nervously tip-toed across to Peregrine's bedroom. He was relieved to find the young Englishman in bed sound asleep, enough moonlight on his face to tell Les he was all right, just out like a light. He watched him for a few moments then tip-toed back out again.

'Peregrine's asleep,' he said, as he opened the car door for Alison. 'He told me he wasn't feeling too good.' Les hit the outside light switch and lit up the barbecue area.

'Hey, this place is really lovely,' said Alison. 'It's so big.'

'Yeah, it's not bad, is it?' replied Les, placing her overnight bag on the table. 'I'll get things organised here, then I'll show you around.'

Before long Norton had the ghetto-blaster playing softly on the table, Alison seated comfortably and a bottle of Moet opened. It was quite cool outside, but after the heat and smoke of the dance hall, it was clear and refreshing.

'Well. Here's to the Yurriki Humdinger Boogie Woogie Ball,' said Les, clinking Alison's glass.

'Yeah, reckon,' replied the little Brisbane waitress, still trying to take in everything around her.

They sipped their drinks and exchanged smiles.

'Anyway, bring your glass and I'll give you a quick guided tour of the bottom half of the house.' Les stood up and got the torch from on top of the fridge.

While he was showing Alison the house, he told her he was a horse trainer in Sydney. Peregrine was thinking of buying the place and turning it into a horse stud and Les was going to work for him. Alison took it all in.

'And this is some sort of a guest's quarters, I think,' said Les, when they came back to the barbecue area. 'You can doss in there for the night if you like.'

Alison peered through the double glass door and let out a strange little laugh. 'Wow. I wasn't expecting anything as good as this.'

Norton looked at her beautiful backside squeezed into the stone-wash jeans. 'No,' he said. 'Neither was I.'

They got stuck into the bottle of champagne, listening to the music, not talking about much in particular. As another glass of Moet went down, Les looked directly at Alison and couldn't help but grin. She caught the big Queenslander's grin and a ripple of laughter went through her body. She was more conscious now of Les than she was earlier in the night, conscious not only of his masculinity, but his sense of humour and easy-going nature. It made her relax and loosen up almost like a small wave breaking over her on a beach. Then again, six beers and half a bottle of French champagne could have had something to do with it too.

Alison looked that good to Les he could have put her on a plate and started eating her there and then, starting with her dainty little toes. They were about to say something to each other when of all things it started to rain. It was only light but steady, making a soothing rhythmic drumming on the timber above their heads.

'Hey, look at that,' said Les. 'Rain. I wonder where that came from?'

The August rain was only gentle but it seemed to put an even more pronounced chill in the air. Alison gave a tiny shiver.

'Ooh!' she said. 'It's starting to get a bit cool out here now.'

'Yeah, you're right,' agreed Les.

Then another genius idea hit him, even better than the one at the dance.

'Hey, Alison,' he said languidly.

'Hey yes,' she replied saucily.

'How would you like a nice warm bubble bath?'

'What?'

Norton looked directly at her again. 'Well, we can't take the party upstairs because Peregrine's asleep. Why don't we go into my room? I can fill that big tile bath full of warm water and soapsuds. And we can lay in it and guzzle champagne while we listen to the radio. I'll give you one of my T-shirts to put on. What do you reckon? It's better than sitting out here freezing our bums off.'

Alison looked at Les for a moment. The way he put it had a little boy's simple honesty about it. And it wasn't a bad idea either. She was still sweaty and her clothes were damp from the dance. There were worse places to be than laying around in that big bath full of warm water with Les.

'Okay,' she smiled. 'But bring another bottle of this grouse champagne. It's beautiful.'

In his room, Norton placed the ghetto-blaster and the champagne on a table near his bed. He gave Alison a big, floppy white Adidas T-shirt to put on and began running the bath. The water pressure coming straight down from the dam was stronger than normal and before long the huge bath was almost a third full of steaming, crystal clear water warming the room and sending misty streaks down the mirrors. Les watched it filling rapidly for a while. When he turned around Alison had changed into his T-shirt and even though it fitted her slim little body like a nightshirt, somehow she seemed to look even more delectable than ever.

'Jesus, it's only just big enough,' he said.

'Yes. I thought I might have had to let the sleeves out.'

Les returned her smile with a wink. 'I'll go and get the soapsuds.'

The rain was coming down harder now; Les watched it for a while as he had a leak then went into the laundry and got a packet of Fab. It wasn't quite the bath crystals he'd been intending to get, but it would do. While he was in the laundry another thought struck him. That bit of pot Marita had given him on Sunday night was still in the pocket of his jeans. He'd thrown them in the laundry meaning to wash them, but hadn't got around to it as he didn't need them on the farm. He'd almost forgotten. It was still rolled up in the piece of gladwrap. Dare I? thought Norton. Champagne. Drugs. The girl's barely out of school. You could go to gaol for things like that. He rubbed his hands together. What a way to go...

The bath was almost full when Les got back. He tipped a liberal amount of soap powder where the water was gushing out of the taps and began beating it with his hand. In no time there were soapsuds two feet thick up the sides of the bath. He turned off the taps, clapped his hands together and blew some suds up in the air.

'Well, what do you reckon?' he smiled at Alison.

'I don't believe it. It looks unreal.'

Norton sat on the edge of the bed and started getting out of his army gear. Alison sipped her champagne while she watched him.

'Alison,' said Les.

'Yes, Les.'

'Do you smoke pot?'

'Yeah. Why?'

'You feel like a smoke?'

Alison's eyes lit up. 'Have you got some?'

Les handed her the gladwrap. 'Here you are. But I got no papers.'

'That's okay. I got a packet of Tally-Ho's out in my bag.'

While Alison went outside to get her bag Norton slipped into a pair of blue shorts with a cord-pull front. He knew what would happen once he got into that bath with Alison and it might be an idea to have them on rather than have embarrassing things poking out all over the place.

'Ooh, it's really coming down out there now,' said Alison,

slamming the door shut behind her and throwing her bag on the bed next to Les. 'I'm glad we're in here.'

'Yeah. Me too.'

She noticed him sitting there in his shorts. 'Hey, you're really solid, aren't you?'

'Yeah,' replied Les. 'But I'm just a softy underneath.'

Alison reached across and kissed him on the cheek. 'You probably are too.'

Norton chuckled and couldn't help a flush come to his cheeks. He watched Alison unwrap the pot. 'You won't need much of that,' he said. 'It's pretty strong.'

'Yeah, it looks good. I'll just roll a greyhound. Where did you get it?'

Norton shrugged. 'Peregrine bought it somewhere.'

The music played in the background while Alison's tiny fingers deftly rolled a joint. Norton watched her intently. There was a beauty and a magic about her that was more than physical — Les couldn't quite explain it.

'Hey, Alison,' he said. 'There's something I've got to ask you.'

'Sure, Les.'

'How old are you?'

'Eighteen.'

'Oh.'

'Well.' She smiled as she licked the gum on the cigarette paper. 'I will be in January.'

Norton had to turn away. Ohh, no Les, he said to himself. Seventeen. Christ! What have I become? What sort of a depraved monster am I turning into? Seventeen. If I was any older it'd be nothing more than legalised incest. He watched the rain pattering against the windows and had a hopeless one-sided battle with his conscience when he felt a tap on his shoulder. He turned around and Alison had the joint lit.

'Here you are,' she said.

There was enough for about four tokes each; but Marita's dope was that good you didn't need much more and it soon did the job. Almost immediately the music got better. If it was at all possible, Alison seemed to become more beautiful. The night intensified.

'Hey, that's a good smoke,' said Alison.

'Is it what,' agreed Les.

They stared at each other for a moment and exchanged ridiculous grins.

'Well,' smiled Alison, nodding towards the steaming bath. 'Last one in's a rotten egg.'

'I hope I don't drown,' chuckled Les. 'That looks deeper than I thought.'

They slid into the warm soapy water and it was fantastic from the word go. The rain coming down outside made it even better. Alison squealed and giggled with delight. Norton couldn't help but sigh with ecstasy, the warm natural spring water was like heaven on his body. He ducked his head beneath the surface and splashed around. Alison did the same, running water through her hair and smearing soapsuds over her face. There was a ton of room, the bath was almost like a small pool. Les got the bottle of Moet and placed it on the tiles behind them. They had another glass or two each while they frollicked around like two baby seals, splashing each other and blowing soap bubbles in each other's faces and doing and saying stupid things you normally wouldn't if you weren't stoned and drunk on French champagne. They settled down after a while and rested their heads on the edge of the tiled bath facing each other while they just took in the luxuriousness of it all. Through the water Les could see the wet T-shirt clinging to Alison's soft smooth body, her delicate pink nipples straining against the wet cotton.

Maybe it was the undertow or the currents in the pool, but somehow Les and Alison seemed to be inexorably drifting towards each other. Before Les knew it she had bobbed up in front of him. He reached out and took her gently beneath the shoulders. Alison's arms went around his neck. Their eyes seemed to burn into each other for a few magical moments then softly, tenderly Les kissed her and their hearts did seem to beat as one.

Alison's lips were an indescribable delight of softness and sweetness. They gently swept across his mouth and brushed his cheek then she kissed him a little harder and the tip of her tongue crept out like a small jet of flame. He returned her kisses, running his hands through her hair and up and down her back. Alison clutched Les's hair and wrapped her legs around his waist. His hands slid down over her thighs and around her ted. It felt like a little sugar cube: sweet, soft, inviting. Les stroked and teased it gently while she kissed him. He wiggled out of his shorts and pushed them to one side of the bath and brought Alison's T-shirt up over her breasts. She straightened her arms and Les slid the T-shirt off over her head. He kissed and ran his tongue over the two delicate pink nipples then lifted her up and went to roll her to one side when she stopped him.

'Stay there,' she said. 'I want to get on top.'

Les lay back against the edge of the bath, Alison wriggled up his chest and her ankles went under his arms. She came down slowly, wiggled her bum a little then Les could feel himself enter her.

Norton groaned; he couldn't believe how warm and firm it was. Alison bobbed up and down, the water supporting her weight, and Les could feel himself sliding deeper insider her. She moaned and sighed while they kissed, pumping slowly as they rocked against the edge of the bath. Les's head swam, he wished this would never end. Then Alison's backside started going up and down, faster and faster. Soapsuds went everywhere. Their discarded clothes swirled around in the warm water. Les felt like his body was going to burst. Alison was beyond description. It was like kissing honey, holding a dream and making love to an angel. The swirling and bobbing intensified, reached a crescendo then slowed. Alison let out a scream of joy. Norton moaned and buried his face into her neck and their love and affection for each other poured out, almost engulfing them in a wave of exhilaration and wicked abandonment.

With shudders still coursing through his body, Les spun Alison around in the bath and gave her one huge kiss.

'Ohh Christ! How good was that?' he panted happily.

Alison drifted back into his arms, smiled and kissed Les's neck. 'I'm not saying anything,' she whispered.

They drank the other bottle of champagne and Les changed the tape. After a while they made love again in the huge tiled bath. But this time it seemed to get a bit out of control, slipping and sliding on the tiles and bouncing off the sides. So they towelled off and finished it in bed.

It was pitch black in the room and Alison was curled up into Norton snoring softly. Her damp hair wisped beneath his chin and Les could feel her heart beating against his. The big Queenslander was smiling to himself yet his mind was in a whirl; he didn't know what to think. There's no such thing as love at first sight — is there? And grown men don't go around falling in love with seventeen-year-old girls — do they?

* * *

APART FROM HIS mate Greg back at Taree, Carrots was the only highway-patrol cop on duty that night; sitting alone just outside of Cundletown on the lookout for speeders or stolen cars. It was bloody cold and there wasn't a great deal around, mainly semis or the odd caravan rumbling up the Pacific Highway, destination unknown. He took absolutely no notice of the white Holden sedan and its three occupants as it went past. Why should he? It was well within the speed limit. There was no excessive noise. Tail lights and headlights were working perfectly. He took even less notice of the one that went past about five minutes later. In fact, if all the cars that went past that night drove as safely as those two white Holdens, Carrots could have taken the rest of the night off.

THE RAIN HAD eased off and the sun was appearing now and again from behind banks of scattered clouds when Norton took his child bride up for breakfast around ten on Sunday morning. They'd woken up earlier, keen for a bit of the other, but the previous night's romp in the bath had left them both a bit on the sore side so they settled for a long shower together instead. Peregrine was in the kitchen wearing his dressing gown nursing a cup of coffee. His hair was unkempt and his face was pallid and he was staring expressionlessly into his coffee as though he had as much to look forward to as Quasimodo's ironing lady.

'G'day, Peregrine,' breezed Norton. 'How's things?'

'Good morning, Les,' replied Peregrine dully. He brought his head up slowly, gave a double blink despite himself when he saw Alison, looked at Les then back at Alison again. With her hair still damp and no makeup on she looked about fourteen.

'Peregrine,' said Les. 'This is Alison. Alison, this is my friend Peregrine.' Norton chuckled at the look on Peregrine's face as they exchanged greetings. 'So how are you feeling, mate? Any better?'

Peregrine shook his head. 'Simply dreadful, I'm afraid.'

'Shit! That's no good. Sounds like you're getting the flu.'

'I doubt if it's the flu. It's all through my back. It's so sore. I've never felt anything quite like this.'

'Mmhh. I'll have a look at it downstairs after we have breakfast. You might have strained a muscle or something. You hungry?'

'I don't think I could eat a thing.'

'What about you, big Al? You fancy some bacon and eggs à la Norton?'

'Sounds good, big Les,' smiled Alison. 'Do you want a hand?'

'All right. You can set the table and keep His Highness company. Make sure he doesn't try to commit suicide.'

Norton soon knocked up a big feed of bacon, eggs, toast and coffee, and they ripped in. Peregrine had a bit of a pick but it was obvious he was ill and off his food. Alison was pretty stoked all round. It had been a good night with Les in the bubble bath drinking French champagne; he'd really looked after her. Now she was getting a hot breakfast on this beautiful big farm. And to think she nearly spent the night in a grungy caravan with no toilet. The bacon and eggs were perfect and Les was getting better all the time.

Les said to leave the dishes and told Peregrine to come downstairs where he could have a look at his back in the daylight. They took their coffee down to the barbecue area where Norton pulled a chair out and told Peregrine to take his dressing gown off and sit down with his arms over the back of the seat. He put his coffee on the table and walked around behind the Englishman.

'Okay. Now let's have a look at this back of yours. You've probably just... Holy bloody hell!'

Alison's eyes followed Norton's. She screwed up her face and sucked some air in through her teeth. 'Oh shit!' she said.

Sitting behind Peregrine's armpit was an ugly, red lump with a black head on it the size of a grape seed. Radiating out from the lump were several thick red lines of about four inches in length. The area around the lump was also red and inflamed.

'What's the matter?' Peregrine asked anxiously.

Norton gave the lump a light squeeze and Peregrine winced. 'You know what's up with you, you stupid prick? You've been bitten by a tick.'

'A what?'

'A tick.' Norton prodded the lump and had a closer look. 'Yeah. That's what these red lines are. The ECM rash. You've scratched the body off, but the head's still in there with the poison. Why didn't you tell me, you wombat?'

'I... didn't really...'

Norton snapped his fingers. 'I would have noticed it only you had your T-shirt on down at the billabong yesterday.' He gave a bit of a laugh. 'You've got Lyme disease, old son.'

'Please, Les. I'm not in the mood for your jokes. I want a doctor.'

'I'm not joking, mate,' laughed Les. 'That's what it's called — Lyme disease, tick poisoning.' He gave Peregrine a light slap on the good side of his back. 'That's one thing I'll never do, Pezz. Call you a limey. You'll always be a rotten pom to me.'

'Thank you. Now take me to a doctor.'

Norton shook his head. 'You're not gonna need a doctor. Alison, get me that lighter out of your bag, will you?' Alison headed for Les's bedroom Les gave the lump on Peregrine's back another squeeze. 'Now where's my Bowie knife?'

'Bowie knife?' howled Peregrine. 'I say, steady on.'

Chuckling like a drain at Peregrine's apprehension, Norton got a safety pin from his first-aid kit. He took the cigarette lighter from Alison and held the point over it till it was red hot. Les was about twenty times stronger than Peregrine at the best of times, but ill with Lyme disease, the Englishman didn't stand any chance at all. Norton forced his chest against the back of the chair and stuck the glowing point of the safety pin into the black head on the red lump in Peregrine's back. Peregrine howled, but the jaws on the tick's head automatically closed forcing it back out of the hole it had dug in the Englishman's back.

'There you are,' smiled Les, picking the head off Peregrine's back. 'One shitty little tick.' He dropped the head on the table and mashed it to nothing with his thumb nail. 'I'll give it one thing, though — it only ate at the best.'

'God, that bloody well hurt,' cursed Peregrine.

'Yeah. For about two seconds.' Les dabbed some iodine on the hole and covered it with a band-aid. 'When I take Alison into Murwillumbah I'll get some stuff from the chemist to draw all the poison out. You'll be as right as rain in the morning.'

'Thank you,' replied Peregrine testily. 'Now I might go back and lay down for a while.'

'Good on you. You want a hand to your room?'

Peregrine shook his head. 'I can manage. Goodbye, my dear,' he said to Alison. 'It's been very nice to have met you.'

'Yeah, you too Peregrine. Take care of yourself.'

They watched Peregrine slowly climb the stairs then Les turned to Alison. 'And now, my dear, would you care for a tour of the estate? Or perhaps madam would prefer another bubble bath?'

Alison slipped her arms around Norton's neck and kissed him. 'The bubble bath sounds like a good idea,' she smiled. 'But I'll settle for a tour of the estate.'

'As madam wishes. Come this way.'

Hand in hand they walked around the fields and the billabongs. Stopping to watch the birds or toss a stone in the creek, have a kiss and a cuddle, a tease and a chase and all the other silly things people are apt to do when they find themselves suddenly falling in love. Sadly before they both knew it, it was getting on for one o'clock and almost time to go. They strolled back to the barbecue area and sat facing each other over a last bottle of beer before leaving.

'God, this place is so lovely,' said Alison. 'The birds. All those trees. That little billabong.'

'You've barely seen half of it.' Les took her tiny hands in his. 'I'm going to be here for another week at least, I reckon. Why don't you try and come back down again before I go back to Sydney?'

Alison nodded. 'I might be able to arrange something,' she smiled.

'Unreal.' Norton's grin faded as he looked at his watch. 'Well, what did the man say? Something about parting is such sweet sorrow?'

'Yeah, something like that.'

Norton finished his beer and looked at Alison. His heart felt like a huge lead weight sitting in his chest. If there's anything sweet about saying goodbye to you, Alison, he thought, it's a mystery to me.

CALL IT THE luck of the Irish, call it coincidence, call it what you like. But the two cells of IRA men couldn't believe their good fortune shortly after they rolled into Murwillumbah around eleven. The trip had been easy and without incident. Taking turns at driving and catching a nap on the back seat, the Irishmen arrived with their eyes a little grainy perhaps, but not all that tired. They had closed the distance between the two cars shortly before they reached Murwillumbah. Patrick was driving the first one with Liam alongside and Logan in the back. They turned left onto the bridge and one of the first shops they noticed when they took the next street on the right was the Tweed Valley Stock And Station Agents And Auctioneers. Liam said to stop and motioned for the others to pull up behind.

'That estate agent's open over there,' he said. 'May as well see what he's got to say while we're here. And remember, we're English.'

They got out of the car, stretched their legs and Liam told the others to wait there while they went over and quickly checked out the estate agency. There was only one person in the shop: he was about five feet tall wearing a white shirt and blue trousers. This person had no reservations whatever about working on Sundays. Saturdays — maybe, but definitely not Sundays, especially if there was a dollar to be turned.

'Yes, gentlemen?' said Benny Rabinski, giving the three Irishmen his oiliest, number one, real estate agent's smile. 'What can I do for you?'

'Good morning,' said Patrick, slipping into an upper class, English accent. 'We're out here from England and we're thinking of investing in some property in this area.'

Benny's round, bald face lit up like the aurora borealis. 'Certainly. Would you gentlemen care to take a seat?'

'Well, actually,' said Patrick, 'to get straight to the point: the property we're interested in is called Cedar Glen, out at Yurriki. Would you happen to know it at all?'

Benny Rabinski beamed even brighter. He made a magnanimous gesture with his hands. 'Gentlemen,' he said. 'Such a coincidence this is! I happen to be the sole agent for Cedar Glen.'

The three Irishmen blinked at Benny then exchanged quick glances. They were barely able to contain themselves.

'You what?' said Logan, without thinking.

'Cedar Glen is on the market. I'm the only agent with that property on his books.'

'I say,' drawled Liam. 'How simply marvellous.'

'An absolutely amazing coincidence,' echoed Patrick.

'Were you gentlemen thinking of going out there now?' asked Benny.

'No. Not today,' said Liam. 'We ... have to go back to where we're staying. We're expecting a call from our broker in London.'

'Whereabouts are you staying?' asked Benny, doing his best to make polite conversation.

'Up at ... ah ...'

'On the Gold Coast,' cut in Patrick. 'Surfers Paradise.'

'Surfers Paradise. Yehh!' Benny grimaced. 'Too gawdy. Too many signs. Down here is better.'

'We couldn't agree with you more,' smiled Liam.

'And when would you gentlemen like to inspect Cedar Glen?'

'How about Wednesday?' said Liam. 'In the afternoon.'

'I'll make sure I'm here,' said Benny. 'Is there a phone number where I can contact you?'

'There is. But I'm dashed if I can remember the number,' smiled Patrick. The others nodded in dumb agreement.

'There's only one minor problem,' said Benny. 'A couple of gentlemen are staying there at the moment, renting with the intention of buying. I'd have to arrange with them for you to inspect the property. Actually one's an Englishman.'

'Really?' purred Liam. 'And who might the other chap be?'

'An Australian. A Mr Norton. You wouldn't know him.' And nor would fine gentlemen like you want to, Benny thought to himself.

'Jolly good,' smiled Liam. 'Anyway, we must be off. And we'll be down to see you on Wednesday. In the meantime, could you give us the address of Cedar Glen, just in case we decide to drive out and take a bit of a look from the outside?'

'No trouble at all,' smiled Benny. 'In fact I'll draw you a map.'

'You're too kind,' said Patrick, returning Benny's smile.

Minutes later they left the estate agency, with Benny's map and his business card. It was all they could do to stop from jumping up and down in the air.

'You'll not believe this,' said Liam, poking his head in the driver's side window of the other car. 'The fockin' yid in that estate agency drew us a map of how to get to Cedar Glen.'

'He didn't?' said Tom Mooney from the back seat.

'Here. Take a fockin' look.' Liam handed Robert, behind the wheel, Benny's map.

'Would you look at that?' said Tom, straining over from the back seat. 'Do you want to go out now then?'

'No. There's no great hurry.' Liam nodded to a large RSL club not far from the bridge and opposite where they were parked. 'I think we should go across to that fine-looking club. Have a pint or two and a decent meal while we discuss this. It's almost lunchtime.'

'Good idea,' said Logan. 'I'm starving hungry and I've the devil of a thirst.'

They drove round and parked in the RSL parking lot.

Whatever their feelings and bitterness towards each other, Irish are still Irish the world over. Take them away from 'the troubles' and they're the happiest, most gregarious people on God's earth. Liam and his two cells may have been the type of people who wouldn't think twice about blowing you apart with a shotgun or shooting your kneecaps off if they had to. But paradoxically, when it came to a friendly beer or a laugh or doing someone a turn, the same men couldn't be there quickly enough.

The Murwillumbah RSL was quite large and modern. The bars were upstairs, with the usual banks of poker machines, a dining room, a bistro and a good sized auditorium overlooking the river. The six Irishmen found a table then Liam and Patrick went to the bar. While they were waiting to be served they couldn't help but notice the two fair-haired young blokes standing next to them in shorts, T-shirts and thongs. Their eyes were bloodshot, they hadn't had a shave for at least three days and even though it wasn't midday they were both laughing like loons and well on their way to getting roaring drunk.

'Having a bit of a celebration, are we, lads?' smiled Liam.

'Yeah sort of, mate,' slurred the young bloke closest to him.

Liam couldn't help but notice the bandaged leg. 'That's a nasty wound you've got there, lad. What ever happened to you?'

'I cut it on a rock and got twenty stitches in it,' was the reply. Then the young bloke and his mate fell about laughing.

'And you're laughing about it? You're a strange fellah, I must say.'

'Ohh, don't worry about it mate,' said the other young bloke. 'That's his million dollar wound. What did we work it out at? Five thousand a stitch. You should have cut your bloody leg right off. We'd both be millionaires.' He hit his mate across the back and they roared laughing spilling beer over the bar.

Liam shook his head and looked at Patrick. Are all Australians as crazy as this? But there was something about the likeable, drunken young bloke that had him intrigued.

'You're talking in riddles, lad. Tell me what happened.'

'I saved some pommy from drowning. And he gave me 'n me mate a hundred grand each. Mate, we've been pissed since Thursday. And we ain't even started yet.'

They both roared laughing again spilling more beer on each other.

'So here's to Sir Pomegranate Normanhurst.'

'At least that's what it said on the cheques,' said his mate, then they burst into more drunken laughter falling against the bar.

Liam exchanged a quick glance with Patrick. 'What was that name you said again?' he said quietly.

'Ohh, I dunno,' said the bloke with the bandaged leg. 'Peregrine. Pomegranite. Normanhurst. Something or other.'

'But, Jesus,' slurred his mate. 'He sure must have had some money.'

'Well,' said Liam. 'You're a fine broth of a lad. And I insist on buying you and your pal a drink. Come on now. What'll it be?'

'All right. We'll force a couple down just to be sociable. Two schooners of Brown Old.'

Geoff Nottage and Brian Byrne had told everyone between Cabarita and Murwillumbah what happened on Wednesday and Thursday so many times half the population of the Tweed Valley had corns on their ears. As they slurped their beers they told a very interested Liam and Patrick what had happened.

'And the big red-headed bloke who was with the Englishman?' said Liam. 'Tell me a bit more about him.'

'Ohh, good bloke,' said Geoff.

'Yeah, bloody oath,' agreed Brian. 'Dunno his name. But top notch, don't worry about that.'

Liam and Patrick listened to their story, shouted them another two beers then said goodbye and returned to the others with the round of drinks.

'What was all that about?' asked Logan.

'Lads,' replied Liam, as he and Patrick placed the beers on the table. 'You're not going to believe this.'

WITH ANY SORT of luck the train might be late, thought Les. With any sort of luck it might have been derailed and not turn up at all. But no. For once the New South Wales Railways had its act together and the 2 pm to Brisbane was right on time.

It hadn't been the easiest thirty minutes or so for Les waiting at the station drinking coffee and softdrinks. He was truly sorry, even sad, to see Alison go. The little waitress from Brisbane had not just plucked at Norton's heartstrings, she'd almost torn them out. It seemed like they'd been together a lot longer than just one night. But it wasn't the end of the world. She'd possibly be down again next weekend and he had her phone number. He could ring her through the week. Now it was time to go. She took her battered overnight bag from Les as they joined the last of the people waiting to board the train. Standing in the crowd, tiny Alison seemed even smaller and the lead weight in Norton's chest seemed to get heavier.

'Well, I guess this is it, big Les.' Alison wrapped her slender arms around Norton's waist and gazed up into his eyes.

'Yeah. I guess it is, big Al.' Norton held her tight, wanting to crush her into him. She reached up and kissed his lips and Les thought his sadness was going to engulf him when he felt her warm teardrops on his cheek.

'Gee, I'm gonna miss you, Les,' she said.

'And I'm gonna miss you too, Al,' replied Norton. 'Like you wouldn't believe.'

They kissed again, then when they looked around they were almost the only people left on the platform. An ominous voice called in the distance. 'All aboooaaaard.' Alison stepped up onto the train, tears staining her cheeks. She let go of Norton's hand and gave a tiny wave.

'Hey, how are you going for chops?' said Les. Alison shook her head. 'Money. You sweet for dough?'

'Yes. I'm all right. Don't worry.'

Yeah, I'll bet, thought Les, looking at her battered overnight bag and worn shoes. He pulled five hundred from the back of his jeans and stuffed it in the front of Alison's.

'Hey, I don't need this,' she said, and started to pull it out.

Les pushed her hand back down. 'Keep it,' he smiled. 'Get me a Brisbane T-shirt and bring it down with you next weekend.' Alison was about to say something when a whistle blew and a second or two later the train jolted forward.

'Goodbye, Les,' she blurted, the tears really flowing now.

'Goodbye Alison. You look after yourself. I'll ring you through the week.'

'You promise?'

Norton had to start walking alongside now to keep up. 'Of course I promise.'

Norton kept walking alongside the train till he was almost jogging. Alison gave another wave and Norton's last memory of her was the tears blending in with the look of complete helplessness on her face. Then she was gone.

Norton gave a last wave as the train pulled out of the station then joined the few other people walking back to their cars. Well, what a bastard, he thought. Little Alison was one in a million, even if she was a bit young. Oh well. He kicked at a stone laying on the road. No good moping around like a lovesick puppy, I've got to get back out to the farm and make sure Peregrine's all right. But as he slowly walked back to the car Les knew it was going to be a very sad and quiet old night back at Cedar Glen.

There was a chemist open a few doors up from the bottle shop where Peregrine had bought all the imported beers. Les got some cotton wool and bandages, Codral Reds and a jar of Icthyol. He told the chemist what had happened and he needed to knock Peregrine out for a good ten hours. Could the chemist . . .? The chemist slipped him six Normison without a prescription. Les left thirty dollars on the counter and a wink. As he was leaving he almost bumped into a small balding figure who had come in to pick up a prescription for his loving wife.

'Mr Norton,' said the figure.

Les looked up from his purchases. 'Oh. G'day Benny,' he replied quietly. 'How's things?'

'Very good, Mr Norton. Actually this is good bumping into you like this. It saves me a trip out to the farm.'

Norton looked quizzically at his old landlord. 'Why? What's up?'

'Oh nothing. Just that some English people were in town today, inquiring about purchasing Cedar Glen. I'd like to bring them out to inspect the property on Wednesday. You and your friend wouldn't mind?' Norton shook his head. 'Good.'

'English blokes, you say, Benny?'

'Yes. Three nice gentlemen. Interested in investing in property around this area.'

Norton nodded despondently. He wasn't really in the mood for talking to anyone, least of all Benny Rabinski. 'Yeah, righto. I'll see you on Wednesday, Benny. So long.'

'Goodbye Mr Norton.'

The bottle shop was open. Les got a bottle of OP rum. He passed a fruit shop on the way home, and he got some more Coca Cola, a capsicum and some garlic. Before long he was back at Cedar Glen.

Peregrine was still in his dressing gown, sitting in the barbecue area sipping a bottle of champagne.

'You're up and about, mate,' said Les, placing what he'd just bought on the table. 'How are you feeling?'

'Still absolutely wretched,' replied Peregrine. 'I just got sick of laying in my room.'

'Yeah, well you'll be okay in the morning. I got all the goodies right here.'

Peregrine gave the bandages and that a scant look. 'You got young Alison away all right?'

'Yeah. Two o'clock train. Right on time.'

'Young would be the correct word there, too. My God, Les. How old was she?'

Norton got a Becks from the fridge. 'Well, she tried to tell me she was fifteen, but I went through her bag while she was asleep and found her school bus pass. She's fourteen.'

'Fourteen! Good Lord. Have you no shame, man? That's absolutely disgraceful.'

'Ohh, I wouldn't say that,' grinned Les. 'I had a pretty good night actually. Anyway you needn't talk. What about those two schoolgirls you had back in your room at Coffs Harbour? And nothing less than an orgy too, I might add.'

'They weren't jolly fourteen.'

'Yeah? So you tell me.' Norton took a good sip of beer. 'Anyway, get into that champagne, Pezz. I want you nice and drunk tonight. You hungry?'

Peregrine shook his head. 'I still don't think I could eat a thing.'

'Well I'm going to barbecue myself a steak while I have a few beers. Then I'll fix up your back.'

Norton got his barbecue together, giving Peregrine a bit of a rundown on what happened the night before, encouraging the Englishman to get stuck into his bottle of Veuve Clicquot at the same time. While he did Peregrine told Les how Colleen drove him home, but he was entirely too ill to do any business, so she left, saying she'd call around through the week. When Peregrine had finished the champagne, Les started applying him liberally with OP rum and Coke. The Englishman complained bitterly, stating that he wasn't a midshipman on Nelson's flagship, but after a while he got the taste for it and they began sliding down a bit more easily. He watched with mild amusement as Les chopped up the garlic and the capsicum, then screwed up his face in disbelief when Les pushed the plate of it over in front of him.

'And just what on earth is that?' demanded the Englishman.

'That,' smiled Norton, 'is garlic, nature's antibiotic. That will help to kill any germs and shit in your system. The green thing is a capsicum. It's packed with vitamin C. That'll build up your resistance. Wash it down as it is with rum and Coke.'

'Oh, bloody wonderful. Then what's next? You dance around me with your face painted, rattling bones and chanting to keep away the evil spirits?'

'No. I keep filling you full of rum then I rug you up and put you to bed with six sleeping pills under your belt. You won't move for ten hours, sweating like a pig with all the rum and vitamins racing around in your system.'

'Oh, good God.'

'Ah yes,' said Norton. 'But that's not all. I cover your back in black-zinc and that draws all the poison and inflammation out of you. Mate, you won't know yourself in the morning. You'll sweat the fever away, the poison'll all be gone, and you'll wake up with a horn a foot long.'

'Oh good God,' repeated Peregrine, taking a slurp of rum and Coke. 'Why me? Why bloody me?'

'Why?' asked Les. 'Because I think you're such a wonderful chap. Isn't that what you told me?' Les pushed the plate of diced garlic and capsicum under Peregrine's face. 'Now, come on. Be a good boy and eat your din-dins. I'm going to put a steak on.'

Over the sound of the radio and Peregrine's complaints Les may have just faintly heard the two cars coming slowly down the road in the distance. If he did, he didn't take any notice. Hidden by the house and trees, he certainly didn't see them pull up at the front gate or see the six dark-haired men get out.

'So, this is where they're holed up, is it?' said Liam. 'Sure and it looks peaceful enough.'

The others gathered around. Patrick handed him a pair of binoculars. Logan checked the lock and chain on the front gate.

'There's no security system,' he said. 'And that lock's nothing. I could fairly bite it off with my teeth.'

Liam took the binoculars while Robert and Brendan checked the road. 'It's nothing but a big wooden house,' he said, running them over the property. There's a set of stables to the right and some sort of a shed behind that old bridge there. This driveway goes right up to the house.' Liam held the binoculars on the smoke coming up from the rear of the house. 'Looks like someone's out there having a barbecue or something.'

'Do you want to go in now?' asked Patrick.

'No,' replied Liam. He peered through the binoculars a little longer then put them down. 'No. We'll come back when it's dark, as we planned. Around eight-thirty. I'm assuming this Norton fellow will have a gun with him, so we'll get the jump on him. In the meantime, we can go and test our own guns. Give you lads a chance to get the hang of these bullpups.'

'Where are you thinking of going?' asked Brendan.

'Remember that rattling old bridge we crossed over on the

way out here? We'll find a spot near that. It sounded like a machine gun going off when we drove over it. No one around will notice a thing. We'll rest there when we're finished. I don't want to go back into town. The less people that see us up here the better. We've thermos flasks of coffee in the car.' He took another look at the house and a malevolent smile creased his face. 'Just one man and that English bastard. Dead easy.' He turned to the others. 'We should be out of here well before ten. Back in Sydney by lunchtime tomorrow, and on the four o'clock plane back to Belfast.' He winked at Logan Colbain. 'Dead easy.'

'Aye,' smiled Logan. 'Dead easy.'

Getting on for six, Les was sitting on a Gosser watching Peregrine who was blind, dribbling drunk on OP rum. He'd managed to get down the diced capsicum, but he'd refused to eat the raw garlic, until Les promised him that if he didn't swallow it he'd force it down his throat like one of those pâté de fois gras geese.

'So how are you feeling now, Pezz?'

'Drunk.'

'Good. 'Cause now comes the best part. Take off your dressing gown.'

'I'm not taking off anything,' replied Peregrine, full of OP rum.

'Peregrine. Take the fuckin' thing off, or I'll rip it off your back.'

'Brute,' sulked Peregrine.

The inflammation had spread a little further across Peregrine's back, but at least the head was out and there was no more poison going into his blood stream. Les removed the band-aid and gave the hole a prod. He got the safety pin from his first-aid kit and poured rum over the point.

'Hey, Peregrine,' said Les. 'What's that over there?'

'Huh?'

Les forced Peregrine against the back of the chair and quickly jabbed ten or so puncture wounds in the inflammation, squeezing open the hole at the same time. Peregrine howled in protest at the pain.

'Good God, man?' he almost sobbed. 'What are you doing to me?'

'Just putting in a few more holes to help drain the poison away. You'll live.' Les watched it bleed for a while, then wiped the blood away with a piece of cotton wool splashed with methylated spirits.

'Oh, you rotten monster!' howled Peregrine. 'God that hurt.'

'I'm sure it did,' replied Norton. 'That looks bloody sore. I'm glad it's you and not me. But mate, you've got to be cruel to be kind.'

Les scooped enough Icthyol out of the jar to liberally cover the inflammation then placed a wad of cotton wool on top. He then covered that with a bandage and stuck the lot down securely with elastoplast.

'There you go, mate,' he smiled, giving Peregrine a pat on the shoulder. 'Put your dressing gown back on.'

Peregrine was almost in tears as he winced his way back into his dressing gown. 'Now kindly leave me alone, you bloody great oaf.'

'I know you didn't mean that,' grinned Norton. 'You love me. Now throw these down your screech.' He took the six Normisons from the small packet the chemist had given him and handed them to Peregrine.

'What are these?'

'I told you. Sleeping tablets.'

'Six of them?'

'They're only mild. Come on, get them down. Then you can take a couple of painkillers before you go to bed.'

Peregrine swallowed the sleeping tablets with a glass of rum and Coke. 'God, this is primitive,' he slurred.

'Yeah, I got to agree with you there,' said Les. 'But you'll feel heaps better in the morning.' He made the Englishman another rum and Coke and got himself another beer. Well, I reckon another fifteen minutes or so and those pills should start working, thought Les, checking his watch as he smiled at Peregrine staring moodily into his drink.

Peregrine took a mouthful then morosely shoved it out on the table in front of him. 'God, I wish my Stephanie was here.'

'Your girl back in England?' replied Les. 'Well I'm sorry but she ain't mate. There's just me. Stephanie doesn't even know where you are.'

'She knows where I am.'

Les took a mouthful of beer and looked at Peregrine over the bottle. 'How would she know where you are?'

'I sent her a card.'

Les thought for a moment. 'That was at Coffs Harbour. When you weren't exactly being faithful to her, I might add.'

'I sent her a card from Yurriki.' Peregrine gave a drunken laugh. 'I sent them all a card.'

'You sent her a card from Yurriki. When?'

Peregrine had to think for a moment. 'Friday before last.'

Les had to laugh. 'Well she'd be bloody lucky to get it by now. In fact, knowing Australia Post, she'd be bloody lucky if she ever gets the thing at all.'

'Oh, she's got it all right. I had it especially couriered.'

'You what?'

'When one has absolutely scads of money, old boy,' replied Peregrine, 'it's amazing just what one can do.'

Peregrine explained the deal he'd worked out with the local postmaster's son and his courier service. Actually he'd been meaning to send more, but they never seemed to get into Yurriki during the day. And when they did he had other things on his mind. When he'd finished Les did a little adding and subtracting of the days in his mind. He wasn't real rapt in the end result.

'You're a bloody dill, Peregrine,' he said seriously. 'If she or any of your mates start telling people where you are, and the bloody IRA find out, it'd take them five minutes to send someone up here. They might even fly out themselves. Jesus, Peregrine, I wish you'd use your head at times.'

'Oh, bloody stupid Irish. Bugger the Irish. Half the time those paddys wouldn't know what day it is.'

'Yeah? Don't you believe it,' said Les. 'Where did you send the card? The boutique? Her place? Where?'

But it was too late. In Peregrine's weakened state and drunk on rum, the Normisons started taking effect quicker than Norton had expected. The Englishman's face suddenly started to look like one huge smile button. He grinned at Norton, raised his glass then started to slump down in his seat.

'Cheers, Les,' he mumbled. The glass fell out of his hand and he pitched forward onto the table.

'Peregrine.' Les gave his shoulder a shake. 'Peregrine.' Norton was wasting his time. Sir Peregrine Normanhurst III was completely out of it.

Shit! Norton cursed to himself. He looked at Peregrine face down on the table snoring. Oh well. He picked the Englishman up over his shoulder, carried him up to his room and placed him gently on his bed.

Les removed his dressing gown then rugged him up in all the clothes he could find: pullovers, jackets, tracksuit pants. There was an extra couple of blankets near the bed so he threw them over him as well. I reckon that should make him sweat, thought Les. He'll be lucky if he doesn't dissolve. I'd hate to smell his breath in the morning. Oh well. Goodnight, sweet prince. He turned off the light and left Peregrine dead to the world with *Portrait Of A Chinaman* by Ernest Norman Toejam for company.

Back in the barbecue area over a fresh beer, Les began to think he may have overreacted a bit to the postcards. Even if the Irish did find out where he was, they wouldn't get out here that quickly. Then there was Peregrine's cousin Lewis to take into account. Still, maybe towards the end of next week, things could be a bit different. I'd better slip into Yurriki and ring Eddie. Les looked at his watch. I'll wait till seven. He usually goes out with Lindy and the kids on Sunday afternoon.

'GOD, BUT THESE are a good weapon, Liam,' said Robert, holding the still-smoking bullpup to his shoulder. 'You can scarcely miss with them, once you get the knack of it.'

'Aye,' replied Liam. 'It was truly decent of the British army to let us have them. We'll see that they're put to good use.'

It was a delightful little spot they'd chosen to test fire the bullpups. A quiet bend in the river with the water flowing past, no houses, plenty of trees and a few hundred metres away the rattling of any cars going over the old bridge covered the staccato blast of the sub-machine guns.

'Here,' said Liam. 'Have one more shot then we'll clean them and start loading some magazines.'

He tossed a piece of wood mid-stream. Robert sighted on it and pressed the trigger. There was a flash of flame, a chattering bang and the piece of wood disintegrated in a spray of water and a shower of splinters and bark.

'Nice shooting,' said Tom Mooney.

Robert nodded in acknowledgement and brought the weapon down. 'How can you miss?' he smiled. 'I certainly prefer these to the AK-47s. They're lighter too.'

'Good,' said Tom. 'Now you other lads know what to do? Magazine in here. Safety catch here. Cocking mechanism here. Now let's start loading those magazines.'

'Then we'll get a bit of rest,' said Liam, 'before we go out and visit our British friend and his Aussie mate.'

The six Irishmen walked back to their separate cars and started cleaning their weapons.

* * *

THERE WAS A scattering of people in and around the hotel, but apart from that Yurriki was like a ghost town when Norton pulled up outside the town's only phone-box around seven. He rattled some coins into the slot. Eddie answered.

'Les, how are you, mate?' he said at the sound of Norton's voice. 'I only just walked in the door.'

'Not bad,' replied Les. 'Still hanging in up here.'

'Good on you. How's his nibs?'

'He's all right. He got bit by a tick and I put him to bed early.'

Eddie laughed momentarily. 'Listen mate. I've got a bit of bad news for you. And for Peregrine.'

'Yeah? What's that?'

'His cousin Lewis got blown up by a landmine in Ireland. He's all right. But the army's going to have to send another team in to get that Frayne brother and his mates.'

'Shit! That's nice.'

'Yeah. So you might have to stay up there another week or so. Can you handle it?'

Les thought moodily for a moment then smiled. An extra week at Cedar Glen. He could get young Alison to join him. He'd pay her to take the time off work. Yeah, he could handle it all right. Don't know about Peregrine. But that Colleen reckons she's coming back out. Sweet.

'I suppose I'll have to, Eddie,' replied Les.

'Yeah. But I reckon they'll get that shit sorted out in Ireland before long. If they don't, I'll bloody well go over and do it myself.'

'I reckon you would,' chuckled Les. 'Listen, Eddie. There's a couple of things I've got to tell you.'

Les told Eddie about how Peregrine had the postcards couriered to Stephanie and his mates in London. He also mentioned about the three blokes inquiring about buying Cedar Glen. The place *was* on the market, but it just struck him as curious that they were English.

'Jesus! The stupid prick,' cursed Eddie. 'He still thinks this is all a lark. Fuck him.'

'Yeah. But we'd only been here a day. He mightn't have been thinking.'

'Does he ever? The fuckin' goose. Anyway, don't worry about it. But if anything looks a bit suss up there, or you're a bit uneasy about anything, give me or Price a yell straight away.'

'Okay.'

They chatted for a while longer then Les hung up telling

Eddie he'd ring him every day from now on. He sat thinking in the car for a few moments then drove back to Cedar Glen.

Les was right earlier when he said it would be a quiet and lonely night on the farm. As he sat in the barbecue area sipping a beer he found his thoughts constantly drifting back to Alison. Jesus, wouldn't it be grouse to have her out there with him right now? He was even missing Peregrine for someone to have a mag to. He fiddled with the radio dial to try and find some better music. Anyway, look on the bright side. Another two weeks in the fresh, clean air and Alison was a big chance to come down for the weekend. Things weren't all that bad. It was just the mood he was in. He finished his beer and switched to bourbon and Coke. A bloody TV would go well though.

Headlights off, the two Holden sedans cruised quietly up to the gates of Cedar Glen. Liam gave the property a quick but thorough peruse through the binoculars; the house was in darkness but he could just make out the light coming from the barbecue area at the rear. He nodded to Logan who got out of the car and with a large screwdriver easily snapped the lock holding the chain to the main gate. As quietly as possible they turned the cars around and reversed down the driveway, ready for a quick get away if something should go wrong. Logan shut the gate behind them. They switched off the engines then opened the boots and began removing the weapons.

'Now, remember what I told you,' said Liam, shouldering the RPG-7. He had the two remaining shells in their webbing holders and the bullpup in his right hand. 'Patrick, you take your lads and go left of the house. We'll move to the right. They're still out the back drinking or whatever and we'll get them in a crossfire. Don't mess about. Just chop the bastards to pieces.' He looked up at the sky. There was very little moonlight, nearly all clouds with a patch or two of stars here and there and no wind. 'We've got everything in our favour. There's bugger all light. They're not expecting us. And we've got the firepower.' The others nodded silently. 'You right then?' The look in Liam Frayne's eyes answered that question for them. 'Okay then, lads. Let's go.'

Liam slipped on his balaclava and so did the others, then after a last quick check of their weapons they split up into two groups and began walking along the driveway towards the house, Liam and his cohorts from Belfast on the right, Patrick and the Irish from Stanmore on the left.

The fourth bourbon and Coke put Norton in a bit of a better mood and he was sitting down chuckling to himself about Peregrine. Poor bastard. For all the fun they'd had on the trip he'd still done it pretty tough at times. Almost getting involved in a pub brawl. Going that close to drowning it didn't matter. Getting attacked by leeches. Not to mention that awful prank he'd played on him with Carrots. Now he was as sick as a dog with tick poisoning. I was a bit rough on the poor bludger too when I come to think of it. But you have to be to get that shit out of your system. Be interesting to see how he brushes up in the morning, though. He took a sip of his drink. Yeah, when it's all boiled down he's not a bad bloke, young Peregrine. I could think of a lot worse blokes to spend two weeks on a farm in the middle of nowhere with. Norton's gaze wandered from his drink to the edge of darkness around the barbecue area. Funny. The possums are a bit late getting here tonight. The little pricks are generally around by now looking for a handout. I'd better get them another bag of apples tomorrow too. He took a larger swallow of drink. I know what I'll do. I'll go and feed those silly bloody owls. Bunter and his mates; as Peregrine calls them. They're always good for a laugh. Les picked up some scraps of sausage and steak and still carrying his drink walked around to the front of the house.

Bunter and his two mates were in their customary position in the pine tree not far from the second gate. They spotted Les and their comical, round orange eyes blinked audaciously. Ahh yes, you're here, you pie-eyed wombats, Les chuckled to himself. Sorry your old china Peregrine can't be here to feed you. Les placed the meat scraps on the ground and waited for the three fat birds to swoop down and grab them. They watched him for a while but didn't move. Les was about to say something to them when unexpectedly all three birds took off with a startled flapping of wings to quickly disappear into the night sky. That's funny, thought Les. I didn't do anything to frighten them. Wonder what's wrong? He looked angrily and suspiciously beneath the surrounding trees. Jesus, there better not be another one of those bloody feral cats around.

Suddenly it seemed very quiet. The crickets had stopped, so had the frogs; even the calling of the nightbirds had tapered off. Then Les heard it. The faint, but unmistakable sound of footsteps carefully crunching on gravel. It seemed to be coming from where the driveway crossed the small billabong down from the second gate. Les listened through the trees. There seemed to be more than one set of footsteps. He bristled slightly. What the —? Revved up a little from the bourbon, and not really thinking, he moved across to the gate. Better see what's going on. Might only be Ronnie and a mate come round for a drink. At this time of night, though?

Les stood at a pole supporting the gate and called out. 'Hey! Anybody down there?'

The footsteps suddenly stopped and it was deadly silent. This really made Les suspicious. 'Hey! Who's there?' he called out again.

Logan gripped Tom Mooney's arm and motioned for the others to stop. 'Christ!' he whispered urgently. 'The bastard's spotted us.'

Norton peered down the driveway thinking he could hear whispers. Something told him to stay on that side of the gatepost.

'There he is,' whispered Tom Mooney. 'Standing next to that gatepost. What do you want to do?'

Liam thought for a moment. 'Fock it. Let the bastard have it.'

Les strained his eyes into the darkness. Christ, he cursed. How would you know what's going on? It's blacker than three feet up an Hassidic Jew's arse down there. 'Hey,' he called out again. 'Is there somebody down there? What do you want?'

This time Les's challenge was answered by two spurts of orange flame and the crashing chatter of Liam and Tom's sub-machine guns.

'Holy fuckin' hell!' yelled Les. He dropped his drink and hit the ground as a fusillade of bullets screamed past his head and smashed into the gatepost. 'Shit!' Another two bursts of machine gunfire spurted along the driveway and into the gate-post, showering him with gravel and splinters of wood. Fuck this, thought Les. On his hands and knees and moving like a lizard, Les scurried back along the driveway to the house. When he reached the car he stood up and broke into a crouching run.

'Did we get him?' said Tom.

'I don't know. I don't think so. Damn!' cursed Liam.

'What do you suggest we do?' asked Robert.

Liam thought for a moment. 'We go after him same as before. But stop at that gate first. See if we can spot where the bastard went.'

Norton's adrenalin was racing and so was his anger when he made it to the side of the house. He crouched down behind the station wagon, his mind going ninety to the dozen. That fuckin' Peregrine, he cursed to himself. Dopey fuckin' pommy cunt. I always said he was an idiot. Sending postcards to his dopey fuckin' sheila. They should have let the prick drown. Fuck it! Now they've found us! He wiped some pieces of gravel and wood splinters from his tracksuit. One thing's for sure, whoever's out there isn't here to hand out the *Watchtower*. Jesus! What am I gonna do? And prickhead's sound asleep. Hah! Just as fuckin' well. He'd only get in the road anyway. Christ! There's no phone: I can't ring the cops. I don't know how many's out there. Why isn't bloody Eddie here? Eddie! The gun. Norton darted across to his room and got the blue bag from under the bed.

The Irish raced up to the top of the driveway and crouched down by the two gateposts where Les had been standing.

'Can you see anything?' Liam said to Robert.

'There's music coming from that light at the back of the house. I thought I saw movement.'

'Well don't just look at it,' snapped Liam. 'What do you think you've got that gun for?'

Robert raised the bullpup and fired a long burst towards the barbecue area. Brendan and Tom Mooney did the same.

Norton came out of his bedroom holding the overnight bag. He snatched up the torch from the table and reached across to turn out the light. As he did a hail of bullets blasted noisily around the barbecue area. Norton gave a yelp and rolled on the ground under the table. Several hit the station wagon, several others ricocheted off the walls behind the fridge and smashed into the ghetto-blaster spinning it off the table in a shower of broken plastic.

'Fuck!' cursed Les. 'There goes my $300 radio-cassette.' He lay under the table in the sudden, darkened silence for a moment, then made a sprint for the stairs at the rear of the house. He took them in three bounds, burst through the door, slammed it behind him and jammed a chair under the handle. Crouching low he did the same to the door facing the driveway and the one facing the front gate. Norton's hands were shaking slightly as he opened the bag by the soft light of the torch. One clip was empty, but the other was still full. Thank Christ we didn't start firing bullets all over the place. There's still about two hundred rounds there. He jammed the full clip into the butt of the Robinson and took it and the bag over to the kitchen window.

Thumbing bullets into the spare clip, he stared out of the window trying to spot the Irish — when the clip was full he placed it near the kitchen sink. S'pose I'll have to break the bloody glass to get a shot at them, he thought. Oh well, here goes the bond money. He brought the butt of the Robinson down hard against the window. Instead of smashing, it just made a dull, thumping sound. Huh? Les was more than just a little mystified. He brought the butt of the gun down again — harder. Still the same dull sound. The windows downstairs were all glass. What's going on here? Then it dawned on him. The *Playboy* article. Cedar Glen was built like a fortress. That colonel must have used some sort of reinforced glass or perspex upstairs. And the only way in was from the outside. Even if the Irish got in downstairs, there were no stairs, they couldn't get to him. Behind the bulletproof windows set in logs and huge reinforced beams in the top half of the house Les was relatively safe. Norton's stocks rose a little. But how do I take a shot outside? He snapped his fingers. The air vents. The latches on the sides of the windows. They doubled as rifle holes. Harcourt, you're a deadset American genius. Les opened one of the latches and poked out the wire mesh. Ah yes. This is a bit better.

Norton's eyesight was good and in the faint starlight he thought he could detect movement near the gateposts. Oh well. Better let the boys know Uncle Les means business. He aimed the nose of the Robinson in that direction and squeezed the trigger.

'DO YOU THINK we got him?' asked Robert.

'How could you tell? It's as black as the devil himself out there,' replied Tom Mooney.

'We must have knocked out the light,' said Brendan.

'Brilliant deduction, Brendan,' said Tom.

There was a sudden burst of orange flame from the top corner of the house and a spray of bullets slammed into the gateposts and ripped up the driveway sending the six Irishmen sprawling for cover. 'Jesus Christ!' cursed Liam. 'The bastard's got a machine gun up there.'

Another burst from the house hit the gateposts and sprayed gravel over the Irishmen. Brendan let out a yelp of pain.

'Oh fock! I've been hit in the leg.' He cursed again.

'Is it bad?' asked Liam.

Brendan felt round the blood soaking into his trouser leg. 'It's not too bad. Just gone through the calf muscle. I can bind it up with my hanky.'

'Those shots came from the upper right hand corner of the house,' said Logan.

'Is that a window up there?'

'It is.'

'All right, all of you,' said Liam. 'Aim for that window. Give the sonofabitch something to think about.'

The Irishmen took aim and the bullpups opened up into a hammering roar as they each emptied almost an entire clip at the window. There was a lot of noise and great shards of wood ripped away but definitely no sound of breaking glass.

'What the fock?' said Liam. 'Again.'

Once more the bullpups erupted in sheets of orange flame and an almost deafening din. Still no sound of breaking glass.

'What in God's name?' said Logan.

'Christ! What sort of a place is this?' said Patrick.

NORTON HEARD BRENDAN'S cry of pain and grinned to himself. Yeah. How did you like that, you potato-eating bastards? Want to kill Uncle Les, do you? Well like my old grandma said, you can't eat a mango without getting some juice on your chin. Les moved away from the latch, slipped another clip into the Robinson and began reloading the other one. He'd just started when he heard the bullpups open up and what sounded like an unbelievable hailstorm hitting the side of the house. The window bucked and rocked as the bullets thumped against it and into the side of the house; but it held firm. There was a pause for a few seconds then another burst hit the window and the house, several came in through the latch and pinged around the shelves in the kitchen. Norton winced and pulled his head in. But his stocks rose slightly again. Behind these logs and beams and the bulletproof windows there was a possibility of surviving. If he could just keep them at bay with the Robinson. He had less than two hundred rounds and dawn was a long way off, but at least he had a chance till he could think of something. And what did Eddie once say at work about firing machine guns in combat situations? Short controlled bursts. Well righto, fellahs. Here's a couple right now.

Les crept across and opened one of the latches behind the study facing the front verandah. He poked the Robinson out and fired two quick bursts in the direction of the gateposts.

'Jesus! They came from the other end of the house,' said Tom.

He fired a burst at where he'd seen the jet of orange flame as Norton's volley smashed into the driveway around them. The others opened up as another burst of gunfire from the house pinned them down behind the gateposts.

'The bastard knows what he's doing, too,' said Logan.

'There's something strange about all this,' said Robert. 'Something bloody weird.'

Beneath his balaclava Liam was starting to sweat a little now. He ground his teeth and spat onto the ground. 'Patrick,' he said. 'You and Robert make a dash for beneath the house. Get inside and see how you get upstairs. We'll give you covering fire. You right then?' The two men nodded. 'Okay, go.'

Robert and Patrick sprinted for the house. Les spotted them and emptied the magazine. The bullets whacked and whined angrily as they kicked up sparks around the shrubs and rockeries. Next thing Les heard a rattle of gunfire and the sound of smashing glass as the two Irishmen got in downstairs. Well, that won't do you much good fellahs, he mused. There's no way up. Les reloaded the Robinson and fired another quick burst at the gateposts then kept an eye on the back door just in case they came up the stairs.

'Christ! It's as black as pitch in here,' said Robert.

'Keep your bloody voice down,' replied Patrick.

Finger on the trigger, Patrick nosed the bullpup down the tiled hallway towards the Davy Crockett room. Robert started searching around the other room. Outside they could hear Les firing from upstairs and the returning fire from the gateposts sounded as if the whole side of the house was being blown away as the bullets slammed into the walls above their heads.

'What's down there?' said Robert when Patrick returned.

'Nothing. Just a bathroom and bedroom. There's no staircase.'

'There's nothing here, either. I just climbed those steps there and there's nothing up there but some sort of a bed.'

'What's through here?'

With Patrick leading they crept into the laundry. Outside more bursts of gunfire came from the house and the gateposts. Patrick opened the laundry door, stepped outside and had a quick look in Norton's bedroom then came back.

'What's there?' asked Robert.

'There's no staircase. The only way up is from those stairs at the front and those ones there.' He motioned with the bullpup to the staircase running up from the barbecue area. 'I think there's another set of stairs where that side door is too. Come on, let's get back to the others.'

'Good idea. I don't like it down here,' replied Robert.

There was another burst of gunfire from the gateposts, then silence. Les heard the crunching of footsteps on broken glass downstairs and raced to the latch near the study. He was just in time to see two shadowy figures racing for the gateposts. He raked them with machine gunfire and an angry, satisfied grin creased his face as he heard an oath of pain.

'Shit! I'm hit.' Robert dropped his weapon and clutched at his ribs as he and Patrick sprawled behind the gateposts.

Liam saw the blood seeping through Robert's fingers. 'How bad is it?'

'It's gone through my side. But I'm all right.'

'Shit! So what did you find under the house?' Liam asked Patrick.

'There's no way upstairs from beneath the house,' gasped Patrick. 'You have to use the outside stairs.'

Liam listened as Patrick told him what he and Robert had found under the house. He cursed his luck. No easy access upstairs. Apparently bulletproof windows. Two men down. This 'dead easy' operation was starting to get out of hand. He spat an oath and turned to the others.

'Right,' he said. 'This has gone fockin' far enough. When I tell you, I want you to give me all the covering fire you can.' He picked up the RPG-7, made sure the rocket was secure in the muzzle and checked the rear sight. 'Okay, Mr Norton, or whatever your name is,' he said, shouldering the weapon as he took cover behind the gatepost. 'Let's see how you like this.'

The spare clip was by the other window. Les retrieved it and the bag still sitting in the middle of the dining room and started reloading in the study. He was feeling a little more confident now. He was certain he'd got two of them. His ammo was still holding out. They couldn't get to him without one hell of a fight. Norton slapped one clip into the Robinson and put the other in his pocket as an intense barrage of bullets sprayed the side of the house. He stood up to return the fire through the latch when the house was rocked by an ear-splitting explosion and the kitchen lit up in a sheet of orange and purple flame. The concussion thumped around the room, hitting Norton in the face and knocking him right off his feet. His head spinning and his ears ringing, Les rolled into the dining room.

'What the fuck was that?' he spluttered.

Temporarily deafened, Les blinked through the smoke at the kitchen. The window was blown out, shelves were torn from the walls, and pots, pans and broken crockery littered the floor. A few tongues of flame crackled briefly before extinguishing themselves in the specially treated wood. Although the window was gone, most of the damage was superficial and the wooden beams and foundations had held firm. Les shook his head and his hearing and senses returned just as another volley of bullets came through from where the window had been, slamming off the walls and up into the ceiling. Norton let out another oath as his head cleared. Don't know what that bloody well was. But at least I'm still alive. The Robinson was still in his hand. Les looked at it for a second then shook his head. Better let the bastards know it. He got up, poked the barrel out of the latch in the study and let go another burst at the gateposts.

'I RECKON THAT might have got the sonofabitch,' said Patrick, smiling towards the house.

'I should damn well think so,' replied Liam. He was about to get to his feet when Norton's volley of bullets tore up the driveway. 'Jesus Christ!' he roared, dropping down behind the gatepost.

He was about to say something else when Logan cut him off. 'Who the fockin' hell is it in that house?' he said. 'Fockin' Rambo?'

From behind their balaclavas the others exchanged looks of disbelief. Liam spat out another oath as the Irish in him really started to boil now.

'Fockin' Rambo,' he swore. 'I'll give him fockin' Rambo.' Liam pushed another rocket into the RPG-7 and shouldered it again. 'Where did those last shots come from?'

'The other end of the house,' said Logan.

'Right, then. Give me some more covering fire. Let's see how fockin' Rambo likes another one of these.'

NORTON WAS STARTING to get a bit concerned now. That bomb, or whatever it was, and the hole in the wall where the window used to be had taken away any slight advantage he might have had. If they fired enough bullets through that hole they were bound to hit him sooner or later: if they didn't, the ricochets would. Les pondered his situation for a moment.

I wonder if I can get a better shot at them from the window? He picked up the bag of ammo and crawled through the debris to the kitchen. He was about to stand up and take a quick look when another intense volley of machine gunfire raked the side of the house. Shit! thought Les, rolling up in a ball and covering his ears. I think I know what that means.

There was another violent explosion and a sheet of purple flame as the windows around the study area were blown apart. Debris and shrapnel splattered around the dining room and kitchen pinging off the walls and ceiling as it rained down on Norton's back. There was silence for a second, then another fusillade of bullets slammed into the study end of the house; some came through the hole, thumping into the cedar walls around Peregrine's bedroom.

Les took his hands from his ears and shook his head. Well, at least he'd been ready for that one. He peered through the smoke which was now thick inside the house. There was debris and small pieces of smouldering wood laying around, but the house wasn't on fire and the walls had held firm once more. He took a deep breath, jumped up and fired two quick bursts through the kitchen window at the Irish.

'Saints preserve us! I don't believe it,' said Liam. He fell back down as the first burst of bullets chopped pieces out of the gatepost just above his head. 'Those bastards must have nine lives.'

Another quick burst made them all keep their heads down.

'He's bloody well got something,' agreed Tom Mooney.

Liam let go a string of oaths. 'Okay,' he said grimly. 'I've got one shell left. I'm going to go to the rear of the house and blow a hole in the back wall. Logan, you come with me. But stay at the left end of the house in case he comes to that hole up there. Robert and Brendan, you stay here and keep firing at those two holes. Patrick, you and Tom go over by that car and watch those steps by the driveway. Whoever it is in there, he can't guard three holes at once and I'm tipping he'll make a break for it, either to the car or out the back. One of us has to get him.' Liam's eyes were blazing beneath his balaclava as he looked at his men. 'You got that, then?' There was a brief nodding of heads. 'Then let's go.'

Norton just had time to see the four Irishmen running for either end of the house when a hail of bullets raked both windows. He fired a burst at whoever was running towards the driveway. The gun emptied out after four shots.

'Shit!' cursed Les.

The Irish were at either side of the house now. He wasn't sure how many, but it looked like two at both ends and there were definitely two guns firing at him from the gateposts. He shone the torch in the bag and reloaded. Christ! He'd fired off more rounds than he thought. He'd be flat out having a hundred bullets left. And now he was almost surrounded. But the sides of the house were still sound, the only way they could still get to him was through the holes in the front. Unless they... Oh shit!!

'Right,' said Liam, when they made it to the house. 'You stay here and put a couple of bursts through that window above. I'm going round the back. I'm thinking this last shell should do it.'

'Okay,' nodded Logan. He waited till Liam was at the rear of the house, then let go half a clip at the study window.

Crouched down behind the station wagon, Patrick and Tom were tempted to open up on the windows above too; they could hear and almost see Les firing out the front. But they waited as Liam instructed.

Liam ran to the opposite side of the barbecue area. After a quick look around he tipped the table over and, keeping it between himself and the house, loaded the remaining shell into the RPG-7. Smiling grimly beneath his balaclava he rested the muzzle on the upturned table and took aim at the windows behind the back verandah. Okay, Rambo or Norton or whatever the devil your name is — try this for size.

Norton ducked down as more bullets hit the house from the gateposts. He was about to return their fire when the burst from Logan smacked into the study window and tore up into the ceiling. As he recoiled from that Les was certain he got a glimpse of movement down in the driveway.

Shit! They're closing in on me now. Norton didn't know what to do. He wasn't panicking, but the sweat was now starting to drip from his brow and his lips were dry. This little gun's fairly accurate. Maybe I can get whoever's under the study. Les had just got to his feet when the back windows disintegrated in another ear-splitting explosion and again the house lit up in a blinding sheet of orange and purple flame. The beams and logs supporting the interior of the house took most of the shrapnel and broken glass, but Les wasn't ready for this one and took almost the full force of the blast. It lifted him off his feet and slammed him backwards into the kitchen. He cannoned off the sink and landed on the floor facing the hole where the rear windows had been, his back against the sink cupboards. Pieces of broken glass had torn through his track-suit, some other smaller pieces had cut his face. Nothing was broken, but he was concussed and badly winded almost para-lysed. It felt as if several people had thumped him on the chest and stomach with baseball bats. The Robinson was on the floor in front of him. Les tried to reach for it but found he couldn't move. All the strength had been temporarily knocked out of him. He fought to get his breath back as he blinked through the thick acrid smoke and prayed that no one would come at him from the back stairs. But it didn't look good. Norton had run out of time. He was almost gone now.

The last thing Les was expecting to see was the house and the surrounding area suddenly light up in a brilliant, purplish white glow almost as bright as day. The glow was accompanied by an eerie whistling sound. Norton lolled his head back and looked up through the smashed-in kitchen window. Floating down from the night sky was a flare suspended by a tiny parachute. What the . . . ? Then came the sound of more machine gunfire. But this was a different sound from the long, hammering rattles he'd been hearing all night. This was more of a harsh, quick bark coming from over by the stables. And it was coming in definite, short, controlled bursts.

THE PURPLE FLARE fluttering down was the last thing Logan Colbain ever saw in his life. He just had time to tilt his face to the sky when a burst of bullets ripped through his body. Four blew apart his chest; two hit him in the throat, almost taking his head off. The bullpup went one way, Logan went another to land like a broken doll, his life's blood oozing out along the concrete path.

Patrick and Tom Mooney also spun around at the flare's light. They barely had time to exchange looks of worried surprise when several short bursts of machine gunfire almost tore them to pieces as it raked through them and into the station wagon. They spun crazily along the side of the car leaving a sticky, bloody smear against the white paint before falling in two lifeless, blood-soaked heaps near the front wheels.

Crouched behind the gateposts Robert and Brendan could make out the darkened figures in the flare's glow, firing from near the stables. They managed to get a couple of quick bursts away in that direction before three machine guns opened up on them. A hail of bullets tore up the driveway and smacked into the gateposts. There were two screams of pain, then silence.

Still holding the RPG-7 Liam looked up at the flare coming down and couldn't believe how everything could go so bloody wrong. Around him he could hear the sudden bursts of machine gunfire and the screams of his men as they fell. He dropped the rocket launcher and picked up his bullpup. It was obvious someone had arrived; who or what he didn't know, but the game was now up. The only thing left was to try and make a run for it. Liam Frayne's wild Irish eyes narrowed. Not a fockin' chance. He'd come all this way to get the British bastard that had murdered his brothers, and by God he would. Even if it was the last thing he ever did on this earth. He gritted his teeth and slowly, carefully, climbed the stairs at the rear of the house.

Norton's head cleared and he could slowly feel his wind coming back. He knew from the screams and noise outside that help had arrived and it appeared he was safe. He gave a silent prayer and reached for the top of the sink to try to stand up when he saw the figure in a balaclava and black leather jacket appear in the shattered doorway with a sub-machine gun in his hands. The figure spotted him, looked at him for a moment then raised the machine gun to his shoulder to make sure he couldn't miss. Les raised his arms in front of him in a vain effort to shield himself. So near and yet so far. He stared at the whites of the two eyes behind the balaclava and Les Norton prepared to die.

There was a quick burst of machine gunfire. Les braced himself for the bullet's impact. Instead of being torn to bits he saw the gunman's chest rip open and heard him scream as he dropped the machine gun and reached for the beam above him. Another shorter burst spun him around. A final one took his legs from under him and he tumbled head first down the back stairs.

Norton gasped in disbelief for a moment. He couldn't possibly explain the feeling going through him. He had been a second away from death. Now he was alive. Battered, shaken and bruised, but definitely alive. The flare flickered out as he climbed to his feet. He lurched to the doorway and held onto one shattered side for support. It was eerily quiet now after the hammering of the machine guns and the roar of exploding rockets. The dead Irishman was sprawled at the foot of the stairs. Standing next to him, holding a funny looking little machine gun with a drum magazine, was a short figure in khakis and a black woollen type of beanie with his face blackened. The short figure nudged the dead Irishman with his foot then looked up at Norton.

'You all right, Les?' he called out.

Norton mumbled a reply, nodded and gave a brief wave.

'You can come down now, Les,' said the figure. 'The area's secure.'

Norton blinked and shook his head. He couldn't make out the blackened face. He thought he recognised the voice. But it was impossible. Slowly Les came down the stairs.

'How you feeling, Les? You all right?' asked the figure in the beanie when Norton reached the bottom.

Les had to blink again at the tight, blackened face. 'Ronnie?'

'Yeah,' replied the little caretaker. 'You okay are you? Where's Peregrine?'

Peregrine. Shit! In all the noise and confusion Les had forgotten all about him. 'He's in the front bedroom.'

Madden ran up the stairs leaving Les staring at what was left of Liam Frayne. He'd taken almost ten bullets. His chest was blown apart and half his face was missing. Laying there seeping blood, the dead Irishman was a dreadful sight.

Ronnie came back down the stairs scratching his head. 'I don't believe it,' he said. 'He's sound afuckin'sleep!'

'That figures,' replied Les. Then despite himself, Norton started to laugh. 'Ohh yeah, that figures. That fuckin' figures all right.'

'Christ,' exclaimed Ronnie. 'If he could sleep through that, he could sleep through anything.'

'I'll tell you about it after. Right now I just want to sit down for a minute.'

Norton couldn't believe how buggered he was. It wasn't so much tiredness; he was drained. His body ached and his head was still ringing from the explosions. He was also completely confused. And on top of that he'd been no more than a split second from death. The sight of Liam Frayne's mangled body didn't help much either. It was by no means the best Sunday Les Norton had ever spent in his life. He picked up the overturned table and found a chair. The barbecue lights were still working; he switched them on and sat down.

'You've got a bit of blood on your face,' said Ronnie. 'You sure you feel all right?'

Les nodded. 'Yeah. I'm a bit bruised, that's all. And my head's still ringing a bit.'

Ronnie picked up the RPG-7 and dropped it on the table.

'Why wouldn't it be? You copped three of these. We heard the explosions coming over the hill.'

Norton looked at the rocket launcher. 'I've seen them on TV. On the news.'

'Yeah. They're Russian design. They're bloody deadly. You're lucky to be alive.' Madden gave a bit of a chuckle. 'Or lucky old Daniel J. put plenty of reinforcement in the house.'

Norton didn't quite know what to say to that. 'How do you fit into all this, Ronnie? You were about the last bloke I was expecting.'

The little caretaker's chuckle turned into one of his wheezy laughs. 'Yeah, I figured that. I'll explain it all to you in a minute.'

Les looked up at the sound of footsteps coming from the driveway. Another two 'soldiers' appeared. One was tall and skinny. The other wasn't much taller than Ronnie, only more solidly built. Like Ronnie, they too were wearing fatigues, sneakers and black beanies. And like Ronnie, their faces were blackened and they carried the same odd little sub-machine guns.

'What's the situation?' asked Ronnie.

'There's two dead noggies in the driveway,' said the tall one. 'And another by the corner of the house.'

'There's two WIA's near the front gate,' said the solid one.

'I got one KIA here.' He motioned to Liam's body. 'How bad are the WIA's, Ray?'

The solid bloke shrugged. 'Pretty bad. They've both been shot through the legs. One's got a bullet in his stomach. The other's taken one in the face.'

Madden seemed to think for a moment. 'Do you think it might be best if you went and took another look at them, Ray?'

The solid bloke nodded slowly. 'Yeah. That might be the best idea,' he said, and walked off.

No one said anything while he was away. Ronnie and the other bloke just stood there. Les stared at the table, moved his jaws and worked on getting his hearing back. Suddenly two quick gunshots rang out in the still of the night.

'Shit! What was that?' said Les. Ronnie and the other bloke still didn't say anything. The solid bloke returned. 'What happened?' asked Norton.

The solid bloke looked at Norton impassively. 'They tried to get away,' he replied briefly.

Les was going to say something but changed his mind. 'Yeah, righto,' he said, with a quick nod of his head.

'I'll tell you what,' said Madden cheerfully. 'All this shootin' and runnin' around's thirsty work. I notice the fridge is still in one piece. Any chance of a beer, Les?'

Norton made a brief gesture with his hand. 'Help yourselves.'

'You gonna have one?'

'Yeah, why not?'

Ronnie went to the outside fridge and got four bottles of assorted beers. He opened them and handed them around. 'Well, cheers,' he said.

'Yeah — cheers,' was the general chorus. The four men each took a hefty swallow.

'Les,' said Ronnie. 'I want you to meet a couple of mates of mine. This is Ray and Lennie.'

'How are you, fellahs?' said Norton, shaking their hands. 'Pleased to meet you.'

'We've heard a fair bit about you,' said Lennie, the tall one.

'And seen you in action at the local pub,' smiled Ray. 'You go off all right, don't you?'

'He didn't put on a bad show here either, just quietly,' said Ronnie. 'Six blokes. And he was on his own.'

'Yeah,' agreed Ray. 'And they had bloody bullpups too. I wonder where the fuck they got those?'

'Before we go any further,' said Les. 'I just got to say one thing. Thanks, fellahs. You saved my bloody neck.'

'Ahh, don't worry about it,' replied Lennie.

'Yeah, well, thanks anyway. I owe you one.'

'Well in that case,' said Ronnie, draining his beer. 'We might take that one right now.' The little caretaker got another four beers from the fridge and handed them around. 'So,' he said, smiling at Les after draining almost half a bottle of Lowenbrau. 'I suppose you're wondering what's going on and how we got here?'

'Well,' agreed Les, 'I am more than a bit curious, yeah.' Norton watched as the three men exchanged glances then settled back into their chairs.

'Okay. I'll do my best.' Madden took another swig of beer and belched. 'The three of us are vets. Eddie was our platoon sergeant in Vietnam first time around. I won't go into all that rattle. But when we got back, it just wasn't the same for a lot of us. It was almost like being a stranger in your own country.'

'Yeah, some fuckin' homecoming,' said Lennie. 'We marched

up George Street and some sheila stepped out of the crowd and spat in my face.'

'It's a bit hard to work out, Les,' added Ray. 'You're in a jungle one week fighting Vietcong. And you come home and find university students running around waving North Vietnamese flags.'

Norton shook his head in disbelief.

'Anyway, we teamed up again after we got back,' continued Ronnie. 'I bought a few acres up here years ago to get away from every cunt. Built a bit of a shack on it and Ray and Lennie joined me. It was more or less a coincidence Harcourt lobbed here and built his joint. We knew him in Vietnam. Eddie did a bit of business with him the second time around. And we did a bit of work for him when he got the duck farm going. Anyway, we all owe Eddie a big favour from Vietnam and he's been good to us with a quid since we been up here. And it was just by another coincidence that Peregrine lobbed in not long after Harcourt put the place on the market.'

'Where did he go?' asked Les.

'We honestly don't know, Les.' Ronnie had another mouthful of beer. 'We'd been talking to Eddie on the phone about the place saying how we'd like to buy it. Make it a sort of a halfway house for vets having a bit of trouble. But none of us had the money. Not long after, Eddie rings back saying he needs somewhere to snooker that Peregrine bloke and why. What about here? And would we keep an eye on things if something should eventuate. Well, like I said, we all owe Eddie a favour. So here you are and here we are.' Madden shrugged and took another mouthful of beer. 'And that's about it, Les.'

'Yeah. But how come you knew there was going to be trouble here tonight?'

'We didn't, really,' replied Ronnie. 'But Eddie rang around eight and said Peregrine had been sending postcards from here back home. Said some pommy blokes had been sniffin' around and to really keep our eyes open from now on. Actually we were up home getting into the piss when we heard all the fireworks start.'

'Why, where's your place from here?' asked Norton.

'Only about two klicks the other side of the stables,' said Ray.

'Oh.'

'We knew you were pretty sweet inside the house,' said Ronnie. 'So we didn't break our necks arming up and getting ourselves together. But when we recognised those RPG-7's, we knew you were in trouble. So we got our fingers out.'

'If they hadn't have had those, you'd have been sweet,' said Lennie. 'This place is built like a fortress.'

'Yeah. It sure is,' agreed Les.

'Anyway, we double-timed down the hill. And I guess you could say,' the little caretaker broke into another one of his wheezy laughs, 'the cavalry arrived just in the nick of time.'

Norton flashed back to the figure in the doorway aiming the machine gun at him and a chill ran down his spine. 'You can bloody well say that again. And I reckon I owe you blokes a drink, too.'

'Ahh, don't worry about it,' said Ronnie. 'Eddie'll probably shout us one. Plus we got six bullpups and a rocket launcher.'

'Yeah. And they've got to have left a car round here some-where,' said Ray. 'We'll keep that. Change the plates. Bodgie up the rego.'

'Yeah, whatever,' said Les. 'But if you blokes want something — anything — just ask.'

'Another beer'd go well,' winked Ronnie, finishing his bottle.

'Help your bloody selves,' said Norton. This time Lennie got them.

Norton watched as the three Vietnam veterans enjoyed another cold bottle of beer, completely oblivious to Liam Frayne's body laying not much more than six feet away. He knew all along there was something about Ronnie Madden that wasn't quite right. The way he eluded questions. The way he answered others. The way he changed the subject. Now all the questions seemed to be answered, but it was all too cut and dried. Les took another thoughtful sip of beer as he watched the little caretaker.

'How come you never told me all this in the first place, Ronnie?' he asked.

Madden shrugged his shoulders. 'I just want to leave the past behind me, Les. There's a few vets living up here apart from us and we'd all rather have it like that. Me and Eddie honestly thought the less you knew the better. He's been ringing me every day to make sure you're all right. Besides, from what I can gather, that Peregrine can be a bit of an egg roll at times. And he might have done something stupid, especially with that Robinson laying around.'

'Sending cards back to London telling everyone where he is was dumb enough,' said Ray. 'Especially with the IRA wanting him like that.'

'Yeah,' agreed Ronnie. 'And watching youse running around

in those tiger stripes and jungle boots was enough.'

Les gave a self-conscious laugh. But the pieces had fallen into place now, there was nothing else he really needed to know, leave it at that; it was bad enough that he had to force Ronnie and his two mates to relive unpleasant memories to save him and Peregrine. Norton sipped on his fourth beer and began to unwind; even his head was starting to clear up now. He looked curiously at one of the strange-looking little guns Ronnie and his mates had placed on the table. Tiny little things — they almost looked like children's toys. Black metal, no butt. The two handles were just metal frames with a strange double trigger mechanism. They were lucky if they were half a metre long and even with the drum magazine, they wouldn't have weighed much more than two kilos.

'Where did you get these things?' he asked. 'I've never seen nothing like these before.'

'They're Seggerns,' replied Ronnie. 'They're American. They make 'em in New Jersey.'

'Or Noo Joisey, as Harcourt used to say,' laughed Lennie.

'We called round for a drink one day,' said Ronnie, 'and Harcourt had a crate of them sitting there. He gave us one each. Fucked if I know where he got them from. Didn't bother to ask. But they're the grouse for wild dogs and feral cats.'

'Hey, there's something I want to know, Les,' said Ray. 'Where's bloody Peregrine?'

Norton laughed. 'Asleep.'

'Asleep? How the fuck could anyone sleep through that?'

Les explained about Peregrine being bitten by a tick and how he'd filled him up full of rum and sleeping tablets. Even with all that under his belt the boys still conceded that it still wasn't a bad effort to sleep through a mini-war. Though in all probability it had worked out for the best.

Ronnie finished his beer and dropped the bottle in the Otto-bin. 'Well, this sitting around drinking piss is all right,' he said. 'But what are we going to do with these six dead noggies?'

'What do you suggest?' said Lennie. 'You're the caretaker.'

'I reckon dump 'em where Harcourt was going to put his swimming pool.' Ronnie motioned to the hole behind them. 'There's some quicklime in the shed. Cover 'em with that then I'll get the tractor and bulldoze the edges in. Couple of weeks and there'll be nothing there but fertilizer and a few teeth.'

'Good idea,' said Ray.

'You want to give us a hand to drag 'em over Les?'

'Yeah, righto,' replied Norton, trying not to sound too unenthusiastic. 'I'll go and get the ones by the front gate.' He finished his beer and headed in that direction as the others rose from the table.

Robert and Brendan were laying face down almost next to each other; their clothes were a torn bloody mess and it looked like they had nearly been shot to pieces round the legs. At the base of their skulls, just above the neck, two neat, almost identical holes had been drilled into the backs of their black balaclavas. Not bad shooting, Ray, mused Les. A pitch black night, two blokes running away. Yeah, not bad shooting at all. Les gingerly picked up the two dead Irishmen by the collars of their jackets and started dragging them back to the barbecue area. It was quite an unpleasant task and worse was to come.

When he got back Ray and Lennie had the other four bodies by the edge of the hole. In the distance the lights in the toolshed were on where Ronnie was looking for the quicklime.

'Strip them now, Les,' said Ray. 'Leave their clothes here. Toss any ID, rings, watches, wallets and that on the table.'

'Tag 'em and bag 'em, Les, as the Yanks would say,' smiled Lennie.

Norton swallowed hard. 'Yeah, righto,' he said.

Stripping and searching the bodies in the moonlight was a miserable and macabre experience for Les. The Seggerns had done a horribly efficient job and it wasn't long before Norton's hands were covered in blood, pieces of flesh and other matter. Ronnie chugged over in the tractor and turned off the motor. Sitting in the scoop was a hessian sack; he dropped it on the ground and cut the string sewn across the top. Before long the six blood-caked bodies were laying naked at the edge of the hole; their clothing was in two black garbage bags, their personal effects sitting on the table. Lennie was examining a gold ring, the front of which formed two initials.

'Not a bad ring, this,' he said. 'I wonder what the LF stands for?'

'Which one did that come off?' asked Les.

'The one at the end.'

Les strolled over and looked impassively down at the body by his feet. So you're Liam Frayne, eh? You're the reason five of your mates are dead. He shook his head. Dopey bastard. You should have stayed in Ireland. Les turned round and the others were standing behind him.

'We've got to place them in the hole now, Les,' said Ronnie. 'Neatly and side by side. So I can get a good covering of quicklime over them.'

'Righto.' Les took one of the bodies by the wrist, Ronnie took the ankles, and they carried it down into the hole.

Soon the six Irishmen were lying face up in a few inches of smelly water at the bottom of the hole. Ronnie gave the bag a shake and walked over to the tractor.

'You gonna say something first before you bury them?' said Les. 'After all, they are Catholics,' he added with a shrug.

Ronnie looked down from the seat of the tractor, smiled and turned to Ray. 'What was it that big black sergeant said that day up at Bearcat? When the Yanks had just filled that pit with dead VC?'

'Yeah, I remember,' laughed Ray. He took off his beanie and stood solemnly at the edge of the hole. 'Hail Mary and all that jive. If you cats could shoot straight you'd still be alive. Amen.'

Ray put his beanie back on and Ronnie started the tractor. 'I should have this done by the time Eddie gets here,' he called out.

'Eddie gets here?' said Les. 'How's Eddie gonna get here? He's in Sydney.'

'Dunno,' shrugged Ronnie. 'When I told him what was going on as we were leaving, he said he'd get here as soon as he could. That was over two hours ago.'

There was a hiss, the blade in front of the tractor dropped and Ronnie started bulldozing the earth piled up by the sides of the hole. Norton washed his hands and joined Ray and Lennie going through the dead Irishmen's personal effects.

'I might go and see if I can find where they left their car,' said Lennie.

'Righto, mate,' said Ray.

Les got two Coronas from the fridge, handed one to Ray and watched quietly as Ray began stacking separate piles: wallets, cash, ID, jewellery etc. Norton couldn't quite come at touching it so he sat there in silence. It didn't seem long before Lennie was back. He was jubilant.

'Hey, it's better than I thought,' he said. 'There's two near new Holdens down by the main gates. The keys are still in them and everything. One's only got 12,000 on the clock.' He looked at the piles on the table. 'How are you going?'

'Grouse,' replied Ray enthusiastically. 'Six good watches. Around four and a half grand in cash. Three Australian driver's licences. Some of this jewellery's not bad either.' He winked at Lennie. 'At least we'll get a good drink for our trouble.'

'Reckon. What a ripper.' He went to the fridge, got a beer and drank it while he watched Ray reading a piece of blood-smeared paper.

Ray finished it and shook his head. 'Fuckin' idiot,' he muttered, and handed it to Lennie.

Lennie read it and shook his head too. 'What a nice fuckin' dill,' he said, and handed it to Les. 'Here. Read this.'

Norton took the piece of paper: it was printed neatly in biro. *My dear Stephanie. How goes it old pip* it started. It was as good as a detailed map on how to get to Cedar Glen. That was bad enough. But when Norton got to the part that said . . . *He's a complete wally* he was less than impressed.

'No wonder they knew where to find him, the dill,' said Ray. 'That must have been on the card he sent his sheila. And somehow those IRA blokes have intercepted it.'

Norton's jaw set. 'Do you mind if I keep this?' he said mirthlessly.

'Go for your life,' replied Ray.

They sat and drank beer while they watched Ronnie filling in the hole; Les was more inclined to sip his and think, the other two were ripping in. There was plenty of earth piled around the sides of the hole which had been softened by the previous night's rain and the little caretaker knew how to handle a tractor with a scoop on the front. It didn't seem like all that long before the hole was filled in and levelled over, Ronnie had switched off the motor and was joining them for a beer.

'I hope you bastards haven't drank all the piss,' he said, adding his usual wheezy laugh.

'There's still plenty there, mate, don't worry about that,' said Ray.

Ronnie got a bottle of Gosser and poured about half of it down his throat. 'S'pose we may as well sit around and see if Eddie shows up,' he belched, as he took a seat next to Lennie.

'How long did he say he'd be?' asked Les.

Ronnie shrugged his shoulders. 'Dunno. But knowing Eddie, it won't be all that long. Doesn't worry me though, how long he takes,' he added, with another wheezy laugh. 'I'll sit here and drink piss all night.'

'Yeah. Me too,' said Lennie.

'Well, there's no shortage,' said Les. 'In fact, how would you boys like a nice chilled bottle of French champagne?'

'Hey, shit! That sounds all right,' said Ray.

'Coming right up,' said Norton. He hustled up four glasses,

opened a bottle of Veuve Clicquot and topped them up. 'Well,' he said, raising his glass. 'Here's to... I don't know. What do you want to drink to?'

The three vets looked at each other. 'I dunno,' said Ronnie. 'Let's just drink to drinking piss.'

'Righto,' said Les. 'To drinking piss it is.'

They raised their glasses and all took liberal swallows. 'Hey, this bloody stuff's all right, ain't it?' said Lennie.

They knocked that bottle off, plus another one and some more beers. It wasn't long before Les was half drunk and in a much more relaxed frame of mind. The boys exchanged yarns about the war and life in the Tweed Valley. Les told them different things about life in Sydney around the Cross and Bondi and how he'd got the job of minding Peregrine. He told them about some of the funny things that had happened to them on the trip and how he'd ripped off Benny Rabinski and his brother years ago. Les was telling them about how Peregrine had almost drowned at Cabarita on Wednesday when he noticed not far up in the night sky a bright white light and a small flashing red one fast approaching the farm from the south-west. A few seconds later came the unmistakable swoosh-swoosh-swoosh of a helicopter's blades. The vets' ears pricked up and they appeared to stiffen at the evocative sound. They stopped drinking momentarily then turned to see where it was coming from.

'I reckon that's Eddie now,' said Ronnie.

The little caretaker walked across to where he'd filled in the hole as the helicopter roared overhead, banked a few hundred metres and came back. Ronnie started making criss-cross motions with his arms above his head then brought them down by his sides motioning the helicopter to land. The helicopter hovered a few metres above him for a while as if the occupants were checking everything out; in the still of the night it seemed to make a dreadful racket tossing up leaves and dust and the landing light seemed to bathe the whole valley in its white glow. Eventually the pilot brought it down not far from where the hole used to be, sat there for a moment and killed the engine. The blade whined for a few seconds as it slowed down and once again there was silence. The passenger side opened and out jumped Eddie in his customary black jeans and black leather jacket. Slung under his shoulder was a Uzi machine pistol. The pilot's door opened and Les couldn't mistake the neat moustache, the black leather jacket and scarf and the World War II, peaked leather pilot's cap. It was Kingsley Sheehan.

Eddie had his arm around Ronnie's shoulders as they walked across to where the others were sitting. He hesitated for a moment as if he didn't quite know who to speak to first. 'G'day Ray, Lennie,' he said to the two vets, who greeted him back. Then Eddie turned to Norton. 'Hello, Les,' he said, a little more slowly. 'How are you mate, you all right?'

'Yeah, terrific Eddie,' replied Norton. 'It's been great. I wouldn't have missed it for anything.' Les looked at the pilot who was now standing alongside Eddie. 'G'day, Kingsley. How are you, mate?'

The usual impish smile crinkled the corners of the pilot's eyes. 'Hello, George,' he said. 'Long time no see.'

'Yes,' replied Norton. 'It's been a while. I didn't know you owned a helicopter?'

'I don't,' replied Kingsley Sheehan. 'Eddie made me steal the bloody thing.' He turned and smiled at the three vets. 'Hello, fellahs,' he said. 'Haven't seen you for a while. How have you been?'

'Pretty good, Kingsley,' was the general reply.

Well, thought Norton, at least everybody seems to know each other. He could see Eddie looking at him and the blood on his face.

'I got here as fast as I could,' said Eddie. 'But it looks like you've got everything under control, thank Christ.' His eyes ran across the four faces at the table. 'So, what happened? Where's all the Irish?'

'You just walked over them,' said Ronnie, nodding to where the hole had been.

Eddie had a quick look at the freshly-turned earth. 'And where's dopey fuckin' Peregrine?'

'Still asleep,' said Les.

'Still asleep? What do you mean — *still* asleep?' Eddie noticed the RPG-7 and the bullpups stacked neatly near the table. 'Shit!' he said. 'Where did all this crap come from?'

'Why don't you have a beer?' said Ronnie. 'And I'll fill you in on what happened after I rang you.'

'Yeah, righto,' replied Eddie, as Ronnie got up and went to the fridge. 'At least it's a bit warmer up here. It was bloody freezing when we left Sydney.'

'Ohh I don't know,' said Kingsley. 'It was all right back at my place with the Lufthansa stewardess — till you dragged me away.'

Eddie and Kingsley found a couple of chairs and sat down while Ronnie told them how he, Ray and Lennie had come over the hill just in the nick of time, and about the quick gunfight and how they'd stripped and buried the bodies. Les then told them his side of it, how he'd got Peregrine pissed and full of Normisons and put him to bed. He showed Eddie the piece of paper with the copy of what Peregrine had sent on a postcard to his girlfriend in London. Eddie was far from impressed and said he wouldn't have minded going up and putting a bullet in Peregrine's aristocratic arse right there and then. Les took them upstairs and showed them where he'd held off the Irishmen till they rocketed the windows. The power was on but all the globes in the kitchen and dining room had been shattered; by the light from Norton's torch they could see the damage and the spent cartridges strewn amongst the debris on the floor. The little Robinson was still lying where Les had dropped it; Eddie picked it up and put it back in the blue bag. Les took them down to the gatepost where the shooting had started, then back to the barbecue area via the driveway and where the two Irishmen had shot the windows out when they got in under the house. Back in the barbecue area Eddie and Kingsley were quite impressed. So were the others.

'That was a bloody good effort, Les,' said Eddie. 'One bloke against six, with just an old World War II machine pistol.'

'It was a bloody good thing I had that,' replied Les.

'I'm only sorry it had to come to all this,' said Eddie, then turned to the others. 'You too, fellahs. Thanks for everything.'

'Ahh, that's all right,' said Ray.

'Anyway,' said Eddie. 'You haven't done too bad on the night. You're four and a half grand in front. You've cracked it for two near new cars. There's enough bloody guns there to start a revolution. And here's something to have a drink with.' Eddie threw a large envelope full of money on the table. 'There's another six grand. That ought to keep you going for a while.'

'Shit, thanks Ed,' said Ronnie. There was a chorus of thank yous from the others.

Eddie took a look at his watch. 'Well, it's all over here,' he said. 'If you blokes want to get home to bed, you may as well get cracking.'

'Yeah, it's not getting any earlier,' said Lennie, yawning and stretching. 'And I am getting a bit tired.'

'At least we don't have to walk home,' grinned Ray.

The three Vietnam veterans rose from the table, picked up the Irishmen's weapons as well as their own. Before they took the two garbage bags full of clothing to burn back at their place, Les removed two small articles, saying he wanted to keep them for a souvenir. There were handshakes and goodbyes all around. Eddie said he'd ring them later in the week to make sure everything was okay and he'd more than likely call back up before long. Ronnie told Les he'd probably call round tomorrow. He did have to go to Murwillumbah, but if not, he'd call round for sure on Tuesday. Les thanked the boys once more and they were gone.

It was quiet in the barbecue area after they'd left; the stars had reappeared and once again the nightbirds were calling to each other across the valley. Eddie said they'd have time for one more beer then Kingsley had to get the helicopter back before the owners — some mining company — missed it.

Les took a mouthful of beer, reflected into it for a moment then looked at Eddie and Kingsley. 'Jesus, Eddie. That was bloody close,' he said seriously. 'Another half a second and I could've been fuckin' dead. I'll be seeing that gun coming up at me for the rest of my bloody life.'

'Yeah, I know just how you feel,' replied Eddie. 'It's scary all right.'

'But bloody little Ronnie the caretaker.' Norton had to shake his head. 'He was the last bloke I was expecting to see.'

'Ohh, don't worry about Ronnie Madden. He was a bloody good soldier. One of the best.'

'Yeah. He was telling me you were his platoon sergeant in Vietnam. Did you know Harcourt too?'

'Sort of. I used to get him stuff for his troops. Camouflage uniforms. Rations. Booze. This and that.'

'I lined him up with a couple of Australian sheilas once,' said Kingsley. 'Couple of entertainers. They said they wanted to see some fighting. So Harcourt got me to fly him and the two sheilas into the middle of a battle. He was a good bloke.'

Norton took another swig of beer. 'But bloody Ronnie. I can't get over it. I mean, he's the biggest pisspot I ever seen.'

'He wasn't once,' said Eddie reflectively.

'Did it happen over there?' Eddie nodded. 'You want to tell us what happened?'

Eddie looked at his watch. 'All right. I'll tell you while I finish this beer then we'll piss off. It was at a place called Nui Ba Dinh. Up in the Tay Ninh province. We were on a patrol. Funny thing was, we weren't even supposed to be there. The yanks had the place. Our platoon was going through this valley looking for VC and NVA regulars, who we were sure were in the area. Anyway, there's this old house almost like a bunker, off to our left. Some noggie's taken a shot at us from a tree and we thought it came from the bunker. So Ronnie's charged it, lobbed a grenade in the window and shot the joint up inside. At almost the same time the NVA artillery opened on us and a shell hit the house, burying Ronnie inside. Next thing, a regiment of NVA regulars hit us from the mountains. We were there for two days before the yank airforce and the NZ artillery bombed them all out. When we dug Ronnie out of the house, all that was in there was a Vietnamese family. Mum, dad, grandma and five kids. Ronnie had killed the lot and got buried in there with them for two days. Two of the little girls had died with their eyes open and Ronnie was pinned alongside them. Two days and two nights. Two dead little girls staring at him. I reckon that'd be just about enough to unnerve anybody. It unhinged Ronnie.'

'Christ!' said Norton. 'The poor little bastard.'

'Yeah. So if you reckon Ronnie's a pisspot, well, now you know why. Every day and night of his life he still sees those two little girls staring at him.'

'Jesus!' Norton pictured Ronnie at the barbecues, pouring beer down his throat. No wonder. 'And what about Ray and Lennie? They seem all right.'

Eddie gave a cynical laugh. 'Ohh, yeah. They're as good as gold. They only got sprayed with Agent Orange. They live on a shitty invalid pension. With a bit of luck they might live another five or ten years.'

'Fuckin' hell!' Norton had to shake his head again.

'Don't worry, Les,' continued Eddie. 'There's plenty of Rays and Lennies running around. With a lot of fat-arsed public servants in Canberra doing their best to forget about them. It was a prick of a war, Les.'

Norton noticed Kingsley staring at Eddie. 'Some of us managed to adapt to it though,' said the pilot.

Eddie caught Kingsley's eye and gave another laugh. A strange one. 'Yeah, some of us managed to adapt to it.' His gaze switched directly to Norton. 'Some of us even got to like it.' He downed what was left of his beer. 'Anyway, we'd better get cracking.' Eddie and Kingsley rose from the table. 'Can you drive shit-for-brains back to Sydney all right? Tomorrow or whenever? And we'll piss him off back to England first chance we get.'

'Yeah, righto,' nodded Les. 'Does O'Malley know what's been going on up here. Would he know about tonight?'

'I rang Price just before we left. And I'll ring him as soon as we get back. I imagine he's been in touch with Canberra. Who gives a fuck now anyway? I'll see you back in Sydney. I'll have a good yarn to you then.'

'All right. See you Eddie. You too Kingsley.'

The pilot extended his hand, the almost permanent smile flickering in his eyes. 'Okay, George,' he said. 'Good to see you again, anyway.'

Les walked across to where the hole had been and watched as Eddie and Kingsley climbed into the helicopter. A few seconds later it whined noisily into life, kicking up dust and leaves and forcing Norton to back away from the prop wash. He gave a wave as the tail rose, then the chopper lifted off, banked across the valley and soon disappeared into the night sky. He watched it for a moment then went back to the table and finished the last of his beer as he stared at the two objects he'd retrieved from the plastic bag and at what was left of his ghetto blaster. So much for a quiet Sunday night at Cedar Glen. He dropped the empty bottle into the Otto-bin, switched off the lights and went to bed.

LES WASN'T QUITE sure what time it was when he went to bed, but after a very ordinary night's sleep, not bothering to shower and still in his ripped tracksuit, he was still tired when he got up around seven. He didn't bother to shave, but a long hot shower revealed the cuts on his face weren't all that bad, though he was thankful he didn't get any splinters or slivers of glass or perspex in his eyes. Apart from that and a few bruises it wasn't too bad. He threw on a T-shirt and jeans and went upstairs, where Peregrine was still asleep.

Daylight revealed just what a mess the kitchen, dining room and study were in. The walls were still all right, but the second blast had completely wrecked the study windows and blown nearly every shelf from the walls. Debris littered the dining room and kitchen. Shelves were lying everywhere amidst pots, cutlery and broken crockery. There was no gas leaking but the stove looked stuffed, although the fridge was still working and all the cupboards under the sink were intact. Les found the electric-jug and took that, some Nescafe and other stuff down to the barbecue area and made a huge, steaming mug of coffee. While he drank it he decided to walk around and check out last night's battleground.

The Robinson may have only been tiny, but it sure had

made a mess. Dozens of small holes were chewed into the driveway and there were gritty white patches everywhere where the bullets had smashed into the rockeries. The two gateposts looked as if a flock of giant woodpeckers had gone crazy on them. Behind one rockery, dull, red patches of congealed blood showed where Robert and Brendan had been wounded and then summarily executed. Les grimly took a mouthful of coffee and walked to the corner of the house. There was another patch of dried blood where Logan Colbain had been shot; it was almost as big as the two bloodstains at the gateposts combined. Behind that, panes of shattered glass lay all around the bottom of the house where the Irish had tried to get in downstairs. Les scuffed some with his feet, drank some more coffee and walked around to the driveway. A sticky red smear along one side of the station wagon and more clotted blood on the driveway showed where Patrick and Tom Mooney were machine-gunned. The car itself looked like something out of a Bonnie and Clyde movie. Four neat holes were drilled in the windscreen. There were another half dozen in the bonnet and about twenty along the side panels and windows. Miraculously, the headlights were undamaged and even more miraculously the car started when Les got behind the wheel and turned the key in the ignition. Even the windscreen wipers and radio worked. Well, at least it'll get us back to Sydney, thought Les.

Norton was sick of looking at patches of blood when he came to the last ones running down the back stairs and on the path next to the barbecue area. It was the biggest of the lot and looked as if Ronnie had chopped Liam Frayne up with an axe. Those three final bursts from the little caretaker's Seggern echoed through Norton's mind again and again he pictured those deadly little black guns in the Vietnam veterans' hands. He made a fresh cup of coffee and sipped it while he stared absently at his two souvenirs sitting on the table. Then a couple of thoughts occurred to him. Firstly, how was he going to explain all this damage to Benny Rabinski? The rapport between himself and his Jewish ex-landlord was lower than a Greek spongediver's arse as it was. This would really put the icing on the cake. Can I have the bond money back, Benny? Certainly Mr Norton. Just explain to these nice policemen what happened out there. Then secondly, what was he going to say to poor Bill Kileen at Kileen's Prestige Kars? Yeah, I'll look after the car for you, Bill, no worries. I just loaned it to Al Capone for a couple of days while I was up there, that's all.

As usual Les had been left to carry the can again. Norton was brooding moodily about this when footsteps coming down the kitchen stairs made him turn towards the driveway. It was Peregrine in his dressing gown.

The Englishman's eyes were a little puffy from too much sleep and he looked dishevelled, but most of the colour had returned to his face and it appeared Norton's rough treatment had worked. He was moving around slowly though it seemed to be more with bewilderment than anything else.

Les watched him approach and a tight smile formed around his mouth. 'Hello, Peregrine,' he said, a syrupy malevolence dripping from his voice. 'Feeling better, are we?'

'Yes. Quite, thank you,' replied the Englishman hesitantly.

'Oh well, isn't that good?' said Les. 'I'm so glad.'

Peregrine stared at Norton. 'What on earth happened upstairs? The house looks like a bomb hit it.'

Norton couldn't believe what he was hearing. 'What did you just say Peregrine?' he asked.

'The house,' replied Peregrine innocently. 'I said it looks like a jolly bomb hit it.'

'Well isn't that a coincidence?' smiled Norton. Then the tone in his voice rose to a crimson-faced, veins-in-the-neck-bulging roar. 'Because that's exactly what did hit it, you fuckin' idiot! A fuckin' bomb! Three, to be exact. Plus about five hundred thousand rounds of fuckin' machine gunfire.'

Peregrine flopped down in a chair. 'I... I don't quite understand.'

'Because of you. You fuckin' imbecile!' roared Norton. 'The Irish arrived last night. Six of them. With machine guns and a fuckin' bazooka. I'm fuckin' lucky to be alive.'

'Oh dear.'

'Yeah. Fuckin' oh dear.'

'Well... what happened?' asked Peregrine. 'Where are they now?'

'Where are they? You want to know where they are? Come here, and I'll fuckin' well show you, you goose.' Les took Peregrine by the front of his dressing gown and shoved him out to the middle of where the big hole had been. 'Here's where they are. Right fuckin' here. You're standing on them. I had to help Ronnie the caretaker and two of his mates bury them last night. If you don't believe me, grab a shovel and dig down about ten feet. You'll find the bodies. Full of bullet holes and covered in quicklime.'

Peregrine looked around him at the freshly turned soil and

the realisation that Les wasn't joking dawned on him. 'But . . . I mean. How on earth did they find out where we were?'

Les looked at Peregrine like he was going to eat him. This was the moment he'd been waiting for. 'How did they find out where we were?' He grabbed Peregrine by the dressing gown again, shoved him back to the table, forced him back into his seat and thrust the blood-smeared piece of paper in his face. 'Here, Einstein. Read this. I got it off one of the bodies.'

With Les watching him like a maddened tiger, Peregrine blinked at the piece of paper, then his face began to colour noticeably. 'Oh dear,' he said, then coloured some more. 'Oh dear.'

'And I'm a fuckin' wally, am I?' hissed Norton.

'I . . . I didn't really mean that, Les. I mean, we had only just got here when I sent that. I . . . I was thinking differently then.'

'Think!' snorted Norton. 'When did you ever think, you fuckin' imbecile?' He poured Peregrine a mug of coffee and thrust it at him. 'Here. Bring that. And I'll give you a guided tour of what happened last night. You'll love it.'

With their coffees in their hands, Les took Peregrine around where he'd been earlier and told him exactly what had happened after he'd put him to bed. From the Irishmen opening up on him at the front gate, holding them off with the Robinson and the rockets hitting the house. The cavalry arriving, in the form of Ronnie and his two mates, the execution, burying the bodies, right up to a not very happy Eddie Salita arriving by helicopter. By the time they got to the last patch of blood on the stairs Peregrine was just about ready to throw up. Any colour that had returned to his face had disappeared and it was back to a chalky white.

'And if you don't fuckin' believe me about how deadly Ronnie and his two mates are,' said Les, back in the barbecue area. 'Have a little look at this.' Norton picked up one of the souvenirs he'd retrieved from the garbage bag: a black balaclava with a bullet hole drilled neatly into the back. He poked his index finger through the hole and it came out red and sticky from the still-damp blood. 'How do you like that, Peregrine?' he said, holding it about an inch from the Englishman's face. 'Not a bad shot, eh?'

That was enough for Peregrine. He rose unsteadily from the table and brought up all his coffee on the grass, then stood there for a while dry retching before sitting back down again.

'It's no good being nice to you, Peregrine,' continued Norton, his diatribe now coming to a climax. 'You're nothing but a fuckin' idiot. A bloke ought to put one right on your chin. Because of your plain fuckin' stupidity we both nearly got killed last night. We're deadset lucky to be alive. And you can thank poor little Ronnie the caretaker for that. So fuck you, Peregrine, you cunt. Get fucked.'

Tears began to well up in Peregrine's eyes. No one had ever spoken to him like that before, never. But then again he'd never been in a position like this before, totally alone in a strange country in the middle of nowhere. He felt lonely, dejected and thoroughly miserable. 'Oh God, what can I say?' he choked. 'I feel such a fool. I'm so sorry.' Then the tears came. 'I wanted so much to be your friend, Les. I really did.'

Peregrine buried his face in his hands and great sobs racked his body as the tears poured out. Les looked at him with disgust. Then Les began to feel disgusted with himself. Standing over poor Peregrine who was half his size and sick as a dog as well. And abusing him like that. For one little indiscretion that was really only meant as a joke anyway. What about all the fun they'd had together? And what about what he'd done for those two battling lifesavers? Now the poor little bastard's sitting there crying his eyes out just because he's not a tough hard nutter like you. Big man, Les. You really showed that Hooray Henry, didn't you? Why don't you punch him in the head and be done with it?

'Ahh, don't worry about it, Peregrine.' Les sat down next to the Englishman and patted his shoulder. 'It's all over now and we're safe. And that's the main thing. We're still mates.'

'I am sorry, Les,' sniffed Peregrine. 'I really am.'

'I know you are. And so am I. I shouldn't have gone on like that. I'm just in a bit of a shitty mood, that's all.'

'I nearly got you killed.'

'Ahh, forget about it. I'm still here, ain't I? Happy and smiling as ever.'

'Are we still friends?'

'Bloody oath we are.' Norton put his arm around Peregrine's shoulders and gave him a hug. 'Come on, I'll make you another cup of coffee. You want one?'

'Yes please.'

Les put the jug on and got some more coffee going. Peregrine's tears dried up, though he was still more than a bit upset. But he did realise that what he had done was quite stupid. Norton settled down and was pleased that the rapport was back between them. It was pretty hard to hate Peregrine, even if at times he was a shocking dill.

'So, how's your back now?' asked Les. 'Is it any better?'

'Yes it is, actually,' replied Peregrine. 'I still don't feel quite one hundred percent. But I'm not nearly as stiff and sore as I was. And my headache has completely gone.'

'Good. That's all the poison sweated out of your system. Anyway, drink this and I'll have another look at it in a minute.'

They finished their coffee and Les got Peregrine to take off his dressing gown. The Icthyol and the rough treatment had done their job. The redness was almost gone — all that remained was a nasty-looking small black sore. Les decided to give it a clean with some methylated spirits and apply a bit more black zinc.

'What's really amazed me,' said Peregrine, 'is Ronnie. I wouldn't have picked him to be a Vietnam veteran.'

'No, me either,' said Les. 'Actually it's a bit of a sad story about Ronnie and his two mates.'

While he fixed up Peregrine's back Les told him the story he got from Eddie and why it turned out Ronnie drank so much.

'Oh my God,' said Peregrine. 'That's absolutely horrendous. Two days trapped in the rubble with all those bodies.'

'Yeah,' nodded Norton. 'And it looks like his two mates have got some sort of cancer.'

'Dear me.'

'It's not the best, is it? And yet we owe our lives to those same three blokes.'

'And what did they want to do? Buy this place and make it into some sore of rehabilitation centre for vets?'

'If they had the money. But between them I don't think they've got a pot to piss in. Evidently they live just over that valley. Ronnie's got a bit of an old farmhouse. I don't think it's anything too flash.'

'Tch!' Peregrine shook his head. 'Those poor chaps. What an absolute shame.'

'Yeah,' agreed Les. 'But I guess that's just the way it goes.'

Norton finished Peregrine's back and told him to put his dressing gown back on. The Englishman seemed to brighten up considerably and most of the colour had returned to his face.

'Well, that looks all right, mate,' said Les. 'Just try and keep it dry and I'll change it again tonight.' He rubbed his huge hands together. 'You feel like a bit of breakfast?'

'Yes. I could eat a little something. But not much.'

'Well, scrambled eggs are off the menu, old mate. The stove's fucked. But I reckon I could knock up some toasted cheese sandwiches on the barbecue. How does that sound?'

'Splendid. I'll get cleaned up. Do you need a hand?'

'No, she's right.' Les watched as Peregrine climbed slowly up the back stairs, doing his best to avoid the patches of dried blood. 'Hey Peregrine,' he called out. 'I wasn't pissed off at you for bringing the Irish around.'

'No?'

'No. I just didn't like you telling your girlfriend I was a wally. That's all.'

Peregrine smiled from the top of the stairs. 'You're definitely not a wally, Les. Never. Though you can be a bit of a wombat at times.' He disappeared inside the house.

Les shook his head and laughed to himself. How can you win? At least he's got his bulldog spirit back. While Peregrine was under the shower Norton brought the food down from upstairs and got the barbecue going. On the open fire with sliced onion, tomato and chives, the toasted cheese sandwiches didn't turn out too bad. Now dressed in his fatigues and Reeboks, Peregrine managed to get down two sandwiches, plus more mugs of coffee laced with local honey. He looked completely different from the half-dead creature moping around the farm the day before. Norton was feeling about ten times better than when he had got out of bed that morning.

'So what do you want to do now, Les?' asked Peregrine. 'Are we going to stay here a while longer? There's no real hurry to leave is there?'

'No. Not really,' replied Les. 'But there's not much point in hanging around. And I don't particularly want to be here if that estate agent comes out. Unless you want to try and explain the damage to him.'

'I concede the point,' agreed Peregrine.

'So I reckon we might get going sometime tomorrow. Probably at night. If the cops see that car going past they'll probably pull me over.'

'Yes,' agreed Peregrine again. 'It looks like it belongs to Elliot Ness.'

They sat around sipping coffee listening to the birds and watching the sun rising higher over the valley; both men lost in their own thoughts. Soon they would be leaving the tranquil beauty of Cedar Glen, a place with which they each now had a unique affinity, and then they would be going their separate

307

ways. It was hard to imagine that it was finally over.

'Ohh yeah, Peregrine,' said Les. 'That's what I meant to tell you. I got a little bit of bad news for you. Your cousin Lewis got hurt in Belfast.'

'Oh dear. What happened? Is it serious?'

'No, nothing too bad,' lied Les. 'Just a freak car accident. He broke a leg and he's in hospital and can't get around. Eddie told me. Your father rang the Attorney General — your god-father. And he rang Price, my boss.'

'And Lewis is all right?'

'Yeah, sweet. So you never know, Peregrine. Maybe this whole shemozzle has turned out for the best.'

'Yes. Quite possibly.' Peregrine's voice faded away slightly. 'Les, I really am sorry about what happened. I just honestly didn't think those scoundrels would follow me all the way to Australia. That's all.'

'No, neither did I, Peregrine, to tell you the truth,' grinned Norton. 'I thought this would be a bit of a lark. The last thing I was expecting was six blokes trying to shoot me.'

'Yes.' Then Peregrine's face broke into a grin. 'But by Jove, we've had some fun at times, haven't we?'

'Yeah, we sure have mate,' agreed Les. 'We sure have.'

Suddenly Peregrine's grin turned into a frown. 'Ooh,' he said twisting his face up. 'I don't know what's in those cheese sandwiches. But I have to . . .' He rose quickly from the table.

'Got a twenty-five pounder jammed in the breech have you, mate?' said Les.

'Something like that,' replied Peregrine, hurrying for the bathroom.

Les watched him going up the stairs. 'Just mention my name up there,' he called out. 'And they'll give you a good seat.'

Smiling to himself Norton took his coffee over to the barbecue and watched the coals glowing as they were fanned by the gentle sou'wester coming across the valley. So it's finally over, eh? He looked across the gently rolling hills to Mt. Warning standing supreme in the distance. I'm gonna miss this bloody joint. Yeah. I really am. Les was musing on this and watching a couple of currawongs who were staring back at him from the grass, when he heard the sound of cars approaching from the driveway near the main road. Hello, who's this? Les put down his coffee and walked across to the driveway at the side of the house. He wasn't there long before two white cars pulled up near the rockeries: a Ford Fairlane and a new Holden. The Fairlane had Commonwealth number plates.

There were two men in each car. They looked briefly at Norton, said something to each other then got out; two walked towards him, the other two watched him from across the car rooves. All appeared to be in their mid-thirties and were wearing sunglasses with sober suits, sober shoes and almost the same boring striped ties. Norton didn't need to be a Rhodes scholar to see they had walloper written all over them. Oh well, mused Norton. It had to happen sooner or later.

'G'day,' he said, as the first two approached.

The taller, fair-haired one on Norton's left nodded briefly. 'I'm Detective Inspector Ledgerwood, Commonwealth Police,' he said, producing a badge on a wallet. He gestured to his darker, balding offsider, who produced a badge too. 'This is Officer Renwell from ASIO. You must be Les Norton.' Les nodded just as briefly. 'We've come for Sir Peregrine Normanhurst. Is he here?'

'Yeah. What's up? Is he under arrest, is he?' said Les.

'No. Nothing like that,' intoned Ledgerwood. 'We've come to drive Sir Peregrine to Brisbane. Is he here?'

'Yeah, he is,' replied Norton breezily. 'If you want to wait a second I'll go and get him. His Highness happens to be on the throne at the moment.'

Norton trotted up the kitchen stairs into the house where Peregrine was coming out of the bathroom. 'Hey, Peregrine,' he said. 'There's some coppers downstairs want to see you.'

Peregrine looked concerned as he straightened his fatigues. 'Police? What on earth do they want?'

'Fucked if I know. Come on.'

They went down the stairs to the two cops, who seemed to stiffen as Peregrine approached.

'Sir Peregrine Normanhurst?' asked Detective Ledgerwood. The Englishman nodded. 'Your godfather, the Attorney General, would like to speak to you. Would you mind coming to the car, please.'

Peregrine nodded but still didn't say anything. Ledgerwood took him to the Fairlane, handed him a car-phone then rejoined Renwell and they both stood looking at Norton.

Les looked back at them. 'Nice day,' he said. The two cops looked back expressionlessly and didn't reply. Norton twigged what they were on about. 'You want to take a look around?' he said, indicating the blown-out windows above him and the patch of dried blood on the pathway. No answer was the pofaced reply. 'Would you like to take down a statement?' The two cop's mouths were starting to turn down a little now. 'No,

I didn't think so,' said Norton. 'Be different if I was selling illegal eggs or something though, wouldn't it?' Fuckin pricks, thought Les. There's been six killings and all you are, is a team of glorified chauffeurs. The two cops stared icily at Norton's grin till Peregrine eventually returned.

'That was Uncle Laurence,' he said to Les. 'He wants to speak to you.'

Les gave Ledgerwood and Renwell a quick once up and down. 'Would you excuse me for a moment? I have to speak to the Attorney General.' Norton walked across to the Fairlane where one of the other cops handed him the phone then stood next to him. Les glared at him then motioned with his head for him to piss off. The cop glared back then moved out of earshot.

'Mr O'Malley,' said Les into the phone.

'Is that you, Les, is it?'

Even over the car-phone Norton could recognise the Attorney General's voice from radio and TV. 'Yes, it is,' he replied.

'A mutual friend of ours has told me a lot about you. I think you know who I mean.'

'I think I do, Mr O'Malley.'

'He also told me what happened up there.'

'Ohh, yeah. The holiday cottage hotted up for a while there.'

'From what I hear, that's putting it mildly. He can be a shocking dill at times, young Peregrine.'

'Ahh, he's not all that bad.'

'Don't worry, Les. Even his old man reckons he could do with a good boot right up the arse.'

'I got to admit, Mr O'Malley,' laughed Norton. 'He went close a couple of times.'

The Attorney General laughed back, then his voice took on a more serious tone. 'I'd like to thank you personally for what you did, Les.'

'I didn't do all that much,' replied Norton.

'You're far too modest, my boy. I owe you one. And I'll personally see to it, through our mutual friend, that it's made up to you.'

'Whatever. But I wouldn't worry about it too much.'

'Anyway, shit-for-brains will be coming back to Brisbane with my men so you'll be rid of the little prick soon.'

Norton laughed again. 'You never know, Mr O'Malley. I might just miss him.'

'Well, if you can be like that, you're a better man than even our mutual friend said you were. Goodbye, Les. And thank you again.'

'Goodbye, Mr O'Malley.'

Les put the phone down and walked back to Peregrine who was talking to Ledgerwood and Renwell.

'Well, it looks like you'll be going back to Brisbane with these blokes,' he said.

Peregrine made a helpless sort of gesture with his hands. 'Yes. But it's not quite what I expected. Or wanted. I was hoping to spend a couple of days in Sydney with you.'

Norton shrugged. 'Ah well, mate. You never know, maybe it's for the best.'

Renwell made a discreet cough. 'There's no immediate hurry, Sir Peregrine,' he said. 'But the Attorney General did say to get you back there as soon as possible.'

Les gave Peregrine a pat on the shoulder. 'Come on, mate,' he said quietly. 'I'll give you a hand to pack.'

In his bedroom Peregrine appeared lost and confused. There wasn't a great deal to pack but he was fumbling and mumbling around and it was clear the idea of leaving so suddenly had upset him somewhat. Les made a joke or two as best he could and told him not to worry, he'd soon be back in England with his girl and all his friends, only this time as safe as a mouse in a maltheap. But Les was feeling a bit melancholy too. He would have liked to have shown Peregrine around Sydney under more relaxed circumstances. Before long Peregrine was packed. All that remained was *Portrait Of A Chinaman* by Ernest Norman Toejam hanging on the wall.

'What about your painting?' said Les.

'Yes,' replied Peregrine. 'Do you think the estate agent would miss these old blankets?'

'I doubt it.'

'Then I might wrap it in a couple.'

'You're going to a lot of trouble for a lousy thirty dollar painting, Peregrine,' said Les.

'It's just the uniqueness of it, Les,' smiled the Englishman. 'Just the uncanny uniqueness.'

Norton found some thick string in the kitchen and before long the painting was securely bound in the two old grey blankets. Les picked up Peregrine's suitcase, the Englishman had a last look around his bedroom of two weeks and they walked down to the Fairlane where Ledgerwood had the boot open.

They placed everything carefully inside then Peregrine grinned at Les and took out his camera. 'Come on,' he said. 'A couple of quick photos before I leave.'

'Okay,' smiled Norton.

'Would you mind?' said Peregrine, handing the camera to Ledgerwood.

'Not at all, sir.'

'How about in front of the station wagon?' suggested Les.

'Good idea,' agreed Peregrine.

Renwell joined Ledgerwood and they both looked decidedly uncomfortable as Les and Peregrine mugged it up in front of the blood-smeared, bullet-holed station wagon. Ledgerwood shot off four photos then Peregrine took his camera back.

'Could you give us a few minutes?' he said.

'Certainly, sir,' replied Ledgerwood.

The two cops walked over and got into separate cars, leaving Les and Peregrine alone in the driveway. There was an awkward silence for a moment, then Peregrine spoke.

'Well I guess this is it, Les,' he said.

'Yeah. I guess it is, mate,' replied Les.

In those six words Norton had summed it up simply and succinctly. No deep and meaningful relationship had developed between the two men or any of that bullshit — they had simply become, to use the Australian vernacular, just that: good mates.

'What can I say?' said Peregrine.

'Yeah,' nodded Les. 'What can you say?'

'We've had some fun.'

'Yes, we sure have,' nodded Les again. 'You've got me into six fights. I've been shot at. Blown up. I'm half deaf in one ear. My ghetto-blaster's fucked and I'm barred from the local pub. Yeah, it's been great, Peregrine. Don't forget to let me know when you're coming out again.'

'Les, you are absolutely incorrigible,' grinned Peregrine. Then he extended his hand and his handshake was as warm and almost as strong as Les's. 'Promise me you'll come and visit me in England. I'd love you to.'

'You know, I might even do that, Peregrine.'

'You've got my card. Tell me when you're coming, I'll send you the plane ticket. There'll be a limousine waiting for you. You'll have a car over there. I'll guarantee you the time of your life. And you won't spend a penny.'

'Sounds good, Peregrine. I reckon I'd be a mug to knock that back.'

'You certainly would.'

'Anyway, come on. Dick Tracy and Sam Catchem are waiting for you.'

Les walked Peregrine to the car, they shook hands once more then Peregrine got into the back seat of the Fairlane.

'Goodbye, Les Norton,' he grinned, as the window slid down.

'Goodbye, Sir Peregrine Normanhurst — the Third,' Les grinned back. 'You take care of yourself.'

'You too, Les.'

The two engines growled into life then slowly the cars circled the driveway around the house to come past Les again. Norton waved and the last he saw of Peregrine was the Englishman's face, smiling and waving to him as the two government cars headed for the front gates.

Norton watched them disappear then went to the barbecue area, got a beer and sat down. Well, I guess that's that, he mused. And there's heaps worse blokes than Peregrine around, I reckon. Before he knew it he'd finished that beer and was into a second. Well, what'll I do? Hang around here for another day? There's no TV, no phone and now I got no radio and no cunt to talk to. And Rabinski could put his head in at any time. It's all right with those federal cops, but the state ones could be a different kettle of fish altogether. Especially when they find out who I work for. Norton finished beer number two and drummed his fingers on the table. His gaze drifted across to where the big hole had been and the six Irishmen were now rotting away under ten feet of earth. No, fuck it. I'll give the place a bit of a clean up, leave a note for Ronnie, if he doesn't call around, and piss off tonight. Les had one more beer and started to do just that.

THE TRIP BACK to Sydney wasn't bad, but it was by no means good either. After packing the car with whatever groceries and booze were left over, giving the place a tidy up and leaving a note for Ronnie with his phone number, Les had a couple of hours snooze in the afternoon and left around eight. He dropped the keys in at Rabinski's without a note and after that it was an all-night drive peering through a half-shattered windscreen. There was a greasy hamburger at Coffs Harbour, a quarter of a chicken and chips at Kempsey and nothing else but staring into darkness and oncoming headlights as the miles went by. Les stopped for a coffee and more petrol at Bulahdelah, and the thin rays of the winter sun were just starting to come up when he got to the outskirts of Newcastle. He reached the harbour bridge around eight-fifteen, just in time for the morning peak hour rush. After the clear balmy weather of the Tweed Valley, Sydney was cold, cloudy and polluted. The sou'westers had blown most of the industrial pollution out to sea but a couple of hundred thousand cars and trucks spewing out clouds of carbon monoxide more than made up for it. Then there was the noise. The only good thing was he'd picked up a bit of mud and dirt on the trip which covered the bullet holes apart from the ones in the windscreen, and he'd hardly got a second look from any of the cars alongside him. Stiff, sore and tired, he pulled up outside his semi in Cox Avenue some time after nine. It was good to be home, or at least to get out of the car.

Norton's old Ford was still intact, which after sitting in the one place in Bondi for two weeks is a bit of a plus. Les shivered in the cold as he looked at the sky; banks of clouds coming in from the Blue Mountains suggested it could rain before the day was out. He shivered again as he got his bags out of the station wagon, hurried straight inside and dumped them in his room. Warren's room was empty and a cup and saucer in the rack and a warm kettle in the kitchen said he must have only just left for work. That's what I'll do, thought Les, have a nice hot cup of tea and some toast. When that was ready Norton somehow seemed inexorably drawn into the lounge room to look at something he hadn't seen for two weeks. TV. He switched it on and flipped around the channels, eyes grainy but too tired to sleep. It was all there before him. 'Here's Humphrey'. 'Play School'. 'Mulligrubs'. 'Fat Cat And Friends'. 'General Hospital'. All the things he'd missed. Before Les knew it, Bill Collins was winding up the pitch for his midday movie, *Four Faces West* with Joel McRae, Francis Dee and Charles Bickford, and Les had started to wake up to himself.

'What the fuck am I doing watching this shit?' he asked out loud.

Les switched off the TV and debated what to do. He decided against ringing Price or any of them and letting them know he was back. He didn't feel like talking to anyone at the moment; even his own house seemed strange to him and somehow he couldn't stop his thoughts drifting back to Cedar Glen with its trees, birds and billabongs. Ah well, better unpack my gear and get the rest of the stuff out of the car. Then I might go for a walk, get some meat and vegetables and make a casserole. And have a bit of a think. I'm buggered if I'm going to bed.

It was late in the afternoon and getting colder by the minute when Les got back home. He'd ended up walking to Bronte cemetery along the cliffs, gazing out at the flat blue sea, avoiding people as he tried to get the peaceful openness of the colonel's property out of his mind and readjust to Sydney and the crowds and what now seemed to be new noises. For an old country boy he was finding it a lot harder than he thought and at times he felt like getting back in the car and driving back up there. Ah, maybe I'm just tired, he mumbled to himself. The blade steak casserole was ready and Les was sipping a bottle of Gosser when the front door opened around six; there was no mistaking those nimble footsteps coming down the hall.

'Well, bugger me,' grinned Warren from the kitchen doorway. 'The bloody landlord's back. How are you, mate?'

'G'day Woz,' replied Norton. 'How are you going?'

'Good. When did you get back?'

'This morning. I drove all night.'

'Hello. Have to make a fast get away did we? Where's Prince Charles?'

'He went back to Brisbane. Flew back to England from there.'

'How come?'

'He just did.'

Warren went to the other side of the kitchen and placed a pizza near the sink. He noticed the stew simmering on the stove and smiled.

'So, what happened up there? Did you have a good time? Was there any sheilas? Did Peregrine get over his nervous breakdown?'

'You ask many questions, grasshopper,' replied Les tiredly. 'Why don't we have some tea and I'll tell you all about it?'

'Okay.' Warren opened the fridge for a soft drink. 'Jesus Christ!' he exclaimed. 'What's all this? Stella Artois. Gosser. Becks. Bloody Corona. Even three bottles of French Champagne! And not a can of Fourex in sight.' He looked at Les in bewilderment. 'What the fuck's going on? Have you caught some rare tropical disease or something?'

'No,' sniffed Norton. 'I've just re-educated my drinking habits, that's all,' he added with a yawn.

'You've *what*?'

'Re-educated my drinking habits. I just find that Australian beer can be a bit, I don't know, rebarbative at times.'

'What? Ohh, don't give me the shits. You must have won this in a raffle. Or stole it.'

'You are a peasant, Warren, there's no two ways about it.' Norton shook his head. 'Come on. Let's get into that casserole.'

'I wish I'd known you were coming home,' said Warren. 'I wouldn't have bought that bloody pizza. How come you never rang anyway?'

'We didn't have the phone on at the farm,' yawned Les.

'Oh.'

They had a beer each and started on the stew. With every mouthful Norton's eyes seemed to keep closing. By the time they'd finished he was almost asleep at the table.

'Are you all right?' said Warren. 'You look rooted.'

His eyes half-closed, Les rose from the table. 'Will you clean up, Woz? I'm going to bed.'

'Bed? It's not even half past seven.'

'I don't give a fuck,' mumbled Les. 'I'm going to bed.'

'Well, what about the trip? What about what happened?'

'I'll tell you about it tomorrow. G'night, Woz.'

Norton shuffled off to his bedroom and left Warren sitting there. Despite cars going up and down the road, sirens screaming in the distance and people walking past his window, Les slept like the dead.

AFTER NOT MOVING all night, Norton woke up feeling fresh as a daisy around six-thirty the following morning. There was no hanging around in shorts and a T-shirt like at Cedar Glen. This was Sydney in August, the house was cold and it was straight into a tracksuit and thick woollen socks. The bathroom scales told him he'd put on nearly three kilograms while he was away, pigging himself on steaks and gallons of imported beer, so a hard run and some even harder exercises were in order. It was too bleak for the beach; Centennial Park would be the go, besides, the ponds and trees might bring back memories of Cedar Glen. Might.

It had rained overnight and all the mud and dust had washed off the station wagon revealing the bullet holes, which looked bigger and brighter than ever. Les wasn't too keen to be seen driving it around and figured that the sooner he got it back to Bill Kileen the better. He replaced the spark-plug leads in his own car, it kicked over almost first time and Les headed for Waverley. When he got back, red-faced and streaked with sweat, Warren was in the kitchen finishing his second croissant and coffee over the *Telegraph* before going to work.

'Hello, mate,' he said brightly, as Les came through the door. 'How was the run?'

'Good,' replied Les. 'Jesus, it's cold outside, but.'

'Yeah. It's been freezing the last couple of weeks. What was it like up there?'

'Grouse. We were swimming and sunbaking in a billabong nearly every day.'

'Yeah I noticed you had a bit of a tan up.'

Norton went to the fridge and got some mineral water. 'So what have you been up to during the landlord's absence? Been having any wild parties while I was away? I hope you haven't been dragging any low molls back here.'

'I don't drag low molls back here, Les,' replied Warren, continuing to read the paper. 'I might invite a young lady back for a drink now and again. The low molls are your department, and the riff raff you rub shoulders with in your occupation as chief thumper and knee-cap dislocater at Kings Cross.'

'Ha-ha-ha,' said Norton. 'So what have you been up to?'

'Not much really. Just work. Been out to dinner a few times, couple of parties. In fact there's a party on up at Mojo this Friday night. If you're lucky I might take you.'

'And why wouldn't you take me?' said Les. 'I'm a fuckin' male model.'

'Yes,' agreed Warren. 'Indeed you are. The face that launched a thousand bottles of poofy wine cooler.' He pushed the paper to one side, then got up and rinsed his cup. 'Anyway, I have to get to work. You going to be home tonight to tell me all about the trip?'

'Yep. Sure am,' nodded Les.

'Righto. I'll see you about six.'

'Okay, Woz. See you then, mate.'

The front door closed and Warren was gone. Les was glancing at the front page of the paper and having another glass of mineral water when he heard the door open again. Footsteps sounded in the hallway and he looked up to see Warren staring at him.

'Is that white station wagon out the front the one you drove up north?' he asked, trying not to raise his voice.

'Yep,' replied Norton, continuing to look at the paper. 'Sure is.'

'It's full of bloody bullet holes.'

'You noticed, Warren.'

'What the bloody hell happened?'

'I got into a machine gun fight. That's all.'

'What? You're joking.' Warren blinked as Norton looked at him expressionlessly and shook his head. 'Jesus Christ! I don't believe it.'

'I'll tell you all about it tonight, Woz. In the meantime, don't tell anybody about the car, or where I've been. All right?'

Warren shook his head as he left. 'Christ! Who am I living with? Dirty Harry?'

'No. Dirty Les. I'll see you tonight, Woz.'

Les checked up on the football results then decided to make a couple of quick phone calls and get cleaned up before he cooled off too much. He rang Price and got his answering service, so he left a message. He rang Billy Dunne and got his wife. Billy wasn't home — he was having a run and workout with some blokes from North Bondi Surf Club. She'd get him to ring him when he got back. Les had a bit of a chat to Louise for a while then hung up and got under the shower. He'd just finished breakfast and was sitting there in a clean tracksuit reading the paper again when the phone rang. It was Billy.

'Hello, Les,' he said happily. 'How are you, mate?'

'Good, Billy. How's yourself?'

'Terrific. When did you get back?'

'Yesterday. But I was too tired to ring anyone. How's it going at the club?'

'Good as gold. Danny's still up there. So you can come back when you feel like it.'

'I tried to ring Price. He's not home.'

'No. He's in Muswellbrook looking at some horses.'

'Oh. Listen Billy, can you do me a favour?'

'Sure. What is it?'

'I got to take that car back to Bill Kileen's. Can you follow me out and bring me back?'

'Yeah, no sweat. Can you give me a couple of hours? I just walked in the door and I've got to run the young bloke over to his grandma's.'

'Okay. Do you want to have a feed and a beer after?'

'Righto. You can tell me about the trip.'

'Okay, mate. See you then.'

Norton hung up and thought for a moment. That's what I can do. Wash all my dirty gear from up there. He did that, tidied up the house, made some more coffee and before long he heard Billy's knock on the door.

'Hello, mate. How are you?' was the first thing he said.

'G'day Billy,' replied Les. 'Come in, mate.'

Billy propped at the door. 'You took a white Ford station wagon up there, didn't you?' Norton nodded. 'Is that it out the front?' Norton nodded again. 'It's full of fuckin' bullet holes. What happened?'

'Didn't Eddie tell you?'

'Eddie's in Melbourne.'

'Oh. Well, come in and I'll tell you about it.'

Billy took another look at the car over his shoulder then followed Les into the kitchen.

'You want a cup of coffee?' asked Les.

'I wouldn't mind a beer.'

'Yeah. I might have one myself.' Les got two beers from the fridge, opened them and handed one to Billy. 'That silly bloody Peregrine sent his sheila in England a postcard telling her where we were. Somehow those IRA blokes got hold of it and followed us up there. I ended up in a machine gun fight. I'm dead set lucky to be alive.'

'Bloody hell!'

'Ohh mate, you should have seen it. It was like something out of a Vietnam movie. Grab a seat.'

Billy sat down and Les told him all about the gunfight. How Ronnie saved the day, burying the bodies, Eddie getting up there by helicopter. The last thing he did was go to his bedroom and get the two balaclavas.

Billy sat there open-mouthed, shaking his head. 'God strike me,' he said, picking up one of the balaclavas. 'That's almost unbelievable.'

'Yeah,' nodded Les. 'And the bloody little caretaker — most inoffensive bloke you'd ever want to meet. He saved my neck.'

Billy poked a finger through one of the holes. 'Doesn't look like his mates were too inoffensive.'

'Funny thing,' said Les. 'If they walked in the door I wouldn't even recognise them, with all that black shit they had on their faces.'

Billy kept shaking his head and staring at the two balaclavas.

'But it wasn't all drama,' smiled Les. 'I had a bloody good time as well.'

'Did you?'

'Reckon. But how about we piss that car off and I'll tell you all about it over a couple of beers?'

'Righto.'

* * *

THE SAME TATTY flags were fluttering in the breeze and the same *Free Firewood* sign was wired to the fence when they pulled up outside Kileen's Prestige Kars at Tempe. The back driveway was open, Les swung the car straight inside. Billy parked in front of the entrance. Kileen was just getting off the phone when Norton strolled into the office.

'G'day, Les,' he said brightly. 'How are you mate? How was the trip?'

'Real good,' replied Norton.

Kileen spotted Billy. 'G'day Billy. How are you?'

'Not too bad, Killer. How's yourself?'

'Terrific.' Kileen turned to Les. 'So you had a good time, did you?'

'Yeah,' nodded Les. 'It was tops. Weather was grouse.'

'Car go all right?'

'Like a Swiss watch.'

'Like a Swiss cheese'd be more like it,' said Billy, looking at the wall.

'Anyway, thanks a lot, Bill,' said Les. 'Here's the keys and the rego papers. We gotta get going. I never had a chance to get it greased, and it needs a wash. But everything else is all right. Okay?'

'Yeah, that's nothing,' replied Kileen. 'I'll walk out the front with you.' Kileen got to the door of his office, propped and gave a double, triple blink. The first thing he saw was the windscreen. He gave another double blink and walked across to the station wagon as if in a trance. 'What the... What's all this?' he said, and walked around the car. 'Jesus! They're all over it.'

'Ohh, yeah, those,' said Les. 'Well, there was a bit of trouble up there at one stage.'

'A bit of trouble?' wailed Kileen, still looking at his bullet-riddled car. 'Where did you fuckin' go? Afghanistan?'

'No, just up the coast a bit,' replied Norton innocently. 'But the car still goes all right. And those holes are sweet. No rain gets in.'

'No rain gets in.' Kileen was starting to spin out. He kept looking at the station wagon in disbelief. 'Where did these all come from, for Christ's sake?'

Billy poked a finger in one of the holes. 'From a gun, I'd say,' he said, very matter of factly. 'More than one, too, by the look of it.'

'Oh, Christ!' howled Kileen. 'How am I bloody well going to sell this?'

'Easy,' said Billy. 'Just shove a price ticket on the window and stick it out the front. You own a car yard, don't you?'

'Ohh great,' said Kileen, closing his eyes for a moment. 'And who am I going to sell it to?'

'Buggered if I know,' shrugged Billy. 'Why don't you take it out to that mosque at Lakemba? Sell it to one of those Lebanese. All the cars look like that in Lebanon. They wouldn't know the difference. They'd probably snaffle it up 'cos it reminded them of home.'

'Oh shit!'

'Maybe one of those punk bands might buy it,' suggested Les. 'They go for that bad, mean look. Run some studs into the upholstery. Slash the interior up a bit.' Les and Billy exchanged rum looks as Kileen still stood there shaking his head. 'Anyway, we got to get going, Bill,' said Les. 'Thanks again. And if you got any beefs, give Price a ring.'

'Yeah. If he can't come out, he'll probably send Eddie,' said Billy.

'See you mate,' said Les.

'Ta ta, Killer,' said Billy.

As they walked to Billy's car, Kileen's body seemed to shrink as his face got longer. Out of consideration and sheer good manners Les and Billy waited till they were about five hundred metres up the road before they burst out laughing.

'Poor bastard,' said Les.

'Don't worry. He'll be up there attacking Price's bourbon after this,' answered Billy.

They were still laughing when they reached the turn off at St. Peters.

'So, where do you fancy going for a feed, Billy?' asked Les.

'What's wrong with The Diggers? We can have a few beers as well.'

'Okay,' nodded Les. 'I might even shout.'

'Jesus,' said Billy. 'What were you smoking while you were up there?'

'That's another story too,' winked Les.

IT WAS ALMOST five when Les and Billy left The Diggers. Billy had a T-bone, but after two weeks of barbecues at Cedar Glen, Les couldn't look at another steak so he went for the roast pork and vegetables. The rest of the afternoon was spent drinking steadily and doing their best to avoid the eyes of the other drinkers in the club who kept looking over their way and wondering what the two rather solidly-built gentlemen were roaring about, especially the shorter, dark-haired one.

Les didn't big note too much about the sexual romps, but he did give Bill a blow by blow description of what happened with Marita and Coco. He also gave Billy a blow by blow description of the two fights at the local pub, which Billy loved. Billy made Les give him another bullet by bullet account of the gunfight at the farmhouse, with Billy seriously concluding it was a bloody close thing. Both he and Les raised their glasses to that. By late evening both of them had a reasonably good head of steam and Billy said he'd better get home, have a quick nap and get some coffee into him to be ready for work that night. Les picked up a barbecued-chicken when Billy dropped him off; stuff cooking anything — he still had to relate the entire story to Warren yet. He told Billy if he didn't see him later in the week he'd give him a ring over the weekend.

WARREN ARRIVED HOME with a bottle of Jack Daniel's around six and a look of expectation and hunger on his face to find Norton pottering around in the kitchen.

'Righto, Les,' he said. 'I want to know exactly what happened up there. From the moment you left and how that car got to be in such a state.'

'Okay,' nodded Les. 'But get changed first and then have something to eat. A lot of this you shouldn't hear on an empty stomach.'

'All right then.'

Warren had a quick clean up and got changed into a pair of jeans and a jumper.

'What's for tea anyway?' he asked, returning to the kitchen.

'Roast chicken, mashed potatoes with mayonnaise and my special salad.'

'I thought you might have cooked another casserole. It's cold enough.'

Norton looked at Warren impassively. 'Woz, we had that last night. Do you seriously think I'd serve stew to a gourmet advertising executive two nights in a row?'

'I never thought of that,' considered Warren. 'It appears that between myself and Sir Peregrine not only your manners but also your code of ethics is improving. Slowly. But definitely improving.'

'Have a beer anyway,' winked Les.

'Yeah. Good idea.'

The meal was washed down with Stella Artois. After they'd cleaned up, Les sat back down at the kitchen table and opened two bottles of Corona.

'Okay, Woz,' he said, taking a mouthful. 'Where do you want me to start?'

'Right from the beginning. The morning you left here.'

Norton thought for a moment. 'All right, then. You know that surf photographer who hangs out at Tamarama? Tony Nathan...'

IT WAS ALMOST midnight when Les finished giving Warren the entire story of the trip. They finished up in the lounge room with the heater and the stereo softly on 2MMM where they managed to knock over four more beers, all the Jack Daniel's and two bottles of Möet. At one stage Les thought he was going to have to get an oxy-viva for Warren he was laughing so much, especially at the part when Les told the girl from Port Macquarie that Peregrine had Melon Syndrome and what he did to the one who gave him the flick at the same time, right up to the look on Kileen's face when he took the station wagon back covered in bullet holes. Warren even got a laugh out of the shoot-out, until Les showed him the two balaclavas. They finished up with Warren still wheezing with laughter and Les half-falling off the lounge.

'So, Woz, old mate,' he slurred. 'That was my two quiet weeks in the country with Sir Peregrine Normanhurst III. Who is now back safely in England recovering from his tick bite with his sheila Stephanie whatever-her-name-is, and his precious painting of the Chinaman. And bloody good luck to him too. There's a lot worse blokes in the world than me mate Pezz.'

Warren wiped his eyes and tried to talk, but found he was too drunk and his throat was too sore to speak. There was a drunken silence between them for a while, broken only by the soft music from the radio, when Norton spoke.

'Warren,' he hiccupped. 'If I can make it to my room, I am going to bed. I am that drunk I can't even scratch myself.'

'S'orright for you,' mumbled Warren. 'I got to go work in the morning.'

Norton heaved himself up from the lounge. 'G'night, Woz. Will you turn the lights and the heater off?'

'If I can find the switch.'

Norton weaved his way into his bedroom, crashed on the

bed and dragged the blankets over him. He didn't even bother to take his running shoes off.

THURSDAY MAY HAVE been the first of September and the beginning of Spring, but it could have been doomsday for both Les and Warren. They bumped into each other in the kitchen at about eight-thirty, both feeling as seedy as raspberries and with breath that would have stripped the chrome off a bumper-bar. Warren had the macrobiotic, vitamin-enriched breakfast he usually had when he was hungover: a glass of soda water, two Codral Reds and a cup of black coffee. Les opted for the soda water and a bowl of porridge. They both agreed their condition was worth it in a way as it had been a funny night. After belching and farting around the kitchen like two old molls for about twenty minutes, Warren shuffled off to work and Les told him he'd see him when he got home. Thank Christ I don't have to go to work today, mumbled Les to himself as he heard the front door close.

It was still cold and bleak outside and Les knew the only way he was going to get rid of his hangover was to sweat it out of himself. He couldn't be bothered driving anywhere so he slipped into a pair of shorts and a sweatshirt then jogged from his place down to Curlewis Street and did a lap of Rose Bay golf links. After a few sit-ups back at his place and a shower, Norton was feeling decidedly better than when he got out of bed, if not quite one hundred percent. After a pot of tea and some toasted chicken sandwiches, he was feeling even better again. He was sitting in the kitchen reading the paper when the phone rang. It was Price calling from Muswellbrook.

There was no mistaking his cheery voice over the phone. 'Hello, Les,' he beamed. 'How are you, son?'

'Price,' answered Les. 'I'm good. How's yourself?'

'Terrific. Sorry I haven't spoken to you since you got back. But I've been up here with the missus running around buying horses. I tried to call you yesterday, but you must have been out.'

'Yeah, I was with Billy. We took Kileen's car back.'

Price laughed. 'What did the pisspot say? Eddie said the car was full of bullet holes.'

'He didn't say all that much,' replied Les. 'But he looked like the portrait of Dorian Gray as we were leaving.'

'Good. That'll teach him to come up to the club and drink all my free piss.' Price's voice changed. 'Listen Les, seriously.

I'm sorry about what happened up there. Eddie told me what came down. It wasn't supposed to turn out like that.'

'Yeah, well, maybe it wouldn't have if Peregrine hadn't sent his girlfriend a card telling her where we were.'

'Yeah, the young flip. You'd think he'd have more brains.'

'Anyway it's all history now, Price.'

'Yeah. But I still don't like my boys getting shot at. O'Malley's pretty rapt in what you did too, Les.'

'I was talking to him on a car-phone. He sounds like a good bloke.'

'He's a gem. And if he says he'll do you a favour he will.'

'Whatever. But I'm not worried about it.'

'So have you got any of that five grand left?'

'Yeah. A fair bit.'

'Well, keep that. Danny's up the club with Billy so have a few more days off. Shout yourself a few days up at Surfers or something. Get out of the bloody cold for a while.'

'Jesus, I wouldn't even mind doing that. Thanks, Price.'

They chatted on for a while longer then Les hung up, telling Price if he didn't see him over the weekend he'd see him up the club next week.

Norton looked at the phone for a moment and a thought struck him. I know who I'll ring up. He got Alison's phone number from his bedroom and dialled Brisbane. Alison wasn't home, but a rather suspicious sounding mother was. Les left his phone number and a message for her to ring reverse charges if she wanted. Thank you. When he hung up Norton had a feeling he wouldn't be seeing much more of young Alison. Oh well, you win some, you lose some. But what a top little babe. And a ton of fun. So what'll I do now? It's a prick of a day outside. But I've got around three grand to spend. I know, I'll shout myself a new pair of jeans and a track-suit, and maybe a new pair of running shoes. Les drove up to Bondi Junction and did just that, then sat around in the Plaza drinking hot soup and having a perv. By the time he got home around five with a couple of videos and two slices of rump steak he found Warren home early from the advertising agency.

'So, how are you feeling now, Woz?' he asked when he spotted him sitting in the kitchen.

Warren's eyes said it all for him. 'If I was a greyhound, they'd have me put down. I feel like something that's been condemned by the Board of Health.'

'You had anything to eat?'

'I had a drover's breakfast when I got to work. A cigarette and a walk around.'

'I thought you'd given 'em up?'

'I did. Now my mouth tastes like the grease-trap at Homebush Abbatoirs.'

'Well I got some steaks and a couple of videos.'

'I could eat a steak. What are the videos?'

'Chuck Norris and Chevy Chase.'

'Ohh shit!' Warren shook his head. 'Anyway, it won't worry me. I reckon I'll be in bed by ten. I'm saving myself for the Mojo turn tomorrow night.'

'What time does it start?'

'Four o'clock. It's upstairs in the pub opposite.'

Les cooked tea then after the news they settled down to a quiet night watching videos. Warren felt better after a decent feed and even managed to get down two bottles of beer, which immediately put a head on everything he'd drank the night before. He stayed up to watch Chuck Norris spinning heel kick his way through a multitude of baddies in Los Angeles, then blast whoever were left over to pieces with an assortment of automatic weapons before finishing up with the available piece of crumpet. However Chevy Chase po-facing and one-lining his way around Mexico didn't turn him on all that much and he went to bed, saying Norton's taste in videos was pretty much like his taste in suits. To which Norton replied he didn't have a suit. To which Warren replied that's exactly what he meant. Norton was left to ponder on this as he watched the last of the video and found himself nodding off towards the end. He was glad when it finished so he could get to bed himself.

FRIDAY MORNING WAS cold and sunny with a brisk westerly blowing. Les was up before Warren and missed him when he came back from training, opting for a few laps of Bondi and a hit on the bag in North Bondi Surf Club. The early morning chill had kept it down to the regulars. Les recognised a few familiar faces who said hello Les, haven't seen you for a while, how have you been? To which Les replied good. Which was true. Because he'd worked off the weight he'd put on at Cedar Glen, plus a little extra.

After a shower and reading another newspaper over breakfast plus catching up on the news on TV the last couple of nights, the realisation that he was definitely back in the big city well and truly dawned on Norton. The nation was in the very best of hands — there were around fifteen thousand homeless kids sleeping on the streets and National Parks and Wildlife needed three million dollars to save the koalas from extinction. So the government spent five million dollars on a report to expunge the English language of such words as 'manpower', 'mannerism', 'manoeuvre' etc so any feminists working on the government payroll wouldn't be offended. Which should be very comforting to the next homeless kid sleeping near a manhole cover, thought Les, to know that he is now sleeping next to a personhole cover. The hole in the ozone layer was increasing, along with the greenhouse effect, so the government in its wisdom was going to let the Japanese woodchip all the forests on the South Coast for the next fifteen years. What they didn't destroy, a Canadian mob would — with a billion dollar woodchip plant in Tasmania right beneath the hole in the ozone layer, guaranteed to pollute the surrounding ocean as it turned all the trees into woodchips to be sold back to Australia as cardboard cartons so we could increase out national debt. Some traitor suggested we try recycling our paper. But this was poo-poohed because it wouldn't be cost effective and it was easier to chop down all the trees. Meanwhile the French were doing their bit for the environment by exploding more atomic bombs in the Pacific and blowing up all the bird colonies in Antarctica to build airfields. And because some greenies protested about this outside the consulate, various money-hungry radio broadcasters labelled them loonies, lefties and ratbags. Yes, it's certainly a great world thought Les, reflecting back to those poor simple hippies in the country trying to protect what was left of mother nature. I think I know who the ratbags are.

The state of the nation and the world in general weren't the only things that disturbed Norton that morning. A very strange letter arrived as he was out the front tinkering with his old Ford just before lunchtime. As soon as Les saw the envelope he knew it spelled trouble. Printed on the back was Tweed Valley Stock And Station Agents And Auctioneers. Oh-oh, thought Les — here it is. Well, it had to come sooner or later. Now I reckon I can expect a visit from the wallopers.

Norton frowned darkly as he looked at the envelope and tried to figure out the best thing to do. He could send it back address unknown, or no longer at this address. No, that wouldn't work. They'd get a summons to me sooner or later. No, bugger it, I'm going to have to face this bloody thing. Fuck it. Les opened the letter, quickly read the contents and an even darker frown crossed his face. What the — what's this fuckin' Rabinski trying to pull. Benny might be kosher, but this bloody letter ain't. There's something very wrong here. Les decided to read the letter again inside, over a cup of coffee. He went into the kitchen, made some instant and read the letter again. Slowly.

Dear Mr Norton,

Please find enclosed a cheque for $500 for your bond money. You failed to collect it when you returned the keys to Cedar Glen to our office. The office would also like to thank you for introducing us to Sir Peregrine Normanhurst. To show our appreciation we have enclosed a cheque made out to you for an additional $250. If you are ever in the Tweed Valley area again feel free to visit our office anytime.

Yours sincerely
Benjamin M. Rabinski

Norton sipped his coffee and his eyes narrowed as he slowly nodded his head. Yeah, good try Benny, you miserable little prick. I cash these cheques and that automatically proves I was at Cedar Glen for two weeks. Then bingo! The nice summons. Call into our office Mr Norton — and in two minutes every copper in Murwillumbah would be in there. No, fuck it, I'll give Cameron a ring on Monday and take these up to him. If my ace lawyer Carnivore T. Funnelwebb, can't figure this out, no one can. Les put the envelope on his dressing table, finished his coffee then went back to tinkering with his car. It was a funny one though, especially the cheque for the extra two-fifty. And how did they find out about Peregrine? He never introduced him to them. Norton was still pondering a little on this when he caught a cab to the Mojo party at four-thirty wearing his new jeans, long-sleeved checked shirt and black leather jacket.

Warren could have been namedropping a little or mishandling the truth about the Mojo party. Mojo weren't actually throwing it. They were there, but the party was being thrown by a guy called Harry Madigan who ran an advertising and music agency called Keen As A Bean. Les had got to know Harry through various parties Warren had taken him to and he used to come up to the game now and again for a flutter at the tables or on the roulette wheel. Harry wrote jingles and did a lot of voice-overs because he had one of those husky, crackling voices that at times could make John Laws sound like Tiny Tim.

Like a lot of blokes in their late thirties, Harry's hair had seen better days and his face told of late nights in a lot of recording studios. But he had cheerful, rolling eyes and the razor-sharp wit you need to survive in the cutthroat Sydney advertising scene.

He was standing just inside the back door of the hotel talking to a couple of people when Les walked in. As soon as he saw Norton he smiled a big welcome and extended his hand.

'Hello, Les,' he said, in his familiar deep, gravelly voice. 'How are you, mate?'

'Good thanks, Harry.'

'Warren told me you were coming.'

'Yeah. Thanks for inviting me.'

Madigan winked. 'The party's upstairs. Just go to the bar and order what you like. There's food and all that. I'll see you up there later.'

'Okay. Thanks, Harry.'

Norton stepped lively up the stairs into three large rooms full of comfortable lounge chairs with a small bar at one end and a piano in the middle. There were about a hundred well-dressed people in there, some dancing, most of them talking and laughing in small groups. Les recognised a few musicians and a few heads he'd seen on TV commercials. Everyone seemed to be having a good time and although the party had more or less just started they were all well into it. Warren was in the end room talking to his bosses; he caught Norton's eye and waved. Les got a bottle of Crown Lager from one of the girls behind the bar and walked over.

'Hello, Woz,' he said. 'How's it going?'

'The landlord,' smiled Warren. 'You got here.'

'Yeah,' enthused Les. 'It looks like a good turn.'

'It is.' Warren nodded to his bosses. 'You remember the boys from work?'

'Yeah,' replied Les. 'How's it going, fellahs?'

Warren's bosses knew Les from the Melbourne wine commercial and they shook his hand warmly and smiled; the ad had been a success so there was a good vibe there. After that it was all plain sailing — Norton was one of the chaps.

Les talked to Warren and his bosses for a while then went to the bar and kept filling up on various drinks, then roamed around in general getting pleasantly pissed. There was no shortage of drinks, no shortage of food, no shortage of anything and especially no shortage of good-looking women; and everyone who Les smiled and said hello to seemed to smile and say hello back. One thing Les did notice as he eased his way through the crowd, ear-wigging different conversations, was the number of one-liners flying around. With all this advertising crowd it was virtually one-liners at two paces. Did you hear about the... ? How do you... ? What's the difference between...? Why did the... ? There were some rippers though and secretly he wished he'd brought a notebook with him to write most of them down.

Eventually he finished up back at the bar ordering another bourbon, about the same time as a tall willowy blonde who ordered a champagne with a dash of blended strawberries. She was quite a good sort, late twenties, straight well-groomed hair and a pretty if slightly serious face. She hadn't gone overboard with the make-up and above a thin nose was a pair of probing green eyes which seemed to be thoroughly evaluating everything as she glanced around the room. Soberly dressed in a double-breasted brown jacket and a pleated, cream skirt, she looked like she could have been the editor of some women's magazine or a TV producer. Norton tipped her to be a feminist. So what, he thought, half full of drink. They can't hang you for being polite.

'Hello,' he said, half raising his glass. 'How are you?'

'Good thanks,' replied the blonde. 'Enjoying the party?'

'Yeah,' smiled Norton. 'It's a donger.'

'Who are you here with?'

Les pointed to Warren. 'That guy over there with the fair hair in the red shirt.'

'Oh, Warren,' said the blonde. 'I know him. He's with Wirraway, I think.'

'Yeah, that's him. I share a house with him at Bondi.' Les smiled at the blonde. 'I suppose you're in the advertising game?'

She nodded and gave a little laugh. 'Yes, CRC at North Sydney. What about yourself?'

Les shook his head and grinned. 'No, I'm a doorman. I work in a casino at the Cross.'

'Oh.'

'But I have done a couple of TV commercials,' said Les. 'Through Warren. Only as a joke though, more or less,' he added.

'I think Australia's turning into just one big TV commercial.'

'Yeah,' agreed Les. 'I think I know what you mean. Anyway, what's your name?'

'Janice.'

Norton raised his glass. 'I'm Les. Pleased to meet you, Janice.'

Janice smiled and clinked Norton's glass. 'Nice to meet you too, Les.'

It turned out Janice was a receptionist for CRC and lived at Rose Bay paying off a home unit which she shared with a girlfriend who was a nurse. She was twenty-seven, didn't go out all that much and was into learning the piano; she had one in her unit. Les told her a bit about himself and about Warren; they discussed life in general. Norton appeared to be getting along famously with Janice and wouldn't have minded following up. But he still wasn't too sure where her head was at and underneath the niceness he still had a sneaking suspicion she could have been a down-in-the-mouth feminist. Only one way to find out.

'I notice they don't mind a one-liner around here,' he said.

'Ohh, don't talk about it,' said Janice. 'I have to put up with them all day at work.' She smiled at Les. 'You're not about to hit me with a barrage, are you?'

Norton smiled back and made a little gesture with his hand. 'What's the difference between a feminist and a can of Foster's?' Janice shook her head. 'A can of Foster's is cold but it's not bitter.'

Janice nodded and smiled. 'How do you get fifty Australian men into a Holden sedan?' Norton had to shake his head. 'Put one in, make him a union delegate, and the rest will crawl up his arse.'

Touché, thought Les. Language a little coarse but well put together none the less. 'Why did Frankenstein shave his legs?' he asked.

'Why?'

'Because he got sick of everyone thinking he was a lesbian.'

Janice gave a throaty chuckle and a wave of her hand. 'Ohh, look,' she said, 'let's give the one-liners a miss. Next it'll be Irish jokes. Then Polish jokes. We'll be here all night.'

'Yeah, you're right,' agreed Les.

Les was going great guns with Janice. But unfortunately she had to leave early. She had to meet her flatmate and they were going to visit some other girls who had just moved into a unit at Dover Heights; a sort of drinks with the girls. No, she had nothing planned for tomorrow night. Dinner? Why, that would be lovely. A five o'clock movie beforehand? Why, that would be even better still. Drinks somewhere afterwards? What a delightful way to finish an evening. Janice gave Les her address and phone number. Les said he'd see her about four-thirty. He'd ring before he called over. Bye bye.

The look in Janice's eye when Les gave her hand a light squeeze just before she left suggested to Les she'd much rather be taking him back to her place for a bit more than piano lessons rather than having drinky-poohs and talking shit with the girls. Norton couldn't help but smile to himself as he watched her shapely dark-stockinged legs going out the door. Well, that's not a bad result on the night. Nice and handy to home. Not a bad sort and not bad to talk to either. I'll give her a giant spray tomorrow night with that three grand and you never know your luck, Janice might take me back to her place and let me put my hand on her D-minor.

The party continued. People came and went. Madigan and some musician mates got a bit of a band together, sang songs, sent up commercials and got everyone into a bit of a sing-along. Warren disappeared, probably with a girl. Les ate more choice food, drank more bourbon and white rum and got progressively drunker till around eleven he discovered he was starting to talk in Swahili so it was time to go before he made too big a dill of himself. He said goodbye to one or two people, thanked Madigan again for a top night then stumbled off towards Oxford Street to find a taxi.

LES GOT UP around eight to find Warren hadn't come home. Norton didn't bother to do any training, he'd done enough through the week, so figured he'd just go for a brisk walk after breakfast. He got the papers, cooked some chops and sat around reading while he waited for Warren. The advertising genius steamed in the front door about nine-thirty, badly in need of a shave and a change of clothes, but looking very pleased with himself.

'And just where the fuck have you been all night?' said Les, as Warren walked into the kitchen.

'Sorry I didn't ring, mum,' replied Warren. 'But I was having too good a time.'

'And who was this particular strumpet you picked up on the night?'

'Dunno,' replied Warren, switching on the kettle to make himself a cup of coffee. 'She was just up from Adelaide for the weekend. She was staying at some sheila's place in Randwick.'

'Mmmhh.' Les looked at Warren over his coffee. 'Are you going to have a shower?'

'Yeah, of course. Why?'

'Well make sure you throw plenty of disinfectant around in there after you. And don't use any of my bloody towels.'

'Ohh piss off.'

'And I hope you made sure you used a condom last night.'

'No way, baby,' grinned Warren. 'I ride 'em bareback. The Man from Snowy River, that's me.'

Norton shook his head. 'Fair dinkum, Woz. Don't you believe in safe sex? Don't you watch the ads on TV? If Ita Buttrose found out you had a fuck last night without using a frenchie, she'd have a stroke.'

Warren's grin seemed to get bigger. 'I don't know about Ita Buttrose having a stroke. But I was stroking pretty good about seven o'clock this morning.'

'Bloody disgusting,' huffed Norton, then he smiled up at Warren. 'It was a good turn though, wasn't it?'

'Reckon. Madigan's a terrific bloke.' Warren made his cup of coffee and took a sip. 'So how did you finish up?'

'Good. Drunk, singing and . . .' Les told Warren about meeting Janice and the arrangements he'd made for the afternoon and evening.

'Janice from CRC.' Warren shook his head. 'I don't think I know her.'

'She said she knew you.'

'Well that's only natural,' breezed Warren. 'All the girls know me.'

'Yes, you're right there,' nodded Les. 'Every cracker from Macleay Street at the Cross down to the wall at Darlinghurst. So what are you doing today?'

'Going over the oldies. My sister's down from Newcastle, so Uncle Warren is going to spend the day with his two nephews.'

'Good one, mate.' Norton rose from the table and put his empty mug in the sink. 'Well, I might leave you to it. I'm going for a walk.'

'Okay,' nodded Warren. 'You'll probably be gone when I get back, so have a good time tonight.'

'Yeah. I got a feeling I will. See you, Woz.'

Norton got his tracksuit top from his bedroom and strode off into the brisk morning air. He headed up Bondi Road, skirting around the crowds of shoppers and housewives and members of the Jewish faith, all done up in their coats and hats taking their Saturday walk to the Synagogue. I suppose there's always something to see in the city thought Les, as he passed a couple of good sorts and three weird-looking punks waiting at the bus stop. But I still think I prefer birds, animals and nice clean billabongs to freaks, junkies and overflowing garbage bins. He got as far as Waverley Oval and climbed to the reservoir to have a look out across the ocean and the city. Somehow his thoughts kept drifting back to Cedar Glen, the Humdinger Boogie Woogie Dance, the possums, little Alison. They also kept drifting back to Benny Rabinski and that strange letter. He may have been back in Sydney and miles away from the Tweed Valley but that matter certainly wasn't over yet. He was still thinking about it when he got home just before twelve.

Les was pottering around in the kitchen figuring out what to do till four-thirty when the phone rang. It was Billy.

'Hello, Les,' he said. 'How are you, mate?'

'Not too bad, William,' replied Les. 'How's things with you?'

'Ohh, all right, I suppose.'

Norton wasn't sure, but he thought he could detect something in the tone of Billy's voice. 'So, what's doing?'

'Ohh, not much. I just thought I'd ring you and see what you were up to.'

'Nothing. I'm sitting here reading the paper.'

'What I really meant was what are you doing tonight?'

'Tonight? I'm taking out a sheila I met at a party last night. We're going to the pictures this afternoon then dinner afterwards.'

'Oh.'

Norton could definitely detect something in Billy's voice now. 'Billy, is something wrong?'

Billy sucked in his breath over the phone. 'Yeah. Big Danny had a prang on the way home from work last night. He's all right. But he's got to have his neck in a brace for a few days, and he can't come to work tonight.'

'Ohh, shit! So who have you got?' Les already knew the answer.

'No one. I've tried everyfuckin'where. Balmain, Rozelle, all round the Cross. They're all short-staffed because of that flue goin' around.'

'Shit!' repeated Les.

'Yeah. So it looks like I'm gonna have to do it on my own.'

'Shit!' said Les again. He knew what Saturday night at the Cross could be like. 'And you dead set can't get anyone?'

'No. Not a soul. And I just don't want to grab some mug.'

'Christ!'

'So I just thought I'd ring you and see what you were doing.'

'Well like I said. I was going out.'

'Yeah, fair enough. Look don't worry about it. I'll find somebody.'

'No, hold on.' Before Les knew it he'd capitulated. 'I'll come up. I can probably take this tart out some other time.'

'You sure?'

'Yeah, sweet.'

'Good on you, mate. I wouldn't have asked you, only it's Saturday night and Eddie's still in Melbourne.'

'Don't worry about it. I'll see you about eight o'clock.'

'Good on you, Les. I owe you one.'

'Yeah. I'm starting to think just about everybody does. See you tonight.'

Les hung up and stared at the phone. 'Well wouldn't that fuck you?' he said out loud.

The last thing Norton felt like doing was standing in the cold wind out the front of the casino arguing with drunks all night. Especially with three grand in his bin and a good sort like Janice waiting for him. But what could he do? Billy had guarded his back plenty of times and he would have done the same for him. Imagine if he'd said no and Billy got hurt. But what a lousy rotten break. So, that settled, what to do for the rest of the afternoon? Ring Janice and tell her he couldn't make it, have a snooze, then iron a shirt and get ready for the pickle factory at eight o'clock.

Norton heaved himself off the lounge, got Janice's phone number from his bedroom and reluctantly called her.

'Hello, Janice?'

'Yes.'

'It's Les from last night. How are you?'

'Oh, hello. I'm good. How are you?'

'Not too bad, thanks.' I was till about five minutes ago, thought Norton.

'I'm glad you rang early. Look Les, I hate to do this to you, but I can't make it tonight.'

'Oh?' This took Norton by surprise. Now he didn't know whether to be pleased or have the shits.

'We had a bad scene back here at the flat last night.'

'What happened?'

'Well, I left the girls early last night. Trudy, who I share with, came home later and some guy attacked her as she was coming up the side.'

'Fair dinkum. Jesus, that's nice.'

'She screamed and managed to kick him in the shins. But

335

the bastard near choked her and he punched her in the eye.'

'Bloody hell.'

'Luckily the people above us just arrived at the same time and the headlights of their car made him run off.'

'Did you call the cops?'

'Yes. But they never found him. Poor Trudy. She's got bruises all over her neck and a dreadful black eye. The doctor's put her under sedation. But honestly Les, I couldn't leave her in the flat alone. She's in an awful state.'

'Yeah. I can imagine. Jesus, there's some bastards around.'

'So I'm really sorry, Les. But . . .'

'No that's all right. I understand. I just hope your girlfriend's all right.'

'Thanks. Maybe some other time?'

'Yeah, sure.'

'You do sound disappointed.'

'Well, you know how it is. But I'm just wondering what to do with these flowers and chocolates.'

'Flowers and chocolates? Oh Les, you shouldn't have.'

'Maybe not. But I'm just an old fashioned country boy at heart. And . . . I dunno Janice, I really fancied you.'

'Oh dear.'

'Doesn't matter. I'll give them to old Mrs . . . Kelly, across the street. Her husband's in hospital dying of cancer. It might help cheer her up.'

'Oh, you're sweet, Les.'

'Thanks. I try.' Les looked out the window towards the sky. One day Norton, the bloke upstairs is going to give it to you. One day.

'Look,' insisted Janice. 'We'll have to make this another time. In fact, why don't you give me your phone number, so I can ring you?'

'Okay.'

Les gave her his phone number. They chatted politely for a few minutes, Les said he might even call to say hello tomorrow. Janice said to do that. Then they hung up.

Well, that eases the pain somewhat, thought Les. He was even smiling a little now. Flowers and fuckin' chocolates. Yeah that'd be right. Who does she think I am, Maurice Chevalier? But it is a bit rough when some poor bloody nurse can't even walk up her driveway without some arsehole trying to rape her. Still, this might've all worked out for the best. I can really put the screws into Billy tonight. I reckon I'll be sweet for at least three baked dinners. And he's got to throw in one of Louise's chocolate strawberry cakes. Norton chuckled and looked at his watch. May as well go and have a bet. He got his jacket and despite being more or less stood up, found himself whistling as he walked down to the TAB.

After three races Norton was about square. He'd backed three losers but another two got up, paying well for a place so he got most of his money back. It wasn't long before the cigarette smoke and noise in the TAB got to him; he had a couple of daily doubles and walked back home.

There wasn't a great deal to do at home and the unexpected call back to work had thrown him out a bit. Just keep warm and watch TV till he had a snooze before going to the club. Les did just that. He was drinking tomato soup and watching some unbelievable windsurfing on 'The Wide World Of Sports' when there was a knock on the front door around four o'clock. Hello, thought Les. I wonder who this is? His forehead creased slightly. I hope it's not the cops. He put down his soup and walked to the front door. It was a short, dumpy girl around twenty, in a courier service uniform.

'Mr L. Norton?' she said.

Les hesitated for a second. 'He's not here at the moment. What is it?'

The girl tended a large, beige envelope. 'A letter,' she said. 'Special delivery from England.'

'England?' Norton looked at the name on the back of the envelope and smiled. 'That's all right. I'll take it.'

'Sign here, please.'

Norton signed the receipt book and the girl handed him the envelope. 'Thanks,' he said. The girl nodded a reply and walked back to her small motorbike. Les heard her putter off as he looked at the back of the envelope again. Beneath an Heraldic crest of a knight's head surrounded by chain and a sword and inscribed with something in Latin was: *Sir Peregrine Normanhurst, Abbey Le Grange, Lomanshire, West Sussex, England.* And a postcode. Well what do you know, grinned Les. It's from me old pommy mate. At least he got home all right. Les closed the front door and went back inside. He turned off the TV, got a knife from the kitchen and settled back down on the lounge. Well, I wonder what old Pezz has got to say? He smiled as he slit open the envelope.

The letter was about four pages of beautifully embossed beige paper with the same Heraldic crest above each page.

Dear Les,
How goes it old sausage? it started.

Norton burst out laughing. That's bloody Peregrine all right.
The Hooray Henry's Hooray Henry.

The letter continued:

It is very late Wednesday here and you will have to excuse
any typing errors. Father and I have been running around
together ceaselessly since I arrived home. I have tried to
make this letter as brief and to the point as possible, but
if it gets away on me as you read on I think you will understand
why.

I imagine by now you will have found out I purchased
Cedar Glen. When I was on the way back to Brisbane with
the plod I made them stop at Murwillumbah for two hours
while I finalised all the details. (I might add there was quite
a scene at Brisbane with Uncle Lawrence when I got there
but I won't go into that.) Your Jewish friend Rabinski wanted
$3m for it but I got him down to $2.5m. I imagine he has
turned me over to a certain extent but I was in a hurry
and I still consider it cheap for such a magnificent property.
I gave Ronnie Madden immediate Power of Attorney and
signed everything over to him. So by now Baldric is the
new owner of Cedar Glen and his plans of making it a refuge
for Australian Vietnam veterans should come to fruition I
think under the circumstances, Les, it was the least I could
do.

So, Les, I suppose one could say my brief holiday away
from home has left me somewhat out of pocket: purchasing
the property, the money for those two lifesavers, picking
up the tab at Penguin Resort, paying for all that imported
beer which you managed to pour down your throat with
great gusto, not to mention the clothes I brought from those
two girls at Stokers Siding which I am still waiting to receive.
Probably the best part of three million dollars Australian.
Quite an expensive two weeks in Australia for a poor unsuspecting pom. However, I'm lucky I can afford it, and I
might add I did have one significant stroke of luck while
I was there. I refer to that painting I acquired from you
and for which I still have the receipt.

I thought for a moment there you may have twigged at
my barely concealed excitement. I knew as soon as I saw
that style and those fabulous colours even without checking
the artist's initials that I had come across more than just
another beautiful painting. Father and I collect and deal
in fine art — Father is an expert and it is part of the way

I built up my fortune. When I took the painting back to my room I got a screwdriver and carefully removed the part of the frame where those initials were. Sure enough, there were more initials in front of the ENT. I almost fainted when I found out the artist's correct signing of his work was VINCENT. I hate to tell you this, Les. But that painting is a Van Gogh. I don't know whether you are familiar with fine art or Vincent Van Gogh but he always signed his paintings VINCENT because he detested the way the French pronounced his surname. Some of his works were never even signed at all. Now Les, the plot thickens. How did a Van Gogh end up in Australia? Father and I have been researching endlessly ever since I arrived home by private jet and what we have come up with is absolutely fascinating.

There was a well-known Australian impressionist, the son of a wealthy pioneer, John Peter Russell. In June 1881 he left Sydney for Europe on the *SS Garone* with another Australian artist, Tom Roberts. When they reached England they went their separate ways. In 1884 John Peter Russell enrolled at a famous art academy in Paris called Cormon Atelier. Some of his fellow students were Toulouse-Lautrec, Claude Monet, Gaugin, Rodin the sculptor and, of all people, Vincent Van Gogh. John Peter Russell and Vincent Van Gogh became very good friends. It was John Peter Russell who did the most famous portrait of Van Gogh, which was Vincent's favourite, and now sits in the Gemaenta Musea in Amsterdam.

Around 1887, Van Gogh became interested in Japanese art and woodcuts and was particularly impressed by two famous Japanese artists of the time, Hiroshige and Hokusai — 'Le Style Japonais'. Vincent Van Gogh went through a Japanese period and held an exhibition of his works at the Cafe Tambourin in Paris which was owned by an ex-model and his mistress at the time, Agostina Segatori. This was in 1887, the same time John Peter Russell opened up his own art studio in Paris, the Impasse Helene. It was here that he painted his portrait of Vincent and it was here we believe Van Gogh did his portrait of the great Japanese artist, Hiroshige. John Peter Russell married an Italian model Mariana Mattiocco, who was, according to Rodin, the most beautiful woman in Paris. For this beautiful woman whom he loved, John Peter Russell built a chateau on a small island called Belle Ile off the coast of Brittany. Monet, Rodin and Vincent Van Gogh used to visit him there and his unique and warm friendship with Van Gogh continued over the years. Unfortunately Van Gogh's mental condition deteriorated and in July 1890 he committed suicide. Before he did, one of the last letters he ever wrote was to his Australian friend John Peter Russell. It was written from the asylum at St. Reny. The last paragraph of the letter reads thus:

'If ever you are in Paris, take, if you wish, a canvas of mine from my brother's house, if you are still pursuing the idea of making a collection for your country. You will remember that we have spoken of it already and it is my desire that you be given one for this purpose.'

Sadly this wish was little more than a bequest.

John Peter Russell returned to Australia in 1921 after the death of his wife and it appears that the painting he chose to take with him was Van Gogh's portrait of the Japanese artist Hiroshige painted at John Peter's studio the Impasse Helene in Paris in 1887. John Peter Russell died in 1930 in Sydney. How the painting got to the Tweed Valley and finished up in a second-hand shop is anybody's guess. But who around that time, especially in Australia, would know anything about a colourful painting of a Chinaman by some artist who simply signed his works Vincent? I would say the colonel picked it up more out of a whim than anything else.

So there you have it, Les. *Portrait Of A Chinaman* by Ernest Norman Toejam is actually *Portrait Of Hiroshige* by Vincent Van Gogh. Father and I have taken the painting to two of England's leading art auctioneers where it has been authenticated. We now await the arrival from Holland next week of the foremost expert on Vincent Van Gogh, Professor Konrad van der Hooft from the Gemaenta Musea in Amsterdam. He is the world's leading authority on Van Gogh and it will only be a formality once he sees it. What is the painting worth? Who knows, Les? A brilliant portrait like that with such a unique history, thirty, forty million — pounds. But one could never sell something like that. It will hang here at Abbey Le Grange along with our Titians, Monets and Raphaels. Our one Van Gogh. Like myself, father has always wanted a Vincent. And now he has one. I might add, father said to say thank you very much.

By now, Les, I imagine your face is starting to look like — what is that expression I heard you use? Jedd Clampett's dog? Letting a fifty million dollar painting slip through your fingers. But don't worry. Do you think I would pull off a dodgy stroke like that without throwing a bit of wedge your way? Leave it out, Terry. As soon as Professor van der Hooft clocks this painting on Monday I am forwarding you a cheque for five hundred thousand pounds. With the rate of exchange and all that you will finish up with over a million dollars. Something, Les. A nice little earner for putting up with some potty pom for a couple of weeks. Know what I mean, squire? So you have done it, old porpoise. You are now a millionaire. Or at least you will be next week when I send you the cheque.

In all seriousness, Les, I would like to thank you for what you did. And I accept the fact that my irresponsibility almost cost both of us our lives. I am truly sorry as you know and I hope you will forgive my act of stupidity. I have woken up in more ways than one since my trip to Australia and I have you to thank for it more than anyone else. I would consider it an honour, Les, if you let me call you my friend. And that invitation to come to England anytime still stands, more than ever.

And now it is very late and I am very tired. Like I said earlier, father and I have been horrendously busy all week. I am looking forward to a quiet weekend. I am going to Scotland — my uncle, Lord Myleford has a houseboat on a lake up there. I am taking the painting with me to show him and spend the weekend fishing. He's my favourite uncle. Goodbye for now, Les, I will write to you again next week when I send you the cheque.

Your friend,
Sir Peregrine Normanhurst III

Underneath was scrawled — Pezz.

Norton just stared at the letter in his hands and blinked. To say he was somewhat taken aback would literally be the understatement of the year. It completely blew him out. It blew him out that much he had to read it again, and again. After the third time Les didn't know whether to laugh or cry, kick a hole in the wall or jump straight up through the roof. That fuckin' stupid painting. Les didn't know Van Gogh from Van Halen. But he did know that just about every time he watched the news on TV one got auctioned somewhere in the world for about a hundred million dollars. And he'd just let one slip through his fingers. But how was he to know? And if he had brought it back with him — which he wouldn't have — he would have only got sick of looking at it after a while and tossed it out. A hundred million dollars! Norton stared at the letter and shook his head. But what about Peregrine buying Cedar Glen and giving it to Ronnie Madden? What a champion bloke. However there was one part of the letter Les had to read a fourth, fifth and sixth time. A part which put a grin on his craggy face and made him warm all over — a feeling he could hardly explain. *'So you have done it, old porpoise. You are now a millionaire.'* Norton had finally done it. He'd cracked it. He was never short of a dollar, but now he was a millionaire. He'd never have to work another day in his life. No more Kelly Club, no more arguing with drunks, no more getting home at dawn and sleeping half the day away. No more fights, no more hassles with coppers, no more getting shot at, no more having to work when he would have liked to have had the night off. From now on his life was pure gravy. He'd still keep his house and rent it out to Warren then buy a property in the bush somewhere miles from the nearest city and live happily ever after; watching the sun rise through the trees in the morning and watching it set behind them in the evening. This was after he'd taken that trip to England with a big pocketful of traveller's cheques. But millionaire or not he still had to go to work that night: he couldn't let Billy down. But he'd definitely be telling Price what he could do with the Kelly Club. Maybe not exactly in those words. But tonight would be his last night at the Cross.

It was all very heady. Very confusing. Les wanted to have a drink and celebrate, but found he couldn't get off the lounge. All he could do was read the letter over and over again and stare into space. He was still sitting on the lounge staring into space when Warren came home just before six. Norton didn't hear him open the door or his footsteps coming down the hall. The big Queenslander was in another dimension.

'Les?' said Warren, as he walked into the lounge room. 'What are you doing here? Why aren't you out with Janice?' Norton shrugged his shoulders and kept staring ahead. 'I know.' Warren burst out laughing. 'She's stood you up. She was drunk last night. Now she's sobered up and realised what she'd done. Ha!'

Norton nodded his head slowly and kept staring ahead. Still he didn't say anything.

'The great lover,' laughed Warren. 'Wouldn't get a fuck in a brothel with a suitcase full of fifties and a bunch of roses. Ha-hah! You fuckin' wally.'

Norton continued to stare into space. The silence and the weird half smile on his face finally got to Warren. 'Are you all right?'

Norton nodded almost imperceptibly. 'Couldn't be creamier.'

'No, you're not,' said Warren. 'Something's wrong. What's going on?'

'Big Danny couldn't make it so I have to go to work tonight.' Norton's voice was slightly indistinct and sounded like it was coming from far away.

'Ohh, what a bastard.'

'Yes, isn't it dreadful?' Norton turned to Warren with the weirdest grin on his face. 'Isn't it . . . a shame?'

Warren shook his head. 'I'm going to make a cup of coffee. You want one?'

'No thank you, Warren.'

Warren made himself a cup of coffee then came back into the lounge where Les was still staring into space. Warren looked at him for a moment then glanced at his watch. 'You mind if I switch on the news? It's almost six o'clock.'

Norton gestured towards the TV set. 'Be my guest, Warren. Watch whatever you like. Watch the news. Watch 'Sesame Street'. Watch re-runs of 'The Don Lane Show'. Take the TV set into your room and crawl inside it.' Norton made a crazy little laugh. 'Do whatever you wish.'

Warren shook his head again. He could understand Les having the shits about going to work when he could be taking a nice girl out. But generally when he was put out he ranted and raved around the house and carried on like a good sort. This mood he was in was most unusual to say the least. He ignored him and switched on the TV.

There was the usual promo for the station followed by the theme music for the news then the teletext printing out across the screen and the voice-over seemed to be concentrating on the main story.

'IRA bomb outrage stuns Royal Family.'

There were two other minor news items, then the camera cut to a po-faced Jim Whaley. The backdrop on the screen behind him was a Union Jack, part of an Irish flag and a figure in a balaclava superimposed over that.

'Hello, what's this?' said Warren. Even Norton seemed to come out of his strange mood at the sight of the figure in the balaclava.

Whaley was at his deepest and most serious. 'Members of the Royal Family were plunged into grief today at the assassination of Lord Layton Myleford in Scotland,' he intoned.

'Did he say Myleford?' said Norton, sitting up on the lounge.

'Quiet, Les,' replied Warren.

'Lord Myleford was killed instantly,' continued Whaley, 'when his houseboat was blown to pieces by a remote-controlled bomb on Lake Dundenfillitch near the Scottish town of Linskygill one hundred and sixty kilometres from the English border.'

The camera then flashed to a picturesque blue lake scattered with wreckage. Police boats and police divers were probing the wreckage, helicopters were hovering overhead, army units were searching and patrolling the shoreline.

'Also missing, believed killed in the blast, is Lord Myleford's nephew and baronet in line to the throne, Sir Peregrine Normanhurst III.'

Les and Warren exchanged brief shocked looks then returned to the TV screen.

'Sir Peregrine, who was only recently in Australia, was fishing with his uncle when the blast went off in the early hours of the morning, completely destroying the houseboat. Members of the Royal Family are unavailable for comment at the moment, but a spokesman for Buckingham Palace said the assassination is a particularly tragic blow because Lord Myleford was a revered member of the Royal Family and a favourite uncle of Prince Charles, who has been forced to cut short an official visit to Spain.'

The camera switched to a grim-faced Prince Charles arriving at Heathrow Airport and being hurried into a Jaguar saloon.

'Police divers have recovered the body of Lord Myleford but are still searching Lake Dundenfillitch for the remains of Sir Peregrine. No one has claimed responsibility for the blast but police say the method and type of bomb used point to the IRA.'

The camera then flashed to Buckingham Palace, film of Lord Myleford and a photo of Peregrine.

'Meanwhile,' continued Whaley, 'a tight blanket of security has been thrown around all members of the Royal Family in case there may be further attempts on their lives.'

The camera rolled onto more film of Lord Myleford, another photo of Peregrine while Jim Whaley spoke of Lord Myleford's war record, and a little more about Peregrine's trip to Australia.

Norton wasn't listening to any of this. He just stared at the TV set as if in a trance, Peregrine's letter still clutched in his hand.

'Jesus Christ! Can you believe that?' said Warren. 'Poor bloody Peregrine. They got him.' He turned to Les. 'All that trouble you went to, he wasn't home five minutes and the IRA blew him up. Jesus! I don't believe it.'

Norton still didn't say anything. He kept staring ahead almost as if he was in a coma.

'God almighty,' Warren shook his head. 'And to think he was only in this house a couple of weeks ago.' He turned back to Norton and noticed something strange. Funny little sobs were coming from Les, jerking his chest like small whimpering coughs. From where Warren was sitting it was hard to distinguish whether Norton was laughing or crying. It was a strange sound. 'Les, are you all right?' he asked.

Then Les turned to Warren and Warren's jaw dropped. Two tiny teardrops were slowly squeezing themselves from the corners of Norton's eyes. They were having a hard time getting out, but eventually they did and rolled down Norton's cheeks like two tiny diamonds.

'Les!' said Warren. 'You're crying. I don't believe it.'

Norton's face was now pure misery. He gave an almost imperceptible nod of his head as the same strange sob shook his chest and stomach.

'Les Norton crying.' Warren shook his head in amazement. 'Well, I'll be buggered.' He watched as another two teardrops forced their way out of Norton's eyes and rolled down his cheeks. 'I knew you and Peregrine finished up good friends, Les. But Jesus! I never knew he meant that much to you.'

Norton's face looked so miserable it was hard for Warren not to laugh. 'Warren,' he said. 'You'll never know just how much Peregrine did mean to me. Here,' he wailed, and handed Warren the letter. 'Fuckin' read this.'

AND IN A grimy tenement house, squashed in amongst a row of equally grimy tenement houses not far from The Falls Road in Belfast, a grey-haired old lady and her grandson were sleeping soundly. If the police or the authorities had been near Lake Dundenfillitch earlier in the day they may have seen the old lady and the little boy playing with a remote-controlled toy aeroplane at the lake's edge. If they had looked into her car they may have wondered why she had a spare remote control console for the aeroplane. They may also have wondered why the old lady threw the lot into a ravine when she drove home to her Belfast house through the police roadblocks, barbed wire, boarded-up houses and burnt-out cars to watch the news on TV. But the sight of killings in the street and bodies being pulled out of a lake didn't worry old Mrs Frayne too much. She was well used to that sort of thing by now.

Robert G. Barrett
You Wouldn't Be Dead For Quids

*As far as fighting went, Les wasn't really a scientific
fighter and for all he knew the Marquis of
Queensberry could have been a hotel in Parramatta.
Whenever Les went off it was anything goes ...*

Look out Sydney – Les Norton has just hit town!

You Wouldn't Be Dead For Quids is a series of
adventures involving Les Norton, a big red-headed
country boy from Queensland who is forced to move
to the big smoke when things get a little hot for him
in his hometown.

Working as a bouncer at an illegal casino up at the
Cross, Les gets to meet some of the fascinating
characters who make up the seamier side of one of
the most exciting cities in the world – gamblers,
conmen, bookies, bouncers, hookers and hit men,
who ply their respective trades from the golden
sands of Bondi to the tainted gutters of Kings Cross
... usually on the wrong side of the law.

As raw as a greyhound's dinner, Les is nevertheless
a top bloke – fond of a drink, loves a laugh and he's
handy with his fists. And, just quietly, he's a bit of a
ladies man too ... Les Norton is undoubtedly
Australia's latest cult figure.

Robert G. Barrett
The Boys From Binjiwunyawunya

*The big Aussie Rules player hit the roadway in a
tangle of arms and legs. His head came up just in
time to see Norton come leaping out of the tram and
the Cuban heels of his R.M. Williams riding boots
land on his chest, with fifteen stone of enraged
Queenslander behind them. If the earlier onslaught of
punches hadn't done Rick's internal organs much
good, the final serve completely destroyed them. He
gave one hideous moan and passed out.*

Les Norton is back in town!

There's no two ways about Les Norton – the
carrot-topped country boy who works as a bouncer
at Sydney's top illegal casino. He's tough and he's
mean. He's got a granite jaw, fists like hams, and
they say the last time he took a tenner from his wallet
Henry Lawson blinked at the light.

Lethal but loyal, he's always good for a laugh. In this,
the third collection of Les Norton adventures, Les
gets his boss off the hook. But not without the help of
the boys from Binjiwunyawunya.

Les then finds himself in a spot of bother in Long Bay
Gaol then in a lot more bother on a St. Kilda tram in
Melbourne ...

Robert G. Barrett's Les Norton stories have created a
world as funny as Damon Runyon's. If you don't know
Les Norton, you don't know Australia in the eighties.

Robert G. Barrett
Between the Devlin and the Deep Blue Seas

Okay, so it looks like the Kelly Club is finally closing down – it had to happen sooner or later. And it isn't as if Les Norton will starve. He has money snookered away, he owns his house, and his blue-chip investment – a block of flats in Randwick – must be worth a fortune by now. Except that the place is falling down, the council is reclaiming the land, there's been a murder in Flat 5, and the tenants are the biggest bunch of misfits since the Manson Family. And that's just the good news, because the longer Les owns the Blues Seas Apartments, the more money he loses.

This time Les Norton's really up against it.

But whilst he's trying to solve his financial problems, he still has time to fight hate-crazed roadies, sort out a drug deal after fighting a gang of bikies, help a feminist Balmain writer with some research she won't forget in a hurry, and get involved with Franulka, super-sexy leadsinger of an all-girl rock band, The Heathen Harlots.

And with the help of two ex-Romanian Securitate explosive experts, he might even be able to sort out his investment.

But can Les pull off the perfect crime? Of course – and why not throw the street party of the year at the same time?

Robert G. Barrett
White Shoes, White Lines and Blackie

All Norton wanted was a quiet coffee and Sacher cake at the Hakoah Club in Bondi, and to be left alone to sort out his troubled love life. How he let notorious conman Kelvin Kramer talk him up to Surfers Paradise for five days, Les will never know. Supposedly to mind KK and his massively boobed girlfriend, American model Crystal Linx, in Australia to promote her latest record. Though it did seem like a good idea at the time. Apart from the President of the United States arriving and Norton's domestic problems, there wasn't much keeping him in Sydney.

Norton went to the Gold Coast expecting some easy graft in the sun, an earn and possibly a little fresh romance. Les definitely got the earn. He certainly got the girl. But what Norton mainly got in Surfers Paradise was trouble. *In a size 40 Double-D cup.*

Robert G. Barrett
And De Fun Don't Done

They don't call him Lucky Les for nothing. A ticket in a raffle and Norton was off to the US of A – Siestasota, Florida, where it turned out hot, red hot, and it wasn't just the weather.

Night club brawls, mafia hitmen, too many girls called Lori, gun crazed Americans and the whole lot washed along in a sea of margaritas. Even for Les Norton it was just too hot to handle.

So it was off to 'greener' pastures – the Caribbean – for reggae, rum and Rastafarians, not to mention Sultry Delta, sweet-lipped Esme, and Millwood Downie, schoolteacher, historian and would-be stand-up comic, who helps Les trace his family tree and possibly uncover the biggest earn ever.

The world is finally Norton's oyster. All he has to do is get the shell open.

Robert G. Barrett
Rider on the Storm and Other Bits and Barrett

For more than a decade now, Robert G. Barrett has been entertaining Australians with the cocky Queenslander Les Norton and his outrageous exploits. In this collection, as well as more great Les Norton stories, Robert G. Barrett offers his views on getting published, getting famous, getting the dole, and getting a date.

Barrett on acting:
'You get instant fame and recognition: drunks want to fight you everywhere you go.'

On getting published:
'If you are seriously thinking of making a living out of writing in Australia, make sure the people in your local dole office read your books. And hope to Christ they like them.'

On *being* published:
'I'm convinced if you took a sandwich into some publishers' offices they'd take the filling, scrape off the butter and leave you with the dry bread.'

Rider on the Storm and Other Bits and Barrett is Les Norton at his worst and Robert G. Barrett at his best – as a columnist, feature writer and short-story teller.